DREAMS OF KELL

Christopher Mitchell is the author of the epic fan̶ ̶ ̶ ̶ ̶ ̶ ̶ ̶ ̶ ne Magelands. He studied in Edinburgh before living for several years in the Middle East and Greece, where he taught English. He returned to study classics and Greek tragedy and lives in Fife, Scotland with his wife and their four children.

For Chelsie

ACKNOWLEDGEMENTS

I would like to thank the following for all their support during the writing of the Magelands Eternal Siege - my wife, Lisa Mitchell, who read every chapter as soon as it was drafted and kept me going in the right direction; my parents for their unstinting support; Vicky Williams for reading the books in their early stages; James Aitken for his encouragement; and Grant and Gordon of the Film Club for their support.

Thanks also to my Advance Reader team, for all your help during the last few weeks before publication.

THE PEOPLES OF THE STAR CONTINENT

There are five distinct peoples inhabiting the Star Continent. Three are descended from apes, one from reptiles, and one from amphibians. Their evolutionary trajectories have converged, and all five are clearly 'humanoid', though physical differences remain.

1. **The Holdings** – the closest to our own world's *Homo sapiens*. Excepting the one in ten of the population with mage powers, they are completely human. The Holdings sub-continent drifted south from the equator, and the people that inhabit the Realm are dark-skinned as a consequence. They are shorter than the Kellach Brigdomin, but taller than the Rakanese.

2. **The Rakanese** – descended from amphibians, but appear human, except for the fact that they have slightly larger eyes, and are generally shorter than Holdings people. They are descendants of a far larger population that once covered a vast area, and consequently their skin-colour ranges from pale to dark. Mothers gestate their young for only four months, before giving birth in warm spawn-pools, where the infants swim and feed for a further five months. A dozen are born in an average spawning.

3. **The Rahain** – descended from reptiles. Appear human, except for two differences. Firstly, their eyes have vertical pupils, and are often coloured yellow or green, and, secondly, their tongues have a vestigial fork or cleft at their tip. Their heights are comparable to the Holdings and the Sanang. Skin-colour tends to be pale, as the majority are cavern-dwellers. Their skin retains a slight appearance of scales, and they have no fingerprints. They are the furthest from our world's humans.

4. **The Kellach Brigdomin** – descended from apes, and very similar to the Holdings, they are the second closest to our world's humans. Their distinguishing traits are height (they are the tallest of the five peoples), pale skin (their sub-continent drifted north from a much colder region), and immunity to most diseases, toxins and illnesses. They are also marked by the fact that mothers give birth to twins in the majority of cases.

5. **The Sanang** – descended from apes, but evolved in the forest, rather than on the open plains that produced the Holdings. As a consequence, their upper arms and shoulders are wider and stronger than those of people from the Holdings or Rahain. They are pale-skinned, their sub-continent having arrived from colder climates in the south, and they occupy the same range of heights as the Holdings and Rahain. The males bear some traits of earlier *Homo sapiens*, such as a sloping forehead and a strong jaw-line, but the brains of the Sanang are as advanced as those of the other four peoples of the continent.

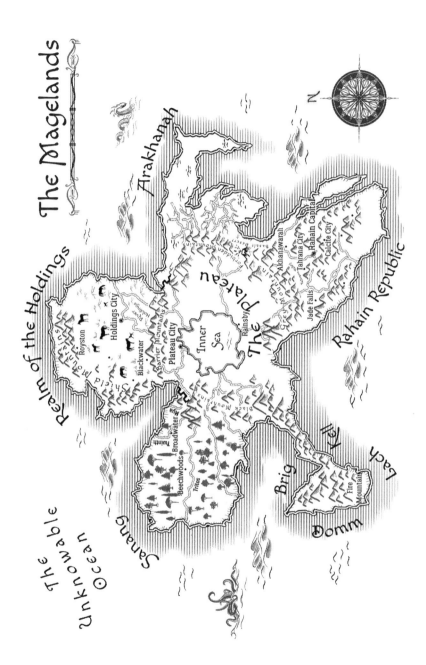

The Magelands

The Plateau

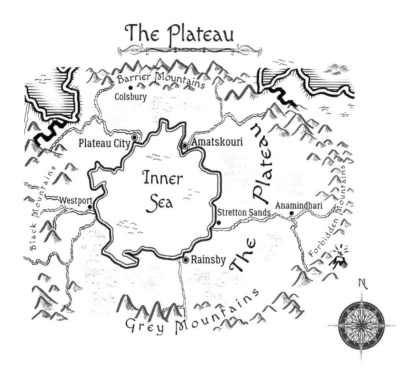

Kellach Brigdomin

CHAPTER 1
SPLENDID ISOLATION

C olsbury Castle, Republic of the Holdings – 1st Day, Last Third Spring 534

Karalyn slid the Weathervane into the side of the Sextant, and the wagon-sized device thrummed into life. Karalyn stood, her eyes studying the intricate mesh of wheels, pipes and cogs. She took a final draw of her cigarette, stubbed it out into an ashtray, then placed her right hand onto the thick glass surface covering the Sextant.

What is your desire, Karalyn?

The tall woman smiled. The voice was different to the one she had heard from the Quadrant she had stolen from Agatha, before her mother had broken it. The small device had asked her for a command, while the Sextant wanted to know her desires. The voice had been a comfort at first, and had led her to believe that she would be able to use the Sextant as easily as she had used the Quadrant; but it had been an illusion. The Sextant might ask her what she desired, but it seldom granted her requests.

Corthie had told her that Belinda had been able to wield the Sextant. She had transported thousands to other worlds with it, despite having no knowledge or training that she could possibly remember; and yet the huge device had been stubborn in its refusal to do as

Karalyn asked. She decided not to argue with it. It could show her the worlds it had created, and that was all she wished. Her mother was continually asking for news of her younger daughter Kelsey, and would nag and complain if Karalyn had been remiss for a few thirds. Half a year had elapsed since the last time Karalyn had checked on her sister, and it had been over double that since she had looked in on Sable. Her thoughts soured as she recalled her rogue aunt. No one ever asked her to check how Sable was doing – in fact, except for Corthie, no one seemed to care whether she was still alive or not.

A mixture of guilt and loathing swamped Karalyn's thoughts. She had taken Sable to Lostwell and had abandoned her there, leaving her to her fate. It had been cruel, but it was more generous than the Empress had thought necessary. Bridget had seemed robbed by Sable's escape from the noose, and even Daphne rarely disagreed.

Alright, she thought; she would spend five minutes observing Sable before looking for Kelsey.

Show me Dragon Eyre, she ordered the Sextant.

Her vision clouded, then cleared. She was looking down at a chain of mountainous islands, their steep slopes covered in forests, while the sky was a deep blue.

Show me the temple where Sable lives.

It was a vague command, she knew, but she had no idea what the islands were called. The Sextant would show her places, but she could hear nothing, nor could she intervene in any way. It was frustrating, but her entire experience with the Sextant had been frustrating. Her vision began to sweep across the vast ocean, until it reached another island. It raced over the barren countryside, and Karalyn gazed down at the thousands of greenhides roaming the interior. Her vision slowed at the southern tip of the island, where a walled compound stood.

Karalyn frowned. The temple area was deserted. The last time she had visited, Sable had been living there, along with two dragons and a few humans, but the orange groves were empty, and the workers' cottages deserted. Sable had been badly injured; had she succumbed to her wounds? Did Karalyn care? Part of her didn't. Part of her would not mourn the death of the woman who had forced Lennox to burn down a hospital.

And yet; Sable was family. Karalyn felt the irony of being one of the few people who did care if Sable was alive, despite being the one who had been hurt most deeply by her aunt's actions.

Show me where Blackrose lives.

She waited as the Sextant shifted her vision. Mile after mile of ocean passed beneath her in a blur of speed, along with several islands large and small, until her vision slowed by the coast where a town stood. Karalyn had seen the town before, when she had been exploring Dragon Eyre, and knew that Blackrose and Maddie lived in a huge palace built onto a bridge. Dragons were soaring over the town, while dozens of humans were clearing up rubble from down by the harbour. Had there been an earthquake? Much of the town's centre looked fire-damaged, though the bridge palace appeared to be unscathed. Karalyn's vision descended, and entered the palace. She sped through the empty hallways, until she reached the large, domed chamber where she had previously seen Blackrose. The large black dragon was there, along with a few others, and Karalyn saw Maddie standing next to a small group of humans. They were talking, but Karalyn could hear nothing. If only she could use her powers, then she would be able to discover Sable's fate in minutes. She attempted to lip-read, but soon gave it up. Sable wasn't there.

Let me enter their minds.

The Sextant didn't respond.

How do I enter their minds?

Silence.

Karalyn ground her teeth in annoyance, and remembered why she disliked the Sextant. Her initial joy at seeing the worlds it had created had faded into a sense of helplessness the more she had used it. Seeing was fine, but being unable to act made her want to tear her hair out.

A low, guttural noise permeated her thoughts. Had one of Colsbury's farm animals got into the Great Keep? She lifted her hand from the surface of the Sextant, and her vision of Dragon Eyre disappeared. Karalyn glanced round the large chamber where she kept the Sextant. Through an open window she could see the clouds in the sky above Colsbury. Rain was on its way, she thought, then she heard the noise again, followed by a long peal of laughter. Karalyn frowned. She recognised the owner of the laugh, and began walking. She stopped herself when she was halfway across the room, then returned to the Sextant and removed the dark blade, silencing the low hum from the device. She placed the Weathervane on top of the Sextant, then left the room. She strode down a narrow corridor, and entered a sitting room. At first, no one paid her any attention, and she stood by the doorway. The twins were sitting on a large, thick rug. Kyra's face was frozen in concentration, while Cael was shaking with laughter and excitement. Reclining on a low couch opposite them was Shella, tears of mirth rolling down her cheeks as she watched the old Sanang man in the centre of the rug. He was down on all fours, his head raised as he grunted like a wild boar.

'Make him bark like a dog!' cried Cael.

Karalyn raised her hand, and severed the powers linking her young daughter to the man. He collapsed onto the rug, panting, as sweat formed on his forehead.

All eyes turned to Karalyn. Cael seemed a little nervous, while Kyra glared at her mother.

'That's enough,' said Karalyn. 'What have I told you about teasing your Uncle Agang?'

'Don't be a spoilsport,' said Shella.

Karalyn turned to the Rakanese woman. 'You were supposed to be looking after them, not encouraging them.'

'And how am I meant to stop them?' said Shella. 'I'm just glad it wasn't me this time.'

Agang lifted his head. 'Thank you, Karalyn.'

She stepped forward, and helped Agang to his feet. The old Sanang man tried to smile, but his eyes betrayed his anger.

'Sorry,' said Karalyn.

'No harm done,' he muttered. 'Please don't punish the twins on my account.'

'I'm afraid they'll have to be punished,' she said. 'I can't keep giving them final warnings.' She glanced down at the twins. 'No cakes or biscuits today; and I want you to tidy your room.'

'But, mama,' yelled Cael; 'that's not fair. I didn't do anything.'

'You know the rules. I've told you both a hundred times; you are not to play tricks on people.'

Kyra narrowed her eyes. 'Thorn never punished us.'

'Aye? Well, I'm not Thorn; I'm your mother.'

'Thorn was a better mother than you,' said Kyra.

Karalyn bit her lip as the anger within her rose, and the atmosphere in the room chilled.

Shella stood. 'I think it's time for lunch.'

'That's a good idea,' said Agang.

'I still haven't checked on Kelsey,' said Karalyn.

'You have plenty of time for that,' said Shella. 'It's been thirds since you last checked on her; another hour won't make any difference.'

'But I'm supposed to be giving the twins lessons this afternoon; they're behind on their reading.'

Shella rolled her eyes. 'Karalyn, you have no job; you have all the time in the world, and yet you never seem to relax.'

'Bringing up the twins is a fulltime job, Shella. Look what happens if I leave them alone for a few minutes. I can't bring in any tutors for them; the twins would turn their minds inside out. I have to do it all myself; how can I relax?'

Shella leaned over to a wall and pulled on a rope. A bell tinkled through the Great Keep, and the twins got to their feet, Cael rubbing his hands together at the prospect of lunch. Agang opened the door to the room, and they filed out. Karalyn lowered her gaze, and followed them. She loved Colsbury, but it was starting to feel like a prison. The twins were controllable, as long as Karalyn was physically present to stop them from using their powers on others, but she could never leave them alone for long. Her entire life seemed to revolve around protecting others from her children, as she tried her best to guide them into adulthood. They would turn eight at the end of summer, which meant that she had another decade before she could relax. She tried not to think about what they would be like during adolescence.

Shella led them all into a large dining room, where servants were preparing the table for lunch. Karalyn kept her senses alert, in case either of the twins tried to enter the minds of those setting out the plates and bowls. Kyra was still glowering, while Cael was eyeing a plate of delicate cakes that had been placed next to a large coffee pot.

They took their seats, and the servants departed. Agang poured coffee for the three adults, while the twins got glasses of apple juice, squeezed from the orchards in the gardens of the small island. A silence hung over the table as they all filled their plates.

'Put that cake back,' Karalyn said to Cael.

The boy stared at her. 'But...'

'You heard what I said. I told you not to bother Agang, but you didn't listen to me. How else are you supposed to learn?'

Cael's temper flashed, and Karalyn felt it; the boy's emotions rippling through his mother's senses. He placed the cake back onto the plate in the centre of the table, and sat in a seething silence. Next to him, Kyra was ignoring Karalyn; acting as if her mother wasn't there.

'What were you doing, then?' said Shella.

Karalyn blinked. 'What?'

'If you weren't looking for Kelsey, what were you doing?'

'Oh. I decided it was time to see what Sable was up to.'

The Rakanese woman nodded as she sipped her coffee. 'And?'

'I couldn't find her.'

Shella nodded. 'Is that good or bad?'

'How could it be good?'

'Well, everybody hates her.'

'I don't hate her,' said Kyra.

'You've never met her,' said Shella. 'Sable did some terrible things.'

Kyra smirked. 'Like you? You've killed lots of people, Aunty Shella.'

'You've got me there, kid,' said Shella. 'Let me put it another way; Sable fought for the bad guys.'

'Is it all right to kill bad guys, Aunty?'

Shella nodded. 'Yeah; I guess it is.'

Karalyn said nothing. Kyra and Cael both knew what their mother had done to the Rahain army after Agatha's death, and had used that knowledge against her many times, bringing it up without fail whenever Karalyn had tried to teach them right from wrong. How could she explain to them that she had acted while blinded by grief for their father? The slaughter of the Rahain army had been roundly celebrated by the relieved inhabitants of the Plateau, yet it pressed down upon Karalyn's shoulders like a weight.

'The pork is lovely,' said Agang. 'You know, I've been thinking.'

Shella groaned. 'Here we go.'

Agang ignored her. 'I was wondering if it would be alright if I stayed in Colsbury a little longer?'

'Why are you asking Karalyn?' said Shella. 'I own Colsbury.'

Agang frowned at her. 'You don't own it, Shella. The Holdings government allows you to live here.'

'But you've already been here a year,' said Shella. 'Have you nowhere else to go?'

'I cannot return to Sanang,' he said, 'not after the Mya enclave was absorbed into the rest of the Matriarchy. I've thought about travelling to Plateau City, but I like the peace and quiet here. It's the perfect place to spend a retirement.'

'Yeah, but it's *my* perfect place,' said Shella.

'I have no objections,' said Karalyn. 'I'm more worried that the twins will drive you away.'

'It's fascinating to live alongside two young dream mages,' he said. 'What's more, I like having children around – they brighten up the place. If that means I occasionally have to grunt like a wild boar, then so be it.'

Karalyn thought back to some of the awful things she had done as a child, and knew that forcing Agang to behave like an animal was the least of what the twins could do to him if they tried.

'Okay,' muttered Shella. 'You can stay, but not because I like having you here. I might fall down the stairs and break my hip, and it'd be handy having you around to heal me.'

'I'll let my mother know,' said Karalyn.

'I'd rather you didn't,' said Shella.

'Why not?'

'Because she has to step down next year as First Holder,' said Shella, 'and the new government might decide to evict me from Colsbury. As Agang helpfully reminded us, this place is still owned by the Holdings.'

'They're not going to evict you, Shella.'

'You don't know that.'

Karalyn smiled. 'To evict you, they'd have to evict me, too – and I'm not going to allow that to happen. Colsbury is my home.'

Shella narrowed her eyes. 'Do you mean that?'

'I do.' She glanced at the twins, who were both eating. 'My only alternative would be to take them into the Holdings desert; far away from other people. That's what happened to me. The difference this time is that the twins have someone around who can stop them from interfering in the minds of others; well, most of the time. You know, my family is rich enough to buy Colsbury from the Holdings government; maybe I could persuade mother to purchase it.'

'But then I would become a tenant of the Holdfasts,' said Shella. 'Is that any better?'

'The only thing wrong with Colsbury,' said Agang, 'is the lack of any news from the outside world. Even in the Mya enclave, I could keep up to date with what was happening in the empire, as messengers were always passing between Plateau City and Sanang.' He poured himself a glass of water. 'Sometimes, I enjoy the isolation, but it would be nice to hear what's going on elsewhere.'

Shella glared at him. 'We allow you to stay, and the first thing you do is complain?'

'I'm not complaining,' he said.

'It sounded like a complaint.'

'It's my fault,' said Karalyn. 'I could spend a few minutes each day finding out what's happening, but I don't have any interest in what goes on beyond the walls of Colsbury; not any more. I have two young dream mages to raise.'

Agang smiled. 'But, maybe, just now and again, you could send your vision to Plateau City?'

'I could take you there, if you wanted.'

'It's funny,' he said. 'You have the power to go anywhere, and see anything, and yet you are content to live on this small island.'

'Look what happened the last time I involved myself in the politics of this world.'

'You saved us all, if I remember,' said Agang.

'Yes, but at what cost? Anyway, Agatha and her coterie of gods are dead, and the other gods have no way to get here. I'm not needed any more.'

'All three of us have done enough,' said Shella. 'Let Bridget deal with the empire.'

'I agree,' said Karalyn. She nodded towards the twins. 'Right; you two. Go and tidy your room. I couldn't see the floor when I last walked in.'

'Not now!' cried Kyra. 'I want to play.'

'You can play when your room is clean.'

Each twin glanced at the other, and Karalyn felt their powers mingle as they communicated with their minds.

Go, she ordered them.

Cael and Kyra got up from their chairs and stormed out of the room.

'I'll be keeping an eye on you,' Karalyn called out, before the door was slammed.

Shella shook her head. 'Those two are a handful.'

'That's the understatement of the year,' said Karalyn. 'Thank you both for being patient. I know that it can't be easy living with two children who can read your every thought.'

'It certainly livens things up,' said Shella. 'I'm lucky I don't have any dark secrets.'

'All my secrets came out a long time ago,' said Agang.

Karalyn pushed her empty plate away from her and stood. 'I'd better get back to looking for Kelsey. I shouldn't be too long, and the twins should be occupied until then. Come and get me if they do anything... rash.'

'No problem,' said the Rakanese woman, as she lit a stick of dreamweed.

Karalyn frowned for a moment, then left the room and returned to the study containing the Sextant. She lit a cigarette, and tried to remember where Kelsey had been the last time she had looked at the world where she lived. The world of the City, or the Salve-World – it didn't really have a name, and Karalyn wondered how anyone could live within such a restricted space. Colsbury was different. If Karalyn wanted to, she could travel to any corner of the Star Continent, but on Kelsey's world the people had to be content with living behind thick walls, while millions of greenhides lurked beyond.

She walked to the window and gazed out. The room looked to the east, and she could see the little bridge that connected the isle of Colsbury to the mainland, where a small village stood. Drizzle was falling from the heavy clouds overhead, but it would be summer soon, and the days were already getting warmer, even up in the mountains. She stubbed out the cigarette, and went back to the Sextant. The black blade of the Weathervane was glistening on the glass surface of the device, and she picked it up and slid it into position. She heard the low thrum, and put her right palm onto the Sextant.

What is your desire, Karalyn?

I desire a lot of things. How about the ability to talk to people through the Sextant?

The device fell into silence.

Thought not. Alright; show me Kelsey's world.

Her vision blurred, then she saw the City spread out in front of her. She was looking down onto a large bay, ringed by towns and suburbs.

Instantly, she knew that something was wrong. Smoke was rising from several locations, and hung heavy in the red skies. She counted at least four fires raging through the towns around the bay, while more smoke was coming from other locations out of sight. She had intended to search the western bank of the Straits, as that was where Kelsey had been living the last time she had visited. She remembered seeing her little sister on the back of her silver dragon, as they toiled to reclaim the ruined town from the greenhides; but that had been six thirds before, and a lot could happen in six thirds.

She descended a little. Across from her was the town built from red sandstone. From Aila, she knew it was called Pella. She even knew the name of the palace there – Cuidrach, as it had once been Aila's home, and the demigod had drawn her a rough map of the various places enclosed by the Great Walls that protected the City. She narrowed her eyes. Cuidrach Palace was in smoking ruins, its roofs gone, and its walls blackened and half-collapsed. In front of the palace was a long line of stakes, where dozens of corpses were hanging. Most had cut throats, while some had been mutilated. A pyre was burning in an open courtyard next to the palace, incinerating a great pile of bodies.

A keen sense of helplessness rose within her. The City was in turmoil, and there was nothing she could do to intervene. She couldn't tell her mother what was happening, not without finding out more, and yet she had no idea where to start. Kelsey could be anywhere. She scanned the skies, looking for dragons, but saw nothing flying. She glanced towards another town, one called Tara, and saw the palace there in flames. She moved in closer, and saw a bustle of activity in one of the palace's large courtyards. Wagons were lined up, and militia soldiers were rushing around. A figure emerged from the palace – a tall, broad figure, dressed in a full set of armour. He was as tall as Corthie, and seemed just as powerful, and was carrying a fearsome axe, its blade as black as that of the Weathervane. As he was giving orders to the militia, another figure stepped out from the palace, and Karalyn gasped. It was a greenhide, though larger than any she had seen before. She felt certain that the monstrous beast would attack the humans, but, instead, it stood docile next to the armoured man, as if awaiting his commands. Karalyn looked closer. In the huge man's left hand was a Quadrant, its copper-coloured surface glinting in the reflected glow of the burning palace.

Had the gods found the City? Karalyn knew that they were searching for it, just as they were searching for her own world. She needed to help Kelsey; she needed to do something – but what?

How do I intervene? she said to the Sextant. *I desire to intervene.*

There was no response.

A dragon swooped overhead, but it wasn't the silver one that Kelsey loved; then the wagons started to move off down the steep hillside towards the lower town. The armoured man climbed into one of the carriages, and disappeared from sight. Karalyn moved her vision down to the bottom of the cliff. In a central square, a large platform had been erected, and hundreds of civilians were gathered there, surrounded by militia soldiers and dozens of greenhides. The platform had a row of stakes, stakes that looked the same as those in front of Cuidrach Palace. There was going to be a mass execution, and there was nothing Karalyn could do about it.

She lifted her hand from the Sextant, and the vision cut off. Karalyn stared at the huge device. Using it felt much the same as having one of her visions. Like them, it granted knowledge without power; one could witness, but never participate. What was she going to do? She couldn't tell her mother what she had seen; that would make the situation ten times worse. Her mother would demand action. Karalyn's thoughts went to the presence of Shella and Agang in the Great Keep. With their combined power under her control, Karalyn might be able to travel directly to the world of the City, but she remembered what had happened when she had gone to Lostwell. She had lost four years in the blink of an eye – four years of her children's lives; gone forever.

There had to be another way. She removed the Weathervane from the side of the Sextant, then she walked back to the dining room. Shella and Agang were still there, working their way through the plate of cakes.

Shella raised an eyebrow. 'What's that look on your face for? Did you see something bad? Is Kelsey alright?'

'I need you to look after the twins for the afternoon,' Karalyn said.

'Why?' said Agang. 'Are you going somewhere?'

'I have to visit my mother.'

'If there's bad news, don't keep it from me,' said Shella.

'It might be bad; I don't know.'

'Then why do you need to see old Daffers?'

'I need to borrow something.'

'What?'

'The God-King's Quadrant.'

CHAPTER 2
RITUAL HUMILIATION

Outside Plateau City, The Plateau – 1st Day, Last Third Spring 534

'I know this isn't what you want,' said Thorn.

Keir stared out of the carriage window.

'All I am asking,' his wife went on, 'is that you give it a chance. Your mother has entrusted me with a great responsibility. I don't want to let her down.'

'What about letting me down?' Keir snapped. 'Don't I matter? You know, I've heard all this before. It was what you told me when we moved from the Hold Fast estate to Holdings City; and now, two years later, you're telling me the same thing again.'

'It was true then, and it's true now. I learned an awful lot working for your mother in Holdings City.'

Keir said nothing, his eyes on the countryside. In the distance ahead, he could see the high walls of Plateau City approach – their new home, whether he wanted it or not.

'Great things could happen to us here,' said Thorn. 'Plateau City is the centre of the empire, and we'll be at its heart; right next to the Empress.'

'You'll be next to the Empress, you mean,' said Keir. 'We're not travelling all this way because of me. You are the one with the fancy new job title – what am I?'

'You can be whoever you want to be, Keir. You can carve out your own position; the Empress is in need of competent advisors and administrators. For a start, I imagine her Majesty will desire you to take over the reins of vision communication within the empire. Her current vision mages are distinctly lacking in that department. By all accounts, Mage Sanders gets exhausted quickly, and Mage Tabor's range is decidedly limited. You could make yourself essential to the Empress within a couple of thirds.'

'I don't want to be Bridget's pet vision mage.'

He felt Thorn's gaze pierce him. 'No?'

'No.'

'How about doing it to support your wife?'

Keir laughed. 'You're deluding yourself. My mother has sent you to Plateau City because she doesn't want to be there in person. You may think you have a wonderful new job, but the Empress will see through it in a second. I wouldn't be surprised if Bridget sends you packing within a few days.'

Thorn shrugged. 'I am at her Majesty's service.'

'No; you're my mother's lapdog. You would do anything to please her, wouldn't you? You've been running around after her in Holdings City for two years, hanging on to her every word, and for what? Are you trying to prove to her that you're worthy of being a Holdfast?'

'I am a Holdfast; worthy or not.'

'Only because you're married to me.'

Thorn fell into silence. Keir wondered if he had gone too far, but consoled himself with the knowledge that he was right. Unlike Jemma and Celine, who had both been adopted into the family, Thorn was a Holdfast purely on the merit of her wedding certificate. If they ever divorced, then she would be ejected from the family. Not that he wanted to divorce her, but it was true all the same. He turned from the window to glance at her. Thorn was gazing out of the other window, her expression closed. She was wearing blue again, which annoyed him. She seemed to think that the colour belonged to her. It was a little pathetic, really. His eyes strayed over the folds of her dress, and up to her neatly pulled back hair. She was just as beautiful as the day he had first seen her in the harbour of Rainsby eight and a half years before. He had stuttered and stammered in her presence that day, so over-awed had he been; and the feeling of inferiority had never quite departed. She could choose any man she desired, and yet she had chosen him. He hated her at times, but the thought of her in another man's arms sent him into paroxysms of rage. He would never divorce her; never allow another man to take his place.

Their carriage bumped over the cobbled road surface as it neared a high set of gates. Keir's attention went back to the view, and he gazed out. The gates were wide open, and, while there were a few soldiers on duty, none were checking the traffic passing in and out of the great city. Bridget's city. For twenty-seven years, Bridget had ruled the empire from Plateau City. In comparison, Guilliam's reign as Emperor had lasted a mere three years, though he had been King of the Holdings for a year prior to that.

'I wonder how Bridget remembers us,' Keir said. 'I doubt it's with any affection.'

'I don't require her affection,' said Thorn. 'Respect would be far better, even if it's grudging. A long time has passed since the two witches of Rainsby were disobeying her orders. She hated us back then, of that I am convinced, but will she still hate us now? I don't think your mother would have sent us down here if that were the case.'

'I miss those days.'

Thorn raised an eyebrow. 'I don't.'

'It seemed as though the entire world was at our feet. Do you not miss the adulation of the marines, or the cheers from the people of Rainsby? They thought we were gods.'

'There were a few good moments, such as when we destroyed the Sons of Sanang. There were also some of the worst times of my life, like the trek from Stretton Sands to Amatskouri. I don't regret our actions, but I'd rather not have to live through anything like that again.'

The carriage trundled through the open gates and entered the New Town of the city. Keir stared at the busy streets. Handsome tenement blocks lined the road, and well-dressed citizens were out in large numbers. After a few more streets, Keir realised that he had seen more wealth than existed in the whole of Holdings City, which looked provincial and small compared to the great imperial capital. Neither he nor Thorn had been in the city for several years, and it seemed to have grown ever more prosperous in that time. Their carriage took a left at a major junction, and turned towards the Old Town. On their right was the aristocratic district, where the Holdfast townhouse lay, and south of that, the thin spires of the university complex soared into the cloudy sky.

Ahead of them, the dark walls of the Great Fortress loomed, towering above the other buildings of the city.

'Our new home,' said Thorn.

Keir frowned. 'What?'

Thorn pointed. 'The fortress palace.'

'We're not staying there,' said Keir.

'Yes, we are.'

'No. We'll be living in the Holdfast townhouse. I don't want to be under the constant supervision of the Empress and her soldiers.'

'But, Keir, the whole point of me coming here is to act as your mother's legate. How am I supposed to represent her if I'm not around? I'll have to live in the Great Fortress, so that I'm always available.'

'Why didn't you say this before now?'

'I thought it was obvious.'

'To you, maybe.'

Thorn looked at him for a long moment, then turned away. The carriage continued down a wide, straight road that cut through the heart of the New Town. When they were a hundred yards from the Great Fortress, their driver guided their four horses into a deep layby, where several other carriages and wagons were parked. The carriage came to a halt, and the driver clambered down from the high bench. He knocked on the side door and opened it.

'Mister and Missus Holdfast,' he said, bowing. 'We have arrived at the Great Fortress.'

'Thank you,' said Thorn, extending her hand.

The driver took it, and helped Thorn down to the roadside. Keir stepped down next, and gazed around.

'Shall I have your luggage moved into the palace, sir?' said the driver.

'No,' said Keir.

'Not yet,' said Thorn. 'Please stay with the carriage and bags for the moment, until we work out what's happening.'

'As you will, ma'am.'

He closed the door, and Thorn gestured towards the bridge that crossed the dry moat. Beyond it sat the northern entrance to the Great Fortress. The gates were well-protected by imperial soldiers, but were lying open, and a steady stream of pedestrians were making their way in and out of the massive structure.

Keir and Thorn walked over the bridge, and passed into a large hall, where officials were directing the crowds of civilians into several different queues. A line of desks ran along the left-hand wall, and civil servants were dealing with the various requests, complaints and petitions from the citizens, while soldiers stood guard by every doorway. An official stepped in front of Thorn and Keir as they made their way through the hall.

'Excuse me; can I help you?' she said.

'Yes,' said Thorn, smiling. 'We have an appointment to see the Empress today.'

'I see,' said the official. 'Do you have a letter that I can review?'

Thorn reached into her small bag and passed the official an envelope, sealed with the wax stamp of the First Holder. The official gazed at the seal for a moment, then passed the letter back unopened.

'May I take your names, please?'

'I'm Keir Holdfast,' said Keir. 'This is my wife, Thorn.'

A slight flicker of interest flitted across the official's eyes. 'Wait just one moment, please,' she said. 'I shall send someone to inform her Majesty of your approach.'

Keir opened his mouth to speak, but the official was too quick for him, and she darted away through the crowds. Keir frowned, then glanced around at the inside of the hall.

'This is where I ran away from my father,' he said; 'the day he was murdered.'

Thorn glanced at him. 'I hear that there's a statue of him in the district where he was slain. We should pay it a visit while we're here.'

'This city has several statues of my family. There's father, and there's Aunty Keira as well. There's even a statue of my idiot sister Karalyn.'

'Do you mean the idiot sister who saved the world – twice?'

'She hardly saved the world the first time – she was a damn baby. And the second time, she wouldn't have been successful if she hadn't stolen our powers. Without us, she would have been defeated. Yet, there's no statue of me, or any of the other mages that she drew power from.'

'Saying things like that makes you sound a little churlish, Keir. Did we fight Agatha for renown, or because it was the right thing to do?'

Keir smirked. 'Is it wrong to want both? For a time, you and I were the greatest mages in the world. Where's our statue?'

'You could always build one yourself. You're rich enough.'

The official returned, apologised for the delay, then led Keir and Thorn through a heavily-guarded doorway. They came to a large stairwell, and began to ascend. The lower levels of the Great Fortress were given over to military and administrative personnel, and they passed floors packed with offices and soldiers. Keir lost count of the flights of stairs they climbed, then the official took them along a wide corridor, which ended in a thick oaken door. Two soldiers were on duty outside, and they nodded at the official. The soldiers opened the door, and they passed through, the stone walls and floors replaced by fine tapestries and carpets.

'Welcome to the palace,' said the official.

'We've both been here before,' said Keir. 'This isn't new to us.'

The official smiled, then led them onwards. They entered a vast hall, which was empty, and crossed to a side door. They passed more guards, and walked into a comfortable study, where three people were sitting.

Thorn bowed low. 'Your Majesty,' she said.

The Empress glanced up from her chair.

'May I present Keir and Thorn Holdfast, your Imperial Majesty?' said the official.

Bridget nodded. 'I was expecting them; thank you.'

The official bowed, and left the room.

'Well, well,' said the Empress. 'The wee renegade witches return to Plateau City, eh?'

Thorn reached back into her bag and produced the letter.

The Empress raised her hand. 'No need. Daphne has already told me why you're here. She was in my head this morning, telling me that you would be arriving today.' She shook her head, her eyes tight. 'This is so typical of her. Daphne's been the Herald of the Empire for seven years, and she's spent only a tiny fraction of that by my side. I demand that she attend court, and what does she do? She sends you.'

'Your Majesty,' said Thorn; 'the First Holder is extremely busy governing the Holdings. She felt that...'

'I don't care how she feels!' cried Bridget, her eye flashing. She took a breath, and her features calmed. 'I'm forgetting myself.' She gestured to the two young men sitting on the couch opposite her. 'This is my son Bryce, whom you have already met, and Mage Tabor.'

Thorn smiled at the two men. 'I remember you both. Is Brogan here as well?'

'No,' said Bridget. 'My eldest daughter has gone with Corthie and Aila to Kellach Brigdomin, along with Bethal from the triplets. It was a strange coincidence that Corthie decided to leave when he learned that you two were going to be coming here. He made his plans the same day. I wonder why.' She smiled at Keir. 'Any ideas?'

Keir's temper threatened to boil over.

'I'm sure they'll have a lovely trip, your Majesty,' said Thorn.

Bridget laughed. 'Is Keir not allowed to speak? Do you wipe his arse for him as well, Thorn?'

Thorn lifted her chin a fraction. 'Do you expect an answer to that, your Majesty? With your permission, I would like to get to work right away. As the appointed legate of the Herald of the Empire, I am authorised to take decisions in the name of Daphne Holdfast, and I have several ideas about how to improve communications throughout the empire. I am also ready to take on any extra tasks or assignments that you may feel appropriate. I am here to help, and I am at your service.'

Bridget narrowed her eyes, as if evaluating Thorn. 'I could always do with another hedgewitch. You want to work? I can find you work. Report to the Old Town infirmary, and they will assign you some duties curing the sick and injured.'

'Very well, your Majesty. I will do so, if that is your desire.'

'It is,' said the Empress. She shifted her gaze to Keir. 'What about you?'

Keir blinked. 'Your Majesty?'

'Are you also here to work?'

He frowned, unsure of how to respond.

'It's not a trick question,' said Bridget, 'so you can take that glaikit expression off yer face. Can your vision powers reach Rahain from here?'

'I... I've never tried to reach Rahain from here, your Majesty. I could reach Amatskouri from Rainsby, and I can reach Holdings City from here, so I suppose that...'

Bridget raised a hand to quieten him. 'Good enough. Mage Tabor is decent, but he doesn't have that kind of range. You could be useful to me, if I could trust you.'

Keir's face burned. 'Why wouldn't you trust me, your Majesty?'

Bridget slapped her thigh, as a roar of laughter left her lips. Keir and Thorn stood in silence, waiting for it to subside.

'You're seriously asking me that?' said Bridget. 'You, the mage who continually disobeyed direct orders during the last war? Do you think I'm an eejit? My, how the world changes. You two thought you were going to take over the entire empire, didn't you? And now you're reduced to this. I've half a mind to throw you both out on your arses.'

'Mother,' said Bryce; 'the last war was a long time ago. It's been seven years since Agatha and her Rahain army were defeated; and I remember Keir and Thorn pledging their allegiance to you in Colsbury. Perhaps it's time to forgive, and move on?'

Bridget nodded. 'Maybe.' She glanced at Thorn. 'You should know that Bryce has been working in my court for nearly a year now, handling most of the work that would usually be carried out by a herald. In fact, I'm considering replacing Daphne with him, once he's learned the ins and outs. That way, at least I would have a herald who actually lived here.'

'You are the Empress, your Majesty,' said Thorn.

'Aye, and don't you forget it, Thorn. I know you have half an eye on my job; but let me tell you this – you will never be empress. Understand?' She nodded at the door. 'Now, bugger off. Thorn, report to the infirmary first thing tomorrow; and Keir, come back here in the morning, if you decide that you want to make yourself useful. I have a long list of messages that need sent across the empire.'

Thorn and Keir bowed their heads, then walked from the room. The official from before was waiting for them, and they were escorted from the Great Fortress without another word being exchanged. As soon as they were back out in the open air, Thorn clenched her fists and took a deep breath.

'That bitch,' said Keir. 'All she wanted to do was humiliate us.'

Thorn glared at him. 'Don't call her that. She is the Holder of the World.'

'How can you defend her after what she just put us through? I was right, wasn't I? Coming here was a terrible idea. Let's get out of this city, and head back to the Holdings.'

'No.'

Keir eyed his wife. 'No?'

'That's what I said. Daphne Holdfast has given me a job to do, and I intend to do it. The Empress can humiliate me all she wants; it's not going to stop me from doing my duty.'

She walked off towards their carriage, and Keir followed her.

'Wait,' he said. 'Let's stay overnight in the townhouse, and we can discuss it over a couple of drinks.'

Their driver bowed as they approached.

Thorn smiled at him. 'Take us to the Holdfast townhouse.'

Keir knocked on the front door of the elegant townhouse for several minutes before it was answered. A young woman peered out onto the wide, tree-lined street, then smiled as she saw who was standing there.

'Lord and Lady Holdfast,' she said, bowing.

'Hello, Tabitha,' said Thorn.

'You remembered my name, ma'am?'

'Of course,' said Thorn. 'You were in Colsbury during the siege; how could I forget you?'

'Who else is here?' said Keir.

'It's just me, sir,' said Tabitha. 'No Holdfasts have lived in the townhouse for a long time, and Holder Fast didn't want to waste money hiring staff for an empty house.'

'Didn't Corthie and Aila stay here?' said Thorn.

Tabitha opened the door wider, and stood to the side to allow them to enter. 'No, ma'am. Corthie, Aila and their son stayed in the Great Fortress while they were in the city. They visited the townhouse once, to let me know that they were here, but they didn't stay a single night. How long will you be staying for, ma'am?'

'We're not sure,' said Thorn. She turned to the carriage, and signalled to their driver. 'Please bring the luggage indoors.'

The man bowed, and began pulling large trunks down from the back of the carriage.

'This is Patra, our driver,' Thorn said to Tabitha. 'He will also be staying with us.'

'I shall prepare a room in the servants' quarters for him, ma'am,' said Tabitha.

'Is there any food?' said Keir.

'Not much, I'm afraid, sir. The market in the Old Town will still be open – shall I go out and purchase some supplies?'

'Yes. Make sure you get some wine, from Anamindhari if possible.'

'Yes, sir. I'll show you to your room, and then leave right away.'

The servant led Keir and Thorn through the narrow hallway, passing rooms to their left and right, where the shutters were closed, and every item of furniture was covered in dust-sheets. Keir hadn't set foot inside the building since fleeing from Amatskouri during the war against Agatha, and there were several areas that he had never seen. He was familiar with the spacious quarters that Tabitha took them to, on the first floor. The servant pulled a dust-sheet from the large bed, then opened the doors to the balcony. Keir walked out, and gazed at the view. The sun was lowering in the western sky in front of him, and the Inner Sea was sparkling. Behind him, he could hear Thorn chatting to Tabitha, but he paid no attention. How dare the Empress treat them in such a manner? They were Holdfasts, members of the most powerful family in the world, and Bridget was nothing but an uncultured barbarian from the savage depths of Kellach Brigdomin.

Thorn joined him on the balcony.

'Tabitha's gone out to buy food,' she said, as she leaned on the railings to look at the view.

'Just enough for one night, I hope,' he said.

Thorn said nothing for a moment, then she turned to her husband. 'I'm not leaving in the morning. The Empress assigned me a role, and I am going to do as she asked.'

'What? You're going to serve in the damn infirmary?'

'Yes. If you recall, it won't be my first time. I have healed the sick and wounded for many years of my life.'

'But, you're a soulwitch. Bridget called you a hedgewitch to humiliate you.'

'Perhaps she did.'

'And it doesn't bother you?'

'Not in the slightest. Let the Empress have her little revenge on us; after all, it's been a long time coming.'

'She would have lost the war without us.'

'I know. Regardless of that, we disobeyed her orders, and were never punished for it.'

'So you intend to meekly go along with her idiotic requests?'

'That's exactly what I intend to do; and I advise you to do the same. Tomorrow morning, I will don an apron, and start work in the infirmary. I will be polite, and obedient. I will defer to those in charge, and strive to do the best job I can. My healing skills are in fine shape; it will feel good to put them to use again.'

Keir sighed and shook his head. 'I'll be staying here. The Empress didn't order me to do anything. She requested my help, and I decline the offer.'

'You would be making a mistake.'

'I'm not going to degrade myself for her.'

'Working as her vision mage would in no way degrade you, Keir. Have a little patience. Let's prove to her Majesty that we can be trusted, and that we are here to serve the empire. She's testing us; don't give up at the first obstacle.'

'My mother would be outraged if she knew how Bridget had treated us today.'

Thorn smiled. 'Would she? How do you know that your mother and the Empress haven't planned all this? Daphne has protected us from the wrath of the Empress for many years, and now she is trying to fit us back into imperial society. If a little ritual punishment for the crimes of our youth is the worst we can expect, then I say that we've got off lightly.'

Keir lit a cigarette. 'This is utter bullshit. If we left at dawn, then we would be out of the city long before the Empress discovered our absence. Then we could head back to the Hold Fast estate, avoiding mother in the process, and I can get back to doing what I want to be doing – running the estate. For the last two years, I've had to give up my dreams, so that you could play politics with mother in Holdings City. It's time to do what I want for a change.'

'No.'

'Is that it?' Keir cried. 'No?'

'You can leave if you want to, Keir. I'm going nowhere. If we let this chance slip through our fingers, then we shall never get another one. We would be damned as rebels and have to hide in Hold Fast for the rest of our days.'

Keir shrugged. 'That suits me fine.'

'It doesn't suit me, husband. I spent five years in Hold Fast, caring for Karalyn's children, and suppressing my hopes and ambitions. I don't regret any of it, but I'm not going back. The Empress was right about many things – we have to earn her trust and respect all over again; we have to prove ourselves to her. It won't be easy, but I've never shied away from a challenge.'

'The Empress was wrong. We're Holdfasts – we don't need to prove anything to anybody.'

Thorn shook her head and smiled. 'No, dear husband. The Empress was wrong about one thing, and one thing only.'

'Oh yeah? And what's that?'

Thorn gazed out to sea. 'One day, I shall be Empress.'

CHAPTER 3
HALLOWED GROUND

Northern Pass, Kell – 1st Day, Last Third Spring 534

'This is amazing,' said Corthie, a huge grin on his face. 'The ocean, the cliffs, the mountains. Kell is the most beautiful place on any world.'

'That's great, Corthie,' said Aila, from the side of the carriage. 'Could you give me a hand, please?'

'Eh? Aye, sure.'

He turned away from the view, and helped Aila climb down from the carriage, their child held close in her arms. Behind her, a servant and a soldier also disembarked, while the other carriage was also disgorging its passengers onto the grass a few yards down the track.

Aila placed the child onto the ground, and held his hand as the little boy tried to run away.

'Stay here, Killop,' she said. 'There's a big cliff, and I don't want you falling.'

Corthie laughed. 'The lad would survive a fall. He's immortal.'

'Yes, but who would fish him out of the ocean?' said Aila. 'So, this is the nice part of Kell?'

'Almost,' Corthie said. 'The pass goes right along the coast for a few miles, and then opens up into Southern Kell.'

'I confess that I didn't think much of Northern Kell. It reminded me a little of Lostwell, apart from the terrible weather. All those slag heaps and ruined villages.'

'Aye. It's a wasteland, thanks to the Rahain; but the mines there have made the rest of Kellach Brigdomin prosperous. The mine-owners have to pay a whole range of steep taxes, or so I've heard.'

Aila nodded towards the track, where the two princesses were approaching. The daughters of Empress Bridget had been travelling in the other carriage, and they only met up with the others whenever they stopped.

'What is the significance of this place?' said Brogan, the elder of the two.

'I think there was a famous battle here,' said Corthie. 'It's the Kell Pass.'

'Who cares?' said Bethal, a cloak wrapped round her shoulders despite the sunshine.

'You should,' said her older sister. 'If this is the Kell Pass, then Corthie's father fought here, alongside Mage Keira. They defeated the Rahain here in five-oh-three.'

'Five-oh-three?' said Bethal, squinting. 'In ancient times, you mean. Why is it so cold?'

'It's a beautiful day,' said Corthie. 'Take a deep breath of the fresh air, and feel the sun on your skin.'

Bethal rolled her eyes.

'Look,' said Aila. 'Some people are coming.'

Corthie turned, and saw a small group approach from the south. They were all Kellach Brigdomin, as were the six imperial soldiers who had accompanied Corthie and the others on the long journey from Plateau City. They towered over Aila and the two Holdings servants who had come along to minister to Bridget's daughters.

Corthie raised his hand as the group approached. 'Hello,' he called out.

A middle-aged Kellach man strode towards them from the group.

He glanced at Corthie and the others, then bowed before the two princesses.

'You must be Brogan and Bethal,' he said. 'Welcome to the Kell Pass.' He turned to Corthie. 'And are you Corthie Holdfast, sir?'

'Aye,' Corthie said. 'This is Aila, my wife, and this wee lad here is Killop.'

The man's eyes went down to the child standing by his mother. He crouched down, and ruffled the boy's hair; and for a moment Corthie thought he could see the man's eyes well up.

'Who are you?' said Bethal.

The man got back to his feet and composed himself. 'My name is Conal. I was an old friend of your mother, and served with Killop and Keira right here, thirty years ago.' He raised an arm and swept it over the narrow pass. 'This area might look peaceful now, but back then it was a forest of palisade walls and fortresses. The Kell blocked this pass to the invading Rahain armies, and we smashed them for days. It's the only viable route for an army to cross from Northern to Southern Kell. We would have held out indefinitely, if the Rahain hadn't used winged lizards to get behind us.'

'What happened to the fortifications?' said Corthie.

'The Rahain cleared them all away, once they'd conquered the rest of Kellach Brigdomin. After that, when Keira was leading the resistance, they erected a fort of their own, a couple of miles south of here, to stop the fire mage from reaching the mines in Northern Kell.'

Corthie nodded. 'Where was my father based?'

Conal smiled. 'Right here. We're standing on the spot where your father's squad of soldiers defended a stretch of palisade wall. We lost half of the squad on the first day of the attack, but we didn't budge an inch. My sister Connie was one of the first to be killed, hit by a giant boulder sent over by a Rahain catapult. Her blood, and the blood of all those who fell defending Kell, is now mingled with the soil of our homeland.' He paused for a moment, his eyes lowered. 'Of course, our victory here meant nothing in the long run. Despite defeating the Rahain in the Kell Pass, and at

Marchside, we were overwhelmed, and most of the survivors were carried away in chains. I was put into one of the same wagons as Killop and the future Empress, and we were all taken to Rahain as slaves. All the same, this pass is almost sacred to us few Kell who remain. It is a symbol of hope.'

'Can I take a walk around?' said Corthie.

'Aye,' said Conal, 'though be careful. There are lots of pits and ditches that the wee one could fall into.'

Corthie stooped down and picked up Killop in his arms.

'Here we go, wee man,' he said.

Corthie set off across the thick turf, as Aila walked by his side. They headed in the direction of a high wall of steep cliffs, and Corthie noticed how uneven the ground was under his boots.

'This reminds me of the ruins of Jezra,' he said, 'when Achan, Yaizra and I were scrambling about on the Western Bank.'

'The ruins of Jezra are thousands of years old, Corthie,' said Aila, 'not thirty.'

Corthie's foot stubbed against something, and he leaned down and picked up a long, rust-covered arrowhead.

He smiled. 'I wonder how many of these are lying around here. It must have been some battle.'

Aila glanced up at him. 'Do you miss all that?'

'What, fighting in big battles?' He shrugged. 'You know me, Aila. I'm only good at one thing.'

'Don't say that. You're good at lots of things.'

'Aye? Like what?'

'Being a father, for one thing. Which is just as well, seeing as how there's another on the way.'

'I could almost forget that you're pregnant at times.'

'It's one of the perks of being a demigod. Even giving birth to Killop was easy.'

'So, you're glad that we're having children?'

Aila halted, and raised an eyebrow. 'Glad?' She smiled. 'Glad doesn't begin to cover it. For centuries, I avoided having any relationships with mortals, and one of the main reasons was that I didn't want a mortal child; one that I would have to watch grow old and die in front of me. That's all changed now; my entire perception of it has been turned upside down.'

'Because wee Killop is also a demigod?'

'Yes. I don't understand how, but there's something in you that allows our children to retain their self-healing powers. It's never happened before, as far as I'm aware. Every single child with one demigod parent on my world ended up mortal.'

Corthie grinned. 'Does this mean you want to have more children? I've always wanted a big family.'

Aila nodded. 'Ten? Or maybe a round dozen? I'm never going to go through the menopause, so I can keep going for as long as you can.'

Corthie lowered his voice. 'And what would this world think, if we unleashed a dozen demigods upon it?'

'A dozen Holdfast demigods.'

'It could change everything.'

'Don't worry, Corthie.'

'I'm not worried, but it's a decent enough question.'

'By the time it might become a problem, you... you will...'

'I'll be dead by then?'

Her face fell. 'Yes.'

'Fair enough,' he said. 'To be honest, I have no desire to live forever.'

'I wish I could agree.'

'Let's just enjoy the time we have.'

'I intend to.' She glanced around. 'It's hard to imagine Empress Bridget fighting here, even though it was thirty years ago.'

'She didn't,' said Corthie. 'This battle was fought between the Kell and the Rahain. The Brig didn't get involved until a little later. She fought in the Fire Temple, though, and a lot of other battles.'

'I didn't want to mention this in front of the servants or soldiers,' said Aila, 'but the Empress didn't look well to me.'

'Nor to me.'

'How old is she?'

'Fifty,' said Corthie.

'She seemed older.'

'She's been Empress for more than half her life. The pressure of that has taken its toll.'

'But she doesn't help herself. Her drinking, for instance. I thought you could drink a lot, but Empress Bridget easily matched you. She must be demolishing a bottle of whisky nearly every day. If she keeps it up, then this world might be looking for a new ruler sooner than anyone would like.'

'Nah. Old Bridget is as tough as my leather boots. She's Brig.'

'And Brig don't die, do they?'

'She's easily got another ten years in her; maybe more. Anyway, I'm sure the high and mighty will have something planned.'

'By "high and mighty", I assume you are referring to your mother?'

'Well, her and others.'

'What others? Your mother is ruler of the Holdings, and the Herald of the Empire. In many ways, she's just as powerful as the Empress. And, she'll probably live longer.'

'My mother doesn't want to be Empress, if that's what you're getting at. It was offered to her once, and she turned it down.'

Aila frowned. 'Trouble's on its way. I've lived through enough political intrigues and machinations to sense it. The Empress and your mother don't particularly like each other – that's obvious; and there's no clear line of succession. On top of that, your mother, who, in theory, is supposed to be a loyal and obedient servant of the empire, routinely ignores the Empress's demands, and does whatever she pleases.'

'All this political talk is of no interest to me,' he said. 'Does it matter who sits on the throne? Part of the reason I wanted to come down here to Kellach Brigdomin was to escape all that.'

Aila smiled. 'Really? I thought it was to avoid your brother.'

'Aye, well, that too. Keir does my head in. I'd hoped that a few years might have improved him, but he's just the same as he was when I was younger – a bawbag.'

'Who's a bawbag?' said a voice.

They turned, and saw Brogan and Bethal approach. The younger of the two sisters was shivering in the cold wind that was sweeping across the pass.

'Go on,' said Brogan. 'Who are you calling a bawbag?'

'My brother,' said Corthie. 'You should be grateful you're not in Plateau City if he's living there now.'

Brogan laughed. 'And what about his wife?'

'Thorn's alright,' said Corthie; 'if we forget about her poor taste in men.'

'All the guys say that about Thorn,' said Bethal. 'All I can remember of her is my mother complaining that she was a rebel.'

'She looked after my sister's bairns for four years,' said Corthie. 'She has my respect for that.'

'Bairns?' said Aila. 'We've just entered Kell, and now you've started speaking like one?'

'I'm half Kell; so aye.'

'Corthie's accent is too posh for Kellach Brigdomin,' said Brogan. 'You should hear the way my mother speaks after a few drinks.'

'I've heard,' said Aila. 'I found it hard to understand half of what she was saying at times.'

Bethal laughed. 'One whisky, and every second word she says is "fuck".'

Brogan glared at her little sister. 'I want none of that language from you, little madam.'

'I'm sixteen; you don't control me.'

'We're representing the empire while we're here,' said Brogan.

'So?'

'Don't make me regret bringing you along on this trip,' said her elder sister. 'You need to behave yourself.'

'Or what? Are you going to tell mother if I swear? She would laugh, that's what she would do.'

'Go and wait by the carriage.'

Bethal glared at Brogan for a moment, then turned and strode back to the road.

'Sorry about that,' said Brogan. 'This is Bethal's first time outside

Plateau City since the siege of Colsbury. I think she might be a little over-excited.'

'There's no need to apologise,' said Corthie. 'It's only a word.'

'I'd rather not hear it in front of little Killop,' said Aila.

'You should prepare yourself, then,' said Brogan. 'We'll be in Southern Kell by this evening, and I won't be able to give everyone a telling off.'

They made their way back to the carriages, where Conal was speaking to the soldiers. He turned at their approach.

'Are you ready to move on?' he said.

'Are you our official escort?' said Aila.

'Eh, something like that,' said Conal. 'I was sent up here to welcome you, and to let you know that rooms have been put aside in a wee village not too far from here, at the southern end of the pass. I have a wagon nearby. Bring the carriages up, and I'll lead you down into Southern Kell.'

'Who sent you?' said Corthie.

'An old friend of your father's,' said Conal.

The visitors climbed up into the two carriages, while Conal hurried along the track until he disappeared out of sight. The soldiers mounted the driver's benches, and the carriages set off. Corthie gazed out of the window. In the distance, he could see the ocean crashing against the ragged cliffs that bordered the edge of the pass.

'Have you ever been sailing?' said Aila.

Corthie smiled. 'We sailed across the Inner Sea on our way here.'

She pointed out of the window. 'I meant, have you ever sailed out there?'

'No one sails on the ocean,' said Corthie. 'It's far too wild.'

Aila frowned as she balanced little Killop on her knee. 'Really? No one? Someone must have tried.'

Corthie shrugged.

'Is it because there's no moon, and only seven stars?' said Aila. 'Is it too hard to navigate at night?'

'You're asking the wrong person,' said Corthie. 'Karalyn would probably know the answer to that.'

Another wagon appeared ahead of them on the road, with Conal on its back. He waved at the carriages and then they set off down the pass. After an hour, the road began to descend, and the coastline veered away to the south, while the mountains on their right ended in a wall of rock. The road led down into a wide, green landscape of fields and tiny villages that nestled among the low hills and valleys. The sun came out from behind the clouds at that moment, and Corthie felt a wave of emotion ripple through him at the sight.

Kell. It was a place he had long dreamed about, but never visited. Throughout his four years of training on Lostwell, and then while fighting on Aila's world, he had been sure that one day he would return home; but which home? Hold Fast? The estate where he had been brought up held mixed feelings for him. He had experienced joy there, but pain too, and the endless torment and bullying inflicted by Keir and Kelsey that had blighted his childhood. The mansion also reminded him of his father, but not in a cheerful way. Plateau City had been alright, but he had avoided the Holdfast townhouse, due to the memories it evoked of Laodoc's violent death, and his killing of the god responsible. The Great Fortress was comfortable, and he had got on well with the Empress and her five children, but it wasn't home.

He stared out of the window. Could Kell be home? He had never mentioned it to Aila, but part of the reason for travelling to Kell had been that it might be a suitable place in which to settle, and raise the large family that he hoped he and Aila would have. It was remote from the rest of the empire, but that didn't concern him. If there were no wars to fight, then he needed something else in his life. He pictured a little house next to a small stream, then realised that he was imagining the cottage near Severton where Karalyn and Lennox had lived just before Corthie's abduction. Was that what he wanted?

'Are you alright?' said Aila.

'What?'

'There's a tear rolling down your cheek, Corthie.'

'I... I don't know. What am I going to do with my life, Aila? I'm twenty-two years old, and I feel as if I've already lived a lifetime. I want a peaceful life, but all I know is how to kill.'

She took his hand and squeezed it. 'What's brought this on?'

He turned back to stare out at the view. 'This is as far as this world goes. I look at it, and it's so beautiful that it actually hurts; but there's nowhere else to go. I couldn't relax in Hold Fast, and Plateau City was just temporary...'

'Corthie, compared to the City, this world is enormous. The Star Continent is five or six times larger than the whole of Khatanax on Lostwell. You could travel for months in the same direction, and still not reach the ocean.'

'Do you like it here?'

'Yes. The wide open spaces of the Holdings, the cities, and now this. You're right; Kell is beautiful. In fact, it's the most beautiful place I've ever seen; but there's still Sanang, Rahain, and Rakana to visit – all huge countries with their own histories and cultures. We could spend years travelling around this world, and not see half of it.'

'And what if I wanted to stay in Kell?'

Aila paused.

'Before I met you,' he said, 'the happiest time of my life was down here. Not in Kell; we were over in Domm, right at the far end of the peninsula. I stayed there with Karalyn and my mother; and Jemma and Cole were there, too. We were on the run from gods – Agatha and the rest of them, but I didn't care about any of that. All I can remember is being happy.'

'Let's see how it goes,' said Aila.

He nodded, feeling foolish. He wiped his face, and took Killop from Aila's knee. He held the child up to the window.

'Look at this, wee man,' he whispered. 'Home.'

Two hours later, the wagon and carriages pulled into the dusty tracks of a small village. Cottages lined the road, along with a waterwheel that was turning amid a wide stream that flowed down from the nearby mountains. The sun was still halfway up the western sky, and Corthie felt its warmth on his skin as they climbed down from the carriage.

'Looks like rain later,' said Conal, his eyes on a low bank of dark clouds approaching from the south-west. He glanced at the others. 'It rains pretty much every day in Kell; but be thankful that we're not in Lach – it rains twice a day down there.'

The soldiers helped Bridget's daughters step down from the other carriage, and they walked into a square courtyard, where two dozen people had gathered in front of a low stone building. Conal went to speak to an older woman in the small crowd, then he turned to the others.

'Please welcome two of the Empress's children to the village,' Conal said; 'Brogan and Bethal.'

The crowd clapped, and there were a few cheers.

'It's the first time since Bridget became Empress that any of her family have travelled to Kell,' Conal went on, 'so we have a duty to show them some proper hospitality.'

'Then shut up and get the fucking beers in,' came a voice from the crowd, provoking a few laughs.

Conal cringed. 'Aye, sure; just hold on a wee moment. It's not just the Empress's daughters that are here; we also have Corthie Holdfast, son of Chief Killop; his wife, Aila, and their wee bairn, Killop junior.'

The crowd hushed, and a few mouths fell open. Several rushed forward, ignoring Bridget's daughters, and surrounded Corthie. A few of the older folk had tears in their eyes as they gazed at the child in Aila's arms, as if the mere mention of his name had brought their old chief back to life. Men as tall as Corthie slapped him on the back, and grunted their congratulations.

'Give them some space, ya eejits,' cried Conal. 'They've not come all this way just to get crushed by you, ya dozy bastards.'

The crowd cleared a little, and a path opened up towards the low building. The soldiers next to Brogan and Bethal led the way, and they all piled into the tavern. Two fires were roaring, one by the left-hand wall, and the other in a central hearth, around which several tables had been laid out. Someone shoved a bottle of Severton whisky into Corthie's hand.

'Just a wee gift, son; on the house,' said the old man.

Corthie grinned. 'Thanks.'

'Do you want to say a few words?' said Conal.

'Aye, sure,' said Corthie. He gazed around at the villagers packing into the tavern. 'Thanks for the welcome. I know how much my dad loved Kell, and I'm glad that I could bring my own family to see the place.' His chest tightened a little, and he took a second to compose himself. 'When Chief Killop left Kell, it was empty. It would mean more to him than you can imagine to know that there are Kell living here again.' He picked up his child in his arms. 'There was only one name I could have given our firstborn son. In the Holdings he's called Killop Holdfast, but down here, he's Killop ae Corthie ae Kell.'

The crowd let out a loud cheer. The doors to the kitchens opened, and a stream of serving boys and girls emerged with loaded trays. The villagers took their places at the tables, while Corthie, Aila, and Bridget's daughters sat at a table next to the central hearth. Conal joined them, along with the old woman he had been speaking to in the courtyard.

'Nice speech, son,' said the old woman, as plates were set down onto the table.

'Thanks,' said Corthie.

Brogan leaned forward. 'Should I say a few words? I'd like to pass on my mother's greetings to the people of Kell.'

'You're Brig, hen,' said the old woman.

'Ah, yeah?' said Brogan.

'Well, we're in Kell, if ye hadn't noticed. Save yer words for the Brig.'

Bethal smirked. 'We might be half Kell.'

'Is that so?' said the old woman, peering at her.

'I suppose it's possible,' said Brogan.

'What do you mean?' said Aila.

Corthie chuckled. 'Nobody knows who their father is.'

'I'm sure my mother has a pretty good idea, Corthie,' said Brogan.

Aila blinked. 'Wow. Why did the Empress do that? I mean, why would she want to keep the father's identity a secret?'

'I've asked her about it a few times,' said Brogan. 'She always gives me vague answers; but if I had to guess, it was to prevent him from trying to take power. My mother doesn't wish to share the throne.'

'There might be two different fathers,' said Bethal. 'One for the twins, and one for the triplets. Brogan and Bryce both have dark hair, while me and my sister Berra are blonde, and our brother is a redhead.'

'Two fathers?' said Aila.

'That's a load of nonsense,' said Brogan. 'All five children have the same father, and I know that because it's one of the few details I've managed to get mother to admit to.'

'I wonder if he lives in Plateau City,' said Aila.

'I hope not,' said Bethal. 'It would be creepy to think that he's been watching us for years. Whenever I think of him, I picture him dead.'

Brogan raised an eyebrow. 'Why?'

'Because, if he was alive, then why has he never tried to contact us? I reckon mother had him murdered, to keep him quiet.'

'Don't be ridiculous,' said Brogan. 'If she was going to have him killed, then she would have done it after Bryce and I were born. Yet, five years later, the triplets came along. She must have summoned him back to the city.' She glanced at the old woman. 'Bearing all that in mind, would it be alright if I spoke to the folk in the tavern?'

The old woman shook her head. 'No, hen.'

'Why not? Our father might have been a Kell.'

'Aye,' said the old woman, grimacing, 'but I'm not taking any chances. He might have been a Domm.'

CHAPTER 4
RECOVERED TECHNOLOGY

Holdings City, Republic of the Holdings – 1st Day, Last Third Spring 534

Daphne glanced at the ten men and women sitting around the table.

'I know it's late,' she said; 'and I'm sure you all want to go home, but there is one more item on today's agenda that we need to cover.'

One or two of the Holdings government ministers frowned, and Daphne noted who they were for later.

'In less than a year from now,' she went on, 'the electorate of the Holdings will select a new parliament. I intend to put my name forward as a representative from the Holders, but, as you all know, I cannot be elected for a third term as First Holder. As the constitution dictates, I must stand down from my position on election day, and a new First Holder will be chosen from among those sitting in the new parliament.' She gazed around the table, but no one raised their hand to speak. 'Our main opponents remain in the royalist camp. Despite the failure of Lord Blackhold's attempted coup seven years ago, their influence reaches all sections of Holdings society. The wealthy hope that the return of a monarch will mean a reduced tax burden, while many of the poor still yearn for the old days, in spite of everything my government has done for them. Many of our achievements will be put at risk if a royalist is selected as First Holder, and so we must do everything in our power to prevent that outcome. That means we need a credible candidate to replace me.'

The finance minister raised his hand.

'Yes?' said Daphne.

'Could we alter the constitution, ma'am? We could raise the limit to three terms, thereby allowing you to become First Holder again.'

'That would betray the very notion of democracy that we are trying to protect from the royalists,' said Daphne; 'and our enemies would use it against us at every opportunity. No. There is no alternative; I must stand down, and allow a peaceful transfer of power. I love this country too much to endanger it. You should know that I have also given my word to the Empress regarding this, and have assured her that I will not seek an unconstitutional third term.'

'But you still intend to stand as a representative in parliament, ma'am?' said the finance minister.

'I do. Whether the new First Holder selects me to serve in their government is, of course, up to them, whoever they may be. I will make myself available to serve; that goes without question. Now, who among us sitting here could we all rally around? It should be someone who is already in government, so that they have the requisite experience.'

Weir, Daphne's long-standing deputy First Holder, caught her glance. 'Do you have someone in mind, ma'am?'

Daphne smiled. 'Yes, Weir. You.'

'Me, ma'am?' said Weir, his eyebrows rising. 'But I am not a Holder. The other Holders would never accept me.'

'So? Most of the other Holders loathe me.'

'Yes, ma'am, but you remain one of them. An aristocrat of the highest pedigree. As everyone in this room knows, I come from humble River Holdings peasant stock.'

'Did you not run the caretaker government at the end of my first term? You held this country together while I was being chased across the continent by a horde of demented gods. If I had been killed, then you would have taken over as First Holder by the automatic procedure of the law.' She glanced around the table. 'Does anyone here doubt that Weir has the ability to fulfil the duties of First Holder?'

The minster for agriculture raised her hand.

'Yes?'

'It's not that I have any doubts regarding Weir's abilities, ma'am,' she said, 'but I think he's right about the reaction of the other Holders. They accepted you, ma'am, because Hold Fast is one of the strongest and most influential Holdings in the country. You carry a weight, and an authority lacking in many others. The royalist Holders will do everything in their power to prevent Weir from being elected First Holder, and if they are unsuccessful, then they will obstruct his government at every turn.'

'Yes, probably,' said Daphne. 'Do I look like I care? Let them rail and rant. Their cacophony of fabricated outrage will only serve to prove to the poor of this country that the rich do not have their best interests at heart.' She lit a cigarette. 'We don't have to make a decision tonight. All I ask from you at present is that, firstly, you take some time to mull it over. If you think you have a better suggestion than Weir, then I want to hear it. And, secondly, do not repeat a word of this conversation to anyone else. When we come to the time to announce our favoured candidate, I want the campaign to be fully-funded and ready to go.' She nodded. 'Dismissed, and have a good evening.'

Daphne watched as the members of her government rose from their seats. They each bowed their head to her, then departed through a side door. Weir was the last to go, and he lingered by the table until the others had left.

'Ma'am,' he said.

'Don't you dare tell me that you don't think you're up to the job, Weir,' said Daphne.

Weir smiled. 'What if I don't want it?'

'Do you think I like this job? It's been nothing but a damn burden. I missed seeing my children grow up during my first term, and my second has thoroughly exhausted my patience and my energy. We don't do this because we enjoy it, Weir; we do it for the good of the Holdings. As far as I'm concerned, the fact that you don't want the job is a prime reason to make sure you get it.'

'Thank you for trusting me with this, ma'am.'

'I've trusted you ever since we met in the Sanang forest, Weir. You didn't let me down then, and you've never let me down since.'

Weir gave a slight bow, then walked from the room. Daphne sighed, and enjoyed the silence for a moment. It had been another long day, and she was looking forward to getting into a blisteringly-hot bath back at the First Holder's residence, with a glass of whisky in one hand, and a stick of dreamweed in the other.

The air crackled, and Karalyn appeared in front of her.

Daphne frowned. 'I suppose it was nice of you to wait until the meeting was over, dear.'

'Meeting?' said Karalyn. 'What meeting? Never mind about that; I need the God King's Quadrant.'

'What do you need a Quadrant for? You can go anywhere you choose.'

'Not anywhere, mother. I can't go to the City-world.'

'You mean the place where Corthie was?'

'I mean the place where Kelsey is.'

Daphne sat up straight in her chair. 'Why? Is Kelsey alright?'

'I'm not sure. I couldn't see her when I looked at her world earlier today. What I do know is that there's an extremely powerful god on that world; possibly even an Ascendant.'

'A what?'

'An Ascendant, mother. Someone with the full range of powers, like Belinda before I scoured her, or the Creator. They've been looking for that world, and I think they might have found it.'

'And you would be able to get there with the Quadrant you brought back from Lostwell?'

'I don't know, but it's been there, so it's the best chance we've got.'

Daphne got to her feet, and lifted a coat from a peg by the wall. 'Should I bring a sword?'

Karalyn narrowed her eyes. 'You're staying here, mother.'

'No, dear. If one of my children is in danger, and I have the power to help, then I'm not going to sit on my hands while you do all the work.'

'Where is the Quadrant?'

'I don't have it, dear.'

'What?'

'I gave it to the Empress years ago, so that her experts could try to figure out how to work it.'

'You didn't tell me that.'

'You never asked. To be honest, I didn't think you would ever need it again. You will be taking me with you to Plateau City, dear; I insist.' Daphne hesitated. 'Wait. Today happens to be the day that Thorn and Keir have arrived in Plateau City. Let's not surprise the Empress. I will contact her to let her know we're coming.'

She sent out her vision powers before her daughter could object. Her sight soared south across the darkening fields and towns of the River Holdings, and then over the border into the Plateau. She had visioned that way countless times since becoming Herald of the Empire, and her powers were honed to a sharp edge. Her sight reached Plateau City, and Daphne sped towards the Great Fortress. The upper floors, where the palace was situated, were quiet, with the day's business at an end. Daphne entered the meeting chamber where Bridget often conducted her duties, and saw her elder son Bryce at work, sifting through a tall pile of documents, while Mage Tabor stood by his side. Daphne pushed her vision into the Empress's private quarters, and found Bridget sitting alone in her small study, her feet up on a stool, and an opened bottle of whisky on the little table next to her. Daphne gazed at the Empress for a moment. The worries of the world seemed etched into her face, and she looked tired.

Daphne entered her mind.

Good evening, your Majesty.

Daphne? Are you here to check up on your boy and his wife?

No.

Then, what do you want?

Karalyn and I will be arriving in a moment or two. I thought you deserved a small warning.

You're coming here? My Herald is coming to the capital, at long last? What a great honour; I feel privileged.

See you soon, your Majesty.

Daphne cut the connection, then glanced at her daughter.

'How did she take it?' said Karalyn.

'Fine.'

'What kind of mood is she in?'

'No worse than normal, dear. Shall we go? Take us to her Majesty's little study.'

Karalyn nodded, then the air shimmered and Daphne found herself standing before the Empress, who glanced at her and Karalyn with her good eye.

'Well, this is nice,' said Bridget. 'Karalyn, how are you?'

'I'm fine, your Majesty. Did my mother tell you why we are here?'

Bridget chuckled. 'No. It must have slipped her mind.'

'We're looking for the Quadrant, your Majesty,' said Daphne. 'Kelsey might be in trouble.'

'Straight to the point, as always, Holdfast,' said Bridget. 'Small talk has never been your strong point, has it? Don't you want to know how I dealt with the two young mages you sent my way?'

Daphne shrugged. 'I trust that you have found them suitable tasks to perform, your Majesty.'

'You could say that. Thorn will be starting work in the Old Town infirmary tomorrow.'

'An infirmary?'

'Aye. You got a problem with that? As for Keir, why did you bother sending him as well? It was obvious from the look on his face that he didn't want to be here.'

'I could hardly send Thorn along without her husband.'

'I'm not going to make it easy for them.'

'I assumed that when I sent them here, your Majesty. I'm not asking you to give them any special favours. Thorn and Keir behaved badly when they were younger – even I can admit that. However, they have both matured, and I think they deserve a chance to prove that to you.'

'We'll see,' said the Empress. 'I do have one question, Holdfast. Why did you make Thorn your legate?'

'Thorn is reliable, intelligent, and dedicated. She spent four years looking after Karalyn's twins, and then she spent the next two years working for me in Holdings City. She has a great store of potential within her.'

'She has a great deal of ambition in her,' said Bridget, 'but I'm not sure that's the same thing. Anyway, that's not what I was getting at. I meant – why didn't you give the job to Keir?'

Daphne smiled. 'Ah. I see. What do you want me to say? That I think Thorn is more suited to the role than my own son? Keir would rather be on the Hold Fast estate, managing the business side of things there, which is what he was learning to do under Celine, while Thorn was caring for the twins. He is aggrieved, I think, that he has had to give this up for a while.'

Karalyn frowned. 'Can I hurry this along? You two can discuss Keir and Thorn another time; I need the Quadrant.'

The Empress narrowed her eye at Karalyn.

'Apologies, your Majesty,' Karalyn said. 'What I saw through the Sextant is making me impatient; the salve world is under attack by a powerful god, and I need to help if I can. Kelsey...'

Bridget grunted. 'Fine. The Quadrant is in the university. I handed it over to the Department for the Recovery of Rahain Technology, as there didn't seem to be anywhere else suitable. They worked on it for a while, but I think they've given up. They certainly haven't been able to discover how it works.'

Karalyn glanced at her mother.

'Leaving already?' said the Empress. 'Before you go, I have an ultimatum for you, my dear Herald.'

Daphne frowned. 'Yes?'

'Aye. You have less than a year of your term as First Holder left, Holdfast. For a long time, you have used your position as an excuse to live away from the imperial capital. In the days following the defeat of Agatha, this was a necessary expedient, but those days have long since passed. Once your term is over, I expect my Herald to be by my side. That means you, Daphne Holdfast. If you do not move to Plateau City when your term has expired, I will take that as confirmation that you have resigned as my Herald, and will move to have you replaced. I already have a candidate in mind.'

'Who, your Majesty?'

'My son Bryce.'

'I see.'

'Are we clear, Holdfast?'

'Perfectly, your Majesty.'

'Alright. Now you can piss off and leave me in peace.'

Daphne's surroundings altered before she could reply, and she found herself in the university quad, amid the high, slender spires and towers. Karalyn set off across the cobbles without a word, and Daphne followed her.

'I also looked for Sable today,' Karalyn said, as they entered one flank of the complex of buildings.

Daphne didn't respond.

'I couldn't find her,' Karalyn went on.

'What a shame.'

'Am I the only one who cares about Sable?'

'Probably, dear. No. Corthie also has some misguided notions regarding his aunt. Kelsey did too, if I recall, but she was always the contrary one.'

'Sable is a Holdfast, mother.'

'Yes, I suppose she is. However, we saved her from execution, and I don't feel as if I owe her anything else. You, in particular, owe her nothing.'

They ascended a flight of stairs to an upper level of the university. The corridors were quiet after the day's lessons, and many doors were sealed and locked. They arrived at the end of a long hallway, and Daphne knocked once upon a door, then opened it and strode through.

Two figures were sitting next to a desk, drinking tea.

'Good evening,' said Daphne.

Ravi shot to his feet. 'Lady Holdfast? And Karalyn, em, how do you do?'

The other figure was an old woman, and she got to her feet slowly, and bowed her head.

'So,' said Daphne, 'this is the Department for the Recovery of Rahain Technology, is it? Staffed by Ravi and Nadia. I must say, you don't look particularly busy.'

'We're resting after a long day,' said Ravi. 'Do you want a cup of tea?'

'I'm sure they haven't come all this way for a cup of tea,' said Nadia. 'How can we help you, Holder Fast?'

'We need the Quadrant,' said Karalyn. 'Do you have it?'

'Oh,' said Ravi. 'Eh, yeah. Somewhere.'

'It's in the desk drawer, I think,' said Nadia.

Ravi walked to the front of the desk, opened a drawer, and began pulling out papers and everything else that had been stuffed inside.

'I assume you couldn't make it work?' said Daphne.

'We stopped trying,' said Ravi. 'It was too dangerous.'

'Dangerous?' said Daphne. 'Explain.'

'Well,' he said, 'one time, I accidentally glided my finger across the surface, and the air went all funny, and my stomach lurched. When I opened my eyes, I had moved three yards from where I had been standing, and I was an inch from a thick stone wall. An inch. I lost my nerve after that.'

He pulled out a folded bed sheet, and unwrapped it on the surface of the desk. He removed a few clasps, and revealed the Quadrant, lying in the centre of the sheet.

'Here it is. All the way from Lostwell, or wherever.'

'It used to belong to the God-King on Kelsey's world,' said Karalyn.

Nadia smiled. 'And how is young Kelsey?'

'Yeah,' said Ravi. 'How's she doing? She was always my favourite Holdfast; no offence.'

'None taken,' said Daphne.

Karalyn strode to the desk, and picked up the Quadrant.

'Wait,' said Daphne. 'Tell us what you intend to do before you vanish, leaving me here in Plateau City.'

Karalyn glanced at her. 'I'm going to ask the Quadrant to send me to Kelsey's world. It's been there, so it should know the way.'

'It should know the way?' said Ravi, his brow crinkled. 'What does that even mean? It's a piece of metal.'

'It talks to her,' said Daphne. 'Had you forgotten?'

Ravi's mouth fell open. 'Shit. Yeah, that's right.'

'Is there any need for foul language?' said Daphne.

Ravi shrugged. 'Sometimes.'

'Alright, daughter,' said Daphne; 'here's what we're going to do. You will try to travel to Kelsey's world. If you are successful, you will return immediately, and we will gather a collection of soldiers and mages. Thorn is nearby, and Keir, too. We will go in armed and ready, and deal with any god who stands in our way. We shall then extricate Kelsey, and bring her home. Got it?'

Karalyn narrowed her eyes.

'This is not something you should be doing on your own, dear,' said her mother.

Karalyn glanced down at the Quadrant in her hands. Daphne watched for a moment, but nothing happened.

'Damn it!' Karalyn cried.

'No luck?' said Daphne.

'The Quadrant is telling me that it can't take me there, because *I* don't know where it is.'

'That sounds familiar, dear.'

Karalyn blinked. 'What?'

'Do you remember when you tried to use Agatha's Quadrant to travel to Lostwell? The device had clearly been to that world, and yet it refused to take you there.'

'How did you get to Lostwell, if that was the case?' said Nadia.

Karalyn turned to the old Rahain woman. 'I saw the location of the world in Racine's mind before my mother beheaded her. Then I used the power of the other mages in Colsbury for the strength to travel there.' She shook her head. 'You all know what happened next. I lost four years. I didn't know I had, not at first – the trip to Lostwell seemed to occur instantaneously.'

'Therefore,' said Daphne, 'to travel to Kelsey's world, you need to find someone who has been there, and then use the Quadrant to avoid losing any more time.'

'Great advice, mother. Do you know anyone who has been to the City? And don't say Corthie or Aila – I've already been in their minds. They have no idea how a Quadrant works. The difference with Racine was that she had used a Quadrant to get here from Lostwell – the information I needed was in her head.' She glanced at Ravi and Nadia. 'I'm taking this back with me to Colsbury. I'm not giving up just yet.'

'That's fine by me,' said Ravi. 'If the Empress asks, I'll tell her you requisitioned it.'

'The Empress knows why we are in Plateau City,' said Daphne. 'She'll be expecting us to take it.'

Nadia reached over the table, and wrote something on a scrap of paper.

'What are you doing?' said Ravi.

'Writing a receipt,' said the Rahain woman. She handed the quill to Karalyn. 'Please sign at the bottom, so there's no room for confusion.'

Karalyn scrawled her name on the scrap of paper. She then tucked the Quadrant into her clothes, and nodded at Daphne. An instant later, Daphne found herself standing in a room she knew well.

'Why have you brought me to Colsbury, dear?'

'So you can see Kelsey's world for yourself, mother.'

'And my grandchildren? I haven't seen the twins, or Shella, for that matter, for over a third.'

'One thing at a time, mother.'

They left the room, and went down the hallway to where Karalyn kept the Sextant. The room was in darkness, and Karalyn lit a few lamps, while Daphne peered at the massive device sitting in the middle of the floor.

'Insert the Weathervane,' said Karalyn, as she closed the shutters to the evening sky.

'Do what, dear?'

'Never mind,' said Karalyn. She strode over to the Sextant, and picked up the black-bladed sword.

'Oh, that,' said Daphne. She watched as Karalyn slid the blade into the side of the Sextant. The device began to hum, and seemed to lift an inch off the bare floorboards.

'Place your palm onto the surface of the device,' said Karalyn.

Daphne raised her right hand, and pressed it down onto the cold glass.

'I still don't hear any voices,' she said.

'I know,' said Karalyn, 'but I'm hoping that you will be able to see what I see.'

Karalyn placed her palm onto the device and closed her eyes. Daphne watched her for a second, unsure what was supposed to be happening. Then, without warning, her vision clouded over, and she saw a dark red sky, filled with smoke and flames.

This is Kelsey's world, mother, said Karalyn inside Daphne's head. *Can you see it?*

Yes. It looks awful.

It's quite beautiful when it's not being burned to the ground. I'm going to show you a place called Tara, where I last saw the god I mentioned.

Daphne watched as the scene before her changed. Her vision lowered, then flew over a wide bay, passing a colossal statue of a man on a rocky headland. They reached a town with a harbour. A long line of cliffs sat above the town, where a gargantuan building complex was burning.

That's one of the City's palaces up there, said Karalyn. *For such a small place, they have more palaces than the whole of the Star Continent.*

Never mind that, dear. Where is Kelsey?

I'm looking, mother.

Daphne's vision descended again, and she gasped as a scene of appalling carnage opened up in front of them. They were looking down at a square, where a long platform had been erected, with execution posts spaced a few yards apart. Bodies were covering the flagstones of the square – mangled and torn corpses of humans, along with dozens of the creatures Daphne had been told were called greenhides. Near the platform was the enormous carcass of a dead gaien, its wings ripped, and its eyes closed.

There! Karalyn said.

The view turned to the left, and Daphne saw a crowd of survivors amid the slaughter – soldiers, and a few civilians. Next to them were two other huge gaien, one of them silver in colour, the other red. Standing by the long forelimbs of the silver beast was Kelsey, looking bruised and exhausted, but alive.

My little girl! cried Daphne. *She looks hurt, the poor thing. Oh, Kelsey. Look at her, Karalyn. She's nearly twenty-four.*

Take a look at this, mother.

Daphne glanced over, and saw the headless body of a large man, covered in scorched and broken plates of armour.

This is the god I saw, said Karalyn. *They got him.*

The vision dissolved, and Daphne found herself staring at the Sextant again.

'Why did you stop?' she said. 'I wanted to see more.'

Karalyn shrugged. 'We know that Kelsey's safe; that's the important thing. I wonder how they managed to kill such a powerful god.'

Daphne suppressed her irritation. It had been her first glimpse of her younger daughter in three years, and Karalyn had snatched her away without any warning.

'Come on,' said Karalyn. 'Let's see the twins. Shella and Agang have been looking after them for long enough, I imagine. This morning, Kyra had Agang grunting on all fours like a wild boar.'

'I would have liked to have seen that,' said Daphne.

They extinguished the lamps and left the room. A few doors down,

Daphne heard laughter and yells coming from the chamber within, and she opened the door.

Kyra and Cael were clambering over Agang as if he were a horse. They peered up at the doorway.

'Granny!' cried Kyra.

She leapt off Agang and ran to the door, hugging Daphne's waist.

Daphne smiled and laughed. 'How lovely to see you, Kyra; and you too, Cael.'

Cael sprinted over, and joined the embrace. Daphne crouched down, savouring every moment as her two grandchildren pulled her close.

'Are you alright, Agang?' said Karalyn.

'Yes, yes,' he said, rising to his feet with a grin on his face. 'I was a willing participant this time.'

'All the same,' said Shella, from her comfortable armchair, 'I'm glad you're back. I was dreading having to put those two to bed.'

Karalyn smiled. 'Granny can do it tonight.'

Daphne reluctantly stood. 'Unfortunately, I need to work in the morning, and that means I shall have to return to Holdings City.'

Shella's face fell. 'What? No chance, Daffers. I haven't seen you in ages. Stay overnight, and have a few drinks. We can catch up.'

'As much as I'd love to, Shella, I have a country to run. I haven't even been home for dinner. Karalyn's been taking me all over the place.'

'We can sort that,' said Shella. 'I can have dinner brought up in fifteen minutes.'

'Is everything alright?' said Agang. 'Did you find the Quadrant?'

'Everything's fine,' said Karalyn. 'Thanks for asking, Agang.'

'What's that supposed to mean?' said Shella.

'We saw Kelsey,' said Daphne. 'My little girl is alive. Bruised, but alive.'

'Listen, mother,' said Karalyn. 'If you stay here tonight, I'll take you back to Holdings City at dawn tomorrow. The twins would love it if you read their story and put them to bed; then we can eat and open a bottle of something.'

Shella's eyes lit up. 'Please, Daffers?'

Daphne glanced down at Kyra and Cael. They were so beautiful it made her want to weep. Moreover, the thought of spending a pleasant evening with Shella, Agang and Karalyn sounded like the perfect end to a long day.

'Very well,' she said, holding Cael's hand. 'I'll stay.'

CHAPTER 5
BEGGING

Plateau City, The Plateau – 8th Day, Last Third Spring 534

Keir squinted, his hangover exacerbating the glare coming off the waters of the Inner Sea. He groaned, and lit another cigarette, the ashtray next to him overflowing. He pulled the dressing gown closer to his body as a cold wind swept across the balcony from the west, then scratched his chin. He hadn't shaved for days, and he needed a shower. He had thought that spending so many days drinking, smoking and eating would be an enjoyable experience, but he was bored and fed up. He hadn't set foot outside of the townhouse since they had arrived seven days previously, while Thorn had slipped out each morning before dawn, ready to work another punishing twelve-hour shift in the Old Town infirmary.

That was her choice, he told himself, as a twinge of guilt threatened to divert his thoughts. If his wife wanted to slave for the Empress, that was no one's fault but her own. He blinked, the sun in his eyes. He had emerged from bed in the middle of the afternoon, following another long, solitary drinking session. By the time he had staggered to the bedroom, Thorn was getting up. She had given him a look that had told him exactly what she thought of his behaviour, which was completely unfair. What else was he supposed to do with his time?

He reached back without looking, and pulled a short cord. A few moments later, Tabitha appeared by the balcony doors.

'Can I help you, sir?' she said.

Keir eyed the young woman. She was looking pretty in her servant's uniform, the skirt showing off her legs.

'Get me something to drink,' he said. 'A pint of water and a pot of coffee should do it for now.'

'Yes, sir. Would you care for something to eat?'

'Not now,' he said. 'Maybe later.'

She bowed her head and walked back into the townhouse. Keir watched her go. He hadn't slept with his wife for several thirds, and he felt something stir within him. He frowned. If Thorn caught him misbehaving with a servant it would mean the end of their marriage. He had never been unfaithful to Thorn, but the temptation to stray had been building for some time; and he had been catching himself gazing at any pretty young women who had crossed his path. Plateau City was full of them – Holdings women, Kellach women, Sanang women; though he drew the line at Rahain or Rakanese women – they were just too different. The city was probably full of brothels as well. Would Thorn divorce him if he visited one? Surely paying for sex was far removed from indulging in an affair. He could blame it on her if he was discovered. If she hadn't been so cold to him in recent days, then perhaps he would have had no need to visit a brothel. No. He was a Holdfast. Paying for a woman was beneath him.

Tabitha returned to the balcony, bearing a tray. She set down a flagon of chilled water onto the table next to Keir, along with a coffee pot, a cup, and some sugar and milk. She also removed the full ashtray and replaced it with a clean, empty one. He watched her movements, then entered her mind. At once, he sensed that she knew he had been looking at her, and it filled her with a sense of annoyance bordering on revulsion. She thought he was good-looking, but she had absolutely no intention of consenting to any physical relationship. She liked her job, and she respected Thorn; whereas her respect for Keir was fast diminishing.

Keir turned away, and directed his gaze out over the Inner Sea. His desire thwarted, his anger rose. So, that silly little bitch thought she was too good for him?

'Do you require anything else, sir?' she said, her eyes lowered.

Keir thought of a few cruel replies, but eventually grunted, 'No.'

She bowed her head and left the balcony.

When Keir had been sixteen in Hold Fast, there had been a constant stream of local girls vying for his attention, and he had picked them up and cast them aside as the mood had taken him. Jemma had been one of those girls, but now, thanks to his foolish mother, Jemma was a fully-adopted Holdfast, with the same inheritance rights as him. It had been completely unnecessary. Cole was already a full Holdfast; there had been no need to make Jemma one as well. When she had been plain old Jemma of Hold Fast, he had been able to bully her; but Jemma Holdfast was more than capable of standing up for herself, as he had discovered on multiple occasions following the siege of Colsbury. While Thorn had toiled day and night to care for Karalyn's brats, Keir had made a few half-hearted attempts to get to know his son a little better, but Cole had seemed intimidated by his presence. Keir had tried to win him over, but the boy's stubborn refusal had culminated in Keir losing his temper. He had screamed and shouted at the child, calling him ungrateful and stupid; after that, Jemma had told him to stay away, and he had.

The return of Corthie the golden boy had only made things worse. His mother, Jemma, Celine, and even Thorn had fawned over him, showering the oaf with love and attention. Keir had scarcely believed what he was seeing when he had been re-introduced to his younger brother. Corthie had grown into a giant, even taller than Keir, with broad shoulders, and arms that looked as though they could wrestle a bear into submission. To top it all, when Aila's baby had been born, Corthie had transformed into mush. The fool had actually wept open tears when he had first held his child in his arms, which, naturally, had made the women of Hold Fast even more fond of him. Why couldn't they see that Corthie was nothing but a muscle-bound idiot? He had received virtually no education in his teenage years, and seemed to know next to nothing about whole areas of the academic curriculum that Keir had mastered years before. Apparently, he was rumoured to be good at fighting, but Keir had slaughtered thousands without so much as clenching his fists. No one seemed to care about that. No one ever remembered that Keir had single-handedly saved Rainsby, or that he had stood on the roof of Colsbury's Great Keep during the siege, helping to defeat Agatha, while Corthie had been idling on Lostwell.

A sound behind him intruded into his thoughts. He turned, and saw Thorn sitting on their bed. She looked drained and exhausted, and a bloody apron was gathered up in her hands.

Keir got up and walked to the balcony doors.

'What are you doing back so soon?' he said.

She glanced up at him. 'I was sent home a couple of hours early.'

'Why?'

'The Old Town infirmary is empty, Keir. In the last seven days, I've healed more than a thousand citizens of this city. Tomorrow, they're sending me over to the infirmary in the old peasant district, next to the Kellach Quarter. Have you had a pleasant day?'

'I was hoping you might have a day off soon.'

Thorn gave a weak smile. 'I don't think the Empress has scheduled any days off for me.'

'This is ridiculous. We shouldn't be putting up with this nonsense. We should leave this stupid city at once.'

'I'm staying, Keir, even if I have to heal every sickness and injury in the entire city. The Empress is trying to break me, but I will not allow that to happen.' She lay back onto the bed, her eyes closing. 'I'm so tired.'

'There's fresh coffee out on the balcony. Do you want some?'

'No, thanks. I need to have a decent sleep tonight.' She yawned, then struggled back up into a sitting position. 'I'll have a shower, and then I think I'll go to bed.'

'Already? The sun hasn't even set yet. Can you not use your soul-witch powers to wake yourself up?'

'I've used so much of my powers over the last few days that I need sleep to ensure I can do it all again tomorrow.'

'But I've barely seen you since we got here. Go for a shower, and we'll open a bottle of wine. Twenty minutes, that's all I ask.'

Thorn nodded. 'Alright.'

She got to her feet, then dropped the bloody apron into a laundry basket in the corner of the room. She pulled her clothes off, leaving them in a pile on the floor, then walked over to the bathroom as if in a daze.

Keir tugged the cord and the bell rang.

'Yes, sir?' said Tabitha, entering the room.

'Fetch a bottle of white wine and two glasses,' he said, making sure he didn't glance in her direction.

'Yes, sir.'

The servant left the room, and Keir wandered back out onto the balcony. The sky to the west was resplendent in shades of pink and red, as the sun neared the horizon. To his left and right, Keir could see other inhabitants of the wealthiest street in the city sitting out on their own balconies, enjoying the sunset. They would have noticed that at least one of the Holdfasts was back in the city, and were probably gossiping about him, but he didn't care. He sat and lit a stick of dreamweed, his feet up on the railings.

Tabitha brought the wine a few minutes later, and he dismissed her with a nod. He opened the bottle and filled the two glasses. Moments later, Thorn emerged onto the balcony, a long towel wrapped round her. She sat, and Keir passed her the stick of dreamweed.

'Thanks,' she said. She held the weedstick in her left hand, and began brushing her wet hair.

'Why would you wash your hair if you're about to go to bed?' he said.

She shrugged. 'There was blood in it.'

'You know,' he said; 'I admire your stubborn streak, but maybe you've made your point. Bridget might decide to keep you working in the city's infirmaries for thirds; or forever, if you let her. She hates us. I think we've suffered enough of her games.'

'We?' she said. '*We* haven't suffered anything, Keir. As far as I can tell, you spend your nights drinking, and your days sleeping. Tell me; how exactly are you suffering?'

He glared at her. 'You're the one who wants to be here, not me. My life's been turned inside out because of you. I moved to Holdings City for you; and now I'm in Plateau City. Why? Because of you. A loyal wife would have stayed by my side on the Hold Fast estate; that's what I wanted.' He shook his head. 'And you have the cheek to sit there and say that I haven't suffered.'

'Oh Keir, don't be childish. There's so much you could do in Plateau City, even if you continue to refuse to work for the Empress. But no, you've already decided that you hate it here, so you aren't even going to try. A loyal husband wouldn't attempt to smother his wife's dreams; am I not allowed to have my own dreams?'

'What you call a dream, I call naked ambition. You're only here because of some stupid notion that you'll be sitting on the throne one day. I remember when I used to believe you when you said that you would become Empress. How foolish of me. You had your chance, when thousands of soldiers and marines were worshipping you in Rainsby and Stretton Sands – you had your chance, and you blew it.'

Thorn stared at the sea. 'Do you still love me, Keir?'

'What?'

'It's a simple question. We've been married for seven years. Do you still love me?'

'Yes.'

'You rarely act as if you do.'

'Neither do you. When's the last time we slept together?'

'Is that why you're so angry all the time; because we haven't been intimate in a while? Keir, we spent day after day in a carriage, travelling all the way down from Holdings City, and now I have to work long shifts in a place filled with blood and misery. Is it any wonder that I haven't been trying to rip your clothes off recently?'

'It makes me feel like you don't want me any more.'

'Grow up, Keir,' she said, standing. 'I've had enough of your crap for one evening, thank you very much. Good night.'

She strode back into the apartment, and Keir stormed after her.

'I hadn't finished speaking,' he yelled.

'Maybe, but I've finished listening.'

'You're so selfish at times.'

'Me? You're the one who's sitting bone idle day after day, drinking wine and smoking weed, while I mop up blood, shit and pus from the infirmary floor. You wouldn't last an hour in there; your knees would buckle at some of the things I've seen in the last few days – and you call me selfish?' She clenched her fists and looked as if she was about to scream. 'I want you to go to the palace and tell the Empress that you're willing to work for her.'

'Or what?' he cried.

'Or leave, Keir. If managing the Hold Fast estate is your dream, then I won't stand in your way. But what I will not tolerate is you sitting here on your arse while I work in the city infirmaries day after day. Support me, or get out!'

Keir stared at her. Was she being serious? Would she stand by and watch if he packed his bags and left? His gaze lowered. There was no way he was going to leave her alone in the city. He loved her, despite everything. More than that, though – he needed her.

He tried to smile. 'I'll need a shower before I see the Empress.'

The courtier bowed. 'May I present Keir Holdfast, your Majesty?'

'I know who he is,' said Bridget. 'Leave us.'

The courtier bowed again, then backed out of the chamber. Keir swallowed, keeping his eyes on the thick rug beneath his feet. Bryce and Mage Tabor were standing next to where Bridget sat on a raised throne, but Keir avoided eye contact with them.

'It's a little late in the day for a visit, Holdfast,' said the Empress. 'I was about to go for dinner, so this had better be worth the wait.'

'Good evening, your Majesty,' said Keir in a low voice.

Bridget narrowed her eye. 'Get on with it, Keir. What do you want?'

'I would like to offer you the use of my powers, in your service.'

'The use of your powers, eh? You mean that you've decided you want to work for the empire?'

'Yes, your Majesty.'

Bridget kept her stare fixed on him. 'No, thanks.'

Keir blinked. 'What? Eh, I mean, I'm sorry, your Majesty, but...'

'You're sorry? What for?'

'I don't understand. Are you saying that you don't want my help?'

'That's right. I asked you seven days ago if you wished to assist the empire, but I've seen no glimpse of you since. Do you think I've been sitting here each day, hoping that you'd turn up? We've managed fine without your help for years, and I'm sure we'll continue to manage. Was that everything?'

'But... but, I... I...'

Bridget laughed. 'That's a dreadful stammer, Keir.'

Keir felt a surge of humiliation wash over him. How could he return to the townhouse now? What was he supposed to tell Thorn?

'I... I want to help, your Majesty.'

'Do you? Very well. Perhaps you should consider enlisting in the imperial army? I'm sure you could secure a position as a junior officer.' She frowned. 'You would need to obey orders, and that's never been one of your talents, as far as I recall. You were good at disobeying orders, but for some reason the army don't seem to appreciate that particular skill.'

'If you take me on as a mage, your Majesty, I swear that I'll do as you say.'

'Is that supposed to convince me?'

'Please, your Majesty.'

Bridget sat in silence for a moment, then she nodded. 'Get on your knees.'

Keir felt his face burn with shame. His mouth went dry, then he lowered himself to the floor. He had no choice, he told himself. Thorn would leave him if he failed, and he would be alone, truly alone.

'Good,' said the Empress. 'Now beg.'

'I beg you, your Majesty,' he said, the words almost choking him; 'please allow me to use my powers in your service.'

'What a kind offer!' said Bridget. 'No, thanks.'

Keir stared at her, his mouth open.

Bridget laughed. 'You should see your face, ya wee prick. Fine. I'll take you on as an apprentice mage, for a trial period. You'll be working for Tabor, and will do everything that he asks of you. One mistake, one tantrum, one complaint – and you're out, for good. Have I made myself clear?'

Keir hung his head. 'Yes, your Majesty.'

'Get to work, then.'

'Now?'

'Aye, now. Mage Tabor, please take our new apprentice to your office, and get started on those messages. Make sure Keir sends every last one of them before you stop for the night, then I expect you both here at dawn.'

Tabor bowed low. 'Yes, your Majesty.'

'Remember, if Keir steps out of line in any way, let me know immediately. Keep a close eye on him.'

'I will, your Majesty.'

'Dismissed.'

Keir got back to his feet, then Tabor gestured toward a side door. Keir caught the glance of Bryce as he walked from the chamber, and the son of the Empress gave him a gentle shrug. Tabor led Keir out of the chamber, and they walked down a short hallway, where several doors lay. Tabor unlocked one, and they entered a snug little office, with a single, shuttered window.

'This is where I do most of my work,' said Tabor.

Keir glanced at the desk. Sitting upon it were several piles of documents.

Tabor pointed at the papers. 'This pile here contains messages that need to be sent out to various regions of the empire; while this pile is for messages that have been sent, but which are awaiting a response. This last pile is for messages that have been received from other mages, which need to be processed and brought to Lord Bryce's attention.'

'Why Lord Bryce, and not the Empress herself?' said Keir.

Tabor frowned. 'I hate to have to do this, but I require you to address me as "sir" while you remain my apprentice.'

Keir glared at the younger mage. 'Did the Empress tell you to say that?'

'If you don't call me "sir", then I will have to report it to the Empress. You heard what her Majesty said.'

'You know,' said Keir, 'I remember you from Rainsby.'

'I remember you, too.'

'You were like a lost little child.'

'I was very young back then. I had just turned sixteen when I was assigned to accompany Herald Nyane to Rainsby. As I recall, you were seventeen at the time, and the difference in age between us might have seemed large to you. However, I am now twenty-four, and you are twenty-five. It hardly seems such a big gap, does it? I am going to give you one more chance, Keir. If you fail to address me by my proper title, then I will have to inform the Empress.'

Keir swallowed his battered pride. 'Yes, sir.'

'Thank you. Now, as for your original question – Lord Bryce sifts through the messages that reach me here in Plateau City, and decides which ones need to be brought to the attention of her Majesty. It's a role that used to be carried out by the Herald of the Empire, but, as you are aware, the Herald is not resident in the imperial capital; therefore, the job has fallen to Lord Bryce.' Tabor glanced at a chair. 'Take a seat, and we'll get started.'

Keir sat down, and Tabor lifted some papers from the first pile.

'Can you reach the Great Tunnel from here?' said Tabor.

'Yes.'

'Yes, what?'

'Yes, sir.'

Tabor handed him several sheets of paper. 'A certain Captain Greenhold is based in the fortress at the northern end of the tunnel. She deals with supplies and logistics for the imperial garrison occupying the Great Tunnel, and is currently on duty to receive vision messages from the capital. I want you to contact her, and deliver the contents of these documents. Take your time, as she will need to write down all of the details.'

Keir glanced at the papers. On them were inscribed lists of various supplies, from boots and shields, to shovels and medical kits, next to quantities, and their expected date of arrival at the fortress. Tabor walked over to the window and pulled open the shutters, revealing the dark night sky outside.

'Get started,' he said, 'and I'll have some coffee sent up for us.'

'Can I smoke, sir?' asked Keir.

'Only with the window open. Her Majesty doesn't like the smell of smoke to linger through the palace.'

Tabor walked from the small office, leaving Keir alone with the pile of papers. He lit a cigarette, then stubbed it out and decided to get to work. He sighed. If he had stayed in the townhouse, he would be halfway to getting drunk; instead, he was going to have to perform the most tedious vision work imaginable. He thought about what Thorn had been doing for the previous seven days. The knowledge that she had been working far harder than him should have been consoling, but he still felt cheated. He was the saviour of Rainsby – how had he been reduced to reading out lists of boots to an army captain in a faraway fortress?

One day, he told himself; one day, he would take his revenge on the stupid Empress.

He sighed again, and sent his vision out through the open window.

Midnight had come and gone by the time Keir had worked his way through the first pile of papers. Tabor had kept him supplied with coffee, and had filed away each report as soon as Keir had delivered it. Keir had spoken to over a dozen representatives of the empire, from officials based on the border with Rakana, to agents scattered across the Plateau. Even the harbour-master in Rainsby had a message from the Empress, and Keir had taken a moment to gaze down at the town he had known so well. It had been unrecognisable. The inferno that Keir had unleashed upon Rainsby had devastated the buildings. Many were still in ruins, and only a small area near the harbour had been rebuilt.

Keir's head was spinning as he placed the last sheaf of papers back onto the desk. A dull ache had formed behind his temples, a pain that he hadn't experienced in years. He didn't want to admit it to Tabor, but he was out of practice, and his exertions had exhausted him.

The door to the office opened as Tabor began tidying away that day's work.

'Good evening,' said Bryce, from the doorway. 'I just wanted to see how things were going.'

'Good evening, sir,' said Tabor. 'All outstanding messages have been sent.'

Bryce smiled. 'Excellent. Mother will be pleased; although I'm sure she won't admit it. I'm glad you changed your mind about working for us, Keir. Would you both like to join me for a whisky before you go?'

'Thank you, sir,' said Tabor.

Keir nodded.

'Come on, then,' said Bryce.

The Empress's eldest child led the two mages through the dark hallways of the palace, until they reached a suite of rooms that Keir remembered from a previous visit.

'I stayed here once,' he said; 'along with my sister Kelsey.'

'That's right,' said Bryce, smiling. 'I remember when Thorn stayed here as well, and your brother Corthie, on both occasions when he lived in the Great Fortress. Karalyn used to have the suite next door. All of the Holdfast children have lived here at one time or another.'

He walked over to the wall and lit a few lamps, then opened a cabinet and extracted a bottle of whisky.

'This is Severton's eighteen-year-old single malt,' Bryce said. 'Their finest expression, in my opinion. 'The twenty-four-year-old is a little too oaky for my palate.'

The three men sat down on the couches that surrounded a low table, and Bryce filled three small glasses. Keir took out his packet of cigarettes.

'There's no smoking in here, I'm afraid,' said Bryce. 'I can't abide the smell.'

'Oh,' said Keir.

Bryce glanced at him, then his features softened. 'Come on; we'll head up onto the roof. You can smoke there. Bring your glasses.'

They walked to the rear of the room, where an iron staircase ascended. They climbed the steps, and Bryce opened a door at the top. Keir and Tabor followed him, and they emerged into the large garden that covered the roof of the Great Fortress. The seven stars were shining above them, and the lights of the city were providing enough illumination for Keir to make out the trees, bushes and paths that filled the garden.

'A beautiful night,' said Bryce, his eyes on the view of the city.

They sat on a bench under the branches of a beech tree, and Bryce raised his glass.

'To a new beginning,' he said.

Tabor and Keir raised their glasses, then each took a drink. The whisky warmed Keir's throat, and he nodded in approval.

'It's not too bad, eh?' smiled Bryce.

Keir nodded, and lit a cigarette.

'Listen,' said Bryce; 'about what happened in the audience chamber, when my mother made you beg on your knees. Don't take it personally, Keir. My mother's had years in which to dwell on what happened in the war against Agatha. There was no way she could just allow you and Thorn to walk into positions of influence and authority without making some sort of demonstration about the past. However, I promise you that if you work hard and remain loyal, then things will get easier.'

'I heard some news about Thorn today, sir,' said Tabor.

Bryce nodded. 'Yes? What did you hear?'

'That she's emptied the entire Old Town infirmary, sir. She healed every single patient there. Is it true?'

'Yes. Amazing, isn't it? Seven days it took her; seven. Over a thousand patients, some of whom had been ill and bedridden for years. I'm slightly in awe of her achievement.' He smiled. 'It's almost as if she has something to prove.'

'She's being moved to an infirmary in the peasant district tomorrow,' said Keir.

'I know,' said Bryce; 'it was I who gave the order for her transfer.'

'It's wearing her out. She's exhausted.'

'I'm sure she is, Keir. Regardless, she will remain in her post for as long as the Empress wishes her there. Imagine, within a few thirds, she might heal every sick person in the entire city. Her powers far outrank those of any ordinary hedgewitch.'

'I know,' said Keir. 'Thorn's a soulwitch. She might be the greatest mage Sanang has produced in decades.'

'Without a doubt,' said Bryce. 'Tell me, do you disagree with my mother's decisions regarding Thorn and yourself?'

Keir said nothing.

Bryce sipped his whisky and turned back to gaze at the city. 'You have to consider things from my mother's point of view. Eight years ago, you and Thorn were rampaging across the southern Plateau. You formed your own armed force, made up of imperial soldiers and marines who had all sworn oaths to the empire. You persuaded them to abandon their loyalty to the Empress, and rejected every command issued by your sovereign ruler. There is a word for that type of behaviour, and the sentence for such acts is death. You may feel hard done by, Keir, but believe me, what you are going through is a little better than sitting in the dungeons awaiting execution. Wouldn't you agree?'

Keir didn't want to respond, but both Bryce and Tabor glanced at him, waiting for him to speak.

'Yes,' he mumbled.

'Good,' said Bryce. 'We are in agreement, and that bodes well for the future. You and Thorn will be useful additions to the imperial court, if everything works out.' He sipped from his glass. 'Tomorrow, I want you to try to reach out to the cities of Rahain. Our intelligence regarding that region of the world is patchy at best, and we would like to make contact with the Rahain leadership, if such a thing is possible. Will you try?'

Keir nodded. 'Yes.'

Tabor narrowed his eyes at him.

'Yes, sir,' Keir said, correcting himself.

Bryce smiled. 'Excellent. This has been a useful chat. Go home, Keir, and we'll see you in the morning, bright and early. Tabor will show you out.'

Keir got to his feet. The entire evening had been nothing but one long exercise in humiliation. Still, at least he could tell Thorn that he was now working for the Empress, and his marriage had been saved.

He hoped it was worth it.

CHAPTER 6
THE DREAM MAGE

C olsbury Castle, Republic of the Holdings – 27th Day, Last Third Spring 534

'Colsbury is wonderful at this time of year,' said Agang, as he and Karalyn strolled through the gardens. 'The birds are singing in the trees, and the sun is warm.'

'If it gets too cold and wet for you in the winter, you could always travel north. Winter in the Holdings is like spring on the Plateau; it never gets too chilly.'

'I might consider it,' he said. 'You know, I have yet to visit the Hold Fast estate.'

Karalyn smiled. 'Are you looking for an invitation? You're welcome there at any time, Agang; although, right now, the only members of the family who are there are Celine, Jemma and Cole. You could always visit my mother in Holdings City, if you are in the mood to travel.'

'Thank you, but I know how busy your mother is. And, to be honest, seeing her reminds me of everything I have lost. I still feel a little bitter about how I was forced into handing over the Mya Enclave to the Matriarchy. I governed that region for over twenty years, and transformed it from a deforested wasteland into the most prosperous part of Sanang. I built schools, roads, market-towns, and now the new Matriarch is claiming credit for all of those achievements.'

Karalyn nodded, but said nothing.

'Sorry, Karalyn,' Agang said. 'I must sound like a grumpy old man to you. I am a grumpy old man; however, I am also extremely grateful that you and Princess Shella have allowed me to live here with you.'

'I think you might be the only person who still refers to Shella as a princess.'

Agang shrugged. 'She has never been formally stripped of her royal position, so, technically, she remains a princess. It's strange; Shella and I used to despise each other, back when we were fighting the Creator. We drove each other crazy, and yet here I am. It's a comfort for me to be around someone who was there; someone who remembers what those days were like. And, of course, we're both childless; we share that.'

'Shella would never admit it, but she loves you being here. It's good for the twins too, to have someone else around. Colsbury can seem very isolated and lonely at times. The only period in which it was busy was during the siege.'

'Ah yes, the famous siege, to which I wasn't invited.'

'You were busy in Mya.'

He sighed. 'I know. It sounds foolish, but I wish I had been there, sharing the danger with the other high mages of this world. Shella, your mother, and the Empress were all there. I was the only survivor from the Great Fortress who was absent.'

'You're forgetting Dean,' she said. 'He was with the refugees who fled Plateau City. He wasn't there.'

A cry rang out from the nearby trees, and Karalyn glanced over to see Kyra and Cael swinging from the branches. They were calling out to each other as they played, daring themselves to climb higher.

'Should we stop them?' said Agang. 'One of them might get hurt.'

'No,' said Karalyn. 'Let them play.'

They walked on a little further, and passed through one of the apple orchards, where the new fruit was beginning to grow, replacing the blossom that lay across the grass. They slowed at the far end of the orchard. A graveyard was positioned there, with almost a hundred headstones lying in rows amid the thick grass. The great majority of the graves belonged to marines who had fallen in the siege, but Karalyn's eyes went to the site where the body of Lennox lay. His grave had flowers next to it, placed there by Karalyn the previous day. She had also set flowers next to the graves of Calder, Acorn and Darine, but she always saved the best for Lennox.

'No matter which path through the gardens we take,' said Agang, 'we always end up in this spot.'

'My heart pulls me here,' said Karalyn. 'My mother once told me that what didn't kill you made you stronger, but I don't believe it. It sounds like something my mother would believe, but she's wrong. Nothing good came from Lennox's death; nothing. It didn't make me stronger. All it did was leave a huge void in my life. I look at his grave, and all I feel is regret.' She started to cry. 'I miss him more than ever.'

Agang said nothing. He had watched her cry many times at the grave of Lennox, and had learned that silence was his best response. Karalyn wondered if he begrudged their frequent walks through the gardens, as they usually ended in her tears, but she resisted entering his mind to find out. Some things were better left alone.

'Would you have gone to Lostwell if Lennox had survived?' he asked, after a few minutes had passed.

'Aye,' she said, wiping her face. 'I would have left the twins with him instead of Thorn. I genuinely believed that I would be gone for just a few thirds. There was no other way to find Corthie.'

'Now, you don't have to answer this next question, but why did you choose Thorn? From what I gather, you had hardly spent any time with her before you made your decision.'

'There was no one else available. I could have asked my mother, but I knew that she would be busy running the Holdings, and I also knew that she would help Thorn financially, and allow her to live on the Hold Fast estate. Kelsey was too young. There was also something that happened during the siege. Kyra was wounded, and Thorn saved her. Because of that, both twins looked upon her with affection. It was a risk, but as I said, I thought I would be away for a short time. In the end, it turned out to be one of the best decisions I've ever made. Thorn did a great job, and I'll forever be grateful to her.'

'And to Keir, also, I assume?'

'Keir?' She snorted. 'Keir did nothing. He left the entire burden to Thorn. I should have known, but I'd hoped that the responsibility might trigger a change in his attitude. It didn't. He isn't even capable of being a father to his own child, let alone mine.' She gazed at Lennox's grave. 'The gods deprived my twins of their father.'

'And you made them pay for it, Karalyn.'

'They're still searching for this world; it's not over.'

Agang nodded. 'If they ever find it, please make sure you invite me along this time.'

Karalyn smiled. 'If you insist.'

Kyra folded her arms. 'No.'

'Come on, wee Kyra,' said Karalyn. 'Just read one more page.'

'I don't want to. Cael isn't reading.'

'Cael finished this book yesterday. Just one more page, and then we can go dream-visioning.'

'I want to dream-vision now.'

'If you don't finish this page, there will be no dream-vision lesson today.'

Kyra started to weep.

Karalyn felt like giving up. It would be so easy to let the girl have her way, yet she knew that it would be a mistake to retreat after she had made a threat. There was nothing she could do but dig her heels in. She lifted the book, open at the correct page, and Kyra closed her eyes so she couldn't see it.

'Let's start at the top,' said Karalyn. 'I'll help you. "The wolf said goodbye to the little boy."'

'Wolves can't talk!' cried Kyra.

'It's just a story, wee Kyra; it's not real. Did you know that wolves live in these mountains? High up, where there are no people. Auntie Shella says that she saw one a few years ago, drinking from the lake. That would be exciting.'

'I'm bored,' said Cael. 'What can I do?'

Karalyn turned to her son. 'Have you finished your drawing, dear?'

'Aye,' he said, lifting up a piece of paper.

'That's lovely, Cael,' said Karalyn. 'What is it?'

'It's Uncle Agang.'

'I see. Why have you given him horns?'

Cael laughed. 'They're not horns. They're teeth, growing out of his head.'

'Very nice.' She turned back to the book. 'Come on, wee Kyra. "The little boy hugged the wolf."'

'The wolf would eat him,' said Kyra.

'Maybe that's what happens next,' said Karalyn. 'Open your eyes, and you'll see.'

'That's not what happens,' said Cael. 'The wolf runs away into the forest and the boy goes home.'

Karalyn sighed, and put the book down. 'Who would like to go dream-visioning?'

'Me!' the twins cried.

Kyra opened her eyes, a look of jubilant triumph on her face. 'Where will we go?'

'Where would you like to go? Shall we see what granny is doing?'

'I want to see Cole,' said Kyra.

'Ah, your big cousin? Alright. He's up on the Hold Fast estate. Are you ready?'

The twins nodded.

'Close your eyes. Remember that ordinary vision mages can only use their powers with their eyes open, but we dream mages are special. We don't need our eyes to see.'

She watched as the twins closed their eyes, then she drew on her powers, and her sight left her body. She hovered over the twins, waiting for each consciousness to join her. After a moment, she sensed their presence, then she guided them out of Colsbury, keeping them close as they raced over the mountains. She felt joy course through them as they sped across the wide open plains of the Holdings. The miles unrolled beneath them in a blur, then they slowed as they began to near the Hold Fast estate. The grass was starting to turn brown from the heat of late spring, and the whitewashed buildings of the estate were gleaming in the sunshine.

Karalyn brought the twins to a halt.

Now, she said in their minds, *without looking, try to sense where Cole is. Remember that he has traces of the same powers that we possess, only he doesn't know how to hide them, so you should be able to work out where he is.*

Is Cole a dream mage? said Cael.

Not yet. He might become one when he's older.

I sense him! cried Kyra. *He's on a horse!*

Very good, Kyra. Cael, do you sense him too?

Karalyn felt her son use his powers to search for his cousin.

Aye! he yelled.

They rushed off in the direction of Cole, and found the eight-year-old boy with his mother. They were both on horseback, their mounts trotting across a vast field a few hundred yards from the estate mansion.

Can I say hello? said Cael.

Aye, said Karalyn. *Just for a minute.*

She watched as her children entered their cousin's mind. Cole's eyes widened, and he started to laugh. Jemma glanced at him, an eyebrow raised.

'The twins are in my head, mummy,' he said.

Jemma smiled. 'Tell them to say hello to their mother for me.'

Karalyn waited a few moments, then called the twins back to her. Their thoughts wheeled around, then she herded them together, and they started to speed back the way they had come.

They had almost reached Colsbury, when Karalyn felt something – the tendrils of another presence, like fingers probing across the mountains, looking for something, or someone. Karalyn hesitated, astonished. The powers being used were the same as hers, though they felt a little rawer, as if the mage using them was younger. Before she knew what was happening, a tendril of power surrounded Kyra, and entered her mind, brushing past the many-layered protections set up by Karalyn as if they weren't there.

Karalyn surged her powers, and blasted the presence from Kyra's mind. The strange powers vanished in an instant, replaced by nothing but silence.

Karalyn severed the connection linking their bodies to their vision, and all three of them opened their eyes. Cael was staring at his sister, his mouth open.

'Wee Kyra,' said her mother. 'Did you feel that?'

'Feel what?' said Kyra.

'There was someone else out there with us, just for a moment. Did anyone speak to you?'

'I saw it,' said Cael. 'Was it Cole? Maybe he is a dream mage.'

'It wasn't Cole,' said Karalyn. 'Cole can't do that. Kyra, talk to me. Did you hear anything inside your head? A voice?'

'Aye, mama. I heard a boy's voice.'

'A boy? What did he say?'

'He said "hello", mama; so I said "hello" back. Who was it, mama?'

Karalyn realised that her expression was probably frightening the twins, so she smiled and tried to relax.

'Is something wrong?' said Cael, his eyes betraying his fear.

'No; don't worry,' said Karalyn, trying to sound calm. 'I'm sure every-thing's fine.'

'I hear what you're saying,' said Shella, 'but you must have made a mistake.'

Karalyn lit another cigarette. 'I didn't make a mistake. It was defi-nitely dream powers.'

Shella shrugged. 'It was probably vision powers.'

'I can tell the damned difference, Shella,' said Karalyn. She leaned on the roof parapet, the wind blowing through her hair. 'Besides, there's no way that ordinary vision powers would have been able to enter Kyra's mind. Mother is one of the most powerful vision mages alive, and she can't do it.'

'And Kyra said it was a boy?'

'Aye.'

Shella snapped her fingers. 'What about Corthie and Aila's kid?'

'Killop junior doesn't have those kind of powers.'

'You don't know that for sure.'

'I do know. I've examined every corner of that boy's mind.'

Shella squinted at her. 'Why would you do that?'

'Aila asked me to. She wanted to know what powers to expect. I saw vision – the full range, and the same kind of vestigial dream powers that Corthie possesses. Killop is going to be very powerful, but he's not a dream mage.'

'He's not a mage at all,' said Shella. 'The boy's a demigod.'

'Keep this quiet, but their second child is also going to be immortal. Aila asked me to check that too, when she found out that she was pregnant again.'

'Holy shit. Are you serious? How many brats are they going to have? Are they all going to be little gods?'

'I can't say for certain. I don't know what's causing this to happen. Let's go back to the present problem. We have to accept that there's another dream mage on the Star Continent. He's probably young. That would explain why I've never sensed him before; or he might be far away. Or both.'

'Hang on. I remember that old bastard Kalayne telling me that he was the last dream mage in existence, yeah? He also said that you were a freak of nature – a new dream mage created by the combination of Holdings and Kellach blood. Both of your parents were mages. And Daphne has a few funny powers.'

'So does Sable.'

'Right. So... Shit, I don't know what I'm trying to say. Okay, here goes

– imagine that your grandfather, Daffer's father, had a few vestigial dream powers. That would explain Daffers and Sable. Then, Daffers meets Killop, and out you pop – a full dream mage. How else could one be made?'

'The same way as Kalayne. Laodoc told me that dream mages could arise from either Holdings or Kellach Brigdomin people. It was rare, but possible. If Godfrey Holdfast had vestigial powers, and Kalayne had full powers, then another one could be born in the same way.'

Shella narrowed her eyes. 'Maybe Kalayne had kids of his own that he never told us about.'

'Aye, but he died nearly twenty-seven years ago, so any child would have to be older than that. I can't see how any dream mage could have lived that long without me sensing them.'

'Yeah, but you only sensed him because he was looking for you.'

Karalyn frowned. 'Do you think he was looking for me?'

Shella shrugged. 'It seems too unlikely a coincidence that the only dream mages around bumped into each other by accident. Perhaps he could sense your powers, and headed straight for them. That means he could have been around for a while, but had chosen to remain in hiding. Look, I don't really know what I'm talking about. You should be speaking to your mother about this.'

Karalyn nodded. 'I will. I'm taking the twins to the Hold Fast estate in a couple of days, for the Summer's Day festival. Mother will be there.'

'You're having a party? Why wasn't I invited?'

'You were, Shella. Mother asked you last time she was here.'

'Did she? Oh. I might have been too drunk to remember.'

Karalyn gazed down at the lake, its smooth surface reflecting the side of the mountains. 'Can you and Agang look after the twins for a while?'

'Are you going to use your powers to look for this dream mage?'

'I think I need to go down to Kellach Brigdomin in person; just for a few hours. That's the likeliest place he'll be.'

'You can visit Corthie while you're there.'

'No. I'll leave him in peace to enjoy his holiday. If I talk to him as well, then I could be gone for ages, and I don't want to leave the twins with you for too long.'

'Actually, yes. Don't speak to Corthie. It's not that I don't like looking after the twins, but the longer you're away, the more likely it is that they'll do something... weird. I'm too old to be barking like a dog. My knees can't take it.'

'You don't have to explain – I get it. I appreciate every time you look after them, Shella.'

'Thank you. It's getting harder, the older they get. Sometimes, they frighten me a little, especially when they get that gleam of mischief in their eyes. Agang and I are hardly in the spring of youth.'

'I'll go now, so that there's no drama. They'll be needing their lunch soon.'

'I'll sort it. Go. The sooner you leave, the sooner you'll get back.'

Karalyn nodded, then took a deep breath. It had been seven years since she had travelled to Kellach Brigdomin, though, with four years lost to her, to her mind it felt like three. Lennox had still been alive when they had departed the *World's End* in the Domm Pass, and Corthie had just been abducted. She didn't want to return to the *World's End*, she decided; there were too many painful memories associated with the tavern, but the Domm Pass was a good place to start any search.

Outside World's End, Domm Pass. Go.

The air shimmered around her, and she found herself standing in a muddy street, a gust of cold rain hitting her face. Above, dark and heavy clouds were rolling in from the west, and the town of Westgate was damp and grey in the light. To her left she saw the *World's End*, its sign swinging in the wind. The chill penetrated her clothes, and she started to wish she had brought a raincoat. She stared at the tavern door. Inside, it would be warm and dry.

She felt foolish for standing in the freezing rain, when there was a welcoming tavern. And perhaps she owed an explanation to those who worked inside about the events that had occurred seven years previously. She sighed, and strode towards the door. She swung it open, and a blast of warm air coursed over her.

'Keep that fucking door shut, hen,' someone shouted.

Karalyn stepped inside, and pulled the door closed behind her.

The man who had shouted put down his tray and stared at her. 'Kelpie!' he yelled. 'Come and see who's here.'

Karalyn remembered the man. He had greyed a little, and was carrying more around his waist than the last time she had seen him.

'Hello, Kendrie,' she said.

'Karalyn Holdfast,' he said. 'Welcome back. Are you, eh... are ye here on yer own?'

'Aye.'

'Well, don't just stand there, hen; come on in and grab a seat.'

She walked to the bar, and sat on a tall stool. The tavern was almost empty, but a large fire was blazing in the hearth, and the shutters were half-closed, as rain pelted against the window panes. An old woman walked out from a side door, a stick helping to support her steps.

'Pyre's arsehole,' she cried. 'It's Killop's lass. What are ye doing here, hen?'

'Miss Kelpie,' said Karalyn. 'It's nice to see you again.'

Kelpie eyed Kendrie. 'Crack open a bottle of Severton's finest, lad. Are ye hungry, Karalyn? We could stick on some bacon rolls for ye.'

'That sounds great. Thanks.'

'Right you are,' said Kendrie. 'Give me a minute.'

He turned, and strode through the kitchen door.

Karalyn turned to Kelpie. 'I need to apologise for what happened the last time I was here.' She paused. How could she explain why it had taken so long for her to come back? 'I was, eh, stuck in a place called Lostwell for four years, and then I had the twins to look after.'

Kelpie raised an eyebrow as she sat down next to Karalyn. 'We were pulling the bodies out for days.'

'Sorry. We found Corthie.'

'Did ye? That's good. Actually, word came through a few days ago that Corthie's down here in Kellach Brigdomin, doing some kind of tour round the place. He has two of Bridget's daughters with him, or so I heard. Will they be coming here, do ye think?'

'Well, they're planning on going down to Severton, so they'll have to pass through Westgate. How did you explain what had happened to the local militia?'

'We told them the truth, that a bunch of crazy Holdfasts had attracted some unsavoury attention. There were plenty of witnesses to back up our story. The Iron Brigade was rounded up after that, what was left of them, and they were disbanded. And before ye say anything else, we know about Darine.'

Karalyn's glance fell.

'Carrie was down here three years ago,' Kelpie went on; 'she told us. She also told us that you had been missing for years, and that no one knew if ye were coming back. Carrie also mentioned that yer man Lennox had been killed. She was fair upset about that.'

Kendrie emerged from the kitchen, and set down a plate filled with bacon packed into white bread rolls. He poured a pint of ale for Karalyn, and opened a bottle of whisky.

'I can't get too drunk,' said Karalyn.

'Och, wheesht, hen,' said Kelpie. 'Yer in my tavern, and ye'll do as yer told.'

'You remember Kalayne, don't you?'

'Aye.'

'Have you heard anything recently about another mage down here, who might have the same powers that he possessed?'

'Like you, you mean?'

'Aye, like me.'

Kelpie glanced at Kendrie, and the man shrugged.

'I've heard nothing about that,' said Kelpie. 'Is there a dream mage on the loose?'

'That's what I'm worried about.'

'So that's why yer here?'

Karalyn glanced round the tavern, her eyes lingering on the spot where her mother had butchered a god called Gorman.

'The truth is,' she said, 'that I've been avoiding the *World's End*. Lennox, Darine, Corthie – the memories are too raw. And the twins;

they're both dream mages, and I can't leave them alone for long. They're too powerful.'

'Ye don't need to explain anything, lass. I'm just glad that ye got back safely from wherever ye were. Now, that glass of whisky isnae gonnae drink itself, hen.'

Two hours later, Karalyn staggered outside for some fresh air, her head spinning from the whisky. That hadn't been part of the plan, she thought to herself, but she had felt unable to refuse the generous hospitality that had been forced upon her. She had achieved precisely nothing, but had been able to relax for the first time in years. She wondered if she should start to make a habit of heading down to the *World's End*. She could tell Shella that she was on important business, and slip off for a few hours at a time.

She lit a cigarette. There was still time to sweep the area with her powers before she returned to Colsbury. She concentrated, and allowed her dream vision to rise up from her body. She glanced around at Westgate. The rain had stopped, but the thick clouds foretold that more was on the way. She quietened, and listened, her senses straining for any signs of mage powers. Miles away, down in the Domm lowlands, she felt a tiny flicker of sparker powers, and she was reminded of her father. She aimed her powers in the other direction. Corthie, Aila and baby Killop were somewhere to the east, travelling through Kell. If she could sense them, then she would know that her sweep had covered the majority of Kellach Brigdomin. She pushed her powers out to the edge of their limits, then smiled as she caught a sliver of Aila's self-healing powers. There was no hiding them, as gods and demigods were continually burning their powers at a low level. Once she had fixed on Aila, she was able to sense a fainter version of the same powers, coming from her two-year-old son Killop junior. Corthie was invisible to her, but if he wasn't using battle-vision, then that would make sense. She was tempted to travel down to Kell to meet them, but she knew that she had been away from Colsbury for long enough.

She pulled away from Aila, and listened again. Nothing else was coming from Southern Kell. The empire had a vision mage posted in the northern half of Kell, to keep an eye on the massive mining operations that supplied half of the Star Continent's coal and iron, but Karalyn doubted that her mage-sensing abilities would reach that far. She turned to Brig. Nothing. She knew that no one lived in Lach, but aimed her powers in that direction anyway. Nothing. She sighed. If the dream mage was in Kellach Brigdomin, then she would only sense him if he used his powers, and he could be resting, or sleeping. She was wasting her time.

She pulled her powers back to her body, and stubbed out the cigarette. The wind had stilled, and she gazed out at the view of the Domm lowlands, picturing the little cottage where she had lived with Lennox. If things had been different, she would still be living there. If Sable hadn't forced him to slaughter the innocents of Rainsby, then Karalyn wouldn't have walked out on him, and they might still be together. She stopped herself. There was no point in dreaming about what might have been.

Karalyn turned back to face the tavern, then felt it. A faint, slender thread of dream powers. They whipped up over Westgate, paused close to where she stood, then vanished. Shella had been right – that couldn't have been a coincidence. She had been searching Kellach Brigdomin with her own powers, and to any watching dream mage, she would have shone out like a beacon. She focussed, and sensed the vestiges of the powers that had snaked up close to her. She back-tracked, following them through the Domm Pass, until the trail went cold near Threeways.

There was no doubt. There was a dream mage in Kellach Brigdomin.

And he was looking for her.

CHAPTER 7
UP WITH THE DAWN

Marchside, Kell – Summer's Day 534

Corthie opened his eyes. He was buried under a mountain of warm blankets, and for a moment he forgot where he was. They had been travelling for so long, and had slept in so many different places, that it took him a while to remember that he was in the small town of Marchside, the capital of Southern Kell. Their carriages had arrived in heavy rain late the night before, after a tiring journey, and they had gone straight to bed.

He sat up, and glanced around. A thin ray of light was coming through the slats in the wooden window shutters, and he could see the interior of a small room with stone walls. Aila was sitting in a chair, with Killop on her lap.

'You been up long?' he said.

Aila glanced at him. 'No. Just fifteen minutes or so. Killop was hungry. I've fed him, changed his nappy, and now I think he wants to go back to sleep again.'

'Have you been outside yet?'

She shook her head. Corthie pulled the masses of blankets away from him, and swung his legs off the bed. The air was cold inside the cottage, and his breath misted.

'This is summer in Kell, eh?' said Aila. 'It's freezing.'

'It will warm up when the sun comes out.'

'*If* the sun comes out. It's like Freshmist all the time here.'

'When I was last in Domm, it was winter. This is nothing.'

He pulled on some clothes, then walked over and kissed Aila and the child.

'Where's the bathroom?' he said.

'I don't think this cottage has one, Corthie. Last night, Conal told us that there was an out-building for that, but so far I've managed to resist paying it a visit. Maybe they don't have indoor toilets down here.'

'The house where I lived in Severton had an inside toilet, but I don't mind roughing it a bit. I'm going to take a look outside.'

He walked to the room's only door, and opened it. It led directly outside, and he stepped through the entrance and closed the door behind him. Over to his right, the sun had just cleared the horizon, and the sky was brightening up. In front of him spread a settlement, with single-storey houses lining the unpaved streets. The town was small, but it was the largest he had seen since arriving in Southern Kell. Bunting had been put up, and coloured ribbons were hanging across every street. He heard the sound of running water, and walked round to the side of the little cottage where he, Aila and Killop had slept. He glanced up at the sight of a steep hillside that seemed to rise directly out of the earth. The town had been built at the bottom of the slope, where a small stream flowed. He walked to a little bridge that crossed the stream, and gazed at the hills. He had never seen so many different shades of green. The Holdings was dusty, dry and ferociously hot at that time of year, and even the Plateau would be wilting a little in the heat, but down in Kell everything seemed green.

He wondered why the streets were empty. The sun was up, so where were all the people? He walked back to the cottage and entered the small room.

'No one's around,' he said to Aila. 'Does everyone sleep in on Summer's Day?'

Aila laughed. 'You sleep so much that you haven't noticed what time the sun rises down here. Have you not seen how light it is in the evenings? I'd guess that it only stays dark for four hours or so each night.'

Corthie frowned. 'Really?'

'When you were here in winter, did the sun rise late, and set early?'

'Eh, aye. You're right. It was dark most of the time.'

'Then I guess it's the opposite in summer. You should have a turn getting up to feed Killop; then you might notice these things more.'

'Aye, but you can cure your own hangovers; it's like an unfair advantage. And anyway, you're from a world where the sun doesn't even rise properly – how do you know all this stuff?'

'The sight of the sun crossing the sky each day was a novelty on Lostwell, but I'm used to it by now. I noticed that the nights were getting lighter before we entered Kell. It's not the same in the Holdings – the amount of sunlight there doesn't vary between winter and summer. Karalyn told me it was because this world is slightly tilted, and the further south you go, the bigger the difference between summer and winter.'

Corthie sighed. 'Yet another thing I missed learning about in school. You know, Keir thinks I'm completely stupid. While he was learning all kinds of things, I was training how to kill people.'

'Do you care what your brother thinks?'

'No.'

'And you're not stupid, Corthie. Could a stupid person escape from Tarstation and make it all the way back to the City?'

'I know what you're saying. I can think quickly on my feet, but ask me a question about history or geography, or politics, and I'm lost. But hey! I know lots of ways to kill a man with my bare hands.'

Aila stood. 'Let's go for a walk while the streets are empty. It'll be nice not having a crowd follow us around.'

She put Killop down onto the bed, then strapped the child-carrier to Corthie's chest. He lifted the sleeping boy in his arms, wrapped him in a blanket, then squeezed him into the carrier. Aila grabbed a long coat and a hat, and they went outside.

'It's beautiful, eh?' said Corthie. 'Just look at those hills.'

'Very green,' she said.

'That's what I was thinking! Everything's green.'

'It's because it rains so much.'

He eyed her as they began to walk towards the centre of the town. 'I'm not that stupid. I do know some things.'

She laughed. 'Sorry. You know, a year spent reading would plug all the holes in your knowledge. I meant what I said before – you are far from stupid, Corthie. You have the brains; you're only lacking the knowledge. There were more books in the Great Fortress than in the whole entire City; even better, books are a fraction of the price here. A decent book in Pella was beyond the reach of most people, but you have printing presses, and cheap and plentiful supplies of paper. Mona would love it. I love it. The university library is also supposed to be excellent.'

Corthie nodded, but said nothing. It disconcerted him a little when Aila talked about how much she liked Plateau City. She was a city girl, after all, and he wondered if she would be happy to stay in the relative backwardness of Kell. At the very least, she would want a toilet that was inside anywhere they lived. There were fine houses in Severton, with taps that dispensed hot water, but Corthie was starting to long for seclusion; somewhere nice and quiet, with only Aila, the children, and nature for company.

They reached a square in the middle of the town. A memorial was standing in the centre, with words engraved down one side.

'The Battle of Marchside,' read Aila. 'I remember Conal telling me about this.'

'And I can remember my father going on about it,' said Corthie. 'It was one of his favourite stories.'

Across from the memorial was the village hall, the largest building within the boundaries of the town. It had a newly-built appearance, with a stone ground floor, and an upper level constructed from timber. As Corthie was gazing up at it, he felt a strange sensation ripple through his head. He frowned.

'Did you feel that?' he said to Aila.

'Feel what? Is it starting to rain?'

'No. It was like... as if someone was in my head.'

'Well, the only person who can enter your mind is Karalyn; and her twins, too.'

'Maybe I imagined it.'

'Perhaps Karalyn is checking that we're still alive.'

'She usually stops to say hello when she does that. It didn't feel like Karalyn, to be honest.'

They walked on a little further, and came across one of the town's many taverns. A man was unloading a cart by a side door, and he glanced in their direction.

'You're up early,' he said in the Kellach tongue.

'The dawn woke me,' said Corthie, slipping into his father's language. 'Are you opening?'

'Not for a few hours yet, lad. You look handy; can ye help me lift this barrel?'

'Aye. Sure.'

Corthie transferred the child-carrier to Aila, then strode over and picked up the barrel.

'Where do you want it?'

The man laughed. 'You have muscles like an ox, lad. Take it inside for me and set it down by the bar.'

Corthie carried the barrel into the tavern, and placed it next to the long bar.

'It's for today's big feast, lad,' the man said, coming in behind him carrying a crate of whisky. 'I assume that you'll be coming?'

'Do you know who I am?'

'Of course I do, lad. The whole town knows. Two of the Empress's daughters, and the son of Chief Killop. It's not every day Marchside gets visitors from the outside world. That's why I'm up at this hour; there's a lot to do.'

'Can I help?' said Corthie. 'I'm not going to be able to go back to sleep, not now that I'm awake.'

'Eh, you're a guest, lad. I cannae put ye to work.'

'You've already asked me to carry a barrel; and you'd be doing me a favour. I could do with some hard work, after months in a damn carriage.'

The man frowned. 'Months?'

'Oh, I meant thirds.'

'Fair enough. You can start by unloading the rest of the cart, and bringing everything inside.'

'Let me clear it with the wife, and I'll get to work.'

Corthie walked back outside. Aila was sitting on a bench next to the tavern, her eyes on the nearby hills, while Killop continued to sleep in the carrier.

'I'm going to give the guy a hand,' he said.

Aila smiled. 'Did he bribe you with offers of free whisky?'

'Nah. I need to work off some excess energy.'

'That's fine by me, as long as I don't have to do anything.'

Corthie began unloading the cart, flexing muscles that he hadn't used in a while, as the sun rose in the sky. The clouds stayed away, and it began to warm up a little. When he had finished with the cart, he and the man walked a mile to where he lived, and they pulled another loaded cart back to the tavern.

'The folk here drink a lot, do they?' said Corthie, eyeing the rows of full barrels.

'Aye. Summer's Day can be quite boisterous. Nothing like Winter's Day – that's a different matter altogether. That can last for days. Tell you what, lad. Get this cart unloaded, and I'll pull you and your wife a pint.'

Corthie lifted the first barrel, and carried it into the tavern. When the cart was empty, the man wiped his hands on a rag and walked behind the bar. He lifted three large mugs, and filled them with a pale, golden liquid. Corthie called Aila inside, and she sat down by the bar next to him.

'Here ye go,' said the tavern-keeper, switching to the Holdings language as he set the three mugs down onto the bar.

Corthie glanced at Killop. 'That lad can sleep, eh?'

'Yes,' said Aila, 'but not usually when you want him to.'

'Cheers,' said the tavern-keeper, raising his glass.

'Aye, cheers,' said Corthie, taking a drink. He coughed. 'What is this?'

'It's cider, lad.'

'Cider?'

'Aye. Before the Rahain invaded, cider was all anyone drank in Kell. Then, when Kell was emptied of folk, the old traditions died away, and it's only in the last couple of years that we've starting making it again. The apples for it are grown right here in Marchside. That was the chief's doing – she insisted that we bring back some of the old customs.'

'I like it,' said Aila. 'It's better than that dark brown ale we've been drinking.'

The man grinned. 'Too right, hen. That shite was introduced by the Brig. Smells like sweaty socks, and tastes even worse. Who knows, maybe one day the Lach will start making whisky again.'

'Where is the chief?' said Aila. 'We haven't met her yet.'

'I imagine she'll still be sleeping, hen. Someone will ring the town bell when it's time to get up, and on Summer's Day, that'll happen an hour or so later than normal.' He locked eyes with Corthie. 'So, lad, what's it like to have such a famous father?'

Corthie shrugged. 'Did you know him?'

'Me? Naw. I was one of the lucky ones – I was taken to Domm when the lizards invaded. I've never once left Kellach Brigdomin. Why would I want to? Everything I need is down here. The chief knew him, but.'

'I didn't really understand that my father was well-known in Kellach Brigdomin when I was growing up,' Corthie said. 'He never boasted about it.'

'Don't feel bad about it, lad. Not every son can equal their father's exploits.'

'Corthie might not be famous down here,' said Aila, lines of irritation crinkling her brow; 'but where I come from, he's a hero.'

Corthie's face went red.

The man laughed. 'A hero, eh? I wish my wife thought the same about me, hen.'

'I'm not saying that just because I'm married to him.'

'Alright; keep yer hair on.'

'Sorry; it just annoys me. Corthie has achieved more than anyone else I know, and yet no one here knows the first thing about any of it. Do you realise that he's the greatest mortal warrior who has ever lived?'

The man smirked. 'Is that a fact, doll?'

'Yes, it is a fact, and if you call me doll again I will punch you in the face.'

'What are you anyway, hen?'

Aila blinked. 'What?'

'Yer clearly too wee to be Kellach Brigdomin, but yer skin's too pale to be one of them Holdings folk. Yer tongue has no cleft in it, so yer not Rahain, praise Pyre for that; and I don't think yer one of the frog folk. Who does that leave?'

'I'm not from Sanang, if that's what you mean.'

'The monkey folk, that's right. Fine. If yer not any of them, then where exactly are you from?'

Aila glanced at Corthie.

'Tell him,' he said.

'Alright. I come from a different world altogether. I used to live in the City, a place surrounded by ferocious green monsters, and ruled by gods. I am the granddaughter of the God-King and God-Queen. I met Corthie there, when he was fighting those monsters I mentioned. He killed thousands of them.'

The man looked slightly aggrieved. 'Alright, so ye don't want to tell me the truth.'

Aila's eyes flashed. 'That is the truth!'

'Aye, right.'

Corthie smiled. 'Maybe we should tell folk you're from Sanang.' He glanced at the tavern-keeper. 'Don't call Aila a liar again. I'm grateful for the cider, but I have a low tolerance for anyone insulting my wife.'

The man raised his hands. 'Fair enough, lad.'

'Let's go,' said Aila.

'Aye,' said Corthie.

'Thanks for the help, lad,' the tavern-keeper said, a weak smile on his face.

'Thanks for the cider.'

Corthie and Aila walked outside into the growing sunshine.

'The guy annoyed the crap out of me,' said Aila.

'Aye, I noticed.'

'Does it not bother you? Back in the City, you were a champion; and on Lostwell, you took on two Ascendants on your own. That old fool had no idea who he was speaking to. To him, you're just the son of a famous man.'

'I don't mind.'

'You should, Corthie. I almost wish that this town would suddenly be attacked by greenhides, so you could prove that bastard wrong.'

'It's just the way of things here. I don't think the Kellach like folk bragging, or making too much of themselves.'

A bell rang from a wooden tower on the far side of the square.

Corthie smiled. 'Time to get up.'

'Have you still got plenty of energy to burn off?'

He glanced at her. 'Aye.'

She rolled her eyes. 'Not for that, Corthie. I was thinking that we should climb the hill.'

'Oh.'

'I need to clear my head, before I say something to one of the villagers that I'll regret.'

They took a bag with them, and remained up on the hill for several hours, letting Killop run around on the soft grass while they gazed out at the view over Southern Kell. When they finally trekked back down the slope, the town was packed with people. Farmers from outlying areas had arrived, bringing wagon-loads of food, and children were playing in the main square, chasing each other round the memorial. Tables and chairs had been laid out along each edge of the square, and the nearby taverns were doing busy trade.

Conal leapt up off a chair when he saw Corthie and Aila approach.

'Where have you been?' he cried. 'I nearly had a heart attack when no one could find you.'

'We went for a long walk,' said Aila, 'and by some miracle it didn't rain.'

'It's a braw day, right enough. For once, we might not have to bring out the canopies to keep the tables dry. Anyway, I've had the chief on my back for a while, asking to see you. Can ye spare five minutes? The Empress's daughters are with her now.'

'Sure,' said Corthie. 'Where is the chief?'

'Follow me,' said Conal.

He led them through the square, and they entered the village hall. The interior was as busy as the main square, and they squeezed past several large groups of Kellach. Conal took them to the rear of the hall, and knocked on a door. A reply came from within, and he opened the door. Inside, a woman was sitting behind a large desk, her elbows on the surface, while Brogan and Bethal were seated on the left. All three had glasses of cider in their hands.

'Hi, Chief,' said Conal. 'This is Corthie, Aila, and their wee boy. I managed to track them down.'

'About time, Conal,' said the woman. She glanced at Corthie, as if appraising him. 'My name is Kallie.'

Corthie put on a polite smile. 'Nice to meet you.'

Kallie's eyes tightened slightly. 'You don't know who I am, do you?'

'Eh, no, ma'am. Should I?'

'No, probably not. I was an old friend of your father, long ago.'

'Did you fight alongside him in the war?'

'Aye. And we were slaves together – me, him and Bridget, in Rahain.'

A vague memory came back to Corthie's mind; about something his mother had once told him.

'I also knew your Auntie Keira,' Kallie went on. 'She was some woman.'

'Aye, so I've heard.'

'How's your mother doing?'

'She's fine, thanks. Did you know her too?'

'A little. Anyway, I wanted to welcome you to Marchside. I can't stay for the celebrations, unfortunately, as I have to travel to Threeways for a meeting of the Clan Council. That's why I was anxious for Conal to find you; I didn't want to leave without saying hello.'

'Thank you. Is the Clan Council in the habit of meeting on the holidays?'

Kallie smiled. 'No, Corthie, they are not.' Her gaze turned to Aila, who was holding the child in her arms. 'You must be Aila. It's been brought to my attention that one of our inn-keepers was rude to you this morning; so, apologies for that. I've told the wee prick to keep his gob shut from now on.' She smiled. 'That's a lovely wee boy you have there. What's his name?'

'Killop,' said Aila.

A strange expression flitted across Kallie's face, then she took a breath. 'Appropriate, I suppose. Before I go, I wanted to propose something to the three of you. Conal was telling me that you might be thinking of settling down here in Kell?'

'We haven't made any decisions yet,' said Corthie.

'It's not something you want to rush into. However, if you do decide to stay, then I want to make you an offer. Corthie, you are half-Kell, and therefore you and your family are more than welcome to make this land your home. We're always on the lookout for young families to settle here; it's been my dream for a long time to see Kell re-populated. More than that, though, I would be prepared to gift you a substantial tract of land. It's called Clackenbaird, and it comes with a large stone-built house and a few farm buildings. The house needs a bit of work, but we're talking nearly a hundred and eighty acres of arable land that used to grow wheat and barley. It's situated about ten miles north of here, on the road that leads to the Brig Pass.'

Corthie's eyes widened. 'And you would give this... Clackenbaird to us as a gift?'

'Aye. You don't need to decide now. Conal can take you up there in a few days to show you around. If it suits you, it's yours.'

'But... why? Why would you give me so much land?'

Kallie smiled. 'You're Killop's son. For that reason alone, I would be happy to see you settle here. It might also attract other Kell back, so I do have a wee ulterior motive. Your father loved Kell, and it seems right to me that at least one of his children returns home.'

'I'm a little overwhelmed. We'll certainly think about it. Thanks.'

'Are you still intending to travel to Severton in a few days?'

'Aye,' said Corthie. He gestured towards the two daughters of the Empress. 'We'll visit the town with Brogan and Bethal; pay our respects to the Severed Clan.'

Kallie stood. 'Then I'll see you on your return journey. Conal, is my carriage ready to leave?'

'Aye, Chief.'

'I'm not sure when I'll be back,' she said. 'Everyone, enjoy the festival today.'

She strode from the room.

Corthie turned to Aila. 'What do you think?'

'I'm open-minded,' she said. 'If you think you'd like to try your hand at farming, then we should definitely take a look at this place.'

Bethal laughed. 'Have you any experience of farming, Corthie?'

'Nope,' he said. 'I know a bit about rearing horses, but I doubt that will be of any use. I'm willing to work hard and learn, though.'

'You'll need help with a hundred and eighty acres,' said Conal. 'There are folk here who'd be willing to lend their assistance.' He rubbed his chin. 'You'd also need gold to repair the buildings, and to buy enough seed and equipment. Even with the land being free, it'll still cost a fair amount.'

'The Holdfasts are one of the wealthiest families in the world,' said Bethal. 'I'm sure they could afford a shiny new plough. You know, I'm amazed that Kallie offered this to you, considering her history.'

'What history?' said Aila.

Bethal glanced at Corthie, a faint smirk on her lips. 'My mother says that your mother stole Killop from Kallie. Apparently, Kallie and Killop were together for ages, then Daphne came along, and took him from right under Kallie's nose.'

'I'm sure it was more complicated than that,' said Brogan.

Corthie snapped his fingers. 'I remember now. My mother mentioned this to me, though her version of events wasn't quite the same as yours, Bethal. I'd completely forgotten. Still, it was a long time ago.'

'I remember the days when Kallie and Killop were inseparable,' said Conal, 'but there's more to the chief's history than that. Kallie was on the roof of the Great Fortress the night the Creator was defeated. She witnessed the whole thing.'

'My mother didn't tell me that,' said Corthie.

'That doesn't surprise me,' said Bethal.

'Chief Kallie has never seemed too concerned that her part in that night has been forgotten,' said Conal. 'But, it still annoys her that Kylon's role has been ignored.'

'Who's Kylon?' said Corthie.

Conal smiled. 'Ask your mother when you next see her.'

Brogan and Bethal glanced at each other.

'I take it that you two girls don't know, either?' said Conal.

'I've heard mother mention his name before,' said Brogan. 'He was Mage Keira's boyfriend, wasn't he?'

'He was,' said Conal, 'but there was more to him than that. I'll say no more. Shall we join the party?'

'Aye,' said Corthie. 'One more thing; what's so urgent that Kallie has to leave her own Summer's Day festival?'

Conal frowned. 'There's been another death on the Clan Council. An old representative from Brig this time, found dead in a ditch.'

'Another death?' said Corthie. 'How many have there been?'

'That makes five in the last third,' said Conal.

'Five?' said Aila. 'What's killing them?'

'We don't know,' said Conal. 'The deaths all look completely unrelated. A Domm representative was killed in a drunken tavern brawl, while a Lach drowned in their bathtub. As you might know, there are eight representatives from each of the four clans sitting on the Council, and they're starting to get worried. Chief Kallie is one of the Kell representatives; she's been on the Clan Council for almost twenty years.'

'Coincidences do happen,' said Brogan, 'but this looks suspicious to me.'

Conal nodded. 'It's cast a dark shadow over today's celebrations. It looks like bad luck, and folk are concerned.'

'Who would want to kill off the Clan Council?' said Aila. 'I thought Kellach Brigdomin was prosperous and happy?'

'There are always a few complainers,' said Conal, 'but no one has ever murdered a member of the Clan Council, as far as I know. The only folk with a serious grievance are the bandits who live way up in the Domm Highlands. They preyed on the traffic moving through the Domm Pass from Threeways, but the army went into the glens a couple of years ago and cleared most of them out. I'd be surprised if they had the ability to carry out any kind of murderous operation these days. You know, as Brogan said, it might just be a coincidence.'

They walked out of the room and entered the busy hall, where over a hundred locals were drinking cider and talking. They squeezed through the crowds, and emerged into bright sunshine. The town square was packed with people eating and drinking, while small groups of musicians were setting up in the corners. Corthie smiled. The sun was warm on his skin, and the town looked beautiful. He thought about spending his life as a farmer. While he understood almost nothing about what the job entailed, he knew the work would be hard. Maybe that was what he needed – maybe hard physical labour would eat up his excess energy, and the urge to fight and kill would slowly fade away.

He nudged Aila as they made their way to the large table in the middle of the square that had been reserved for them.

'Could you see me as a farmer, Aila?'

She smiled. 'You know, I can. That sort of thing might suit you, Corthie.'

'That's what I was thinking. But, what about you? Would you be happy living on a farm down here? Would you not miss being in a city?'

Aila lowered her voice. 'I lived in a city for nearly eight hundred years. I'm sure I could manage. If it's what you want, Corthie, then I'd be happy to give it a go.'

Corthie said nothing as they were led to their seats. Aila hadn't spelled it out, but he knew what she meant. He would grow old and die, while she would remain exactly as she was. She had all the time she needed to return to city life after he was dead and gone – what were a few decades to her?

They sat, and large mugs of cider were filled for them.

Aila picked up her mug. 'To Summer's Day,' she said, then she drained it. A few Kellach Brigdomin laughed, while others glanced at the bump on her waist, but said nothing.

'Should she be drinking?' whispered Conal. 'In her condition?'

Corthie laughed. 'Happy Summer's Day, Conal.'

CHAPTER 8
LONG REACH

H old Fast, Republic of the Holdings – Summer's Day 534
Daphne gazed at the paddock. A heat haze was causing the air to shimmer, and it was difficult to count the number of beasts that had been corralled behind the high fence.

'There hasn't been much progress since your last visit,' said Celine, a wide-brimmed hat keeping the sun from her face. 'Winged gaien take a long time to grow into adulthood, or so it seems. Perhaps we need an expert from Rahain to advise us.'

'How soon will they be ready to lift a carriage?' said Daphne, her eyes on the dull-brown scales of the large creatures. 'That's all that really interests me. If we had a few flying carriages, then I could dispense with having to travel everywhere by land.'

'A few of them could probably do it now,' said Celine. 'But I don't have the knowledge to be able to train them. Too many winged gaien were killed in the wars, along with their Rahain trainers and handlers. Do you think there might be someone at the university in Plateau City who'd be able to help?'

'I can ask. The Empress has always wanted her own flying carriages, so she might loan us someone. How long do the beasts live for?'

Celine shrugged. 'I don't know. At least a hundred years, I'd guess.

Every one in that paddock is a juvenile, and some are close to thirty years old. Still, they'll be a fine attraction for the visitors arriving today for the festival.'

Daphne smiled. 'Kelsey rides about on one of these beasts, or so Karalyn informs me. They put saddles on their backs, and they fly them around. Could we try that?'

Celine raised an eyebrow. 'Yes, but Karalyn also says that Kelsey's gaien can speak. I think we might be dealing with a different creature altogether.'

'They're all giant lizards,' said Daphne. 'Though, Kelsey's one is silver. I saw it.'

'Was it speaking?'

'No. It was just standing there. Try putting a saddle on one, and see if it can understand basic instructions.'

'I'll give it a go,' said Celine, 'but I wouldn't get your hopes up. Horses are more intelligent than gaien. We could try to train them in the same way, I suppose.'

Daphne wiped sweat from her eyes. 'Let's get back under some shade before we melt.'

They turned from the paddock, and started walking back towards the mansion. The whitewashed buildings of the estate were too bright for Daphne's eyes, and she squinted, keeping her gaze down at the dry, dusty ground. They passed the main show paddock, where that day's horse riding competitions would take place. Servants were cleaning the rows of wooden benches that surrounded the paddock, preparing them for the masses of people who would turn up to watch. Beyond that, the streets of the estate were full of market stalls selling food, drinks and anything relating to horses. Many of the people there bowed their heads to Daphne, and she gave a curt nod to each of them. The heat was intense despite the early hour, and groups of workers were erecting pavilions to provide shade over the stalls. Celine and Daphne reached the little square in the centre of the estate. It was surrounded on three sides by stables and administrative buildings, while the family's mansion sat on the fourth side, its walls and domes glistening white in the sunshine. Children were running around in the large fountain in the middle of the square, splashing cool water at each other amid shrieks and gales of laughter.

Daphne smiled. She didn't make it back to the estate as often as she liked, but she never missed the holidays.

'Will you be here for the Founders' Festival as well?' said Celine.

'Of course,' said Daphne. 'Just twenty days to go. Summer's Day feels a little like a dress rehearsal for the main event. That reminds me, though; I still have to write a speech.'

'It'll be a bumper year for the herds,' said Celine. 'We'll have more to sell this summer than we've had for a long time.'

'This time next summer, I'll be out of a job.'

Celine smiled. 'You could always help run the estate. With Keir away, I could do with some assistance.'

'You have Jemma.'

'Yes. Can I ask – how likely is it that Keir will return? If I knew that he wasn't coming back, then I could start to train Jemma properly. I think she'd make a good estate manager, but I'll hold off if you want Keir to do it.'

Daphne pondered for a moment as they crossed the square. 'Assume for now,' she said, 'that Keir might not be returning to take over the reins. Give Jemma her chance.'

Celine nodded.

They approached the large mansion, and slipped under the shade of the canopy covering the wide front porch.

'This heat is close to unbearable,' Daphne said. 'I'm glad I'm not in Holdings City. At least there's a slight breeze here.'

They walked into the cool hallways of the mansion, and a servant noticed them.

'Holder Fast,' she said, bowing low. 'The dining room has been set out for the family lunch, as requested; and the guest rooms have been cleaned and prepared.'

'Thank you,' said Daphne. 'Could you bring some chilled water to my study, please?'

'Yes, ma'am. What time will the others be arriving?'

'About noon, I think. They won't be bringing a carriage.'

The servant bowed again, then left them.

'I'm going for a shower,' said Celine. 'I was up at dawn today, over-seeing the transfer of the eastern herds to the estate paddocks.'

'See you at lunchtime, Celine.'

Daphne made her way through the wide corridors of the mansion to her own little study. It had once belonged to her husband, and she had kept it looking the same as when he had used it. She entered and closed the door behind her, then sat in the huge leather armchair. It was too big for her, but it reminded her of Killop.

She had been a widow for almost nine years, she thought to herself as she filled a glass with whisky. During that time, she had kept herself extremely busy – running the Holdings, helping Thorn raise Karalyn's twins, and carrying out a wide variety of functions as Herald of the Empire. In less than a year, her second term as First Holder would be over, and she dreaded having nothing to do with her time. She thought about the Empress's ultimatum. If she refused to travel to Plateau City to live in the Great Fortress, then Bridget would appoint her son Bryce as Herald to replace her, and Daphne would be unemployed. She sipped her whisky. Perhaps she should consider retiring. She was over fifty, and surely deserved a rest, but she knew that retirement would bore her senseless. She needed a project; something she could get her teeth into, but what?

The servant knocked once, then entered. She placed a large jug of cold water onto Daphne's desk, along with a tall glass.

'Thank you,' said Daphne. 'Let me know at once if there's any sign of my daughter.'

'I shall, ma'am.'

Daphne waited for the servant to leave, then she poured herself some water and lit a stick of dreamweed. The Hold Fast estate grew the stuff in large quantities, and the trade in the substance earned the family almost as much as the trade in horses. Bridget had occasionally toyed with the idea of banning the narcotic across the empire, but so far she had kept the sale of it legal.

'Mother, it's not even noon, and you're smoking that already?'

Daphne glanced up and saw Karalyn standing on the other side of the desk.

She lifted her glass of whisky. 'I'm also drinking this, if you hadn't noticed, daughter. It's Summer's Day.'

Karalyn shook her head. 'You never change, do you?'

'I'm too old to change, dear. Where are the others? I assume you haven't come on your own.'

'I left them all in the square next to the stables. Agang said he wanted to buy a souvenir.'

'He decided to come, did he? You'd better watch that the twins don't do anything to upset the estate workers.'

'I'll sense if they use their powers, mother. May I sit?'

Daphne gestured to a chair.

'I wanted to speak to you alone, mother,' said Karalyn.

'I presumed as much. Is something on your mind?'

'Aye. Four days ago, I discovered that there is another dream mage on the Star Continent.'

Daphne blinked. 'Oh. I would ask if you are certain of this, but I know you. Another dream mage? Where?'

'Down in Kellach Brigdomin. I've been down there several times over the last few days, searching for him.'

'You know it's a "him"?'

'Aye. He managed to get inside Kyra's mind, while we were in Colsbury.'

'What? He could use his powers all the way from Kellach Brigdomin to Colsbury? And he was able to breach the barriers you'd erected around the twins? Dear me. What did he want with Kyra?'

'I don't know. I think he sensed us. I think, maybe, he was reaching out to find us. However, I also discovered something else when I was in Kellach Brigdomin, something which puts things into a different light. Five members of the Clan Council have died in suspicious circumstances, all within the last third. The deaths appear to be unrelated, but a dream mage could have easily made it seem that way.'

'Do you have proof that it was him?'

'No, but it can't be a coincidence. Five separate deaths in a third?'

'Have you informed the Empress?'

'Not yet. I wanted to see what you thought first. Should I go down there and carry out a thorough search? I mean, I think I should, but I don't want to leave the twins alone for too long, and I don't want to take them with me, not if he can read their thoughts. He might even be able to manipulate them; I can't take the risk.'

'Did you see Corthie while you were there?'

'No.'

'Where is he?'

'In Marchside, mother.'

'Oh yes; the site of the famous battle.'

'There's a town there now; and that town is run by someone you might remember – Kallie.'

'Oh. She's still around, is she? I hope she doesn't give Corthie any trouble.'

'Why would she, mother? I doubt she's been carrying a grudge for thirty years. She's also a member of the Clan Council, so she might be at risk.'

'Yes. I think you have to go, dear. Even if this dream mage is innocent of the deaths, we should still make contact. We can't be having a rogue mage with that amount of power on the loose. I wonder if he's related to Kalayne.'

Karalyn smiled. 'That's what Shella said. I doubt it, if I'm honest. I get the feeling our new dream mage would be too young to be a child of Kalayne. Laodoc told me that dream mages can arise naturally.'

'Yes, I remember him saying something like that. This doesn't sit well with me. I liked the idea that the Holdfasts were the only possessors of dream powers. Could Shella and Agang look after the twins if you went south for a while?'

'They'd probably say yes, but I can't ask them. It would be too much. They would be at the mercy of the twins, and Pyre knows what state they would be in when I returned.'

Daphne's eyes widened. 'Are you here to ask if I'll take care of them?'

'I couldn't do that to you, mother. No offence, but their powers would run rings round you.'

'Oh, I know that, dear.'

'We have to face facts – there's not a person alive, except for me, who can resist the power of the twins.'

Daphne frowned, wondering if she should speak.

'You have that look on your face, mother. Don't make me go into your mind to see what's causing it.'

Daphne offered her daughter the weedstick, but Karalyn shook her head and lit a cigarette instead.

'There is someone,' said Daphne.

'What? Who?'

'Now, I'm not saying this as a suggestion; I'm merely pointing it out, but your sister is capable of resisting the power of the twins.'

'Kelsey?'

'Yes.'

Karalyn smiled. 'No, mother. Kelsey can block ordinary powers that are sent through the air; we've known that for years, but she isn't that strong.'

'I hate to say it, dear, but you're wrong. When you left this world to travel to Lostwell, that was indeed the case. Do you recall when Thorn healed her in Rainsby? Quite clearly, Kelsey was susceptible to other powers back then, but she was only fifteen at the time. Her powers have grown considerably since then. By the time she was sixteen, Sable was using her as a shield. By the time she was eighteen, Thorn reported that she could no longer sense Kelsey's life force, even when she touched her physically. It was as if she wasn't even there, or so Thorn said. Then, when she was nineteen, she was here, on the estate, and the twins were unable to access her mind.'

'I didn't know that.'

'Why would you, dear? You were in Lostwell at the time. Tell me; when you returned, did you not sense it from her?'

'No. I was too concerned with the twins, and I hardly spoke to Kelsey before she left to find Corthie.'

'By the time she travelled to Lostwell, she could effectively block all powers for a radius of one hundred yards in every direction.'

'I could still use my own powers when she was around. I needed them to send her to Lostwell.'

'Yes, but did you try to read her thoughts?'

Karalyn shook her head.

'I doubt you would have been able to. I'd wager that Kelsey could also block the powers of this new dream mage, and she would be immune to any tricks the twins tried to play on her.' She smiled. 'In other words, she would be the perfect babysitter.'

'I had wondered why no one was trying to heal her; you know, when we looked in on the City, and saw her. She had cuts and bruises, and yet there were demigods going around healing the wounded. It hadn't occurred to me that she might be resistant to their powers.'

'Well, now you know. Little Kelsey has spent her whole life being underestimated, even by her own family.'

'Her powers must have allowed the others to kill that god we saw.'

'Indeed. However, this is all merely academic, since there is no way to travel to that world.'

'I'm not so sure about that, mother. I've been experimenting with the Sextant again, after we failed to get the Quadrant to take us to Kelsey's world. There might be a way to link the Sextant to the Quadrant. If I can figure out how, then the Sextant would be able to read the location from the Quadrant. It might be possible.'

'Take great care, dear. The last thing I want is to lose you again.'

Karalyn lifted her head. 'The twins are causing chaos. I'd better go.'

Daphne stubbed out the weedstick. 'I'll come with you; it's time for lunch.'

They stood, then Daphne found herself outside, opposite the large fountain, the heat from the sun bearing down on her. Splashing about in the fountain was Agang, who was in the process of removing his clothes as dozens of estate workers watched. To the side of the fountain, Cael was shrieking in laughter, as Kyra kept a finger aimed at the old Sanang man. Shella was attempting to get between Kyra and Agang, then, at a glance from Cael, she sat down on the dusty ground, her mouth clamped shut.

Karalyn focussed her powers, and swept those of her young daughter away. Agang blinked as if awakening from a deep sleep, and he stared around, the water from the fountain soaking him.

'Aw, mama!' cried Cael. 'That was funny.'

'No, Cael, it is not funny,' said Karalyn, marching forwards. 'You two should be ashamed of yourselves. Poor Agang.'

She leaned over and helped Shella stand.

The Rakanese woman groaned. 'Your brats are out of control.'

'Sorry,' said Karalyn. 'Sorry, Agang. There are dry clothes in the mansion.'

Daphne watched as Karalyn helped Agang climb down from the fountain.

'Hey, Daffers,' said Shella.

'Good morning, princess.'

'Sometimes, having Agang stay in Colsbury bugs me, but on days like this, I'm glad he's here – otherwise it'd be me dancing naked in the fountain.'

'And I think we'd agree that no one should have to see that.'

'You cheeky cow, Holdfast. How have you been?'

'Getting by.'

'Did Karalyn tell you about the other dream mage?'

'She did.'

'She wants to go off and look for this guy, but I've had to put my foot down. You can see what happens if Karalyn leaves the twins alone for a few minutes; there's no way I'm looking after them for several days.' She sniffed. 'Is that dreamweed I can smell?'

'It was my duty to test this year's harvest; for quality control purposes, you understand.'

'Yeah, right.'

Daphne crouched down as Karalyn led the twins across the square.

'And how are my little grandchildren?' she said. 'Still causing mayhem?'

Cael grinned, while Kyra looked annoyed that her game had been interrupted.

'Is Thorn here?' said Kyra.

'No, dear. Thorn is in Plateau City, along with Keir. Cole's here, though. Do you want to see him?

'Aye!' cried Cael.

'Come on, then,' said Daphne. 'Lunch is waiting for us inside the big house.'

They strode towards the mansion, with Daphne taking Kyra's hand as they walked. Agang was dripping water over the cobblestones, and he looked as though he was barely managing to keep his temper. Daphne smiled to herself, as she listened to her daughter's repeated apologies. Once inside, a servant escorted Agang away to get some dry clothes, and the rest of them went to the main dining room. Jemma and Cole were sitting there with Celine, who looked fresh from her shower.

'Sorry we're a little late,' said Daphne, 'there was a small incident by the fountain.'

Celine laughed. 'I know. We were watching from the window. Agang was lucky that you got to him before he had time to pull his underpants off as well.'

'We were all lucky about that,' said Shella.

They sat, and a flurry of servants entered. They began laying down plates and bowls onto the long table, as Daphne glanced around at her family, wishing that they could all be gathered together. She couldn't remember the last time all four of her children had been in the same room as each other, and with Kelsey on another world, she wondered if it would ever happen again.

'Let's have a little toast for the absent Holdfasts,' she said, raising a glass of Anamindharian wine. 'To Keir, Kelsey and Corthie, and their partners, and little Killop too, of course. Let's hope they're spending Summer's Day with friends and loved ones.'

The adults raised their glasses, and took a sip.

'Do they have Summer's Day on Kelsey's world?' said Shella.

'No,' said Karalyn. 'There are no solstices on that world.'

Daphne frowned. 'Don't ruin my toast, dear.'

'I wanted to speak to you about Keir,' said Jemma.

'If it's about whether or not he will be coming back, then Celine has already had a word with me,' said Daphne. 'As far as I'm concerned, Celine should go ahead with training you up in the running of the estate.'

Jemma bit her lip. 'Does that mean Keir's not coming back?'

'One cannot say for certain.'

'But, if he does come back, and I'm helping to run the estate... well, it might get awkward if he wants his old job back.'

Daphne nodded. 'I don't suppose you would be happy to share the role with him?'

'I'd rather not, to be honest. Keir and I... we don't get on well together.'

'That's a pity, but I understand,' said Daphne. 'Let me ask you – do you want to manage the estate? Is that a job you would be content with?'

'Yes. I've been watching how Celine does it for years, and I think I would be good at it.'

'I agree,' said Celine. 'Jemma's more than capable.'

Daphne nodded. 'Very well. I'm going to make a decision. Celine, please train Jemma to take over the running of the estate. If Keir returns, then I will speak to him, and let him know that he will have to find something else.'

Jemma's face opened in a wide smile. 'Thank you.'

'You're welcome, Jemma.'

Karalyn raised an eyebrow. 'Keir won't be happy when he finds out.'

'Dear, when is Keir ever happy?' said Daphne. 'He seems to be the opposite of Corthie in every respect. Regardless, if my little plan works out, then he and Thorn will be ensconced in Plateau City for some time to come.'

'What plan?'

'Never mind that for now. I...' She paused, as a sensation ran through her head. She blinked. 'Dear, was that you?'

'Was what me?' said Karalyn. She narrowed her eyes. 'Wait. I think I can sense...'

Daphne felt a head-splitting surge of pain behind her eyes, and she cried out, dropping her glass of wine onto the table. Karalyn stood, and the pain ceased. Daphne held her head, gasping.

'It was him,' said Karalyn, her voice high. 'It was the dream mage. He's found the estate.'

Shella gasped, her eyes on Daphne. 'Daffers, are you alright?'

Daphne nodded. 'I thought my mind was about to be scoured. That pain was dreadful. Was he trying to hurt me?'

'Daimon doesn't want to hurt us,' said Kyra.

Every eye turned to the girl.

'What did you say?' said Karalyn. 'How do you know his name?'

'He told me,' said Kyra.

'When?'

'Yesterday, at night, when everyone was asleep. I saw him in my dreams.'

'Are you saying he didn't mean to hurt me?' said Daphne.

'He doesn't want to hurt us; he wants to be my friend. He only wants to hurt the bad people who killed his mother.'

Karalyn sat, looking stunned. 'Which bad people?'

Kyra shrugged. 'I don't know, mama.'

'What else did he say?'

'He knows that I'm a dream mage. He's the same as me and you, mama, and Cael. He wants to find out more about us.'

'Do you know where he is, dear?' said Daphne.

Kyra shook her head.

'That's all we need,' said Shella; 'another damned out-of-control dream mage.'

'Indeed,' said Daphne, 'but what are we going to do about it?'

The door to the dining room opened, and Agang walked in.

'Hey, monkey-boy,' said Shella; 'you just missed the fun. That dream mage...'

Shella stopped as Agang strode across the room. The eyes of the Sanang man were clouded over, and he seemed to be in a trance. He walked up to the table, then came to a halt.

Shella waved a hand in front of his face, but Agang didn't respond. He raised a finger, and pointed at Karalyn.

'You,' he said; 'dream mage.'

Karalyn stared at Agang.

'Cut the connection,' said Daphne. 'The dream mage is inside Agang's head.'

'Wait,' said Karalyn. 'I think he wants to speak to us.'

'You live like royalty,' said Agang. 'You have silver plates, and fine wines, and enough food to feed a village. You live in palaces and castles; you know nothing of suffering. All my life, I have lived in poverty and squalor, while mobs hunted down my family, because of my powers. Why? Why do you live in luxury, while I am chased from glen to glen, fearing for my life?'

'Where are you?' said Karalyn.

'I have hidden since I was a child, but that will change. I want what you have, Holdfasts; I want justice.'

'That sounded like a threat,' said Daphne; 'and no one threatens my family.'

Agang turned to stare at her. 'A threat? If I wished to, I could destroy the minds of everyone in this room, Holder Fast, just as you did to your enemies in the past.'

'Tell me what you want,' said Karalyn.

'I want you to come to Kellach Brigdomin, Karalyn, so that we can meet,' said Agang. 'You must come alone. You have until the end of this third. If you refuse, then I will take matters into my own hands. Remember this, dream mage – you do not want me as an enemy.'

Agang's eyes cleared, and he fell to his knees, groaning.

Shella took a swig of wine. 'Karalyn, I hope you go down there and kill that asshole.'

'Did you not hear what he was saying?'

'Oh, I heard him. He threatened your family.'

Karalyn and Daphne rose from their seats, and assisted Agang to stand.

'What happened?' groaned the Sanang man.

'Your body was possessed by that new dream freak,' said Shella.

'He was speaking through you,' said Jemma. 'It was horrible.'

'Daimon is in pain,' said Karalyn. 'Let's not be too hasty to judge him.'

'I know that you always want to see the good in people,' said Daphne, 'but Shella's right. I will not permit some rogue mage to threaten my family. You're going to have to confront him.'

'I know,' said Karalyn, 'but I'm not taking the twins with me. They'll have to remain here.'

Agang sat, his hands shaking. 'I'm not sure my heart can cope with being left alone with the twins, Karalyn. I'm sorry.'

'No, don't be sorry, Agang. I understand.'

'What are you going to do, then?' said Shella. 'You won't take them, and we can't look after them, not for the length of time you might be away.'

Karalyn glanced at her mother.

'Kelsey?' said Daphne.

'Aye,' said Karalyn. 'Kelsey.'

'But Kelsey is on another world,' said Shella. 'Had you forgotten?'

'Mother thinks Kelsey is the only person alive who can resist the power of the twins,' said Karalyn; 'and Daimon told us I had until the end of the third.'

'Is that enough time to work out how to make the Sextant do as you wish, dear?' said Daphne.

Karalyn glanced at her two children. 'It'll have to be.'

CHAPTER 9
PLAYING POLITICS

Plateau City, The Plateau – 16th Day, First Third Summer 534

Bridget eyed Keir. 'Any questions?'

'No, your Majesty,' said Keir.

'Good. Just remember that the Rakanese won't know that I will have someone who can read minds; so make sure you don't blurt it out, eh? Can you read their thoughts without them knowing that you're in their heads?'

'Yes, I can, your Majesty.'

'Right. Don't do anything unless I give you a nod. Bryce, you take the lead when they come in.'

'Yes, mother,' said the young man.

Bridget nodded to a courtier. 'Let the Rakanese delegation approach.'

The courtier bowed, then opened the double doors of the audience chamber. A pair of soldiers snapped to attention as three Rakanese entered the hall. They walked up to the throne where Bridget was sitting, but failed to bow.

'Good afternoon, gentlemen,' said Bryce, from Bridget's right. 'We received your request for an urgent discussion, and are happy to speak with our friends and allies from the Republic of Rakana.'

One of the delegates smiled. 'We are not allies, and I would certainly hesitate before naming us friends. We have not come here for a cordial chat; we are here to demand that you adhere to the conditions of the treaty signed between our nation and the empire.'

Bryce nodded. 'To which conditions are you referring?'

'Don't pretend that you are ignorant of what I am talking about, Lord Bryce. The treaty expressly forbids illegal population movements between the Republic of Rakana and the empire. The border is supposed to be unbreachable, and yet we have compelling evidence that your soldiers have been flouting the law.'

Bryce gave the delegates a polite smile. 'I'm afraid I don't know what you are talking about, Ambassador. What laws have our soldiers been flouting?'

'Every night, more and more renegade citizens of Rakana have been making their way over the border wall into the Plateau, where criminal gangs from Amatskouri have been waiting to assist them. Some of these renegades are wanted by the Rakanese authorities for various crimes, and yet your soldiers have been turning the other way, and pretending not to see what is happening under their noses. Three nights ago, over two hundred Rakanese crossed the border illegally, and your soldiers did nothing to stop them.'

Bryce nodded. 'It is the policy of the empire to always accept refugees who ask for our aid.'

'These people are not refugees!' cried the ambassador. 'They are citizens of the Republic of Rakana, and they must be returned to us immediately.'

'Will they be placed under arrest if they return to Rakana, your Eminence?'

'Yes, naturally. They have broken the law.'

'Then we shall not be returning them,' said Bryce. 'We do not return refugees to their place of origin if their lives are in danger.'

'You twist everything. The empire is in serious breach of its sworn treaty obligations. Do you imagine for a second that we don't know what you are doing? You are trying to undermine the very fabric of Rakanese society, and endangering our security.'

Bryce smiled. 'But, Ambassador, surely it cannot be the fault of the empire that so many of your citizens are trying to flee Rakana? Perhaps if you improved living standards for your people, then they might not want to leave.'

'How dare you?' cried the ambassador. 'We come here with a reasonable complaint, and you insult our country?'

'Please forgive me if there was a misunderstanding,' said Bryce. 'I wasn't insulting your country. I was insulting your government.'

The ambassador turned his glare to the Empress. 'Does this child speak for you?'

Bridget ignored him.

'Her Imperial Majesty does not respond to those who do not address her correctly,' said Bryce, 'but rest assured that I speak with the voice of the empire. Were you aware that no one ever tries to flee from our lands into Rakana? Why might that be, do you think? And tell me, what manner of nation tries to forbid its own citizens from leaving?'

'Is it any wonder, young Bryce, that the Republic of Rakana refuses to join this nefarious empire, if this is your attitude?'

'Our attitude? And I thought it was because you didn't want your entire population to decamp to the Plateau. Have you visited Amatskouri recently? It's quite amazing how it has recovered from the depredations inflicted by Agatha and her army a few years ago. The Rakanese citizens dwelling by the shores of the Inner Sea are free and prosperous. Can you say the same about those who live in your Republic?'

The ambassador stared at Bryce. 'There will be consequences for this outrage; mark my words. Rakana is an independent, sovereign nation, and we shall not be bullied by you. Good day.'

Bryce nodded. 'Good day, Ambassador.'

The Rakanese delegates strode from the hall.

Bridget turned to her son. 'Perhaps I was a wee bit rash to let you lead, Bryce. As much as I enjoyed watching you eviscerating that numpty, we need to be a bit more diplomatic.'

'Sorry, mother,' said Bryce. 'I got a little carried away.'

Bridget sighed. 'Maybe it was time they heard what we really think of them and their pathetic wee government. I only wish we could do more to help the poor bastards trapped in that dismal country. Letting them slip across the border is nowhere near enough.'

'What else can we do?' said Bryce.

Bridget turned to Keir. 'Well? Any suggestions? Imagine that I asked your mother, the Herald of the Empire. What would she advise?'

Keir frowned. 'My mother would probably advocate a series of targeted assassinations to eliminate the leadership of the Rakanese government, your Majesty.'

'Aye, she probably would. Unfortunately, that approach would only lead to war, and my number one policy is to avoid war at all costs. Rakana cannot hurt the empire. The only folk they *can* hurt are their own citizens. It's hard to believe that they were a democracy before the Migration. Now, they're every bit as bad as Rahain was under Ghorley. Alright, forget what your mother would say, Keir. What do you think?'

Keir smothered his initial response, which was concerned with how much he generally disliked people from Rakana. What would a wise ruler do? He didn't know.

'Maybe we could demolish the border wall, your Majesty,' he said, 'and allow the Rakanese to flood across the border?'

'That would lead to clashes with the Rakanese border forces, and, hence, to war. Try again.'

'We could ask Karalyn if she could use her powers to manipulate the Rakanese leadership into making concessions?'

Bridget smiled. 'Better, but impractical. The days of Karalyn being a dutiful servant of the empire have long since departed.'

Keir's face flushed. 'Then, your Majesty, we should continue with our current policy.'

'Well, you got there in the end,' said Bridget. She yawned and stretched her arms. 'Time to get drunk.'

Bryce glanced at Keir, then they both bowed and left the audience chamber. They wandered up to the rooftop garden, where Keir lit a cigarette as they basked in the heat of the late afternoon.

'I have to admit,' said Keir, 'that was pretty funny; you know, the way you spoke to those Rakanese fools.'

'They're driving their country into the dirt,' said Bryce. 'It's amazing to think that the old Arakhanah was one of the most open societies in the world. Their citizens voted on every little decision. Sure, it was cumbersome, but it worked. And now? It grieves me to know how much the people there are suffering. I wish we could do something, but any intervention by our armed forces would only make things worse.'

'Maybe we should build the wall twice as high, and pretend that Rakana doesn't exist.'

Bryce gave him a look.

'I'm joking, of course,' said Keir. 'I'm as troubled as the next man about the poor Rakanese.'

Bryce seemed to accept that, and Keir smothered his relief, glad that the young man was unable to read his true thoughts. What were his true thoughts? He wasn't sure, except that he had a vague loathing for the Rakanese. The food they ate was disgusting, and they bred too quickly; like flies. There was no solution to the problem of the Rakanese, except, perhaps, mass extermination.

'It's good having you here,' said Bryce, 'especially with Brogan away in Kellach Brigdomin. How's Thorn?'

'Still working long days in the city infirmaries.'

'Yes, well, I know that. But, how is she? Is she holding up?'

'She's too tired to say much when she gets home each night. She usually just wants to eat something, then sleep.'

'She has been showing great resilience; and there are countless families living within the city who will always be grateful for what she is doing.' He glanced at Keir. 'Tomorrow morning at dawn, I would like you to go into the mind of the Rakanese ambassador, and discover what he is planning to do as a consequence of today's meeting.'

Keir said nothing.

'Without access to vision mages or winged gaien,' Bryce went on, 'the ambassador will have to send a message back to Rakana the old-fashioned way, by road. I want you to locate the courier. Find out when he or she leaves the city, and which route they are taking.'

'Are you planning to intercept the courier before they can reach Rakana?'

Bryce glanced away. 'The roads can be very dangerous at times. Not every message that is sent reaches its destination.'

'I understand.'

'Also, the Empress doesn't need to know about this. Her Majesty needs plausible deniability if the courier fails to cross the border. You will report to me on this, and only me.'

'Yes, sir.'

'Excellent. Are you on duty until midnight?'

Keir nodded.

'Then I shall leave you. Remember, it is not wise to interrupt the Empress when she wants to relax. Stay quiet, but available. Good night.'

Bryce turned, and walked away, leaving Keir alone on the roof. The sun was setting in the west, and the sky had turned a deep red. He wondered if the courier would be executed. Bryce would probably utilise one of the empire's shadowy agents to make it look like an accident, and it might take thirds before the ambassador realised that his message had not reached the government back in Rakana. It was the first time that anyone in the palace had asked Keir to do anything that could be considered unethical. Did that mean they were starting to trust him? The short exchange with Bryce had made him feel important, as if he were on the verge of being admitted into the inner circle that existed in Bridget's court. The life of a Rakanese courier seemed worthless compared to that. He smiled. He couldn't wait to tell Thorn.

―――――

Keir spent the next few hours wandering the quiet hallways of the palace, bored. Bryce and Tabor were busy, the Empress was drinking on her own, and Keir had no desire to pass the time with Bridget's younger children. At sixteen, the two triplets who had remained in the palace while Brogan and Bethal had gone to Kellach Brigdomin were practically children. He made frequent trips to the gardens on the roof, and smoked too many cigarettes as he waited for his shift to end. Darkness fell over the city, and the streetlamps were lit, as Keir counted the minutes.

A courtier found him while he was in the palace library, searching for something to read to pass the time.

'Lord Holdfast,' the courtier said, bowing low in front of him.

'Yes?' said Keir, trying to mask his irritation. He had a mere thirty minutes left until midnight, and the last thing he wanted was to be given a job to do.

'The Empress requires your presence, my lord.'

'And where might I find her Majesty?'

'She is in her private quarters, my lord. Shall I escort you there?'

Keir snorted. 'I know the way.'

'Very good, my lord.'

Keir put down a book and strode towards the stairs. He ascended a level, and a soldier permitted him to enter the Empress's personal suite of rooms. A tight coil of anxiety stirred in the pit of his stomach. He dreaded speaking to the Empress when she was drunk, and she had had several hours in which to consume whisky.

He knocked on the door of her little study, and was rewarded with a low grunt.

He opened the door and entered, his glance aimed downwards.

'You summoned me, your Majesty?'

'Aye,' said Bridget, from her armchair. Her cheeks were a little flushed, and she had a glass in her right hand. 'Your sister was here.'

'My sister, your Majesty?'

'That's what I said.'

'But...'

Bridget laughed. 'But she didnae bother her arse to speak to you while she was here? Is that what's annoying you? Ye ken what she's like,

Keir. Karalyn comes and goes whenever she fucking feels like it, eh? She's a Holdfast.'

'What did she say, your Majesty?'

'We've got another dream mage on our hands. As if the Holdfasts werenae bad enough.'

'Another dream mage?'

Bridget sighed. 'Will ye stop bloody repeating what I just said? It makes ye sound like an eejit.'

'Sorry, your Majesty.'

'Of course, Daphne's fucking known about it for ages. I should feel honoured that Karalyn bothered to inform me. Anyway, I want yer opinion on this. You're a Holdfast. What could another dream mage in the empire mean?'

Keir suppressed his anger that Karalyn had been in the palace without stopping to see him. What did the existence of another dream mage mean?

'If this new mage has the same powers as Karalyn,' he said, 'then the empire could be in danger. Karalyn... well, she... I mean, Karalyn is...'

'A right pain in the arse?'

Keir let out a laugh without meaning to. 'Eh, yes, your Majesty. All the same, though, Karalyn has never used her powers to do anything really bad. She was horrible as a child, and she made my life a misery, but, if she wanted to, she could wreak havoc throughout the empire. She can make herself invisible; she can travel anywhere she likes; she can read and manipulate people's minds; and she's immune to other mage powers.'

'I see what yer saying, Keir. We've been lucky that Karalyn isn't a deranged mass murderer, or has designs on becoming Empress?'

'I guess so, your Majesty. We might not be so lucky with a new dream mage. Has this mage arisen from the Holdings or Kellach Brigdomin?'

Bridget eyed him for a long moment. 'Ye know, Keir; you're not as stupid as you look. Sit down and have a whisky with me.'

Keir nodded, then sat across from the Empress. She filled a glass with whisky and passed it to him.

'Nae smoking, mind,' she said.

Keir took a sip. 'Thank you, your Majesty.'

'The new mage is in Kellach Brigdomin,' she said. 'But, and here's the thing, his powers can reach all the way to the Holdings. So far, he's been messing with Karalyn's bairns – going into their heads and so forth, and he took over the body of that auld bastard Agang Garo, so he could send Karalyn a message.'

'I see. Karalyn can't do that. Her range isn't as long. She could vision from Colsbury to here, but not all the way to Kellach Brigdomin. She'll have to go down there in person.'

Bridget nodded.

'But,' Keir went on, 'if she did that, then she would have to leave her children behind, and her children are also dream mages, which means that they could cause chaos while she's away. Karalyn scoured my mind when she was a child. Kyra and Cael could do the same, if they were angry or upset enough.'

'Karalyn says she has a plan to take care of that.'

'What plan, your Majesty?'

'She didnae go into details. Surprise, surprise, eh? Anyway, I now have to consider what to do about the fact that two of my own bairns are down in Kellach Brigdomin. If this dream mage wants to hurt the empire, or me, then Brogan and Bethal are sitting targets. Yer wee brother too, and his wife and bairn.'

'Karalyn has the ability to bring them all home, your Majesty.'

'Aye, that she does. It would look bad, but. It might even set off a panic if Karalyn suddenly whisked them away in the middle of their wee trip. I need to warn them, and then Karalyn can discreetly extract them once the bulk of their trip is over.'

'Do we know if the dream mage harbours any ill will towards the empire?'

'No.'

'Then, this could be an opportunity, your Majesty. You could welcome this new dream mage; he could be very useful, if he decided to pledge allegiance.'

'Aye; that's what I was thinking. Karalyn used to be extremely helpful, back in the days when she worked for me. To have another dream mage working for the empire would be grand, and it would stop me having to beg the damn Holdfasts every time I need a favour. Aye; that would wipe the smirk from yer mother's face. I wouldnae need the Holdfasts if I had my own dream mage.'

'I have an idea, your Majesty. What if you sent Lord Bryce down to Kellach Brigdomin with Karalyn? He could warn Lady Brogan and Lady Bethal, and make contact with the dream mage. Karalyn could protect him. Then, you could see if the dream mage is willing to help you.'

The Empress sipped from her glass. 'Aye, but I need Bryce here.'

Keir smiled. 'There is someone else in the city who could step in, your Majesty. Someone who has been trained to act as your Herald.'

Bridget frowned for a moment, then laughed. 'Fucksake, lad; for a moment there I thought ye were referring to yerself!'

'I meant Thorn, your Majesty.'

'Aye, I ken ye did.' She leaned over, and pulled a cord.

Moments later, a courtier knocked and entered the room.

'Your Majesty?' he said, bowing.

'Send someone to fetch Thorn Holdfast. She's in the New Town infirmary. Have her brought here immediately.'

'Yes, your Majesty.'

Keir waited until the courtier had left the room, then he smiled. 'Thank you, your Majesty.'

'Do ye realise that, if my plan succeeds, then your family might lose a wee bit of its influence and power?'

Keir's smile faded as he thought about the Empress's words. Over the previous few decades, the Holdfasts had pushed their way into a position as the wealthiest and most powerful family on the entire continent, and much of that was due to the vast range of powers possessed by Karalyn. It had been his elder sister, after all, who had annihilated a hundred thousand Rahain soldiers, bringing the war against Agatha to a rapid end. A rival dream mage working for the Empress would undermine all that. Keir realised that he didn't care. He owed his sister nothing. His mother would be angry, but she had removed him from the Hold Fast estate against his wishes, and had sent him to work for the Empress. It would be her fault if his newfound loyalty to the empire hurt the family; not his.

'Should one family be allowed so much power, your Majesty?' he said.

Bridget stared at him. 'Yer mother would have a hairy fit if she heard ye say that, lad!'

'My mother should be here. She is the Herald of the Empire, but she has chosen to remain absent. She will have no one to blame but herself if her absence causes her to lose influence.'

'I'll need to keep a close eye on you, lad.'

She leaned over and pulled a different cord, and moments later, Bryce walked into the small study.

'Mother?'

'I need ye to go to Kellach Brigdomin, son,' said Bridget.

Bryce blinked.

The Empress turned to Keir. 'Step outside for a moment, lad, while I talk to my son.'

Keir rose to his feet, bowed, then left the room. He paced up and down in the corridor outside, fighting the temptation to spy on the Empress's conversation. She would be repeating to Bryce everything she had learned about the new dream mage, but she would also be talking about Keir's advice, and he was curious to know what was being said. He started to worry a little about how his mother would react. If the new dream mage could be won over to the Empress, then Karalyn probably wouldn't care. She might even be relieved. His mother, on the other hand, would be furious at the thought of the Holdfasts' influence diminishing.

The minutes passed. After what seemed like an age, Bryce left the room. He nodded to Keir, then strode away. Keir was about to knock on the study door, when he saw a courtier leading a woman along the corridor.

'Thorn,' he said.

His wife glanced up at him. Her eyes were reflecting her utter exhaustion, while her apron was spattered with blood.

'What's this about?' she said. 'I was in the middle of healing an old woman.'

The courtier squeezed past them, opened the study door, then turned to Keir and Thorn.

'Her Majesty wishes you to step inside, if you please.'

Keir and Thorn walked into the study.

Bridget stared at Thorn. 'Holy shit, hedgewitch,' she said; 'check the state of you. Ye stink of blood and shit.'

Thorn nodded, seemingly too exhausted to speak.

'How long have you been working in the infirmaries, Thorn?'

'Today was my forty-sixth consecutive shift, your Majesty.'

Bridget exhaled. 'I've left ye there that long, eh? My, how time flies by. Well, as of this moment, yer done. I'm removing you from infirmary duties. Take a day off, and then report to me at dawn on the twenty-third. It'll be a trial period, mind. If ye fail to please me, then you can go back to the infirmaries. Understand?'

Thorn frowned. 'I think so, your Majesty. Shall I be working for Lord Bryce?'

'At first, aye. Keir will explain the rest; now beat it, the pair of ye.'

The two Holdfasts left the room, and began to make their way down through the levels of the Great Fortress. Keir waited until they were outside before starting to tell Thorn all about his earlier meeting with the Empress, and she listened as they walked through the streets of the New Town. When he had finished, she remained silent, as if she were focussing on placing one foot in front of the other as she trudged along.

'Well?' he said. 'This might work out great for us. You'll be in the heart of the palace, where you're supposed to be.'

Thorn frowned. 'I'm still letting it all sink in. Did you see Karalyn?'

'No. That silly cow didn't even bother to say hello. Typical. She doesn't give a shit about me, so why should I care if another dream mage comes along and supplants her?'

'And Bryce is going to Kellach Brigdomin, to try to recruit this dream mage?'

'Yeah. It was my idea.'

'This could have serious consequences, Keir. We know nothing about this dream mage. He could be extremely dangerous.'

'Or he might be useful. We don't know yet, but it's worth trying.'

Thorn shook her head. 'We should leave it to Karalyn. She knows what she's doing.'

'But, if I'd done that, then you'd still be stuck in the infirmaries.'

'I'd rather be in the infirmaries than risk damaging the Holdfasts, Keir. If the Empress gets her way, then at best the Holdfasts will be side-lined. Your mother will probably lose her position as Herald, since Bridget will have no need to appease her any longer, and the entire family will become expendable. At worst, the new dream mage could bring the empire to its knees.'

'I did it for you,' Keir said. 'Why do you have to be so negative about it? Once you're installed in the Empress's court, then you can start to wield influence. I thought that's what you wanted.'

'The cost is too high. As soon as a new dream mage enters Bridget's court, then she can ignore us. Everything you can do, the new dream mage will be able to do better. And with Daphne relieved of her position, any authority that I might have held will crumble into dust.'

Keir said nothing, his face falling.

'The Empress played you, Keir,' Thorn said. 'Even drunk, she's more than a match for you. She's going to use this dream mage to push the Holdfasts to the fringes of power; and you helped her do it.'

'Shut up,' he muttered; 'just shut up.'

Thorn glanced at him, her eyes piercing his soul, then she looked away without a word.

CHAPTER 10
BREAKTHROUGH

Colsbury Castle, Republic of the Holdings – 21st Day, First Third Summer 534

Karalyn closed her eyes in frustration and stifled a scream. Across from her sat the Sextant, humming as if it were alive. She felt as though it were mocking her. No matter what she had tried, nothing seemed to work, and she was no closer to being able to reach Kelsey's world than she had been at the start. For twenty days, she had done little else but try to coax the stubborn device into submission, but had got nowhere.

She got to her feet and strode to the window. She threw the shutters open, and sat on the ledge, lighting a cigarette. If she had to listen to *What is your desire, Karalyn?* one more time, she might jump out of the window. The damned device knew what she desired, and yet refused to grant it. Restless, she walked back to the Sextant and picked up the Quadrant from where she had placed it on the surface of the larger device.

Command me, Karalyn, the Quadrant said in her mind.

Take me to the salve world. Go.

Silence.

She went back to the window, sat, and stared at the engravings marking the surface of the small copper-coloured device. They were the key, she felt. When others used a Quadrant, they touched specific places on its surface, so the engravings had to mean something. Karalyn had never needed to pay close attention to how the device was supposed to work, but she wished she had done. If she had only read the contents of Agatha's mind before killing her, then she might have learned how to use a Quadrant correctly.

She was running out of time. Daimon had demanded that she meet him before the end of the third, and only nine days remained. On top of that, Keir had sent her a message from the Empress, demanding that she take Bryce along with her when she next returned to Kellach Brigdomin. Karalyn had been too surprised to refuse, and Keir hadn't lingered. As soon as he had delivered the message through Shella, he had vanished. First things first, she told herself. She needed to bend the Sextant to her will, and then she could worry about Bryce.

She walked back to the huge device, and laid her left palm on it, while keeping hold of the Quadrant in her other hand.

What is your desire, Karalyn?

Can you sense the Quadrant in my hand?

Silence.

Can you connect to a Quadrant? Karalyn said, trying again.

Yes.

How?

Deliver the Quadrant unto me.

Alright, but how do I do that?

Deliver the Quadrant unto me.

Karalyn lifted her palm from the Sextant, and felt like crying.

'Mama!' came Kyra's voice from the hallway.

Karalyn placed the Quadrant back onto the Sextant and opened the door. Kyra was standing outside, her face red.

'What is it, wee Kyra?' said Karalyn.

'Cael pinched me!'

'Where? Does it hurt?'

The girl held her arm out, but Karalyn could see no blemish or injury.

'He pinched my arm,' the girl said.

Karalyn sighed. 'Alright. I'll speak to him. Where is he?'

Kyra ran off down the corridor, and Karalyn followed. They went into a play room set aside for the twins, but Cael wasn't there.

'He was here a minute ago,' said Kyra. 'Will you play with me?'

'I can't just now; I'm busy.'

'Why do you never play with me, mama? Thorn always played with me.'

'You need to stop using Thorn to make me feel guilty, Kyra. Now, stay in here while I go back to work.'

Kyra gave her mother a look of anger, and Karalyn left the room. She would make it up to the girl later. She walked back to the chamber holding the Sextant, and saw Cael sitting on the floor next to the huge device. He had the Quadrant gripped in both hands, and was ramming it into one of the many gaps in the side of the Sextant.

'Cael!' Karalyn cried. 'Stop that at once.'

Cael jumped in fright. He let go of the Quadrant, but one end was lodged into the side of the Sextant. Karalyn ran over, and crouched down to check that the little device hadn't been damaged. She pulled it from the side of the Sextant, and examined its surface.

'You could have broken it, Cael,' she said to the cowering boy.

'Sorry, mama.'

'And you have to stop pinching Kyra.'

'She started it. She poked me in the eye.'

'Go back to the play room, Cael. I'll come and see you soon.'

The boy got to his feet and ran away. Karalyn glanced down at the Quadrant, then her eyes went to the side of the larger device. Cael had been shoving the Quadrant into a hole that lay beneath the slot where the Weathervane fitted. Karalyn lifted the Quadrant, and measured its size against the many other slots and holes that marked the side of the Sextant.

Damn it, she thought; maybe she had been doing it all wrong, and it was Cael who had the right idea. She carefully slid the Quadrant into an empty gap. Nothing happened, but how would she know if it had worked or not? She half-stood, and placed her palm onto the surface of the Sextant.

What is your desire, Karalyn?

Can you sense the Quadrant now?

Silence.

Karalyn removed the Quadrant, and placed it into a different gap.

Now?

Silence.

Karalyn sighed as she counted the places where a Quadrant could potentially fit; then she carried on. On her fourteenth try, something changed.

Sextant, how about now?

Yes.

Karalyn blinked in shock. She glanced at the Quadrant sitting snugly in a hole a quarter of the way down the flank of the larger device, unsure of what to say or do next.

What is your desire, Karalyn?

Show me Kelsey's world.

Her vision clouded over, then she saw the City spread out before her. She glanced around, wondering where Kelsey might be. She saw a group of soldiers standing outside the ruins of Cuidrach Palace.

Here goes, she thought. She focussed her powers, and tried to enter one of the soldiers' minds. Her vision soared down, and passed through the man's eyes, and she could see his thoughts. Almost trembling with excitement, she read through some of the soldier's memories, looking for traces of Kelsey. It was easy. Kelsey Holdfast was known to nearly everyone in the entire City – she was a hero, one of those who had helped to kill Simon, the powerful god that Karalyn had seen on her previous visit. She was living with a man called Van Logos in a mansion in Tara.

Karalyn withdrew from the soldier's head, turned, and raced over the waters of the bay towards Tara. She knew where the mansions lay – up on the hill next to the ruins of another palace. She found them quickly, and scanned the area. It took her fifteen minutes to locate

Kelsey. She watched as her sister walked out of one of the large mansions, and began heading up the tree-lined road in the direction of the ruined palace.

Despite everything her mother had told her, Karalyn attempted to enter Kelsey's mind. She pushed down with her vision, but her sister's eyes repelled her powers, and there was no way through. Kelsey kept walking, unaware of what Karalyn had attempted. She turned right, close to the palace gates, and began striding along a path lined with bushes and hedges. Karalyn spotted another woman, heading in the other direction, and entered her mind instead. She gently pushed the woman's consciousness to the side, and took control of her body. She looked out from the woman's eyes, and saw her sister peering at her.

'Are you alright?' said Kelsey.

'Kelsey.'

'Um, aye? That's me. Do I know you?'

Karalyn laughed. 'I can't believe that this is working. For the last two years, I've watched you, but I've not been able to communicate or do anything to help.'

'What?' said Kelsey, a frown planted on her lips. 'You've been watching me? Who are you?'

'The Sextant is so complicated,' Karalyn said, 'but I've had a break-through, and I can now use it to push my dream vision powers into people's heads. Well, not your head, obviously; some things never change.'

Kelsey stared at her. 'Karalyn? Is that you in there?'

'Aye. It's your sister, Kelsey. I'm in Colsbury Castle, but I'm speaking to you here, in the City. Corthie wasn't kidding; the sky really is red.'

'Corthie made it back?'

'Aye, and Aila too. She's had a baby. Anyway, listen.'

'Don't worry; you have my full attention.'

'Good. Something's happened.'

'Something bad, I assume?'

Karalyn nodded. 'Kelsey, I need your help.'

'Um, sure; I guess. How can I help?'

'I'm going to try to travel to your world, and then I'll attempt to bring you back with me.'

Kelsey backed away. 'Hold on a minute, Karalyn. I have a life here now. You can't just march in and expect me to drop everything and go back with you to the Holdings, or wherever.'

'It'll be temporary, Kelsey. If you like, I will bring you right back here. I'm not trying to disrupt your life. Please wait there, and I'll see you in a minute or two, in the flesh; I hope.'

Karalyn severed the connection with the young woman whose mind she had been controlling, and gazed down at the City.

Alright, Sextant. If I travel to this world, will part of my mind remain here, with you?

Yes.

Can I take others with me?

Yes.

Karalyn hesitated. If the next step went wrong, then she would be stranded in the City with Kelsey, with no way to return. She swallowed.

Take me to the City. Go.

The air around her vision crackled, then she realised that she was standing on the same path as Kelsey.

Her sister laughed. 'Pyre's arse, Karalyn. You're here.' She reached forward, and prodded Karalyn with a finger. 'You're really here.'

'Stop poking me.' She smiled. 'So, who's Van?'

'You know about Van, eh? What about you? Are you seeing anyone?'

'Come on, Kelsey; I have two dream mage children to look after. Where would I find time to meet anyone?'

Karalyn gazed at her sister, then reached out to hug her. Kelsey stepped back a foot.

'Why does everyone try to do that?' Kelsey said. 'Corthie tried to hug me as well, on Lostwell. How is the giant oaf?'

'He's wondering what to do with his life now that he hasn't got any greenhides to kill. Aila had a wee boy, and she's already pregnant again. Keir...'

'Did I ask about Keir?'

'Well, no, but...'

'Who gives a flying shit about Keir?'

'Thorn, I guess.'

Kelsey laughed. 'Has she not divorced him yet? So, what's the plan?'

'That depends. How long would you be willing to live in Colsbury for?'

'Hmm. I don't know. A few months, at most. I was serious before – I like my life here in the City. I have Van, and Frostback, and, you know, I'm a bit of a local celebrity, after helping to defeat Simon. That's two Ascendants I've had a hand in killing. Him, and Leksandr on Lostwell. Not that I'm counting, of course. Come on, let's speak to Emily, and we'll see what she says.'

'Emily?'

'Aye, the Queen.'

Karalyn smiled. 'It's good to see you, Kelsey.'

'Don't get all weird on me. Oh, be prepared. I might have let slip that you're the most powerful mortal ever to exist, so, eh, some expectations have been set.'

'You told them I'm what?'

'They don't have mages here. They have gods, well, they did; quite a few were killed recently, but they don't have any mortals with powers. To most mortals here, you are kind of like a god.'

'It was the same on Lostwell.'

'Oh aye. I keep forgetting you were there. Did you bring me any chocolate?'

'Should I have?'

'Aye. This place is alright, but there are no cigarettes, weed, chocolate, coffee, tea, whisky, sugar. There are cats and opium; that's about it.'

'I have an idea. I want to test something, so I'll pop back to Colsbury, and then I'll meet you and the Queen. Where will she be?'

Kelsey pointed at one of the mansions. 'In there – the Aurelian house. All of the palaces are a little singed at the moment.'

Karalyn nodded. 'See you in a few minutes.'

'Bring chocolate!' Kelsey cried.

Sextant, take me back to Colsbury. Go.

Karalyn blinked, and saw the familiar surroundings of the Sextant chamber in Colsbury Castle. She grinned. She had done it. She hurried to the door and opened it.

'Shella!' she yelled.

The Rakanese woman emerged from a room. 'What?'

'Could you help me for a minute? I need to pack a bag; no, two bags. One with clothes and stuff, and another with treats – chocolate, whisky and cigarettes. Could you handle the treat bag? Stuff it full.'

Shella stared at her. 'What?'

'Have you been smoking dreamweed again?'

'Well, yeah.'

'Get the bag ready for me, please; then meet me back here.'

Shella muttered something under her breath and strode away. Karalyn raced to her bedroom, and packed a bag, including clothes for the twins as well as her own. The vague outlines of a plan were crystallising in her mind, and she was unable to keep a smile from her face. A few minutes later, she met Shella outside the room containing the Sextant.

'Come inside,' said Karalyn.

'How about, "Thank you, Shella"?'

'Thank you, Shella. Come inside.'

They entered the room, and Karalyn swung her pack over her shoulder.

'Keep a tight hold of your bag,' she told Shella, as she laid her palm onto the Sextant.

Tara, the City, with Shella. Go.

The air crackled, and Shella shrieked as they appeared on the path by the ruined palace.

'Where are we?' cried Shella. 'Why is the sky red?'

Karalyn eyed her. 'Do you feel alright? Any strange pains?'

'Eh, what? No, I'm fine, apart from being transported to... wherever this place is.'

'We're on Kelsey's world.'

Colsbury. Go.

They appeared back inside the castle.

'What are you trying to do to me?' yelled Shella. 'I'm too old for this shit.'

'Sorry. I want to take the twins with me for a few days, and so I needed someone to test it on first.'

'What? You mean, I was a subject in your little experiment? Dear gods, Karalyn; what if I'd completely disappeared, or been reduced to a pile of ash?'

'Then I would have known that it was too dangerous to risk the twins.'

Shella shook her head. 'You cold-hearted bitch.'

She threw the bag at Karalyn and stormed out of the room. Karalyn waited a moment, then peered out into the corridor.

'Kyra, Cael!' she yelled. 'Come here.'

The two children ran out of the play room, glancing at each other as if they were in trouble.

'Would you like to go on a little holiday with me to see Aunty Kelsey?' Karalyn said. 'Just for a few days.'

'Aye!' cried Kyra.

'Come on, then,' said Karalyn. She led them into the room, and stood them next to the Sextant. 'I have a few rules,' she said to them. 'No going into people's minds, and you must stay where I can see you. Aunty Kelsey is far, far away, and I don't want you to get lost. Are you listening?'

Neither of the twins responded.

'There is one person, just one person, whose mind you are allowed to enter.'

That got their attention.

'Who?' said Kyra.

'Aunty Kelsey. If you manage to get into her mind, tell me, and I'll give you a biscuit. Alright? Oh, and if you see any colourful winged gaien, don't be scared of them.'

'Why would I be scared of a gaien?' said Cael.

'Because these ones can talk and breathe fire.'

The twins stared at her.

Karalyn placed her palm onto the Sextant.

All three of us. Tara, the City. Go.

The air sparkled, and they found themselves in the same lane as before. The twins gazed around, their mouths open.

'This way, children,' said Karalyn, and they walked along the path to the main road. On their right were the iron gates of the burnt-out palace, while the road stretched along the top of the ridge to their left. Huge houses lined the road on both sides, though many were half-hidden by trees and hedgerows. Karalyn was trying to remember which mansion to approach, when she saw Kelsey waiting for her by a drive-way, along with two men in military uniforms.

Karalyn smiled, and led the twins along the road towards Kelsey. The twins broke free, and ran at Kelsey, nearly knocking her over.

'Aunty Kelsey!' Kyra cried, her joy uncontained.

Kelsey laughed. 'Look at the size of you two!'

While Kelsey was embracing her nephew and niece, Karalyn's eyes went over the two men. The shorter of the two seemed a little awkward, almost nervous, while the taller one was half-smiling, as if he knew a secret that was incredibly funny.

Kelsey straightened herself.

'This is Van,' she said to Karalyn, gesturing at the shorter man.

Van stuck out his hand, and Karalyn shook it.

'It's an honour to meet you, Karalyn,' said Van, bowing his head.

'Stop acting weird,' said Kelsey. 'She's my sister, not the queen of the greenhides. She's not going to eat you, Van.' She pointed at the taller man. 'And this numpty is Lucius Cardova. If you want to make a friend for life, give him a cigarette.'

'I have cigarettes with me,' said Karalyn, holding up the bag Shella had packed. 'And chocolate, and a few other things. Coffee and so on.'

She rummaged in the bag, and brought out three packets of cigarettes. She offered them to Kelsey.

'Nah,' said her sister. 'I quit smoking in Lostwell.'

Karalyn noticed Cardova staring at the cigarettes in her hand, so she passed them to him.

'Tall, strange woman,' he said; 'I think I love you.'

'Don't call my sister strange,' said Kelsey. 'She is strange, but only I get to call her that.'

Cardova laughed. 'I meant strange, as in I don't know her; not strange, as in weird. You're the weird one, Kelsey. Everyone in the City knows that.'

'Shut it, Lucius.'

Lucius Cardova looked Karalyn in the eye. He was slightly taller than her, which annoyed her a little, for a reason she couldn't fathom.

'Do you have a light?' he said, a cigarette in his hand.

'Why are you so tall?' she said, then her cheeks flushed. 'Sorry. I have no idea why I said that.' She dipped a hand into a pocket and passed him a box of matches.

'I keep telling Lucius that he'd pass for a Kellach back home,' said Kelsey, 'but, of course, he has absolutely no idea what I'm talking about.'

'I rarely know what you're talking about, Kelsey,' he said, though he kept his eyes on Karalyn. He lit a match, put the flame to the end of the cigarette, and inhaled.

Kelsey elbowed Van in the ribs. 'Why are you being so quiet, eh?'

'I guess I'm a little intimidated,' Van said. 'I'm in a relationship with a woman whose older sister is the most powerful mortal who has ever lived. I'm just hoping she doesn't take a dislike to me.'

Karalyn cringed. 'I'm not that powerful. Kelsey's been exaggerating.'

'Are you sure?' said Kelsey. 'I mean, really sure? You didn't kill one hundred thousand Rahain soldiers with the power of your mind, then? Oh. I must have imagined it.'

'Please, Kelsey. I don't want to talk about that. I was... I was... very angry.'

'Why are we standing here?' said Cael. 'I'm bored.'

Cardova crouched down, so that his face was level with the twins. 'Shall we go and see the Queen?'

'Is she pretty?' said Cael.

'Oh yes,' said Cardova. 'Here's a little tip. Tell her you think she's beautiful when you see her. It'll make her day.'

Kelsey furrowed her brow. 'I didn't know that you fancied the Queen, Lucius.'

'I don't fancy her,' he said, standing. 'I was just teaching the lad to be a gentleman.'

'Let's go,' said Van. 'Her Majesty is waiting for us.'

'Is Daniel there too?' said Kelsey, as they began to walk up the driveway towards the huge mansion.

'I think he's in Pella this morning,' said Van. 'Looking over the ruins of Cuidrach.'

Karalyn went into Van's mind. She didn't mean to, not exactly, but if Kelsey was in love with him, then she wanted to check that he wasn't deceiving her. She had a quick look around his thoughts and memories, and saw how deep his love for Kelsey ran. He would do anything for her. Satisfied, she withdrew, and saw Kelsey scowling at her.

'Did you have to do that?' said Kelsey. 'You've only been here five minutes.'

Karalyn shrugged. 'Just looking out for my little sister.'

'We're the same age now.'

'No. I'm still a few thirds older than you.'

'So? We're both twenty-four, and that's what matters. How's dear mama?'

'Exactly as you'd imagine.'

They passed a few soldiers at the entrance to the mansion, and walked inside. Kelsey led them past a fine kitchen, and along a hallway towards a large room at the end. A large table dominated the room, and a young woman with blonde hair was sitting, along with a few others.

'Your Majesty,' said Van, bowing. 'May I introduce Miss Karalyn Holdfast, and her children, Kyra and Cael Holdfast? Karalyn, this is her Majesty, Queen Emily Aurelian.'

The Queen of the City smiled. 'At long last, I get to meet the fabled Karalyn Holdfast. Did you use the God-King's Quadrant to get here?'

'No,' said Karalyn. 'I have a Sextant. In theory, it could take me to any world that it created.'

'You have a Sextant?' said Cardova. 'A real, proper, functioning Sextant?'

'Aye.' She glanced at the Queen. 'I have some gifts, from my own world.' She held up the bag, and unloaded its contents onto the table. 'A bottle of whisky, some more cigarettes, chocolate, coffee...'

'Chocolate?' said Kelsey. 'Oh, Queenie, you have to try some of that. Please.'

'I concur,' said Cardova.

Emily scanned the array of items on the table. 'Thank you very much,' she said. 'Let me finish the introductions first.' She gestured to her left. 'This is my mother, Lady Omertia, and my mother-in-law, Lady Aurelian.'

Karalyn smiled at them. Lady Omertia smiled back, while Lady Aurelian kept her expression guarded.

'Are there no gods or demigods here?' said Karalyn.

'There aren't very many left in the City,' said Emily. 'Two are living in Port Sanders, while a couple of others are scattered here and there. One of them is in the dungeons beneath the ruins of Maeladh Palace. May I ask if you have news of Lady Aila of Pella?'

'She's doing well,' said Karalyn. 'One baby, and another on the way. She and Corthie got married.'

'How wonderful,' said Emily. 'Unfortunately for Aila, none of her siblings survived the recent troubles.'

Kelsey looked as though she was bursting to say something, but kept her mouth closed.

'We were visited by an Ascendant,' Emily went on; 'and it took a long hard struggle to put an end to his reign of terror. Now, I understand that you wish to take Kelsey back with you for a while?'

'Aye,' said Karalyn. 'I need her.'

'Will it be dangerous?' said Van.

'Not for Kelsey,' said Karalyn. 'She'll be safe.'

'You're right about that,' said Kelsey. 'Do you know why, sis? Because I'll be bringing my dragon with me.'

Karalyn glanced down at the twins. 'Give me a moment. Kyra, Cael – have you tried to do what I asked?'

'Aye, mama,' said Cael. 'I can't get inside Aunty Kelsey's head.'

'Kyra?'

The little girl shook her head. 'It's like Aunty Kelsey isn't even here, mama.'

Karalyn nodded, then turned back to Emily. 'Alright. I'll need Kelsey for a few thirds...'

'Months,' said Kelsey.

'Aye, months. And then I'll bring her back. Before that, though, I was hoping to stay here for a few days. It'll be good for the twins to see a new place, and it's only fair that Kelsey has some time to say goodbye.'

'You are very welcome to stay,' said Emily. 'There's space in one of the mansions here on Princeps Row. We'll have it cleaned and prepared for you. Lucius can organise a tour of the City, if you like.'

'That sounds great,' said Karalyn. 'Thank you.'

'I want Lucius to come with us back to my home world,' said Kelsey.

Van blinked. 'You want Lucius to come? What about me?'

'I'll explain later, Van; trust me on this.'

'I'm afraid I need you here, Van,' said Emily. 'There's too much work to spare you. I can, however, spare Lucius.'

Cardova frowned. 'Ma'am?'

'Don't take it the wrong way, Lucius,' said Emily; 'you know how much I value everything you have done for me and this City. You're the best soldier I have. I want you to guard Kelsey, so that she can return to Van in one piece.'

Cardova stood to attention. 'As you will, your Majesty.'

Kelsey smiled, then leaned across the table and picked up a bar of chocolate. She opened the wrapping, broke off a chunk, and slipped it into her mouth.

'Pyre's hairy arse,' she groaned. 'Queenie, please have some of this. It'll change your life.'

Emily took a piece from Kelsey, sniffed it, then placed it onto her tongue. She sat still for a moment, then her eyes widened. Van and Cardova exchanged a glance, then laughed.

'You two are from Implacatus,' said Karalyn.

'Yes,' said Cardova. 'We were stranded on Lostwell, and then suddenly we were here, along with another forty thousand refugees. The vast majority are natives of Lostwell, but there were three thousand Banner soldiers as well.'

Karalyn narrowed her eyes. 'Banner soldiers? The ones Corthie told me about?'

'That's us,' said Cardova. 'My old Banner fought your brother in Lostwell, in the caverns under Yoneath.'

'And now they fight for me,' said Emily. 'Whatever disagreement the Holdfasts may have had with the Banners in Lostwell do not apply here.'

Karalyn kept her gaze on the two soldiers. 'I'm not sure my brother would agree.'

'I knew Corthie well on Lostwell, ma'am,' said Van. 'He understood that the Banners are strictly professional mercenaries. We sign contracts with employers, and then we remain faithful to those employers. I once had a contract with Corthie himself – to protect Kelsey. Furthermore, if Captain Cardova accompanies Kelsey back to your world, then he will be under a similar obligation.'

'Let me put it more simply, sister,' said Kelsey. 'If the Banner are employed by bawbags, then they'll act like bawbags. Here, they're employed by the good guys.'

'I have an idea,' said Cardova. 'I'm happy to leave with Karalyn and Kelsey, but perhaps we also need someone with a wealth of experience to join us. Someone who has travelled, and fought, on many different worlds.'

Emily frowned for a moment, then her eyes narrowed. 'I see, or at least I think I do. Are you referring to Caelius Logos?'

'Got it in one, your Majesty. He's always on the lookout for something new to do.'

'I'll speak to him,' said Van, 'but I think you might be right, Lucius. Sending my father along with you would keep him out of trouble here.'

'Missus Queen,' said Cael.

Emily smiled. 'Yes?'

'You're beautiful.'

'Thank you very much.'

'When's dinner?'

'Are you hungry?' said Emily. She glanced at a soldier by the door. 'Prepare lunch for our guests, please; for, say, half an hour's time.'

'At once, ma'am,' said the soldier.

Kelsey glanced down at the children. 'Do you want to see a dragon?'

'What's a dragon?' said Kyra.

'It's one of those talking gaien I mentioned,' said Karalyn.

Kyra's eyes widened. 'Can they really breathe fire?'

Kelsey grinned. 'Let's find out.'

CHAPTER 11
UNABLE TO RESIST

Severton, Domm – 22nd Day, First Third Summer 534

Corthie waved at the crowds from the back of the wagon as it was pulled through the streets of Severton. The two imperial princesses were in the lead wagon, while Corthie and Aila were in the one following, along with Conal and a few town dignitaries.

Aila gazed at the handsome stone tenements that lined the road. 'After all of the villages and farms, I wasn't expecting a town like this to appear down here.'

'The distillery certainly brings in the money,' said Conal. 'Every legal bottle of whisky sold throughout the empire is made in Severton.'

Aila nodded. 'But where did they get the money to build it in the first place?'

Conal glanced at Draewyn. The old woman had once been the provost of Severton, but had retired a few years previously. She smiled.

'The Severed Clan were very lucky,' Draewyn said. 'When we got here, we discovered that Daphne Holdfast had left all of her gold behind when she ran off. Pyre's arse, that girl was rich. And there was almost no gold to speak of down here, just a few tiny bits and pieces. That hoard funded the building of the distillery, and the distillery funded everything else.'

Aila raised an eyebrow. 'Daphne Holdfast's gold? Did you know about this, Corthie?'

He shook his head. 'I don't remember hearing that.'

'Bridget was responsible too,' said Conal. 'She prevented the hoard from being frittered away.'

'Aye,' said Draewyn. 'A few folk thought that the gold should be dispersed here and there, but Bridget insisted that we use it all to build the distillery. She was a smart lassie, even back then.' She nodded towards the lead wagon. 'It's marvellous to see the two princesses; but it's a shame that Bridget herself has never been back to the homeland.'

'Running the empire takes a lot of work,' said Corthie.

'I'm sure it does, son,' said Draewyn. 'I wasnae criticising the Empress; we all know she's busy. Still, it's a shame, but. The folk down here would go wild if Bridget turned up.'

Corthie pointed down a wide street, flanked by large townhouses. 'That's where we lived,' he said. 'In one of those houses.'

'That's right,' said Draewyn. 'The house ye were in is occupied now, but we've arranged a similar house for ye to stay in while yer here.'

Aila's eyes lit up. 'Does it have an inside toilet?'

Draewyn laughed. 'Aye, hen, and it flushes. And it's got hot water that comes out of pipes, and everything you city folk like. We're not all savages down here. This is Domm.'

Conal gave her a look. 'Marchside will be like this one day.'

'I'm sure it will, Conal,' said Draewyn, 'in fifty years, maybe.' She glanced at Corthie. 'The rumours are saying that you and yer family are thinking of settling down here, son. If that's the case, then I hope ye'll pick Domm. If it's inside toilets yer after, then Domm's the place.'

'Thanks,' said Corthie, 'but we haven't decided anything yet.'

Draewyn nodded. 'What did they clowns in Threeways offer ye?'

Corthie smiled. 'They said they would give us a big house in the middle of the town, if we wanted to live there. We had folk offer us shares in their merchant businesses, and someone offered us some land along the Domm Pass.'

'Pyre's tits, son. It sounds like ye've got the whole of Kellach Brig-domin trying to get ye to stay. Did eh, did Kallie offer ye anything?'

Corthie nodded. 'A farm. A hundred and eighty acres.'

'Shit. Right. I'll speak to the new provost, and see if we can beat her offer.'

Aila shook her head. 'I'm not sure why every town and village is trying to get us to stay.'

'Come on, hen,' said Draewyn. 'Look at the crowds that have turned up just to watch ye get pulled through the streets. They're not all here to see the Brig princesses. And anyway, everybody kens that those two lassies will be heading back to the Plateau once their wee trip is over. It's a constant battle, hen. So many young folk decide that they want to see the big city where the Empress lives. They leave, and hardly any of them come back. If somebody of Corthie's name and heritage decides he wants to move in the other direction? Well, it's a sign to the young folk that it's worth staying down here. I guarantee ye, hen, that if you and Corthie stay, then we'll be able to hold on to more youngsters.'

'Is the population falling?' said Corthie.

'Nah, it's rising,' said Draewyn, 'but slowly. We used to get waves of refugees coming in, especially from Rahain, but they've all dried up in the last few years. For every three bairns born, one heads off to the Plateau as soon as they're old enough, and we've a long way to go before we come close to matching the population level that existed before the Rahain invasion. I mean, Lach's still a deserted wasteland, and very few folk live in Brig. Still, it's a comfort to know that there are a hundred thousand Kellach Brigdomin up on the Plateau, even if few of them will ever come home.'

The wagons pulled into the town's main square, where two larger-than-life statues stood. Corthie glanced at them. He remembered seeing them before, when he had stayed in Severton with Karalyn, Jemma and his mother.

'Are they the Empress and your father?' said Aila.

'Aye,' he said.

'Why is the Empress pointing to the west?'

'It was Bridget who guided the Severed Clan all the way here from Rahain,' he said. 'I guess she's pointing towards the homeland.'

'Ye know yer history, lad,' said Draewyn.

'My father told me stories about the Severed Clan,' he said. 'I only wish I'd listened more.'

A platform had been erected between the two large statues, and the occupants of the lead wagon were ascending the steps to the top. Standing next to the two princesses was Brady, the town's new provost. Once empty, the lead wagon moved off, and the rear wagon pulled up in front of the platform. Corthie took hold of Killop and clambered down to the cobbles, then he reached up with a hand to help Aila climb down. Her baby bump had grown over the first third of summer, and her pregnancy was obvious to anyone who saw her.

Conal helped Draewyn down from the wagon, and they walked through the crowd to the steps, then joined Brady and the princesses up on the platform.

The provost raised his hands, and the crowd quietened.

'Today,' he said, in a loud, clear voice, 'the town of Severton is honoured to welcome Princess Brogan and Princess Bethal, two of the Empress's daughters. They have travelled all the way from Plateau City to visit Kellach Brigdomin, so let's make sure our wee town gives them the hospitality they deserve. Also visiting us today is Corthie ae Killop ae Kell, only this time he's brought his wife and wee lad along. Some of ye might remember him from the last time he was here, nigh on nine years ago.' He smiled. 'Some of ye might even remember how drunk his mother got at the Winter's Day festival, but that's another story, eh? Now, Princess Brogan has kindly agreed to say a few words to mark the occasion, and then we can make our way to the taverns before the rain starts.'

Brogan looked a little nervous as she stepped forward. 'Thank you,' she said. 'Let me just say how much my sister and I appreciate the welcome, so thank you, Provost Brady. It's been a dream of mine since I was a wee girl to come down to Kellach Brigdomin, to see the lands where my mother was born and raised. Not a day goes past that my mother doesn't remember where she came from. She once said to me that if a Brig girl from a peasant village could make it all the way to the imperial throne, then there's hope for everyone. For twenty-seven years, a Kellach Brigdomin has ruled the empire, and I hope my mother continues to reign for another twenty-seven years. Thank you.'

She fell silent as the first drops of rain fell from the dark clouds that hung over Severton. The crowd applauded politely, then Provost Brady stepped forward.

'That's the rain on, folks. See you in the taverns!'

Corthie, Aila and the princesses spent the next three hours touring the many taverns of Severton, accompanied by the provost, Draewyn and Conal. Each tavern they visited was packed out, and Corthie began to suspect that the town was paying for everyone's drinks. He was handed a generous measure of whisky in each place, and he was almost staggering by the time they reached the final tavern, which was nestled into the side of the massive distillery. The building complex dominated the western half of the town, its blackened walls towering over the tenements. Wagons and barrels were lined up in long rows by the distillery entrance, but no one was working that day. Brady led them to a large table at the end of the tavern that had been reserved for them, and they sat.

'You look a little worse for wear,' said Aila, glancing at Corthie.

'I've lost count of the number of taverns we've been to.'

'Thirteen,' said Conal.

'Why am I the only one who looks drunk?'

Conal smiled. 'Because you were the only one who finished every whisky they were given, lad. I'm amazed yer still standing.'

'He doesnae get that from his father,' said Draewyn. 'Killop was never a big drinker.'

'You didn't know him in Hold Fast,' said Corthie. 'He liked a drop of whisky in the evenings. My mother can drink like a fish, though. She's as tough as any Kellach.'

'Aye, I remember,' said Draewyn. 'She ordered gin at the Winter's Day festival. Gin! Can ye imagine? She's in the home of whisky, and there she was, knocking back a whole bottle of gin like it was water. Folk talked about that for ages.'

'Do you make gin here?' said Aila.

'Och aye,' said Draewyn. 'And then we send it all up to the Plateau, eh? The folk up there cannae get enough of it. You look like ye could be a gin drinker, hen; no offence. Do ye want some?'

Conal leaned forward. 'I'm not sure wee Aila should be drinking, Draewyn. Not in her condition.'

'Aye. I suppose yer right,' said Draewyn.

Aila frowned, but said nothing. Corthie wasn't sure which had annoyed her more – being denied alcohol, or being called 'wee'.

'I had my first drink in Severton,' said Corthie; 'at that festival you were talking about.'

'What age were you?' said Aila.

'Fourteen.'

Aila nodded. 'That explains a lot.'

'Is Corthie fond of the booze, hen?' said Draewyn.

'You could say that. He drank his way through Lostwell, in amongst all the fighting.'

'I'm a simple man,' said Corthie, 'and those were trying times.'

'Tell us a wee story about this Lostwell place,' said Conal. 'What was it like there?'

Corthie paused, trying to think back to the last six months he had spent on a world that no longer existed. He had hated Lostwell – the earthquakes, the unrelenting heat, the poisonous deserts. Had it all been bad? He recalled Belinda, and the sacrifice she had made in order to send him and Aila home; then he remembered dying at the hands of the two Ascendants in the caverns of Fordamere, and the slaughter of the civilians of Yoneath by the Banner soldiers.

'Ye don't have to, lad,' said Conal. 'Not if ye don't want to.'

Corthie stared at the table. 'Lostwell's gone.'

Conal frowned. 'Eh?'

'The gods destroyed it,' said Aila; 'they destroyed the entire world. We were lucky to escape. Millions weren't.'

'Millions?' said Draewyn. 'Pyre's knackers. How did ye get away?'

'A god called Belinda helped us,' said Aila; 'just as the world was falling apart.'

Corthie felt his eyes start to well. It might have been due to the whisky, but he didn't want to break down in front of a tavern full of people. He got to his feet.

'I'm going to get some fresh air for a minute.'

Draewyn raised an eyebrow. 'But it's raining outside, lad.'

Corthie eased his way through the crowd and strode out in to the street. The rain was falling steadily, but he didn't care. An image of Belinda throwing herself at the Sextant as two ballista bolts ripped through her body flashed across his mind, and he stared up at the dark sky, his raw emotions in turmoil, as the rain ran down his face. Why did he seem to be the only one who still cared about Belinda? Even Karalyn had accepted that her old friend was dead and gone, and yet, despite the destruction of Lostwell, and despite the ballista bolts, Corthie had never been able to fully believe that Belinda was really dead. And, as long as that tiny glimmer of hope remained, he had found himself unable to move on, unable to properly mourn.

'What are you doing out here?' said Bethal.

Corthie glanced to his right, and saw the younger of the two princesses standing next to him.

'Just getting some fresh air,' he said.

'In the rain?'

'Aye. It's only water. Why are you out here?'

Bethal frowned. 'Because Brogan's cut me off. She says I've already had too much to drink, and that I'm not getting any more. But I heard you say in there that you were drinking when you were fourteen. It's not fair.'

'So you stormed out in a huff?'

'Yeah, something like that.'

'Brogan's a good sister. You should listen to her.'

'Not you as well, Corthie? I thought you were different. Brogan's trying to control me as if I were her daughter, and I'm sick of it.'

'The Empress told her to look after you; it's not her fault.'

'Let's go back inside. I hate getting wet.'

They turned, and walked into the warm tavern. Corthie glanced over at their table and saw Aila with Killop on her knee, talking to Draewyn and Conal. A little to their left, Brogan was engaged in an animated conversation with an older man, his red hair flecked with grey. Corthie squeezed through the crowd of people, and reached the table. He was about to speak to Aila, when Brogan lifted her hand and slapped the red-haired man across the face. Corthie shoved his way forward, and blocked the man from reaching out for Brogan.

'Keep your hands to yourself, mate,' he said to the red-haired man; 'or it'll be me punching you next.'

'You don't understand,' said the man, his palms raised. 'I wasn't trying anything sleazy; I just need to talk to the princess for a minute.'

Corthie glanced at Brogan. By then, the closest half of the tavern had fallen silent, as eyes turned towards the town's guests of honour.

Brogan said nothing. She was staring at the red-haired man, her eyes wide.

'What's happening?' said Bethal.

The man turned to face the other princess, and he seemed to choke back a sob.

'Bethal?' he said. 'What a beautiful young woman you've become.'

Bethal snorted, then glanced at her sister. 'Who is this prick?'

Brogan swallowed, her eyes still drawn to the man. 'He says he's our father.'

The entire tavern fell into utter silence. Provost Brady got to his feet, his cheeks reddening.

He glanced around at the watching faces. 'Eh, maybe we should take this discussion into the back room?'

'I would be most grateful for that, Provost,' said the red-haired man.

'He's a liar,' said Bethal. 'We should throw him out of the tavern.'

'Hold on a wee moment,' said Draewyn. 'Let's not do anything rash. Unlock the back room, Brady, and we'll get our guests inside. Conal, give me a hand.'

149

Conal and Draewyn began ushering Corthie and the others towards the rear of the tavern, where Brady opened a door. They went into a comfortable room, laid out with couches and padded benches, and Brady opened the shutters to let in some light.

'Everybody sit,' said Draewyn. 'We're going to have a civilised conversation.'

'That's all I wanted,' said the red-haired man.

Brady eyed him as they all sat. 'Really, Brannig? I've known you for what? Ten years? And you spring this on us? Just what are ye playing at?'

'You know this man?' said Brogan.

'Aye,' said Brady. 'He owns a fleet of wagons that transports whisky and other goods to the Plateau. He has a contract with the distillery.'

'He's not our father,' said Bethal. 'He's a con man.'

'Let him say his piece, hen,' said Draewyn. 'Out with it, Brannig.'

The red-haired man bowed his head. 'I am these girls' father, and I'm the father of Bryce, and Berra, and Bedig, too.' His voice broke on the last name, and he lowered his eyes.

'You're either a liar,' said Brogan, 'or an oath-breaker. I've asked my mother a hundred times about the identity of our father, but she's told me nothing. One thing she did say, though, was you had sworn an oath to never reveal yourself.'

'I swore two oaths,' Brannig said. 'Once for the twins, and then again for the triplets. Bridget insisted that I never return to Plateau City, and that I never told a soul the truth.'

Draewyn narrowed her eyes. 'Did she pay ye?'

Brannig turned. 'What?'

'I always wondered where ye first got yer money from. Did the Empress pay ye to keep quiet?'

'She gave me a sum of gold, to start a business. I invested it in a fleet of wagons.'

Brogan shook her head. 'This is too much. Tell us something about mother that only you would know.'

'Alright,' he said. 'She still loves my brother, even though he's been dead for nearly thirty years. She never loved me. She wanted me to father her children, because I was the closest thing there was to my brother. I was reluctant, at first. But she told me that it would be me, or no one. So, I agreed, and she fell pregnant with the twins. And then, a few years later, I was back in Plateau City on business. I was desperate to see the twins, so I approached the Empress. She wouldn't let me see them, but she wanted more children... And then she fell pregnant with the triplets. I left the city before they were born; it was part of the agreement.' He gazed at Brogan and Bethal. 'This is the first time in my life that I've seen any of my children.'

'What was yer brother's name?' said Draewyn. 'I mean, I can guess, but I want to hear you say it.'

Brannig kept his eyes on the princesses. 'My brother was called Bedig. We were twins.'

Draewyn sighed. 'Pyre's arse.'

'Do you believe him?' said Corthie.

'I think I'm starting to, lad.'

'I don't,' said Bethal. 'This could all be a pile of horseshit. If it's true, then why has he waited so long to see us? And if he swore an oath, why's he decided to break it? He's after money. He wants us to pay him so he'll shut up.'

Brannig raised his hands. 'I don't want your money. I'm already wealthy; why would I need more?'

'Answer my sister about the oath,' said Brogan. 'Why have you broken your word?'

Brannig rubbed his face. 'I knew you were coming down to Kellach Brigdomin; the news has been talked about for thirds. I should have stayed away, but I thought that this might be the only chance I would ever get to actually see you. I was in the crowd today, in the town square. I heard your speech, Brogan. After that, temptation got the better of me, and I waited in this tavern, knowing that you would be coming here last. I guess I couldn't help myself.'

'Ye couldnae help yerself?' said Draewyn. 'Pyre's tits, Brannig, do ye ken the damage ye might have just done to Bridget? Word will spread, mark my words; in fact, word will have probably already spread across Severton, and it'll be in Threeways by the end of the third. Could ye not have kept yer big mouth shut for another few days?'

'I'm sorry,' said Brannig.

'What now?' said the town provost. 'Draewyn's right – there'll be no keeping this quiet. Folk have wondered about the identity of the father of Bridget's bairns for years.'

'I want to see the rest of my children,' said Brannig. 'Just once, while I still live. Just once.' He glanced at Brogan. 'Would your mother understand?'

'My mother's going to rip your head off,' said Bethal. 'How dare you do this to us? You completely humiliated us in front of a packed tavern, and now, as soon as we walk out of this room, folk will be staring at us, wondering if it's true.'

'It is true, Bethal,' he said. 'I know why you're angry with me. I never married, did you know that? How could I, when I had five children living in Plateau City? Can I come back to the city with you, when you leave? I don't want any money, and I certainly don't want to interfere in your mother's work. All I want is to see my children.'

Bethal stared at him with nothing but rage and contempt in her eyes, then she started to cry. Brogan put a protective arm over her sister's shoulder, and the room fell into silence, punctuated only by the sound of Bethal's tears.

Aila nudged Corthie. 'Should we leave?' she whispered. 'I feel like we're intruding.'

Corthie got to his feet. 'We'll get out of your way,' he said. 'This is family business.'

'We should leave, too,' said Provost Brady.

'Draewyn, can you stay?' said Brogan. 'I want someone else to be here.'

'Of course, hen,' said Draewyn.

Brannig, the two princesses and Draewyn remained seated, and the others filed out of the room. Brady closed the door behind them, then turned to face the crowd that had gathered in the tavern.

'There's nothing to see here, folks,' he said. 'Let's give our guests some privacy.'

'Is it true, but?' someone shouted. 'Is Brannig their da?'

'No comment,' said Brady. He nodded to a woman behind the bar. 'Stick a couple of burly guys on the door, hen, to keep any nosy bastards from interrupting the princesses.'

'Aye, boss,' she said.

Brady slipped a set of keys into Corthie's hand.

'These are for the house where you'll be staying, Corthie,' the provost said. 'The address is on the key ring. Will we be seeing ye tomorrow for the tour of the distillery?'

'Aye,' he said. 'See you then.'

Corthie took Killop from Aila, then he shoved his way through the tight press of people packed into the tavern. He and Aila emerged on to the street, where it had stopped raining. They strode away from the tavern, leaving the mass of people behind.

'I wasn't expecting that,' said Aila. 'Poor Brogan and Bethal. Imagine discovering who your father was in that way.'

'I'm not sure he was telling the truth,' said Corthie. 'He might be trying to pull a scam, just like Bethal mentioned.'

'That was no scam, Corthie. I could see it in his eyes. Bethal knew it, too. She might have doubted it at the beginning, but she believed it by the time we left. Could you not see the family resemblance? Brannig looks like an older version of Bryce, apart from the hair.'

'Bridget's going to go mental.'

'Yes, that's what worries me. She's kept that secret quiet for over twenty years, and he's blown it open in a few minutes.'

Corthie shifted Killop to his other arm, and checked the address written on the key ring. They walked through the wet streets of Severton, then halted in front of a tall townhouse.

Aila gazed up at it. 'Is this all for us?'

'It certainly appears so,' said Corthie. They walked up the steps to the front door, and Corthie unlocked it. Inside, was a house as palatial as anywhere they had stayed on their entire trip. The ceilings were high, and the rooms elegant and spacious.

Aila laughed. 'This is slightly better than the shack where we slept in Marchside. It reminds me of the interior of the Royal Palace in Ooste.'

'Whisky must bring in a ton of gold,' said Corthie.

'Could Severton tempt you, as a place to settle?'

He shrugged. 'Too many people here.'

'Yes, but we could live in a place like this. Inside toilets, Corthie.'

They walked into a large sitting room, where their luggage had been set down. Corthie placed Killop onto the thick rug, then sat on a huge couch. He put his head back on a cushion and closed his eyes.

'I think I'm still half-drunk from all the whisky.'

He heard Aila sit down next to him.

'It's funny,' she said; 'when Brannig was giving us his version of events, I kept thinking that it had nothing to do with us. Not *just* on a personal level – on a personal level, of course it has nothing to do with us. But, as far as Bridget and the empire goes, I was thinking, this doesn't matter to us, because we're not going back to the Plateau. The princesses will head back, and Brannig might too, and all the drama that will unfold will happen hundreds of miles away.'

He opened his eyes. 'Is this your way of saying that you've made up your mind? You think we should live down here?'

'Why don't we give it a try? I think we should take Kallie up on her offer, if you don't want to stay in Severton. We could learn how to be farmers in Clackenbaird. We can hire some help, and settle down to raise an enormous number of children. We would need to rebuild the farmhouse, but I seem to have married into an exceedingly rich family, so money shouldn't be a problem.'

'Are you serious?'

'Yes. Farming might be the answer, Corthie; for you, I mean. Maybe hard, physical labour is what you need.'

'And it'll keep me in good shape in case any wars happen.'

She raised an eyebrow. 'That too, I suppose. Though I certainly hope that there won't be any wars, at least in the near future. And, I have one other condition.'

'Let me guess – an inside toilet?'

She smiled. 'There are several things that Lady Aila of Pella will not do, Corthie, and one of them is pee in a ditch.'

CHAPTER 12
FAVOURITES

Holdings City, Republic of the Holdings – 24th Day, First Third Summer 534

Daphne sipped her coffee as she read a copy of the morning newspaper. The dawn sun was shining through the large bay windows of her dining room in the First Holder's official residence, and it would soon be time to close the shutters, to keep out the ferocious heat of summer in the Holdings. It was pleasant at dawn, though, and Daphne was usually up early to enjoy the brightness of each morning before it got too hot.

She put down the newspaper and glanced at her daily schedule. It was empty. Parliament wasn't due to sit again for another few days, but even so, her days were normally filled with back-to-back meetings, and yet she had nothing planned for that day. It was a symptom of her final year in office. People were courting favour with her possible successors, and treating Daphne as if she were already out of office. She flicked the pages of her diary, and saw a mere handful of meetings scheduled for the following days.

She sighed. Maybe she should go up to the estate, rather than be seen idling in the capital. It was a dispiriting end to her twelve years as the elected head of the Holdings government, as well as the years when she had ruled under emergency decree. Altogether, she had been in a position of authority for as long as the Empress had been on the throne. She recalled a conversation she had had with Corthie after he had returned from Lostwell. He had been telling her that he felt empty without a war to fight, and she had told him not to be silly. Now, she was starting to know how he felt. When you were only good at one thing, and then that one thing was snatched away from you, what was left?

Bridget clearly expected her to resign as Herald of the Empire at the same time as she stepped down as First Holder. The Empress's so-called ultimatum had been her way to let Daphne know that Bryce would be replacing her, as they both knew that Daphne would never move to Plateau City. She would stop being the second most powerful person in the empire, and her status would diminish to that of just another wealthy Holder. For many people, that would be enough, but not for Daphne Holdfast.

The air shimmered in the corner of the room, and Karalyn appeared.

'Good morning, Karalyn,' said Daphne. 'Thank you for interrupting a bout of self-pity.'

'You? Self-pity?' said Karalyn.

'Exactly, dear. It's what comes from contemplating a future in which I seem to have very little to do.'

'Well, I can't help with that, but I do have a surprise for you.'

'Have you managed to get the Sextant to work?'

'Come with me to Colsbury, and you'll see.'

Daphne stood, and walked to the main doors. She opened them and looked out onto the hallway, catching a servant's eye.

'I shall be away from the residence for a while.'

The servant bowed. 'Very good, ma'am.'

Daphne closed the doors and turned back to Karalyn. 'Colsbury it is, dear.'

Karalyn smiled, and a moment later, Daphne found herself standing in the chamber in Colsbury where the Sextant was located.

Daphne glanced at the device. 'Am I here to see Kelsey again?'

Karalyn laughed. 'Aye.'

Daphne walked up to the Sextant, and placed her palm onto its glass surface.

Karalyn kept laughing.

'Really, dear?' said Daphne. 'Whatever is so amusing?'

Her daughter glanced towards the door. 'You can come in now.'

The door opened, and Kelsey strode in. Daphne blinked, then put her hand to her mouth.

'Hi, mother,' said Kelsey. 'Did you miss me?'

Daphne stepped forward and embraced her daughter with her good arm. Kelsey spluttered, and tried to resist, but Daphne's grip was unyielding.

'Let go, mother; you're going to break my ribs.'

Daphne laughed, and released Kelsey. 'My little girl; look at you! Happy birthday. I know it was a third ago, but all the same.'

'It's been three birthdays since I was last here,' said Kelsey.

Daphne wiped a tear from her eye and glanced at Karalyn. 'Well done, daughter. How did you do it?'

'I'll explain later,' said Karalyn. 'There are more people waiting outside in the hallway.'

Daphne frowned. 'Why?'

'I didn't come alone, mother,' said Kelsey.

Daphne's eyes widened. 'Did you get married?'

'No.'

'She's seeing someone, though,' said Karalyn.

'Aye, but I didn't bring him. The Queen needs him in the City.' Kelsey glanced at the doorway. 'You can come in, lads.'

Two men walked through the door. The first was as tall as any Kellach, while the other was Holdings-sized. Both had the air of veterans about them, though the taller man was younger.

'This is Lucius Cardova,' said Kelsey, gesturing to the taller man. 'He gave Karalyn and the twins a tour of the City.'

He waved. 'Hello.'

'And this is Caelius Logos,' Kelsey went on, pointing at the other man.

Caelius walked forward. He took Daphne's right hand before she could pull it away, and kissed it.

'Kelsey never mentioned how beautiful her mother was,' he said, 'I look forward to making your acquaintance, my lady.'

'My,' said Daphne. 'That was a touch forward, but not altogether unpleasant.'

Caelius smiled, his eyes holding her gaze.

'That's enough of that,' said Kelsey, grimacing. 'Maybe we should send Caelius back to the City if he's going to do that.'

'The Queen wouldn't thank us,' said Cardova, trying to suppress a laugh.

'And why have you two gentlemen come along?' said Daphne. 'Would I be right in saying that you are both military types?'

'You have a keen eye, ma'am,' said Caelius. 'Indeed, both Lucius and I are soldiers. However, while I spent many long years as a sergeant, Lucius here has risen all the way to captain. My son Van is the commander of the Banner forces in the City. He's a major-general, as well as Kelsey's romantic partner. Kelsey's a wonderful girl – my son's done very well for himself.'

'That's all very fascinating, Caelius, but you didn't answer my first question.'

Caelius puffed out his chest. 'We are here to protect your daughter, ma'am.'

'I see.'

'We'll be discreet, ma'am,' said Cardova. 'We're not here to make a nuisance of ourselves. This is the first time Caelius or I have been on this world, so any materials that might help to orient us would be useful. Maps, books, and so on.'

'Colsbury has a small library,' said Daphne, 'though I wonder if you would be able to read its contents? Are the languages in the City the same as here? That would seem a little unlikely.'

'They all speak and read Holdings in the City, mother,' said Kelsey.

'We're not speaking Holdings,' said Cardova. 'Right now, we're all speaking the language of Implacatus. The divine tongue, as it were. I have been led to believe that the Fourth Ascendant, Nathaniel, created this world, and in doing so, he must have imparted his own language into at least one of the dominant sub-created species of humans.' He glanced at Karalyn. 'Have I got that right?'

'How would I know?' said Karalyn. 'Half of what you said made no sense to me.'

'I didn't come all this way for a linguistics debate,' said Kelsey. 'Aye, Lucius – you'll be able to read the books here, but that can wait. There's someone else that mother has to meet, and she'll be wondering where we are.'

'Someone else?' said Daphne. 'Send her in.'

Kelsey laughed. 'She won't fit inside this room, mother. Let's go up onto the roof.'

'The roof?' said Daphne.

'Shella, Agang, and the twins are already up there,' said Karalyn.

'Did you leave the twins here while you fetched Kelsey?'

'No. I took them with me to the City. You were right, of course; they can't read Kelsey's thoughts. She's immune to their powers.'

'Have you told her why we need her?'

'Not yet. I was saving that for after the introductions. Come on.'

They left the Sextant chamber, and made their way to the stairs that led to the roof of Colsbury's Great Keep. They climbed the steps, and emerged into the sunshine. Daphne smiled as a warm wind brushed her cheek, and was glad that she had escaped the furnace of Holdings City. She spotted Shella and Agang standing by the lead-lined dome that sat in the centre of the roof. Next to them, Kyra and Cael were running around, shrieking as they played.

'Where is the other person?' said Daphne.

A shadow passed overhead, and Daphne looked up. Her mouth fell open. A huge silver gaien was flying above them, its long wings outstretched as it wheeled and banked over the island fortress. The sun was making its scales glisten and sparkle, and it looked more elegant than any winged gaien Daphne had seen before. It swooped down, and she felt the air rush over her from the beat of its wings. Great talons came from its four limbs, and it alighted onto the side of the roof, then swung its long neck round to gaze at the humans, its eyes glowing.

'Mother,' said Kelsey, 'say hello to Frostback.'

Daphne stared at the wild creature.

'Greetings, mother of my rider,' it said, its voice melodious and low.

'It... it can speak.'

Kelsey glared at her. 'Don't call her "it". She, mother; she. She can speak. She's a dragon.'

'I did not take offence, rider,' said the dragon. 'It is clear that your mother has never witnessed the grandeur of my kind before, and I realise that we can be quite intimidating to little humans.'

'Frostback can breathe fire!' cried Cael.

'And she ate a goat in one giant gulp,' said Kyra. 'I heard the bones crunching.'

Daphne kept her eyes on Frostback. 'I remember Karalyn and Corthie telling me about dragons, though I scarcely believed what I was hearing. How did you meet my daughter?'

'I met her on Lostwell, Kelsey-mother,' said the silver dragon; 'and Aila, too – Corthie's mate. Kelsey saved my life from the powers of an Ascendant. I knew she was special from that moment, and nothing has happened since to change my mind. As I honour her, I honour all her kin, especially you, Daphne Holdfast. You gave birth to my rider, and for that you will always have my gratitude and respect.'

'Thank you,' said Daphne. 'I see that not only do dragons speak, but that they are polite and well-spoken. Are there many dragons on Kelsey's world?'

'There are not. A mere five adults survived the coming of Simon, the Tenth Ascendant, along with four infant dragons.'

'Dragons aren't native to that world,' said Cardova. 'They all originally come from Dragon Eyre. There was a colony on Lostwell, and the survivors were transported from there to the world of the City.'

'Dragon Eyre?' said Daphne. 'That's where Sable is, isn't it?'

'Aye,' said Karalyn.

'And how is Sable?' said Kelsey. 'If you were watching me, then I assume you've been watching her as well?'

'I've checked on her now and again,' said Karalyn.

'And?' said Kelsey.

'Indeed,' said Frostback. 'I, too, would like to know the fate of Sable. She and I clashed at times, but she is Kelsey's kin, is she not?'

'She's my half-sister,' said Daphne. She wanted to say more, but the gleam in Frostback's eyes was making her slightly nervous, and she didn't want to anger the beast.

'I sense your contempt for her,' said Frostback. 'A pity. Kin should not quarrel with each other when there are external enemies to oppose.'

'I couldn't agree more,' said Daphne. 'However, Sable found herself working for those external enemies you mentioned.'

'She didn't know she was a Holdfast back then,' said Kelsey. 'Well, sis? Have you seen her?'

Karalyn frowned. 'Not recently. She was badly injured a while ago, and I sometimes saw her recuperating on a small island, along with a few friends. She had a red dragon with her, and a small blue one, along with a man.'

'Sounds cosy,' said Kelsey. 'The red dragon is called Sanguino, and Sable's his rider.'

'One moment, rider,' said Frostback. 'I noticed Karalyn used the past tense.'

'That's right,' said Karalyn. 'The last time I looked, there was no one staying in the old temple where Sable had been living. It was deserted. I couldn't locate Sable.'

Kelsey frowned. 'Did you not use your powers to try?'

'Up until a few days ago, I couldn't use my powers on other worlds. Then, as soon as I learned, I travelled to meet you.'

'And what's stopping you now?'

'Give me a chance, Kelsey. We've only just got back from the City.'

'So you will look for her?'

'Aye.'

'Do you promise?' said Kelsey. 'Look, I get it. No one likes Sable. She's wicked and selfish, and she fought on the wrong side in the war. She did terrible things. But, she was different on Lostwell. She saved Blackrose, and gave her a damned Quadrant, after Karalyn stole hers! Give her a chance to show that she's changed – that's all I ask.'

Frostback raised her head. 'If Sable was a changed woman on Lostwell, then I dread to imagine what she was like before that.'

'Hey!' cried Kelsey. 'You're supposed to be on my side.'

'I once dangled Sable over a pit of lava,' said Frostback.

Daphne laughed. 'I would have liked to have seen that.'

'She had been attempting to manipulate my mind,' the dragon went on; 'and I did not care for it.' She glanced at the twins. 'Just as these two little ones have also been trying to get into my thoughts. So far, they have been unsuccessful, but I wonder how long that will last. I have never encountered children with such power.'

'I can place some protections into your mind,' said Karalyn, 'but the twins will break through if they try hard enough. Dream mages powers come on from birth, as my own mother can attest.'

'Yes,' said Daphne. 'Raising Karalyn had its challenges.'

'That's the understatement of the century,' said Kelsey.

Shella strode forwards, keeping half an eye on the dragon. 'What's the plan? Is everyone going to be staying here while Karalyn does her thing in Kellach Brigdomin? I mean, I like having guests, but I wonder where the dragon would sleep.'

Kelsey raised an eyebrow. 'Kellach Brigdomin? Why would you go down there, sis? Are you going to finally tell me why you need my help?'

Karalyn took out a packet of cigarettes, and distributed them to the people on the roof, with only Kelsey out of the adults refusing one.

'It's so bad that you need to smoke first, eh?' said Kelsey. 'That doesn't auger well. Is it dangerous?'

'No,' said Karalyn. 'You'll be perfectly safe.'

Kelsey looked disappointed. 'Oh. I heard you say that to Van and

Emily, but I hoped you were bluffing. I can do dangerous things, you know. I helped kill two Ascendants.'

Karalyn glanced at her. 'We've discovered that there's a new dream mage, down in Kellach Brigdomin. His powers can reach as far as here, even as far as the Hold Fast estate. He wants me to meet him, and so I'll need to go to Kellach Brigdomin.'

'Alright,' said Kelsey. 'Do you need me to come with you?'

'No. I need you to stay here and look after the twins.'

Kelsey stared at her. 'What?'

'You're the only person apart from me who can resist their powers, Kelsey. I can't leave them with anyone else, and I could be away for a while.'

Rage swept over Kelsey's feature. 'You dragged me all the way here to babysit your kids?'

Karalyn tried to smile. 'Aye.'

'You fucking bitch!' Kelsey yelled, then she stormed from the roof, shoving Caelius out of the way as she ran down the stairs.

'Well,' said Daphne; 'that could have gone better.'

'I confess that I have rarely seen Kelsey that angry,' said Frostback, 'and so I must take exception to your treatment of her. Kelsey has been excited for days, believing that you needed her help for some vital task that only she could perform.'

Cardova started to laugh, and the dragon turned her head to regard him.

'Is this funny, soldier?'

'Sorry, dragon,' he said, 'but yes; it's damn funny. Let me go and speak to Kelsey.'

'Would that help?' said Daphne.

'I think so. I think I understand what's going on. Kelsey acts tough, and, well, she is tough, but she also has a vulnerable side. Let me get this straight. Before now, the only mortals with dream powers were members of this family, correct?'

'Yes,' said Daphne.

'And this new dream mage could be just as powerful as Karalyn?'

'Aye,' said Karalyn. 'And his range is better than mine.'

Cardova nodded. 'Then he presents a credible and potentially catastrophic threat to the stability of this world. He needs to be neutralised or won over. Kelsey's part in this is essential; I just need to convince her of that fact. See you soon.'

The tall soldier strode away. Daphne and Karalyn glanced at each other.

'I like him,' said Daphne.

'He looks like a Kellach Brigdomin,' said Agang, 'although he does not sound like one.'

'He is a fine soldier, and a fine human,' said Frostback. 'For a while, I preferred him to Van, and thought that he would make a better mate for my rider. However, I have noticed the way he has been looking at Karalyn, so perhaps he is destined to become entangled with the Hold-fasts after all.'

Karalyn narrowed her eyes.

'I didn't notice any such looks,' said Daphne, 'and I am usually quite adept at that sort of thing.'

'Yes, Kelsey-mother, but I am a dragon. I can perceive things that lie beyond the reckoning of humans. I have known Lucius Cardova for several years, and he has never once glanced at a young woman the way he has been looking at your elder daughter. It was subtle, but it was there.'

'There or not,' said Karalyn; 'it makes no difference to me. I have no interest in beginning anything with anyone.' She glanced at Shella. 'I was thinking that a remote area, far from here, might be a more suitable place for Kelsey to stay with the twins. Daimon already knows that we live in Colsbury, but I reckon he would be blind to their location if Kelsey was with them. Perhaps the Holdings desert would suffice, though I don't think I should tell anyone here the precise location.'

'The desert would be rather hot at this time of year,' said Daphne.

'I am used to extreme heat,' said Frostback. 'I often travel to the deserts sunward of the City, whenever the miserable weather there gets too annoying to bear. Are there wild animals to hunt?'

'Plenty,' said Daphne. 'The area that straddles the boundary between the desert and the grasslands is teeming with wildlife – deer, antelope, and so on; but you won't be the only predator. There are large, wild cats that also hunt.'

'I shall respect these other hunters,' said Frostback.

Karalyn stubbed out her cigarette. 'Maybe I should go downstairs to see Kelsey. I feel bad that I didn't tell her why I wanted her before we got here.'

'Why didn't you tell her?' said Agang.

'Because I was worried she wouldn't come.'

'I'll go,' said Daphne. 'No offence, dear, but she might not want to speak to you, especially not after what she called you. I had forgotten how coarse Kelsey can be at times.'

Karalyn said nothing, so Daphne made her way to the stairs. She descended into the cool hallways of the keep, and walked to the sitting room. She peered through the entrance, and saw Kelsey in a chair, her shoulders hunched, while Cardova crouched nearby, talking to her in a low voice.

The soldier looked up as Daphne strode across the polished, wooden floor.

'Do you want me to leave, ma'am?' he said.

'No. You may stay. How are you, Kelsey? Karalyn is sorry for not telling you the reason why we needed you; she should have. It wasn't fair.'

'You don't need to baby-talk me, mother,' said Kelsey. 'It's just... well, damn it, my powers are the only reason anyone ever asks me to do anything. And, if they don't ask, then they abduct me, so they can use my powers to protect themselves. Sable, then Amalia, and then Simon. I'm sick of it. For once, it would be nice to be needed for something other than the fact I can block powers.'

'I agree, dear.'

'Frostback isn't like that,' Kelsey went on. 'She likes me for who I am.'

'I love you for who you are, dear.'

'Even though I'm your least favourite?'

'Don't say that.'

'But it's true. You dote on the boys, you always have. The only thing I had was that you didn't like Karalyn, but you adore her now. I've always been at the bottom of the list; maybe that's why I've been so happy in the City. As the only freak Holdfast there, I'm never compared to the others.'

Daphne sat. 'It pains me to hear you say this. I could tell you that I've never had favourites among the children, but I don't think you'd believe me. It's true that I devoted much of my time to caring for Keir, but that was due to his mind being erased by Karalyn when he was a baby. Perhaps I neglected you at that time, and if so, I am truly sorry. However, those days have long gone.'

Kelsey stared at her. 'Keir's not your favourite any more, is he? You've finally opened your eyes to the fact that he's a numpty. It took me a while as well, so don't feel bad about it.'

Daphne decided it would be better not to reply.

'Where's Corthie?'

'He's in Kellach Brigdomin with Aila and their baby.'

'Oh.'

'I sense disappointment.'

Kelsey shrugged. 'I guess I've missed the big eejit.'

Daphne smiled. 'It sounds as though you have a new favourite too, dear. You used to worship Keir, and bully Corthie.'

'I was wrong about Corthie. I spoke to him about it on Lostwell, and made a full and grovelling apology for the way I treated him when we were young.'

'How did he take it?'

'He's Corthie. He forgave me.'

'That pleases me immensely, daughter. I may actually shed a tear about it later. Now, I think you should go back up to the roof. Frostback and Karalyn were discussing your move to the desert. Karalyn thinks that the dream mage wouldn't be able to track you there. Your part in all this is essential, dear; I hope you realise that.'

167

'Lucius has been telling me the same thing,' Kelsey said. She got to her feet. 'Alright, but I'm not going to apologise for what I said. Karalyn deserved it.'

'Karalyn won't be expecting an apology, dear. She's probably forgotten about it already.'

'I don't get her,' Kelsey said. 'Sometimes she can be so caring and thoughtful; and on other occasions she can act like an inconsiderate cow. At least I'm consistent.'

'You certainly are, my beloved daughter.'

Cardova gripped the side of the chair and pulled himself to his feet.

'You stay here, young man,' said Daphne. 'I would like a little word.'

Kelsey laughed. 'It sounds like you're in trouble, Lucius. Good luck.'

Daphne waited until Kelsey had left the room, then she smiled at Cardova, who had a suspicious glint in his eye.

'So,' said Daphne; 'tell me, Captain Cardova; are you married?'

The tall soldier laughed. 'That wasn't the question I was expecting. The answer, ma'am, is no. I used to be, for two years when I was younger, but my wife left me.'

'Why did she leave you?'

'This is getting a little personal, don't you think? Is it relevant?'

'Perhaps. Please answer the question.'

'If you insist, ma'am. She warned me before I left to go on another tour of Dragon Eyre; she said that, if I went, then she wouldn't be there when I got back. Turns out she wasn't lying. I returned to an empty apartment. She'd even taken the carpets. She might have married a soldier, but she didn't want to *be* married to a soldier. She wanted me to quit the Banner, and I refused.'

'I notice you didn't mention children.'

'That's because we didn't have any.'

Daphne nodded. 'Alright, here's my next question – it's clear that you're fond of Kelsey, but what do you think of my other daughter Karalyn?'

'I barely know her, ma'am. Why?'

'The dragon said that you had been looking at her in a certain way.'

Cardova looked alarmed. 'Frostback said that? Oh.'

'Do you deny it?'

Cardova lit a cigarette. Daphne coughed politely, and he offered one to her.

'Thank you,' she said. 'Take your time with the answer to my question; you seem to need it.'

'You're her mother,' he said, 'and I wouldn't want to say anything that you might find inappropriate, so here's what I will say – I am on duty. I'm not on this world to have fun; I'm here to do a job, and I am a professional. I will not act towards your daughter in a way that might lead to anything.'

'So, you're not denying it. You took her on a tour of the salve City, I believe? Did you enjoy being in her company?'

'As I said, ma'am, I will behave as a gentleman should. You have my word.'

'Good, because if you were to hurt her, then I would be most displeased.'

'Understood, ma'am.'

'Walk with me to the roof,' she said. 'Tell me, how many worlds have you visited?'

'Seven, including this one, ma'am,' he said as they walked. 'Caelius has been to more. I think this is world eleven or twelve for him.'

'I will show you the library in a while,' she said. 'There are plenty of volumes on history and politics, and we also have a rather nice collection of maps.'

'I look forward to that, ma'am. There are few books in the City, and I think I've read them all. Are there any books on the Holdfasts?'

'Not specifically, no.'

'Do you have a family tree I could look at?'

'I could draw one up for you. Interested in my family, are you?'

'Your family are legendary, ma'am, on several worlds. You are the only people the Ascendants fear. Did you not realise that?'

Daphne suppressed a wide smile. 'The Holdfasts are spoken about on other worlds?'

'Spoken about, revered, loathed, feared, loved. If you ever decide to take the war to the Ascendants, then you might be surprised at the level of support you will receive.'

'Take the war to the Ascendants? I'm afraid I don't even know what that means. Why would I wish to do such a thing?'

Cardova stopped by the foot of the stairs. 'Because, ma'am, if the Holdfasts don't defeat the Ascendants, then no one will. They will come for the City, and they will come here, if they can. You need to be prepared.'

'Gods have already come here, and we crushed them. Why would they come back?'

'For the Sextant.'

'Oh yes. The Sextant.'

'And,' he went on, his eyes locking with hers, 'to destroy everything and everyone you love.'

CHAPTER 13
ASTRAY

Plateau City, The Plateau – 27th Day, First Third Summer 534

Keir walked into the palace library and went up to where Thorn was sitting by a desk, its surface covered in heaps of books and papers.

'Are you busy?' he said.

Thorn glanced up at him. 'The Empress has given me three days to become familiar with the finances of the empire, so that I can attend a meeting with the imperial treasury. So, yes; I am a little busy, Keir.'

'That sounds unbelievably boring.'

Her attention went back to the thick volume she was reading. 'I find it fascinating. Did you know, for example, that Sanang pays its share of the imperial tax via goods, rather than gold? Instead of cash, they send us tons of produce, including chocolate, which is then sold in markets all over the Plateau.'

'So?'

'And, by head of population, the Kellach Brigdomin actually pay the most tax, but that's because the trade in whisky is so lucrative; they can afford it. The Holdings pay the most altogether, but the least per person.'

Keir sat down next to her. 'Can we talk about something else?'

'What?'

'Anything.'

'Not just now, Keir. I have to get through this book before lunchtime.'

'But I have nothing to do. The Empress doesn't need me this morning, but I have to stay on-call, in case Bryce requires my services.'

'Go up onto the roof for a cigarette and a cup of tea.'

'I've already been up there half a dozen times since I arrived here this morning.'

Thorn sighed. 'I'm sorry, Keir, but I need to concentrate, and you're distracting me. I can meet you for dinner, but I'll have to work until then.'

Keir frowned. 'And I had this silly idea that we would see more of each other if we were both working in the palace. Quite clearly, I was mistaken.'

Thorn narrowed her eyes at him. 'Go and see what Lord Bryce is doing; and leave me in peace.'

Keir got to his feet and strode away without another word. If Thorn would rather read lists of mind-numbing statistics than spend time with her husband, that was her problem. He left the library, then hesitated. He could go back up onto the roof, but Berra and Bedig had been there during his last cigarette break, and he couldn't be bothered having to talk to them again. Sixteen-year-olds were so annoying.

He decided to take Thorn's advice, and check if Bryce needed anything, so he ascended a floor of the palace and walked to the office where Bridget's son conducted his business.

He knocked on the door, and waited for the reply.

'Come in,' said Bryce.

Keir opened the door and strode inside. Seated across from Bryce was a young Holdings woman, a glass of sparkling wine in her right hand. Keir's eyes roved over her dress, then he faced Bryce.

'Good morning, sir.'

Bryce smiled. 'Good morning, Keir. I see that you've already noticed my guest. This is Miss Tilda Holdwain, newly arrived from the Holdings. She'll be working in their embassy, and I invited her along for a chat, so she could see what we do here.'

Keir turned back to the young woman. 'Nice to meet you, Miss Holdwain.'

She raised a hand, and Keir kissed it. 'Please, call me Tilda.'

'And this, as I'm sure you know,' said Bryce, 'is Keir Holdfast. At the moment, Keir is assisting Mage Tabor with running the vision communications across the empire. Keir's range is very impressive – he can see all the way to Rakana and Rahain, and thanks to him, we're starting to get a better picture of events in those two nations.'

'That sound wonderful,' said Tilda. 'I have met you once before, Lord Keir.'

'Really? When?'

'Oh, it was several years ago now. I went to a festival at the Hold Fast estate. You were sitting next to your wife while your mother made a speech. Afterwards, we were introduced, but you probably had to meet many strangers that day.'

Keir smiled as he tried to recall the occasion, but he had attended so many festivals on the estate over the years that they had all blurred into one.

'So, Keir,' said Bryce, 'was there something you wanted to speak to me about?'

'No, sir,' he said. 'I was actually at a loose end, and wondered if you needed anything?'

'It's good of you to ask, but I'm fine at the moment. Wait, I have an idea. I was about to take Miss Holdwain on a little tour of the city, on foot, so that she can get a taste of life here. Would you be interested in joining us?'

'You're intending to walk around the city?'

Bryce laughed. 'Yes. Is that strange? I often go for walks. When you're shut inside a carriage, you can feel insulated from the lives of the citizens. I like to meet them where they live and work. Mother insists that I always take a couple of palace guards along, but I make sure that they wear civilian clothing, and remain a few paces behind me. So far, I have never once needed to call upon their assistance.'

'But, sir, I was informed that my sister could arrive any day, in order to take you...'

Bryce raised a hand. 'I am aware of that. My bags have been packed for a while now, in anticipation of Karalyn's arrival.'

'Are you going somewhere, Lord Bryce?' said Tilda.

He smiled. 'Yes. A short business trip. I should be gone for a few days. If Karalyn happens to appear while I am out walking, then the palace staff will be able to tell her where I am. Well, how about it, Keir?'

'Thank you, sir; I'd be delighted to come along.'

'Good lad. We'll take in a few sights, and then perhaps stop off somewhere for a drink or a bite to eat. There are several excellent cafes and restaurants in the city.'

He got to his feet and removed a summer coat from a peg on the wall. Tilda lifted her hand, and Keir helped her stand. She gave his hand a slight squeeze as she did so, which had Keir wondering if he had imagined it.

Tilda smiled at the two men. 'After such a long time in the Holdings, one can forget how tall the Kellach can grow.'

'Is this your first time in Plateau City, miss?' said Keir.

'It's my second,' she said. 'I paid a brief visit during the Empress's twenty-fifth anniversary celebrations a couple of years ago.'

'That's right,' said Bryce, as he opened the door of his office. 'You came with your father, Holder Wain, if I recall correctly.'

Tilda's face fell.

'Did I say something wrong?' said Bryce.

Tilda remained silent as they walked through the carpeted hallways of the palace.

'I don't wish to dampen the mood,' she said finally, as they descended the stairs that led to the ground floor, 'but my father and I are not quite seeing eye to eye at present. I happened to turn eighteen a few thirds ago, and since then he has been insisting that I either get married or find a job. I told him I wished to do neither, so then he had the impertinence to propose that I marry the third son of some minor Holdings nobility. That was when I applied for the post in the embassy here in Plateau City.'

Bryce nodded. 'I hope it all works out for the best.'

'You should try to look upon this move as an opportunity,' said Keir.

Tilda smiled. 'That is exactly what I intend to do, Keir. I want my entire family to see how happy I am here.'

They quietened as they passed groups of palace courtiers and imperial soldiers on the stairs, then Bryce came to a halt in the hall on the ground floor. He spoke briefly to an army officer, and was assigned two guards, who disappeared into their mess room to change into civilian attire.

'The embassy can give you a pass,' Bryce said to Tilda as they waited; 'and that means you won't have to stand in a queue for hours if you have urgent business.'

'What job do you have in the embassy?' said Keir.

'I am the new assistant to the ambassador's secretary,' she said. 'A fairly junior role; however, one must start somewhere.'

Their two guards emerged from their mess room and walked up to Bryce.

'We are ready, my lord,' said one.

'Very well,' said Bryce. 'You know the routine by now. Stay several paces behind me and my guests, and try not to intervene unless absolutely necessary. Have you been given an allowance for food and drink, in case we stop off somewhere?'

'No, sir.'

Bryce reached into his coat pocket and handed the guard some coins. 'Remember to sit at a different table. Oh, and you can keep the change.'

'Thank you, sir.'

'That's quite all right. We shall be leaving by the Old Town gate, then going through the old peasant district, and into the Kellach Quarter. After that, we shall make our way through the Emergency Wall, and return to the Great Fortress via the New Town gate. Clear?'

'Yes, sir.'

They walked through the lower floor of the fortress, then left through the old gate that led out towards the south. The narrow streets that stretched out in front of them were bustling with people.

Tilda shielded her eyes from the sun. 'When one is in the Great Fortress, one can forget how warm it is outside.'

'It'll be a lot warmer in the Holdings,' said Keir.

'Quite right,' she said. 'At least here there is a soothing breeze coming from the Inner Sea.'

'This is the Old Town,' Bryce said, as they walked. 'It's still the most densely populated part of the city, but nowadays most of its business is concerned with the harbour and the imperial shipyards.'

'It reminds me a little of Holdings City,' said Tilda.

'Indeed,' said Bryce. 'As the original core of the city, it was modelled on its parent in the Holdings. Back then, this was nothing more than a Holdings colony. Of course, it has expanded considerably since those days. Where we're standing now is the spot where Herald Dyam was murdered, back in five-twenty-four, while she was defending my mother during an attempted coup.'

'Is this tour going to be gruesome?' said Tilda.

Bryce smiled. 'Many gruesome things have taken place here; should I ignore them?'

'No. Please continue. I don't mind gruesome.'

'Well, then, this is also the gate used by Mage Keira to enter the Great Fortress on that infamous night when she killed the mad old Emperor. Shortly afterwards, my mother led the soldiers she had rallied in through the same gate, and they fought their way to the roof.'

'And she became Empress?'

'Yes. She was selected by the most powerful high mages in the world – those who had survived the ravages of the Emperor. My mother was reluctant to accept the throne, but she put her own feelings to one side and did what was asked of her.'

Tilda nodded. 'The benefits of being in the right place at the right time.'

A flicker of irritation passed across Bryce's features, then he suppressed it, and they walked on. They went through the busy streets of the Old Town, then turned left at a large crossroads, diverting away from the long row of arches that led to the city harbour. They came to a dilapidated old wall, and passed through its open gates.

'We are now entering the southern expansion of the city, completed after the New Town was erected,' said Bryce. 'This area is commonly referred to as the old peasant district, but its character has continued to change over the years. Like the Old Town, its population is dominated by people from the Holdings, but the Rakanese have a small quarter on the far side of the river. The cavalry also have their headquarters on the other side of the river, close to one of the seven bridges that link the southern bank to the rest of the city.'

'I think my father's memorial is around here,' said Keir.

'It's down the next street,' said Bryce.

They strode on, then turned left down a narrow lane. At a junction where three roads met, there was a tall plinth of granite, and they walked up to it.

'This is where your father was slain,' said Bryce.

'I don't recognise any of these streets,' said Keir.

'The original tenements were pulled down a while ago,' said Bryce. 'Many were damaged in the fire caused by the archmage.'

Keir frowned as he glanced around. There were no traces of the cobbled alleyway where his father had been killed, nor of the tenement where he and Kelsey had hidden. Tilda leaned forward to read the inscription engraved into the side of the plinth.

'It says that he died saving your life, Keir,' she said.

'Yes,' said Keir. 'Can we move on? I don't like it here.'

'Of course,' said Bryce.

'Tomorrow,' said Tilda, still reading, 'it will be exactly nine years since Chief Killop's death.'

Keir started to feel nauseous. It was the first time he had returned to the place where his father had died, and a surge of unwanted guilt swept over him. For years, he had tried not to think about his father. It was true that he had died defending two of his children, but that simple fact had masked the torrid relationship that Keir had endured with him.

Bryce glanced at Tilda, and she seemed to realise how uncomfortable Keir was feeling. She gave him a weak smile, and they moved on.

'Sorry, Keir,' she said, as they re-joined the main road. 'It must still be very painful for you. I hear your father was a great man.'

Keir said nothing. Why did everyone think his father had been great? So he had fought a few battles in his youth – well, so had Keir, and no one called him great.

'My mother adored him,' said Bryce. 'They were best friends for years.'

They walked through a marketplace that ran along a wide street. Stalls selling fresh fruit and vegetables sat across from rows of meat hanging from steel hooks.

'We're approaching the Kellach Quarter,' said Bryce, 'where more than seventy thousand clansfolk live. The Quarter is several times larger than any settlement down in Kellach Brigdomin, and more settlers arrive every year.'

'I'm surprised that they don't all move up here,' said Tilda. 'I hear living conditions are a little primitive in Kellach Brigdomin.'

Bryce smiled. 'And I hear that they're catching up fast. The perception of Kellach Brigdomin is different from the reality. It's the distance that contributes to that, I think.'

They entered the teeming Kellach Quarter. The tenements grew taller, and the streets narrower, while Keir's nostrils were assaulted by a barrage of odours.

'What is that dreadful smell?' said Tilda.

'There's a tannery close by,' said Bryce, 'as well as the city slaughter-houses, where thousands of sheep and cattle are butchered every third. If you look to your right, down that street you can see the start of Duncan Gardens, the largest open space within the walls of the city. On the other side of the gardens is the river, and then the Rahain Quarter. It takes about forty minutes to walk there, so we'll give it a miss today.'

'I wouldn't want to live so close to the Rahain,' said Tilda, 'not after what they did in the war.'

'Unfortunately,' said Bryce, 'many Kellach here agree with that sentiment. At the end of the war, over a hundred thousand Rahain soldiers were encamped in Duncan Gardens. Then, as we all know, Keir's sister annihilated every single one of them. The funeral pyres burned for days, and then the remains were dumped into the Inner Sea. If you think the smell is bad now, then you should have been here then.'

Tilda smiled. 'How does it feel to have a sister who saved the empire, Keir?'

'She stole the powers of others to do it,' said Keir. 'People forget that.'

'And here she is,' said Bryce.

They glanced up, and saw the huge statue of Keira looming before them.

'Not many people in the city realise this,' Bryce went on, 'but the little girl standing next to the fire mage is Karalyn Holdfast.'

'Are there no statues of any Holdings in the city?' said Tilda.

'No,' said Bryce. 'Only the Kellach seem to commemorate their own with statues and memorials. They paid for this and Chief Killop's memorial themselves, as well as the colossal statue of Chief Duncan that stands in the gardens. No other peoples seem particularly interested in such things.'

'I imagine that Daphne Holdfast would quite like a statue of herself in Holdings City.'

Bryce laughed. 'Perhaps.'

Tilda glanced at Keir. 'I'm only teasing you.'

'It's probably true,' said Keir.

They walked up to the statue, so that Tilda could read the inscription. Keir noticed a few locals glancing at him, but as a dark-skinned man of Kellach build, he was used to people staring.

'There are several decent taverns around here,' said Bryce, 'if you would like to stop for a drink?'

As Keir was about to answer him, the air crackled, and Karalyn appeared next to the statue. Tilda jumped in fright, a hand to her mouth.

Karalyn glanced at Bryce, her eyes passing over her brother.

'Are you ready to go?' she said.

'What, now?' said Bryce.

'Aye,' said Karalyn. 'I've already been to the palace and spoken to the Empress.'

'I have luggage,' said Bryce. 'I need to...'

'I've taken care of it,' said Karalyn.

Bryce frowned. 'You've taken my luggage to Kellach Brigdomin?'

'No, Bryce, I've taken it to Colsbury; we're going there first, to discuss our plans.'

'Oh. Right.'

Keir coughed.

Karalyn glanced at him. 'Brother.'

'Karalyn.'

Karalyn's eyes scanned over Tilda. 'I hope you're keeping out of trouble.'

Keir shrugged. 'You know me.'

'Aye, I do. Oh, by the way, I brought Kelsey back from her world, in case you were interested.'

'Kelsey's back?'

'That's what I said. I need her help with something. She'll be staying in the Holdings for a while, but I can't tell you where. Maybe we can all meet up, once Bryce and I have finished. Mother would like that.'

'Mother would.'

'Pass on my best wishes to Thorn. See you around, Keir.'

Karalyn and Bryce vanished.

Tilda stared at the space where they had been. 'How... how...?'

'That's typical Karalyn for you,' said Keir. 'Abrupt, rude and inconsiderate. There's your great hero.'

'She can vanish?'

'She only has to think of a place, and she can appear there. To everyone else, Kellach Brigdomin involves a journey that can take up to three thirds. For her, it's just a thought away.'

'I would never have believed it if I hadn't seen it with my own eyes.'

Keir felt his anger simmer. Karalyn had completely ignored him when she had first appeared, and had barely disguised the contempt in her eyes when she had deigned to look at him. Stuck-up cow.

'What shall we do now?' said Tilda. 'Should we go for that drink?'

'Yes,' he said. 'I could do with a drink after that.'

Keir dismissed the two guards who had been following them, then he and Tilda headed further into the Kellach Quarter, and selected a clean-looking tavern with a large garden attached to its rear. They sat at an outside table in the warm sunshine, and a young serving woman approached them.

'Do you have any wine?' said Tilda.

'Nope,' said the serving woman. 'If it's booze yer after, we have whisky, gin and ale.'

'Bring us ale and a half bottle of whisky,' said Keir, lighting a cigarette.

The woman nodded then strode towards the tavern.

'Could I have one of those?' said Tilda.

Keir handed her a cigarette, then their hands touched as he struck a match and lit it for her.

'You know, Keir,' she said, 'I got the impression that you and your sister are not the best of friends.'

'She annoys the shit out of me,' he said. 'Everyone thinks she's the saviour of the Empire, but she doesn't care about anything that goes on down here. She lives in her own little world.'

'Does she not deserve a rest, after what she did?'

'I told you, she stole the powers she needed to defeat Agatha. I was one of the high mages who was there at the time, and she took my powers as well. Worse, she took them by force – she didn't even ask first. No one should have that much power.'

Tilda smiled. 'Are you jealous?'

'No. Karalyn's a freak of nature. I'd rather be normal any day.'

They paused as the serving woman returned with their drinks. She set down a huge flagon of ale, along with the whisky and four glasses. Keir opened the bottle, and poured out two generous measures of whisky.

Tilda raised her glass. 'We are in the Kellach Quarter, so whisky it is.' She took a large sip, then coughed. 'This is going to go straight to my head. You'll look after me, won't you, Keir?'

He smiled. 'Of course I will.'

She took his hand and squeezed it.

'Sorry,' she said, letting go. 'I probably shouldn't be holding the hand of a married man. How is your wife?'

'I'm not sure; I rarely see her. We've barely exchanged a dozen words in the last third. Sometimes, I think she's forgotten that I'm here. My marriage is... going nowhere.'

'That doesn't sound very good.'

'I'm sick of it, to be honest.'

'You're a Holdfast, Keir. You shouldn't have to put up with that. How long have you been married?'

'Eight years.'

'And you don't have any children?'

Keir frowned. 'Holdings people and Sanang people can't have children together.'

'Oh. I'm so sorry, Keir. How terrible; I hope you'll forgive me for bringing it up.'

'You weren't to know.'

She took another large sip. 'Thank you for being so decent about it.' She removed a clasp from her auburn hair, and let it fall past her shoulders. 'What a beautiful day.'

Keir nodded. He knew he shouldn't, but he eased his vision powers into Tilda's mind, wanting to see how far she would be willing to take their newfound friendship. He plunged into her thoughts, and saw clearly that her intentions towards him were far from pure. She had lied about having seen Keir only once before; in fact, she had been at many Hold Fast festivals, and had watched Keir from among the crowds. She had developed a teenage crush on him at the time, an infatuation that had lasted more than a year. And now, here he was, sitting in front of her, handsome, rich and bored, and clearly unhappy with his marriage. She hadn't wanted to leave her comfortable life in Hold Wain and travel all the way to Plateau City, but now that she was here, she was going to make sure she enjoyed herself, and Keir Holdfast seemed like a good place to start.

Keir withdrew from her mind and relaxed. If he wanted her, she was his.

Tilda finished her whisky, and Keir refilled her glass.

'Are you trying to get me drunk, Keir?' she said, eyeing him with a smile.

He laughed. 'I'm starting to feel the effects of the whisky myself. You know, you're a very attractive girl; you could have any man you wanted.'

'Any man?' she said, raising an eyebrow.

He stared into her eyes. 'Any.'

'Ha. The last thing I'm looking for is to get into a serious relationship. Some fun, that's what I need.'

'That sounds like a good idea.'

Her hand touched his leg under the table. He stared at her, as her fingers traced up his thigh.

'If you want me to stop,' she said, 'just say the word.'

'I know what I want, Tilda,' he said, 'and I think you want the same thing.'

She stood, her face an inch from his ear, and he shivered from the touch of her breath on his neck.

'Follow me,' she whispered.

She started to walk towards the tavern, and he gulped down the rest of his whisky, then got up and went after her. She walked into the tavern, then made her way to the toilets. He followed her into a small bathroom, and she locked the door.

She looked up at him. 'How wicked of us. You aren't planning to tell your wife, are you? I don't want to be mixed up in some game.'

'Shut up,' he said, and pulled her towards him.

Thorn glanced up at him as he walked into the palace library. 'How was your day?'

He shrugged. 'Boring.'

'I looked for you at lunchtime, but I couldn't find you.'

'I went out for a walk with Bryce.'

She smiled. 'That sounds nice. I managed to get through the book I was working on. My head is spinning with numbers.' She stretched her arms, stood, and kissed Keir. 'So, where did you and Lord Bryce go?'

'The Kellach Quarter. Then Karalyn appeared out of nowhere, and, two seconds later, she had vanished, taking Bryce with her. I had to get a carriage back. Karalyn barely even glanced in my direction.'

'You poor dear. Do you want a cigarette on the roof before we go for dinner?'

He nodded, and they made their way through the palace and up the stairs to the roof garden. Keir glanced at the view, but his mind was on the ten minutes he had spent with Tilda in the tavern bathroom, and he had trouble suppressing a smile. He had to be careful. If Thorn ever suspected anything, then who knew what she might do? Tilda had told him the address of her apartment in the New Town, and he wondered how he would manage to concoct an excuse to visit her there. A thrill ran down his spine. Life in Plateau City had been almost unbearably tedious, but now he had a secret, and something to look forward to; something dangerous.

'You look preoccupied, Keir,' said Thorn, lighting a cigarette. 'Is something on your mind?'

'You know that I had my doubts about coming here,' he said, 'but I think we made the right decision.'

'I'm glad to hear it. If we work hard, and do our best, then I'm sure we can make a success of our lives here.'

He smiled back at her. 'You know, I think you might be right.'

CHAPTER 14
DISPERSAL

Colsbury Castle, Republic of the Holdings – 27th Day, First Third Summer 534

Karalyn and Bryce appeared in the wide forecourt between the Great Keep and the Summer Palace of Colsbury. Bryce staggered as he took in his new surroundings, then his eyes gazed up at the fire-blackened exterior of the palace.

'It looks just the same,' he said.

'Aye,' said Karalyn. 'The Summer Palace has been left untouched since the siege; and it's not the only part of Colsbury that bears the scars from those days. The little harbour is still in ruins.'

Bryce turned his gaze towards the tall, needle-like Spire. 'I have nightmares about being trapped inside that tower.'

'You're probably not the only one,' said Karalyn. 'Listen, Bryce; before we go into the keep, you should know that I spoke to your mother about why she wants you to come with me to Kellach Brig-domin, and I think that it's a bad idea. You should let me deal with Daimon, at least until we know how dangerous he is.'

Bryce narrowed his eyes. 'What did my mother tell you?'

'That she wants the new dream mage to serve the empire.'

'Personally, I don't see anything wrong with that idea.'

'It's a fine idea, if it works. However, a dream mage in the Great Fortress could soon have you all wrapped around his little finger, if his intentions were motivated by selfish aims. With the Empress under his influence, he could soon be ruling the empire. Is that what you want?'

'Of course not, but we have to try. What's the alternative, Karalyn – that we persecute him because he might become a threat? Is that not how the Kellach Brigdomin treated dream mages in the past?' He smiled, though his eyes remained cold. 'The easiest solution would be for you to return to Plateau City to resume your duties in the service of your appointed sovereign. If you were working for my mother, then we wouldn't be having this conversation.'

'The empire will always receive my assistance if it really needs it,' said Karalyn; 'but I will not be living in the Great Fortress again, not ever. My hands have enough blood on them.'

Bryce lowered his gaze. 'Are you intending to disobey my mother's orders?'

'No. I'll take you with me, Bryce, but I'm warning you now – I might not be able to protect you from Daimon. If he can enter the minds of my children, then there's no reason why he won't be able to enter yours. If that happens, then he could make you slit your own throat, if he feels like it. Or he could send you mad. You should stay here, Bryce.'

'My mother has given me a task to do. I will not let her down.'

'Alright. Let's go inside; the others will be waiting for us.'

'What others?'

'My mother, my sister Kelsey, mages Shella and Agang...'

'I see. I am about to be surrounded by Holdfasts and their allies. I should have guessed.'

'We aren't the enemy, Bryce.'

'Then why do I feel as though I have walked into a trap?'

Karalyn smiled. 'I don't know. Paranoia?'

Bryce shook his head, then they set off without another word. Karalyn led him into the ground floor of the Great Keep, and they began ascending the flights of stairs to the upper storeys. Karalyn resisted the temptation to read through the mind of Bridget's eldest child, though she doubted that her mother would have any such qualms.

They reached the top floor of the keep, and Karalyn strode towards the stairs that led upwards.

'Where are we going?' said Bryce.

'The roof,' said Karalyn. 'That's where we're conducting these meetings.'

'Why?'

'You'll see.'

They climbed the last steps, and came out onto the square roof of the keep. Chairs had been carried upstairs, and were laid out to the side of the lead-lined dome that poked up from the centre of the roof. Bryce's eyes scanned the people who were already there, then his mouth fell open at the sight of the silver dragon, and he froze.

'That's Frostback,' said Karalyn; 'my sister's dragon. Be polite.'

Bryce remained where he was, his eyes staring at the giant creature. Her scales and wings were shining in the summer sunshine, as her rear limbs grasped onto the parapet that lined the roof. She noticed the appearance of Karalyn and Bryce, and her long neck swung round, until her face was a yard from where they stood.

'You have returned, Karalyn,' the dragon said, 'and you have brought a guest. Is this the eldest offspring of the Empress of this world?'

'It is,' said Karalyn. 'Frostback, meet Bryce.'

'Greetings, Bryce Empress-son,' said Frostback.

Bryce said nothing, his eyes wide.

Kelsey walked towards them, laughing. 'Look at his face. Hi, Bryce; remember me?'

Bryce's eyes flicked over to Kelsey, then returned to the dragon.

'Give him a moment,' said Karalyn, lighting a cigarette. 'I saw Keir while I was in Plateau City and told him I'd brought you back.'

'Oh aye?' said Kelsey. 'What did the numpty say?'

'Not much. I suggested that we all try to get together, once we've sorted the Daimon problem.'

'That sounds like an excellent idea,' said Daphne, striding forwards. 'However, we should press on with our discussion, if you would all like to take a seat?'

Frostback pulled her head back, and Karalyn nudged Bryce in the back. He started, then followed Karalyn and Kelsey as they made their way to the row of chairs. Daphne had positioned her chair to face the others, and Frostback settled down with her head hovering above Daphne's right shoulder.

'As Herald of the Empire,' said Daphne, 'I shall chair this meeting. Any objections?'

She glanced at Bryce, but Bridget's son said nothing.

'Good,' said Daphne. 'We have a few issues to decide, so let's get started. First, we shall deal with Kelsey and the twins.'

'One moment,' said Bryce. 'I recognise most of the people here, but who are the two soldiers?'

'The Kellach-sized one is Lucius, and the other is Caelius,' said Daphne. 'They have come from Kelsey's world. I assume you remember Princess Shella and Agang Garo?'

'I remember Princess Shella very well from the siege,' said Bryce, 'and I know of Agang Garo.'

'Excellent,' said Daphne. 'Let's continue. Kelsey and the twins will be travelling to a secret location, so that the new dream mage cannot find them. It seems clear to me that Frostback should accompany them, as she will be able to protect them from any adversary, and she also has a mild resistance to the powers of the twins. However, with the exception of Karalyn, no one else possesses any resistance whatsoever. Therefore, it would be pointless to send others. The twins would have them barking like a dog as soon as they were left alone.'

'But, ma'am,' said Cardova; 'I swore to protect Kelsey.'

'I understand that, but your presence would only endanger her. Imagine that the twins ordered you to reveal their location to Daimon – you would be unable to resist.'

'Are you asking me to disobey a direct order from my commander, ma'am?'

'She's right, Lucius,' said Kelsey. 'Frostback will be able to protect us. I hereby order you to do as my mother says.'

Cardova frowned, his eyes dark.

'Thank you, daughter,' said Daphne. 'Frostback, Kelsey and the twins shall leave today. Karalyn can transport them to their destination, and then return here.' She glanced at Bryce. 'The next issue to be resolved has been complicated somewhat by the Empress's insistence that her son accompany Karalyn south.' She smiled. 'Lord Bryce, why don't you explain to us the reasoning behind your mother's thinking?'

'Very well,' he said. 'Her Majesty wants me to ascertain if the new dream mage could be persuaded to work for the empire. His powers would be a valuable addition to the imperial court.'

Daphne nodded. 'My elder daughter could ask him for you. Is it necessary for the Empress's eldest child to risk himself in such a manner?'

'My mother believes that my presence in Kellach Brigdomin is indeed necessary, madam Herald.'

'Why? Doesn't she trust Karalyn?'

'I don't think it's a question of trust,' said Bryce.

Daphne laughed. 'If you say so. Either way, my daughter has agreed to take you with her. You must be warned, though; Daimon told her to go alone. He might not take your presence kindly. I propose that Lucius Cardova goes with you both, to provide some measure of physical protection.'

'Why me, ma'am?' said Cardova. 'You must have plenty of soldiers with experience of Kellach Brigdomin.'

'It was Kelsey's idea, actually,' said Daphne, 'but I happen to agree with her. You could pass for a Kellach Brigdomin, Lucius, and Kelsey has been singing your praises as far as your military prowess is concerned. Would it be so difficult for you to protect my elder daughter, instead of my younger?'

Cardova glanced at Kelsey.

'Don't look at her,' said Daphne. 'Kelsey has already confirmed that you take orders from me while you are on this world. Will you obey my commands, soldier?'

Cardova folded his arms across his wide chest. 'I'll need to consult the terms of my contract first.'

'Come on, Lucius,' said Kelsey. 'Van told you to do whatever I say, and I'm telling you to listen to my mother.'

'She's absolutely correct, Captain,' said Caelius. 'I heard my son tell you to obey Kelsey's commands.'

Karalyn glanced at the tall soldier. Despite what Frostback had stated, it seemed clear to her that he didn't want to go to Kellach Brigdomin. Perhaps the dragon had got it wrong. She hoped that was the case; the last thing she needed was Lucius to have a stupid crush on her.

'Well?' said Daphne. 'Will you obey, soldier?'

'I will,' said Cardova, forcing the words out. 'I am at your service, ma'am.'

'Then Karalyn, Bryce and Lucius shall travel to Kellach Brigdomin this evening,' Daphne said, 'once she has transported Kelsey, Frostback and the twins to their location. And, once she has taken me home to Holdings City. Is that quite all right, daughter?'

Karalyn nodded.

Shella elbowed Agang. 'Come tonight, it'll just be you and me left here, monkey-man.'

Caelius raised a hand. 'Eh, what about me? I would like to be of some use. Perhaps I could journey to Holdings City with you, Lady Holdfast? That way I could learn more about this world.'

Shella sniggered. 'Watch out, Daffers; that's not all he wants to learn about.'

'Ignore my vulgar friend,' said Daphne. 'Caelius, you would be most welcome to travel with me. I could find rooms for you in the First Holder's residence, and you could see the city while I work.'

Caelius's eyes lit up. 'That sounds marvellous, my lady.'

'There is one complication we have yet to discuss,' said Bryce.

Daphne turned her eyes away from Caelius. 'And what would that be, Bryce?'

'Your son and two of my sisters are currently in Kellach Brigdomin. My mother thinks that we should warn them about the dream mage, but leave them where there are for now, so that we don't cause any panic. At some point, however, we might have to extract them, if the dream mage turns out to be aggressive.'

'We'll deal with that when we're down there,' said Karalyn. 'Our priority is to investigate the deaths of the Clan Council members. If Daimon is involved, then that will change things. However, so far there has been no sign that Daimon is opposed to the Holdfasts or your family, Bryce.'

'Did he not issue some vague threats when he contacted you?'

'He did, but I think that was to ensure that I went down to meet him.'

'We should keep all options open,' said Cardova. 'If Daimon is a threat, then, for the safety of this world, he will need to be eliminated.'

'Perhaps our places should be reversed, soldier,' said Frostback. 'If I were to travel to this Kellach Brigdomin, then I could take care of Daimon. If I could bite off the head of an Ascendant, then a dream mage should present me no difficulties.'

'No,' said Karalyn. 'The safety of the twins is paramount.'

Frostback's eyes glowed. 'But if Daimon is dead, then the twins shall be safe.'

'Killing him should be our last resort,' said Bryce. 'Daimon could be scared, and lonely. He's reaching out to us, and here we are, discussing whether or not we should murder him in case he turns out to be irredeemably evil. This is not the kind of empire my mother has struggled to forge. Do we murder soulwitches, or high-level flow mages, simply because they possess the potential to kill people? Or are allowances only made for those who ally themselves to the Holdfasts?'

'Watch your words, Lord Bryce,' said Daphne. 'The high mages sitting here have all proved themselves time and again. Four of us were present at the death of the Creator, and a similar number were in Colsbury when we defeated Agatha. Friendship with the Holdfasts has nothing to do with it.'

Bryce's eyes narrowed. 'If you say so, Lady Holdfast.'

'Stop bickering,' said Kelsey. 'The sooner we get this over with, the sooner I can return home.'

'Quite,' said Daphne. 'Karalyn, are you ready to depart with your sister, Frostback and the twins?'

Karalyn stood. 'Aye.'

'Then please do so.'

Karalyn glanced down at her children. 'Come on, you two. It's time for the little holiday I told you about.'

The twins glanced around.

'Is the dragon coming?' said Cael.

'I am,' said Frostback, lowering her head, 'and I shall take you and your sister flying every day, little one.'

Cael grinned.

'Give your granny a hug first,' said Karalyn.

The twins ran towards Daphne, and threw their arms around her.

'Take care, my sweet babies,' said Daphne, 'and do as your Aunty Kelsey says.'

The twins nodded, then Cael pulled away from his grandmother, his eyes wide.

'Is something wrong, Cael?' said Daphne.

The boy said nothing, his mouth open.

Daphne glanced up at Karalyn.

'I'm sure it's nothing, mother. Kelsey, come and stand by Frostback.'

Kelsey stood, then turned to Cardova. 'No hard feelings, eh? And look after my big sister.'

'I can't say I'm happy about this turn of events,' said the tall soldier, 'but you know me.'

'Aye; that's why I know you'll do a good job, Lucius.'

She walked over to Frostback, and Karalyn took a breath.

The Lodge, Eastern Desert. Go.

The air shimmered, then Karalyn appeared in the blisteringly hot desert, the twins close by. Frostback reared up in the heat, extending her wings as she basked in the sun's warmth.

'Pyre's arse,' said Kelsey. 'I'd forgotten how hot the Holdings gets in summer.'

'I love it,' said the silver dragon. She turned her head, then gazed at a collection of whitewashed buildings.

'This is where Laodoc tutored me when I was a teenager,' said Karalyn. 'The Lodge has everything you'll need. I've already brought the luggage, and there's a well in the rear courtyard. I've also arranged for food and other supplies to reach here this evening. I advise that Frostback stays out of sight when the wagons arrive; otherwise gossip will reach the estate, and I don't want anyone to know you're here.'

'I shall take to the air,' said Frostback, 'and survey our surroundings.'

They stood and watched as the dragon ascended into the sky. She circled once, then sped off to the east. Karalyn dropped to one knee, and gathered Cael in her arms.

'Did something happen when you were cuddling granny, Cael?'

Cael moved his head close to his mother's ear. 'Noli's dead,' he whispered.

Karalyn frowned. 'Who's Noli?'

'I don't know, mama, but Aunty Shella is very sad.'

'Cael had a vision,' said Kyra, 'just like Daimon told us he would.'

'What's Daimon got to do with this, wee Kyra?'

'He talked to us in our dreams last night,' Kyra said, 'when Kelsey was out, flying on Frostback. He told us to look into granny's eyes to see the future.'

'That's impossible,' said Karalyn. 'How would Daimon know that you would have a vision of the future?'

'But he was right, mama,' said Cael.

Kelsey walked closer. 'What happened in this vision?'

'Aunty Shella and mama were looking at a grave,' said Cael. 'Aunty Shella was crying.'

'Can I see?' said Karalyn.

Cael nodded, so Karalyn entered her son's mind. He was thinking of the vision he had seen through Daphne's eyes, and Karalyn gazed at the image. Just as he had said, Daphne was watching Shella weep in front of a headstone in the middle of a vast cemetery. Karalyn peered at the engraving on the stone slab – *Noliyalopo 476-534*. A little further away, groups of Rakanese were gathered close to other graves, and the outskirts of a red-brick city were in the distance.

'They're in Rakana,' said Karalyn. 'Mother and Shella.'

Kelsey frowned. 'When? Could you tell?'

'The gravestone said that Noli died this year. I have no idea who this Noli is, though. Her family name was different to Shella's. More than that, though, I don't understand how Daimon could have possibly known what would happen if Cael looked into mother's eyes.'

'Is it possible that he implanted the vision; that it's false?'

'That's what I'm thinking. To what end, though?'

'To distract us? Who knows? Daimon could be a deranged madman, sis. Take care in Kellach Brigdomin.'

Karalyn nodded. 'Why did you suggest to mother that Lucius Cardova comes with me and Bryce?'

'I don't know if Bryce can fight, and I figured you might need a fighter with you.'

'Aye, but why him?'

Kelsey smirked. 'Why not?'

'If this has something to do with what Frostback said, then you and your dragon can forget it, Kelsey.'

'Who says it has anything to do with that?'

'Don't be difficult. Does Cardova like me?'

'I have no idea, sis. None whatsoever. I mean, you hardly know each other. So, he took you on a tour around the City; big deal.'

'Exactly; so why do I get the feeling you're playing games with me?'

'Maybe it was something you ate?'

'I don't need anyone to set me up with a man.'

'You're reading way too much into this, Karalyn. Lucius is a good soldier, and he's one of my best friends. I would trust him with anything. There's nothing more to it.'

Karalyn eyed her sister, then turned back to the twins.

'Be good for your Aunty Kelsey, children,' she said, crouching down and embracing them. 'I'll come and see you in a few days.'

'Bring more chocolate,' said Kelsey. 'No matter how much arrives with the supply wagons, I'll have eaten it all by then.'

Karalyn kissed each of the twins, then stood. 'See you all later.'

She thought about what Cael and Kyra had told her, and made a quick decision.

Rakana. Go.

An hour had passed by the time Karalyn returned to Colsbury, and the first thing she saw was her mother's angry face.

'What took you so long?' Daphne said. 'We were beginning to worry.'

'Fetch Shella and come with me,' Karalyn said.

Daphne's frown grew deeper. 'Why?'

'Fetch her, and I'll tell you.'

Daphne gestured to Shella, and they walked to the far side of the roof.

'What's going on?' said Shella.

'Does the name Noliyalopo mean anything to you?'

'Noli,' said Shella. 'Yeah, she's my sister. She was embarrassed by the family name, so she changed it.'

Karalyn nodded. 'Then I'm sorry, Shella, but your sister is dead.'

Shella put a hand to her mouth. 'What?'

'Cael had a vision of the future; that's why he acted the way he did. I went to Rakana to check, and...'

'You went to Rakana?' said Daphne.

'That's why I was late in returning. I needed to see if Cael's vision was going to occur far in the future. It doesn't. Noli died yesterday, and her funeral is scheduled for tomorrow. In the vision, you two are standing by her newly-dug graveside.'

'Impossible,' said Daphne. 'I have no intention of going to Rakana.'

Karalyn sighed. 'Please don't make me go through this again, mother. You know that these visions always come true.'

Shella glanced up at Karalyn, her eyes welling. 'Will you take me there?'

'Aye,' said Karalyn. 'Today.'

'No,' said Daphne. 'I need to return to Holdings City. I have a country to govern.'

'But, Daffers,' said Shella. 'Noli was my sister. I have to go back.'

Daphne's features clouded with frustration. 'Those damn visions.'

'You don't need to tell me that,' said Karalyn; 'they're a curse; a burden. You cannot fight them, mother. If I take you to Rakana today, then you can attend the funeral tomorrow, and then come back here.'

'You make it sound so simple, dear,' said Daphne. 'Are you not aware that there is an arrest warrant in Rakana with Princess Shella's name on it? She's been wanted by the authorities there for years. If she sets foot back in Rakana, then we could both be arrested.'

'I don't care,' said Shella. 'We could be sneaky.'

'It's not worth the risk.'

'I'm sorry, mother,' said Karalyn, 'but you have no choice. The best way to deal with these visions is to embrace them. Pack a bag.'

Daphne glared at her daughter, then strode away, the anger shining from her eyes. Shella followed her towards the stairs, then the two Banner soldiers approached Karalyn.

'Is something afoot, ma'am?' said Caelius.

'Mother's had to change her plans,' said Karalyn. 'She and Shella will be going to Rakana for a few days.'

'Oh. I see,' said Caelius, his face falling.

'Perhaps Sergeant Caelius should go with them,' said Cardova. 'He could assist them, or watch their backs if it proves necessary.'

'I would be very happy to have such an honour,' said Caelius, a grin on his face.

Karalyn nodded. 'Alright. They're going to a funeral, so keep your features sombre when they come back.'

'A funeral? Who has died, ma'am?'

'One of Shella's sisters, Caelius.'

'You can count on me, ma'am; I shall be the very model of dignified restraint. Please excuse me; I shall gather up my things in preparation for our departure.'

Karalyn and Cardova watched as the Banner sergeant strode away. Cardova lit a cigarette and passed another to Karalyn, and they smoked as they leaned against the roof parapet.

'I think old Caelius might have a soft spot for your mother,' said Cardova.

'Aye? I was hoping he flirted with every woman he met.'

Cardova laughed. 'No. Just your mother. She seems to have made a strong impression on him. Should we warn her?'

'No. Mother can look after herself. Besides, I think she's secretly enjoying the attention.'

Cardova glanced at the mountains. 'I suppose we should discuss your orders for me. What are my priorities, and what is the objective of this operation?'

'I don't have any orders for you, Lucius. I didn't even want you to come along.'

'The feeling's mutual, ma'am. Van's going to rip my head off when we get back to the City – he expressly ordered me to protect Kelsey.'

Karalyn glanced at him. 'Your orders are to look after Bryce. If the dream mage makes any threatening moves, then get the Empress's son out of danger.'

Cardova glanced down. 'Your mother ordered me to protect you, not Lord Bryce.'

'I don't need to be protected. If you don't like my orders, then feel free to stay here.'

'You're not making this easy.'

'I'm not doing this to make your life easy, Lucius. I'm doing it because we have no choice. Do you think I want to get mixed up in the politics and troubles of this world again? All I want is a peaceful life, here in Colsbury with my children.'

'Does being the most powerful mortal in history not bring with it some responsibilities?'

'Don't you dare talk to me about responsibilities. I lost my husband fighting Agatha, and now I have the blood of a hundred thousand Rahain soldiers on my conscience. If I didn't care about my responsibilities, I would have left the new dream mage for the Empress to deal with.'

'And what about the other worlds?'

'What about them?'

'You are the only mortal strong enough to confront the Ascendants, Karalyn.'

'Really? Kelsey and Frostback managed to deal with Simon without me.'

'Yes, but only after tens of thousands of innocents had been slaughtered. If you'd been there, it would have been over in days.'

Karalyn shook her head. 'Is that how you see me? As an avenging saviour, destined to overthrow the wicked Ascendants? I'm not like that, Lucius. I will never be like that.'

'If you refuse to choose this path of your own accord, then, one day, the Ascendants will come here, and they'll force you down that path. Anyway, that's my opinion. Feel free to disagree.'

Karalyn suppressed an angry response, more convinced than ever that Frostback had got it wrong. A noise distracted her, and she saw Daphne and Shella emerge from the stair turret. Behind them was Caelius, weighed down by luggage.

Karalyn left Cardova's side.

'I'm too old for this,' said Daphne.

'Shut your face, Daffers,' said Shella. 'If you're too old, then what does that make me, eh?'

'Much too old,' said Daphne. She glanced at her daughter. 'Let's get this over with.'

Karalyn was back on the roof of the Great Keep less than five minutes later. She had deposited Shella, Caelius and her mother in a quiet back alley of the dilapidated and sprawling city of Rakana, where it had been raining heavily.

'Are we leaving now?' said Bryce.

'Aye,' said Karalyn, shaking the rain from her hair. 'At last.'

'And then I shall be alone,' said Agang. 'I'm going to miss everyone, especially the twins.'

'We might be back sooner than you'd expect,' said Karalyn. She noticed a pile of baggage sitting close to the parapet.

'I brought it upstairs while you were away, ma'am,' said Cardova.

'Thank you,' she said. 'Are we ready?'

Bryce nodded.

Outside Threeways, Domm Pass. Go.

The air crackled, and the first thing Karalyn noticed was that it was also raining in the Domm Pass. The outskirts of the town of Threeways lay a little to their right, while the green mountains towered over either side of the wide pass. Fields and cottages were visible through the rain, though the main road leading to the Domm lowlands was quiet. They picked up their bags and ducked under the branches of a tree.

'Where are we?' said Bryce.

'Threeways,' said Karalyn; 'the capital of Kellach Brigdomin.'

'Is the dream mage here, ma'am?' said Cardova.

'I don't know where he is,' said Karalyn; 'which is why I brought us here. From Threeways, I'll be able to scan Domm, Lach and Brig. Threeways sits at the junction in the middle of those clan territories. If I can't find Daimon there, we can look in Kell. However, the chances are that he'll sense me using my powers. It's more likely that he'll come to us.'

'I hope he does,' said Bryce.

Karalyn frowned at the two men. 'Neither of you seem to realise that

I won't be able to protect you from Daimon. If he comes, the best thing you can do is get out of my way.'

'Understood, ma'am,' said Cardova.

Karalyn glanced away, the constant 'ma'am' from Lucius starting to irritate her. Her thoughts went to her children. They were safe, she told herself; safe and well-protected.

'Let's find a tavern,' she said. 'We can rent a couple of rooms, dry off, and then I can start hunting for Daimon.'

Cardova picked up the luggage. 'Ready when you are, ma'am.'

CHAPTER 15
SOLDIERS

Westgate, Domm Pass – 28th Day, First Third Summer 534

Corthie held Killop over the high metal railings, so that he could look down at the Domm lowlands.

'Some view, eh, wee one?' he said. 'You can see the whole of Domm from up here; well, when it's not raining.'

'Don't let Aila catch you doing that,' said a voice to his left.

He turned, and saw Brogan standing next to him on the path that ran between the *World's End* and the cliffs.

'He's perfectly safe,' said Corthie; 'my arm's holding on to him.' And, he decided not to add, the lad's immortal.

'Well, do it for me, please. I can't bear to see the little boy dangling over a hundred foot drop.'

Corthie frowned and pulled Killop back from the railings.

'Glad to be heading home?' he said.

'I guess so,' she said, 'though we have thirds of travelling ahead of us before we get back to Plateau City. And... there's Brannig to think about.'

Corthie nodded. The girls' purported father had accompanied them back across Domm from Severton. He had shared a carriage with Brogan and Bethal, and Corthie wondered how they had been getting along. From the look on Brogan's face, the answer to that question seemed clear.

'Do you want to talk about it?' he said.

Brogan leaned against the railings. 'What is there to say? Without a vision mage, we have no way of knowing if Brannig is telling us the truth, and until that happens, my life seems to have been suspended. I don't want to say anything personal to him, in case he's lying, but if he's not... My head's a mess, Corthie. You know, I wish you and Aila were coming back with us. Without you two and the baby, it'll just be me, Bethal and Brannig, all the way to the Plateau.'

'Sorry about that, Brogan. Do you want him to be your father?'

'I have no idea. None. I used to dream about the identity of my father. Sometimes, I would look at the palace guards, and wonder if any of them fathered me.' She smiled. 'For a while, I even thought it might be Calder. He and my mother were so close. When he died, she confirmed to me that it wasn't him, after I pestered her with questions.'

'Bethal doesn't seem to be taking it well.'

Brogan nodded. 'She's only sixteen. It's hit her like a brick wall. One minute, she's laughing and joking with Brannig; the next, she's crying and calling him a liar. If he is our father, then he must be wondering what he's got himself into. What possessed him to tell us?'

'It must have been seeing you in person, Brogan. It might have been easy, you know, when you were separated by thousands of miles; but then he sees you, and he can't help himself.'

'Do you believe him, Corthie?'

'Aila does. She's fairly certain that he's being honest; but I'm not so sure.'

'Why is Aila convinced?'

'She thinks he looks like Bryce.'

'Well, she's not wrong. He does look a bit like Bryce. Apart from his hair. He wants to show us his home when we get to Threeways. He even asked if we'd stay the night, before we all leave for the Brig Pass. What do I say?'

'I would say no, Brogan. You have every right to insist on a tavern. If he's telling the truth, then he needs to be patient. Regardless, the truth will come out when the Empress sees him.'

'The fact that he wants to come back with us to Plateau City makes me think he's being honest. Why would he risk that if he was lying? And he seems to be rich, well, for Kellach Brigdomin. He's not trying to rob us. It sounds terrible, but part of me hates him for what he's putting us through.'

Killop let out a cry from Corthie's arms.

'The wee man's hungry or cold,' Corthie said. 'Either way, I'd better take him back inside.'

'Breakfast was being prepared when I left,' said Brogan, as they set off.

'Good. I could eat a gnarly old gaien.'

They walked into the *World's End* and Corthie felt the heat from the roaring hearth. Bethal, Aila and Brannig were sitting by a corner table, while their guards and servants were occupying two others. A boy was carrying a loaded tray, and was placing down plates of hot food next to the soldiers.

'Sausage!' cried Killop, his arms stretching out in the direction of the tray.

'Did you hear that?' said Corthie, beaming. 'I think that might be the first thing he's ever said.'

They walked over to the corner table. Corthie was about to announce that his son had uttered his first word, when he noticed the grim, sullen atmosphere between Brannig and Bethal. The man was keeping his glance down, as if angry and depressed, while Bethal was wearing a mask of pure fury, her arms crossed over her chest, and her head held high.

Aila glanced at Corthie as he and Brogan sat.

'Has something...?' Corthie started, then he stopped at a quick head-shake from Aila.

'My so-called father has been attempting to explain himself again,' said Bethal. 'It's just one pathetic excuse after another. He says that we were better off without him growing up, and from his recent behaviour, he's probably correct. He says he didn't want to hurt us; well, that was a load of old bollocks. He's done nothing but hurt us. He says...'

'That's enough,' said Brogan, her eyes tight.

Bethal glared at her older sister. 'Why do you get to decide when it's enough?'

'You're making a spectacle of yourself. The whole tavern can hear you.'

'So? There's no one here apart from our guards, and the two servants. Is the serving boy going to run off and tell everyone? Frankly, I don't care if he does.'

'We are the daughters of the damn Empress,' said Brogan in a low voice. 'You need to behave in an appropriate manner.'

'Oh, fuck off,' said Bethal, getting to her feet, the legs of her chair scraping off the stone floor.

Brogan stared at her sister, her mouth open.

'That's no way to speak to your sister,' said Corthie.

'What's it got to do with you, Holdfast?' snapped Bethal. 'Stay out of it.'

The tavern stilled as Bethal stormed away. She hurried to the side door and slipped outside. Brogan put her head in her hands.

'She'll come round,' said Brannig. 'She needs time.'

Brogan's temper flared. 'Don't you start!' she cried. 'If you hadn't appeared then none of this would be happening.'

Kelpie walked over to their table, her left hand clutching the stick she used to support herself.

'I don't want to meddle, dears,' she said, 'but is there anything I can do to help?'

'I don't think so,' said Aila. 'Thank you for asking.'

Kelpie sat. 'It's nae bother, Miss Aila.' Her eyes looked over the forlorn figure of Brannig, and she shook her head. 'So, are ye all planning on leaving tomorrow?'

'Aye,' said Corthie. 'We'll be on our way to Threeways at dawn.'

'Ach, really? And I was hoping to get ye drunk at least once in my wee tavern.'

Corthie smiled. 'Maybe next time.'

'Next time? The last time ye were here, son, was well over eight years ago; are ye gonnae wait another eight years before ye come back?'

'Aye, but last time, I was abducted from this very tavern, and sent to Lostwell. This time, we'll only be down in Kell – just a few days away.'

'Ye'll remember to pass on my best to Kallie, aye? Tell her to get her arse up here; tell her that the *World's End* is a wee Kell enclave deep within enemy territory.'

'I'll do that, Kelpie.'

The front doors of the tavern opened, letting in the wind. Kelpie tutted loudly, then turned to see who it was.

Corthie stood. 'Karalyn? What in Pyre's name are you doing here?'

Kelpie laughed. 'That lassie is making a habit of just turning up like this.'

Karalyn walked over to the corner table, and Corthie saw that Lord Bryce and another man were with her.

'Good morning, Kelpie,' said Karalyn. 'Any chance of some breakfast?'

'Of course, hen. You and yer friends can take a seat, and I'll get Kendrie to make up yer order.'

'Thanks,' said Karalyn. She turned to Corthie. 'Brother. How have you been?'

'Good,' he said. 'It's great to see you, but I wasn't expecting a visit.'

Bryce smiled at his sister. 'Hey, Brogan. Is Bethal lurking somewhere?'

Brogan burst into tears.

'Oh. Uh...'

Brannig got to his feet. 'She's crying because of me, lad.'

'Why?' said Bryce, his eyes darkening. 'What have you done to her? If you've hurt my sister, I'll...'

'Son,' he said. 'I am your father.'

Bryce stared at him. 'No.'

Karalyn raised an eyebrow. 'Would someone explain what is going on here?'

Brogan raised a finger and pointed at Brannig. 'Thank Pyre you're here, Karalyn. Read his mind. Is he telling the truth? Is he really our father?'

Karalyn stared around, speechless.

'Do it,' said Brannig. 'I have nothing to hide.'

Bryce tried to speak, but his mouth just opened and closed, with no sound coming from his lips.

'Alright,' said Karalyn. 'I can go into this man's mind, if everyone agrees. Should I?'

'Yes,' said Brogan. 'The not-knowing is killing me.'

Corthie watched as his sister's eyes glazed over for a second. The table fell into silence, as everyone stared at either Karalyn or Brannig.

Karalyn blinked, then she glanced at Bryce. 'He's telling the truth. He is the father of all five of the Empress's children.'

Bryce clenched his fists. 'I don't understand. How did this happen? Where's he from?'

Aila caught Corthie's glance. 'Let's get out of here.'

Corthie lifted Killop and they stood. 'We'll leave you to it,' he said. 'We don't want to intrude.'

'Agreed,' said Karalyn.

'No,' said Brogan. 'Don't go, Karalyn; I have more questions.'

Karalyn frowned, then sat down. Corthie and Aila eased their way past, and bumped into the other man who had entered the tavern with Karalyn and Bryce.

'Who are you?' said Corthie.

'My name's Cardova,' he said. 'I'm one of Kelsey's friends from the City.'

'The City?' said Aila, her eyes lighting up. 'When did you arrive here?'

Cardova glanced at the corner table, where Bryce was pointing a finger at Brannig, his face red.

'Let's find somewhere more quiet to talk,' said Cardova.

Corthie nodded towards the side door, and they walked from the tavern. Bethal was standing outside looking miserable.

'Bryce is here,' said Corthie. 'He's sitting with Brogan.'

'Bryce?' said Bethal.

'Aye. No joke.'

They waited until Bethal had run back into the tavern, then Cardova lit a cigarette.

'I'm not going to ask what any of that was about,' he said.

'Never mind the Empress's family,' said Aila. 'Well? How is the City?'

'Still standing.'

She squinted at him. 'Your accent... You sound like Van Logos.'

He smiled. 'We're both from Serene on Implacatus, so that makes sense, Lady Aila of Pella.' His smile vanished. 'Listen; I hate to have to be the one to tell you this, but Vana and Collo are both dead, along with Princess Yendra, Prince Montieth, Ikara, Yvona, Salvor, Amber and Mona.'

Aila staggered backwards, her mouth open.

'Pyre's arsehole, mate,' said Corthie. 'Did you have to announce it like that?'

'Sorry,' said Cardova. 'I thought it would be better to hear it all in one go, rather than in dribs and drabs.'

Corthie put his free arm round Aila's shoulders. Her mouth was still open, and she looked to be in shock.

'What happened?' said Corthie.

'The City was attacked by an Ascendant,' said Cardova. 'We beat him, but the price was high. Emily is still the queen, but the old royal family was nearly annihilated, along with thousands of civilians and soldiers.'

'I need to...' gasped Aila, her hands shaking. 'I need to go.'

'Where?' said Corthie.

'I don't know. I need to sit down, alone. Yendra?' She started to weep. 'How could Yendra die?'

'Prince Montieth killed her, ma'am,' said Cardova.

Aila shrugged off Corthie's arm and ran back into the tavern. Corthie started to follow her.

'Is that wise?' said Cardova. 'Give her a moment.'

Corthie first instinct was to demand what right Cardova had to advise him about his own wife, then he nodded.

'Lady Yvona, too?' he said.

'Yes,' said Cardova. 'It was a grim business.'

Corthie stared out at the view of the Domm lowlands. 'I should have been there to defend the City.'

'We had Kelsey instead,' Cardova said. 'You should be very proud of her.'

'Does this mean Kelsey's back as well?'

'Yes. She's looking after Karalyn's twins while we search for a rogue dream mage.'

'Should you be telling me this?'

Cardova shrugged. 'You're a Holdfast. I saw you fight in Fordamere; it's something I'll never forget.'

Corthie's eyes narrowed. 'You saw me in Fordamere, and you're from Implacatus?'

'Yes to both. And before you ask, yes, I'm Banner. I was in the Banner of the Black Crown until the Sextant shipped us all to the City.'

'You were in Old Alea when Lostwell was destroyed?'

Cardova nodded. 'And now I'm in the Banner of the Lostwell Exiles, working a contract for Queen Emily. We fought against the Tenth Ascendant.'

'You massacred the inhabitants of Yoneath.'

'We did. Our orders came directly from Leksandr and Arete – two damned Ascendants.'

'It doesn't matter who gave the orders. You slaughtered countless innocent men, women and children.'

'I know.'

'I should kill you.'

Cardova nodded. 'Probably.'

'Can you give me a reason not to?'

Cardova shrugged. 'Yoneath wasn't even the worst atrocity the Banners carried out for the gods. Some of the things we did on Dragon Eyre would sear your soul if you knew about them. The Banners pride themselves on always obeying orders, no matter how awful those orders turn out to be. However, be that as it may, Yoneath was the breaking point for me, personally. I was one of the lucky ones – I didn't have to carry out the slaughter myself. I'm an officer. My role was to hand down the orders from the gods. But I watched, and said nothing, as the blood flowed down the streets. And now I'm a rebel. I cannot return to Implacatus – they would execute me immediately. Van, too.'

'You know Van?'

'He's my commanding officer, and my friend. Thanks to him and Queen Emily, the Banner of the Lostwell Exiles has never been ordered to kill civilians, or any of the other things the gods used to make us do. Still, none of this makes up for what I, and the others in the new Banner, have done in the past. So, if you want to kill me, here I am, Corthie Holdfast.'

'Answer me this first,' said Corthie. 'Why are you here with my sister?'

'It was Kelsey's idea. She wanted someone with military experience to look after Karalyn while she was down here.'

'Kelsey trusts you?'

'Yes. She and Van are my closest friends in the City.'

Corthie turned away in disgust. 'How can I kill Kelsey and Van's friend? I don't like you, Cardova, but if they trust you, then I guess you get to keep your life.'

Cardova laughed. 'You don't like me? You don't know me.'

Corthie narrowed his eyes.

'Have you never killed in anger, Corthie Holdfast?' said Cardova. 'We both have blood on our hands; in fact, I hear that your family has quite a lot of blood on its hands. As far as I can see, only Kelsey has kept her hands clean, but her dragon despatched many misguided Blades who had been forced to side with Simon; does that make her equally culpable? And what about the God-Queen?'

'What about her?'

'She ended up fighting on our side, Corthie; can you believe that? After all of her crimes, she bowed before Queen Emily, and what did

Queen Emily do? She forgave her. If Amalia can be redeemed, then maybe there's hope for me. There might even be hope for the Holdfasts.'

Corthie said nothing, stung by the words of the Banner officer. He thought back to Van. Hadn't Van also done some terrible things in the service of the gods? And yet, Van and Corthie had been friends; good friends, at a time when Corthie had been at his lowest ebb.

'I'm sorry,' he said. 'I shouldn't have judged you.'

Cardova tossed his cigarette butt over the cliff. 'Thank you, but there's no need to apologise to me. We're soldiers.'

'I don't think I'm a soldier any more,' said Corthie. 'There are no wars to fight here, and I'm trying hard to adjust to life as a civilian. I'm going to give farming a go.'

Cardova raised an eyebrow. 'Good luck with that.'

'You think I'll fail?'

'No. Not necessarily. Though, I find it hard to picture you wielding a plough, rather than those wicked-looking greenhide claws you carried on Lostwell.'

Corthie smiled. 'My Clawhammer.'

'Do you still have it?'

'Arete broke the handle in Fordamere, but Belinda had the Banner refurbish it for me in Old Alea. The Banner artificers did a fine job with it, and I got a chance to use it in the final battle, just before the world was destroyed. It's now sitting in a crate on the Hold Fast estate gathering dust. I have to face the fact that those days have gone. It's hard, because fighting is the only thing I'm any good at.'

'I'd be lost as a civilian,' Cardova said. 'I can't even imagine what retiring would feel like. When I wished you good luck, I meant it.'

Corthie glanced at the child in his arms. 'I have to make it work. For Aila, for wee Killop, and for the children yet to come. The problem is that, without fighting, I get bored and depressed, and when I get bored and depressed, I drink. I spent most of my time on Lostwell drinking. Aila loves me, but there's only so much that she'll put up with.'

Cardova leaned in. 'Tell me; do the others know that Aila is a demigod?'

Corthie shook his head. 'The family knows, but we've kept it quiet from everyone else. I'd appreciate it if you did the same.'

'Understood.'

'Let's go back inside,' said Corthie.

They walked back into the tavern. A few more customers had arrived but there was no sign of Brannig, or any of the Empress's children. Karalyn was sitting at the corner table with Aila, who was crying.

'There you are,' said Karalyn, as Corthie and Cardova approached. 'Brother, I think your wife needs you.'

'Sorry,' he said, as he sat down. 'I thought she wanted to be alone. I didn't know she was in here with you.'

'It's fine,' said Aila, wiping her eyes.

Karalyn gave Cardova a pointed look. 'Next time, leave the giving of bad news to me.'

'Why?' said Cardova, sitting.

Karalyn frowned at the soldier, but said nothing.

'Where's everyone else?' said Corthie, taking Aila's hand.

'Kelpie opened up the back room for them,' said Karalyn. 'They're in there arguing.'

'Cardova mentioned that there was another dream mage.'

'Aye. That's why we're down here. He demanded that I meet him before the end of the third, so I spent all night in Threeways trying to find him.'

'Without any luck, I assume?'

Karalyn nodded. 'It can only mean one thing – he didn't want to be found. I used my powers openly; there's no way he couldn't have sensed them. It might be because I brought Bryce and Lucius with me. He told me to come alone.'

'He could be watching us,' said Aila.

'I would sense if he was using his powers,' said Karalyn. 'But, if he's anything like me, then he won't be found unless he wants to be found.'

'What are you going to do now?' said Corthie.

'Well, first of all,' she said, 'I'll be taking Brannig and the Empress's three children back to Plateau City. They've decided to end their trip now. That means I can take you back as well, and save you the long journey overland. Where do you want to go? Colsbury? The Hold Fast estate?'

Corthie took a breath. 'No, thanks.'

Karalyn frowned. 'You want to take three thirds to travel back? Seems a little unnecessary.'

'No, I mean we're going to stay here. We're not coming back. Kallie offered us a farm in Kell, and we're going to live there.'

'What? Please tell me you're joking, brother.'

'When you get back, could you make sure all of our things are sent down here? They're already packed up in my old room in the estate mansion.'

'Let me get this straight, brother – you're going to become a farmer?'

'Aye.'

'But you know nothing about farming.'

'I'll learn.'

'This is one of the most stupid ideas I've ever heard.'

'Leave him be,' said Cardova.

'What's it got to do with you?' said Karalyn.

'I understand what he's going through,' said the Banner officer. 'Corthie is a highly trained killing machine, who has spent years fighting wars and battles, not to mention his work on the Great Wall slaughtering greenhides as if they were rabbits. Have some sympathy; let him be whoever he wants to be. He damn well deserves it.'

'Didn't you used to be enemies?'

'Even former enemies can respect each other. Corthie's trying to do something that I lack the courage to even attempt. Without the Banners, I'd be sitting alone and drunk in a seedy bar in Serene.'

Karalyn sighed, then turned to Corthie. 'Fine. Go and be a farmer. You know that mother will take this badly.'

Aila smiled through her tears. 'Thank you, Lucius. You're the first person I've met here who understands what Corthie is experiencing. No one here knows the first thing about what he's done, or what he's gone through.'

Cardova nodded. 'I'm truly sorry about your family, ma'am. Princess Yendra was the best god I ever met.'

'There were a few members of my family that you didn't mention,' said Aila. 'Can you tell me about them?'

'Certainly, ma'am. Naxor lives, but Queen Emily has him confined to the dungeons of Maeladh Palace.'

'Why? What did he do?'

'He fought for Simon. He betrayed us all, several times over. In my opinion, he is very lucky to be alive. Doria and Lydia are in Port Sanders, keeping their heads down, while Jade turned out to be a hero. She kept the flames of resistance burning when all seemed lost. It was Jade who put an end to Prince Montieth. Also, Amalia is living peacefully on a small estate in Taran territory, after...'

Aila stared at him. 'What? The God-Queen is in the City?'

Cardova nodded. 'Yes, ma'am. She knelt before Queen Emily, and the queen let her go free. Killing Simon required many of us, and Amalia played her part.'

'I don't know what to say to that,' said Aila. 'Kelsey must have been furious.'

Cardova smiled. 'It was Kelsey, ma'am, who advised the queen to let Amalia go.'

'I can take you back there,' said Karalyn, 'now that I've worked out how to control the Sextant.'

Corthie watched as several emotions passed over Aila's features.

'No,' she said finally. 'I think I'll stay here. Maybe in the future, if the offer's still open, then I might go back for a short visit. I don't think I could bear it just now, not without Yendra and Mona. Even Vana's absence would hurt, and we didn't exactly like each other. And I wouldn't want to bump into the God-Queen.'

The door to the back room of the tavern opened, and Bryce emerged, followed by Brogan and Bethal, with Brannig walking behind them.

Bryce approached the table. 'We're ready to go, Karalyn.'

'Are you sure about this?' she said. 'Are you prepared for the consequences once the Empress sees your father?'

Bryce attempted a smile. 'I don't know if anything could prepare us for that. Still, it has to be done.'

Karalyn stood. Cardova started to get to his feet, but Karalyn shot him a glance.

'Stay here,' she said. 'There's no need for you to come with us. I won't be too long.'

'Take care, Corthie,' said Brogan; 'and you, Aila, and little Killop. I'll miss you.'

Aila and Corthie rose to their feet and embraced the two daughters of Bridget, while Brannig stood in the background, his eyes on the floor.

Bryce gestured for their guards and servants to gather round.

'Karalyn Holdfast will be transporting us all to Plateau City,' he said. 'Please go into the back room; we'll leave from there.'

A few of the soldiers looked relieved at the prospect of avoiding the long journey home, and they picked up their things and strode into the back room.

'We'll be leaving Westgate at dawn tomorrow,' said Corthie to his sister. 'Will you be back before then?'

'Probably not, brother, but I will be coming back to Kellach Brigdomin to continue the search for the dream mage, so I might see you around.' They embraced. 'All the best, Corthie.'

He watched as they went into the back room, then the door was closed. Corthie and Aila sat again, and Corthie passed Killop into his wife's arms.

Cardova smiled. 'Sometimes, I get the feeling that I'm not Karalyn Holdfast's favourite person.'

'Don't worry about it,' said Corthie. 'She's kind and loving, but she has erected walls around her. She was less guarded when Lennox was alive.'

'Is that the name of her husband?'

'Aye, and the father of her twins.'

'When did he die?'

'About seven and a half years ago, but to her it will feel like three and a half. She lost four years in an instant, when she first travelled to Lostwell. That's why she looks the same age as me and Kelsey, when she really should be twenty-eight by now. She missed four years of seeing her children grow. That would affect anyone badly.'

Cardova nodded.

'What shall we do now?' said Aila.

'Well, ma'am,' said Cardova, 'it seems that my schedule has been unexpectedly cleared. What would you like to do?'

Aila leaned forward, balancing Killop on her knee. 'I would like you to tell me everything that happened in the City, from beginning to end.'

'I think I can manage that,' said Cardova, lighting a cigarette. 'Though, I might need an ale or two to prevent my throat from drying out.'

Corthie laughed, then glanced over to where Kelpie was standing behind the bar.

'Some ale for the table, please,' he called over.

Kelpie grinned. 'That's more like it, lad.'

CHAPTER 16
ABANDONED

Arakhanah City, Republic of Rakana – 28th Day, First Third Summer 534

'Let me see,' said Daphne, a cigarette poised between her fingers. 'There was Gorman, and then Asher, and then Racine; so, three.'

'Not bad,' said Caelius. 'I wish I had three gods to my name. I have only dispatched one of the beasts, but my one was an Ancient, so I gain extra points for that.'

Daphne raised an eyebrow in the dim light of the abandoned house. 'An Ancient? What's that? I've heard of Ascendants, but not Ancients.'

'Ancient is the name given to any god who has lived for over ten thousand years. There are hundreds of them on Implacatus; it's what most ordinary gods aspire to.'

'I see. And what was the name of the Ancient you slew?'

'He was a despicable creature by the name of Lord Sabat; a nasty piece of work if ever there was one. He was responsible for a tremendous amount of death and suffering on Dragon Eyre, stemming from his time there as governor.'

'Is that why you killed him?'

'I'd like to say yes, but as you can read my mind, lying to you would seem to be pointless, my lady. No, I had a grudge against him because he had the effrontery to disband the Banner of the Golden Fist. That Banner was my entire life, especially after my wife died.'

Daphne nodded from the shadows of the bare room. They were on the fifth floor of the derelict building, and she and Caelius were keeping half an eye on the streets below.

'I had assumed that you were married,' she said, 'what with you being the father of Kelsey's partner. If it's not too painful, could you tell me how she died?'

Caelius nodded. 'She was murdered by a terrorist organisation on Dragon Eyre. They put a bomb inside a tavern, and killed dozens.'

'A bomb?'

'Yes, ma'am. An explosive device. The knowledge of how to make them is kept strictly secret, but they're used in large numbers on Dragon Eyre, by both sides. My wife was also in the Banner of the Golden Fist, so the terrorists saw her and the others as legitimate military targets. Bastards. I'd love to kill every one of them.'

'I'm not surprised,' said Daphne. 'They slaughtered people who were drinking in a tavern? How disgusting. When was the last time you were on Dragon Eyre?'

'Oh, it's been quite a few years now. To be honest, I have very little idea of what's been happening there recently; the authorities on Implacatus were being curiously tight-lipped about events on that world when I left. That's often a sign that things aren't going too well for the gods. They're happy to trumpet their victories, but grow noticeably reticent if things are going wrong. Take Lostwell, for instance – when Lord Renko left to go there, along with my son Van, I might add, the propaganda machine was in full swing. Then, it all went quiet. I later learned from Kelsey that it was because of your son, Corthie. He had wiped out whole regiments of Banner soldiers, and taken out a few gods along the way. He's some fighter, that boy, by all accounts. You know, I'd like to see him in action one day.'

'I hope that day is a long way away, Caelius,' said Daphne. 'Poor Corthie was never meant to become the warrior that everyone seems to either love or fear. He was always such a contented, happy little boy;

kind and always smiling, and without an angry bone in his body. Then a monster by the name of Gadena took him. He put Corthie through years of training, and he's never been the same since.'

'Gadena, you say? I know Gadena. He's been training mercenaries on Lostwell for decades, or, he used to, to be more accurate. A hard man. Occasionally, we used to see his troops fight alongside us in Dragon Eyre. He trained Corthie, did he?'

'From the age of fourteen to eighteen,' said Daphne. 'He took my sweet little boy and transformed him into a killer.'

'A killer? I've heard people say that he's the greatest mortal warrior of all time. He dispatched thousands of greenhides in the City. On Dragon Eyre, it would take six strong Banner soldiers to bring down one of those beasts. Have you ever seen one?'

'Only through the Sextant, and those ones were already dead. I would quite like to fight a live one.'

Caelius nodded. 'You have battle-vision, yes?'

'I do. Corthie inherited that particular trait from me.'

'Did you have your children when you were very young?'

'Why do you ask?'

'Because you don't look old enough to be the mother of four adults, ma'am. You're in fine physical shape, if it's not too forward for me to say. I would guess that you are barely forty years old.'

Daphne laughed. 'Well, that's cheered me up. Forty, eh? My, Caelius, there's no need for such flattery.'

'All right. Forty-two, at a push.'

'I'm fifty-two, Caelius.'

'No.'

'Yes.'

Caelius peered at her through the gloom. 'Do you take salve?'

'What's salve?'

'Never mind; clearly you don't. Well, Holder Fast, let me say that you are aging most wonderfully, like the finest Olkian wine.'

Daphne smiled. She decided not to tell Caelius that she had frequently made use of Thorn's healing powers to keep her body free from illnesses and strains. After all, she reasoned, he didn't need to know.

'I'm fifty-four,' he said, 'and I look it.'

'You seem nimble enough on your feet.'

'Yes, I am now; thanks to a demigod called Jade. I was forced into retiring from active service a few years ago, with a bad back and sore knees; and Jade healed me in a trice. I haven't felt this good since I was in my thirties.'

Daphne nodded towards the window. 'More soldiers.'

Caelius turned, and they both watched as the patrol strode down the street, enforcing the curfew.

'I would hesitate to call those specimens soldiers, ma'am,' said Caelius. 'Look at the way they're marching, and how they're holding their crossbows in the wrong manner. That shows lack of training, and no training usually means no discipline.'

Daphne smiled. 'I agree. However, they are the nearest thing Rakana has to an armed force, and they seem to be enough to cow the local population.' She glanced at the sky. 'It's almost dawn; the curfew will be ending soon.'

'Shall I awaken her Highness?'

'Don't call her that, especially not while we're in Rakana.'

'It is her correct title, ma'am.'

'Yes, but... fine; it doesn't matter. Yes, please wake her up.'

Caelius got up from his rickety chair and walked out of the room. Daphne smiled. She had noticed Kelsey and Cardova both roll their eyes slightly at Caelius while they had all been gathered in Colsbury, but Daphne was starting to like him. He was an old soldier, and a little stuck in his ways, but Daphne could sense that he had a good heart. And who was she, if not an old soldier, also stuck in her ways? Her children probably rolled their eyes at her, too. For years, she had tried to ignore the fact that she was lonely. She had children; she had friends, yet she still missed Killop with an intensity that surprised her. Sitting on her own in the huge First Holder's residence with no one but a couple of servants for company had become an engrained part of her life. Was it wrong of her to yearn for a little companionship? A little tenderness? She told herself to stop being so stupid. Such romantic notions were beneath her. She was Daphne Holdfast, and she had a job to do.

Shella yawned as she trudged into the room where Daphne was sitting.

'Is there any coffee?' she said.

'No,' said Daphne. 'We left it all in Colsbury.'

'Damn it,' Shella muttered. She walked over to the window and sat where Caelius had been sitting. 'Give me a smoke, Daffers.'

Daphne passed Shella a cigarette. Caelius came over, and stood next to the two chairs.

'What time is the funeral?' said the old soldier.

'Two hours after sunrise,' said Daphne, 'but we won't be attending.'

'Oh,' he said. 'I thought that was the purpose of our visit.'

'Yeah,' said Shella; 'me too.'

'If we openly turn up at the funeral, then you will be arrested, Shella dear.'

'But what about Cael's vision?'

'The vision stated that we were at the graveside, not that we were at the funeral itself,' said Daphne. 'These little details make all the difference. Here's what we're going to do – we shall wait until the funeral is over, and then we shall inconspicuously pay our respects to your sister, before slipping out of the city. At that point, I shall contact Karalyn, and she will come and collect us.'

'I want to stay for a few days,' said Shella. 'I haven't seen the city for nearly three decades.'

'We are not on a sight-seeing expedition, Shella,' said Daphne. 'Every day we spend here adds to the danger. Do you wish to live out the rest of your life in prison?'

Shella snorted. 'Prison? They'll hang me if they catch me.'

'May I ask why, your Highness?' said Caelius. 'Have you been convicted of a crime in Rakana?'

'Yeah,' said Shella. 'Treason. The government that rules Rakana is not the same as the last time I was here. Back then, they applauded me and put a nice little crown on my head. The new government got rid of democracy, and decided to dredge up my past – they convicted me for leading the damned Migration; thirty years ago! They've never forgiven me for that.'

'What type of government is now in charge, your Highness?'

'Stop calling me that, Caelius. My investiture as a princess was the biggest joke ever; an attempt by the old Emperor to control Rakana. Anyway, the new government is a dictatorship, run by a handful of old cronies who hate everything that lies beyond the borders, and who seem to hate their own population even more. No one's allowed to leave, or come in; and the jails are full of anybody who complains.'

'I see. Tell me; how many people here do you think would be able to recognise you, if you haven't visited in thirty years?'

Shella took a drag on her cigarette. 'Um... not many.'

'Then our biggest problem would appear to be Holder Fast, not you, Madam Shella. In the vision, were both of you at the graveside?'

'Yes,' said Daphne. 'Why am I the problem? There are plenty of people here with dark skin.'

'You are too tall to be Rakanese, ma'am,' he said. 'As am I. And our eyes are too small.'

Shella laughed. 'Yeah, you bunch of weirdoes.'

'We shall have to wear cloaks and hoods,' said Daphne, 'and hope that no one notices how tall we are.' She smiled. 'In the Holdings, I am deemed to be a little on the short side. It's rather nice to be considered tall for once.'

Caelius laughed. 'It's just as well Lucius Cardova isn't here.'

'Why do you think I chose him to go to Kellach Brigdomin?' said Daphne. 'If he keeps his mouth closed, then no one there will suspect that he's not a local. I do have a cloak that should fit you, Caelius; I packed several in my luggage, just in case.'

'I always like a woman who's prepared for every eventuality, ma'am.'

'Have you two quite finished?' said Shella. She frowned. 'Where did you guys sleep?'

'We've been awake all night, Shella,' said Daphne.

'Oh yeah? What were you doing? Actually, do I want to know?'

'We were talking, Shella. Don't let your imagination run away with itself.'

Shella smirked. 'Talking, eh? That's a likely story. Don't worry; I won't tell the kids.'

'Must you be so vulgar?'

Shella tutted. 'You didn't seem to mind my vulgarity before Caelius turned up. Now, you're trying to act like a proper lady.'

'Daphne Holdfast is a proper lady,' said Caelius. 'She has no need to act; her nobility shines through the way the stars glisten amid the night sky.'

'Dear gods,' muttered Shella.

'That was perhaps a little too much, Caelius,' said Daphne.

The old soldier smiled. 'I find it hard to believe that any amount of compliments would be too much when describing you, my lady. I confess it openly; I have never met anyone quite like you, Daphne Holdfast. You are beautiful and wise, and yet you are also a warrior, hardened in the furnace of conflict. You inspire me to be a better man.'

Daphne felt her face burn.

'That's it,' said Shella. 'Enough. I can't take any more of the way you two are carrying on. Caelius, Daffers is my best friend, and this is our little trip. Save all this bullshit for when we get back, eh? We're on our way to a cemetery, not a party.'

Caelius bowed his head. 'Understood, ma'am.'

'We'd best be going,' said Daphne. 'We have a long walk ahead of us.'

They left the crumbling tenement block as soon as the curfew had been lifted, and made their way to the southern district where the vast cemetery lay. Caelius stayed twenty yards behind Daphne and Shella, a long black cloak hiding his features, while Daphne wore a hood that covered her eyes from any onlookers. The streets grew busier, with crowds of poorly-dressed Rakanese shuffling towards work, their expressions guarded and wary. Militiamen armed with rudimentary crossbows were stationed at every main junction and canal bridge, their eyes on the citizens of Arakhanah City.

'This is the most depressing thing I've ever seen,' whispered Shella. 'So much of the city is in ruins that I want to weep. This neighbourhood used to be affluent, with beautiful willow trees lining the banks of the canal, and look at it now. It's worse than any slum. When I was last here, things were bad, but this is a hundred times worse than I possibly imagined.'

Daphne nodded, her eyes scanning the street ahead for possible threats.

'Why doesn't Bridget do something about it?' Shella went on. 'She's the Empress, after all. She has the power to intervene.'

'Be sensible, Shella,' said Daphne. 'The Republic of Rakana isn't in the empire. Bridget would have to invade with thousands of soldiers.'

'Then, she should.'

'How many would die? A revolution from within would be a better option than outright invasion. If only someone would teach me how to use the Quadrant, then I could remove the upper leadership of the government with a few flicks of a sword. Go straight for the head of the snake, rather than risk the lives of countless imperial soldiers in a costly occupation.'

Shella frowned at her. 'Your daughter could do it.'

'I'm sure she could. However, Karalyn, as you are well aware, detests violence. She got that from her father. Do you remember her reaction to what we did in Rainsby?'

'Yeah, but she slaughtered all those Rahain soldiers; thousands and thousands of them. Surely she could kill a few Rakanese tyrants?'

'One would think so, but she seems to use the Rahain as an excuse to do nothing. She says that she has killed enough people for one lifetime. You know all this, Shella; after all, you spend a lot more time with Karalyn than I do.'

They quietened as they crossed a bridge over a canal, its waters brown and full of rubbish. Militia soldiers glanced in their direction, but said nothing. When they had reached the far side, they turned right, entering another street lined with derelict and abandoned buildings.

'So,' said Shella. 'Spill it, Daffers. I want to hear about you and Caelius. Are you dating?'

Daphne laughed. 'Dating? We're not teenagers, Shella.'

'I could put it less politely, if you want.'

'We're not anything.'

'I wonder how long that will last. The way you gaze at each other makes me want to vomit.'

'I have no intention of starting anything with Caelius Logos.'

Shella snorted. 'Why not? Come on, Daffers; I don't wish to be mean, but when's the last time you had a man salivate all over you?'

'Urgh. That's does not conjure a pleasant image in my mind.'

'You know what I mean. It's obvious he's got a major thing about you. And he's handsome, if a little too soldiery for my tastes. You deserve a bit of fun, Daffers. Are you worried about what the children would say?'

'No.'

'What is it, then? Don't you like him?'

'Can we have this conversation some other time?'

'Why?'

'Because I'm concentrating on the road ahead, in case any soldiers try to arrest us. Look; I've been married, had children, and those children have grown up. That part of my life is over. The very thought of "dating", as you put it, fills me with horror.'

'Really? Picture yourself waking up in your huge bed in the Hold Fast mansion. You turn over, just as the sun is shining through the shutters, and you see Caelius sleeping next to you. Okay? You got it in your mind? Right; how does that make you feel?'

'A little depressed.'

'Why?'

'Because it's never going to happen, Shella. I have responsibilities.'

'Oh, shut up about your damn responsibilities. Weren't you telling me that you'll soon be out of a job? You won't have any responsibilities by this time next year, will you, Daffers? You'll be leading a life of leisure, just like me. I can see it now – we'll be reclining in the sunshine with glasses of booze and enormous weedsticks, while Caelius and Agang act as our butlers.'

Daphne laughed. 'It's quite the picture.'

'It could be our future, Daffers. Who wants to grow old gracefully? I say we go down kicking and screaming.'

'You don't usually talk like this. Has Noli reminded you that you're mortal?'

Shella grunted. 'What a way to bring the conversation down. You're ten years younger than me, and we all know that the life expectancy of the Rakanese is less than people from the Holdings. Let me enjoy these years, without worrying about death.'

'Just make sure that Agang heals you at least once every third, Shella. That way, you'll still have plenty of time.'

Shella frowned. 'How did you know he was doing that? Have you been reading my mind?'

'I don't need to.'

'Did Agang tell you?'

'No. I guessed. But, I've also noticed that you never complain about aches or pains any more. It's a good idea. So good, in fact, that I've been getting Thorn to heal me regularly for years.'

'What?'

Daphne shrugged. 'It's a sensible precaution.'

'Except that she's now in Plateau City.'

'Yes. I wonder if Agang would mind taking over?'

They swept through busy streets, passing thousands of Rakanese, none of whom glanced in their direction. Daphne noticed that she and Caelius were the tallest people on the road, but the Banner sergeant was walking with a deliberate stoop, his shoulders hunched over, and Daphne's height wasn't too far off the average for Rakana. The morning wore on, and the sun had passed its zenith by the time they reached the huge open space that encompassed the cemetery. It was ringed by an iron fence that had been raided for scrap metal, and large sections were missing. Daphne powered up her vision, and scanned the area where Noli's funeral was due to take place.

'The funeral's over,' she said.

'Did you see any of my relatives?'

'I have no idea what they look like, Shella. There were a few people walking away from the grave who might have been them. How many relatives do you have that still live here?'

'Oh, hundreds. I have cousins coming out of my ears. Around half left with the Migration, and the others stayed.'

Daphne gestured to Caelius, who approached the cemetery gates.

'Ma'am?' he said.

'Stay here,' said Daphne, 'while Shella and I visit the grave.'

Caelius nodded, then Daphne and Shella entered the cemetery, keeping to a gravel path that led through its centre. Long lines of identical gravestones went off to either side, and the dark clouds overhead lent the place a dour atmosphere. Daphne had already scouted the location of Noli's grave, and she led Shella along the narrow paths, turning left and right until they reached a freshly-cut patch of earth. At its head stood a gravestone - *Noliyalopo 476-534.*

'Oh, Noli,' said Shella, approaching the grave. 'If only we'd listened to you all those years ago. I should have slapped Obli, instead of following her into Rahain.'

Daphne stayed back a few paces, watching as her oldest friend wiped a tear from her eye. She remembered her own sister Ariel, murdered along with the rest of her family by the Creator. Apart from Daphne and Karalyn, Celine had been the only survivor. At least Noli had a gravestone to mark her passing; the Creator had left no trace of Ariel, Jonah, or Daphne's parents. Their blood had mingled with the soil of the Hold Fast estate, and although there were memorials to each of them in the Holdfast family crypt, the caskets that sat on the shelves were empty.

Shella crouched down, and picked up a handful of soil from the grave, sifting it through her fingers.

'We all go back to the dirt,' she said quietly. 'You're there now, Noli, and I won't be too much longer. I know you hated me, and I'm sorry; sorry for everything. I was young and stupid, and now I'm old and stupid; but you always knew that, didn't you? Goodbye, sister.'

Shella stood, and backed away from the grave. Daphne put her good arm over her shoulder.

'Have I wasted my life, Daffers?'

'Of course not, Shella.'

'Can we go home now? I want to go home.'

They walked back to the cemetery gates, where Caelius was waiting for them.

'I'm sorry for your loss,' he said to Shella.

Shella nodded, but said nothing, her eyes red.

'Let's get back to the abandoned tenement block, and I'll send a signal to Karalyn,' said Daphne.

They set off, walking back the way they had come through a dreary overcast afternoon. They were a few hundred yards from the tenement when Caelius caught up with Daphne and Shella. He kept walking without breaking his stride, then leaned in close.

'A man is following us. Dark blue coat.'

Daphne gave a slight nod to indicate she had heard, then she pushed her vision out of her body, and glanced back down the quiet street. She saw the man that Caelius had identified. He was middle-aged, and Rakanese, but Daphne didn't recognise him.

'Shella,' she said, keeping her voice low. 'I'm going to put an image of a man into your mind. Nod if you know who it is.'

She entered her friend's head, and showed her the image of the man who was following them.

Shella gasped, a hand to her mouth.

'Is he a danger?' whispered Caelius. 'I can do what is necessary, if it comes to it.'

'No,' said Shella, her voice fraught. 'He's not a danger. It's my nephew.'

'Let's lead him to the tenement,' said Daphne, 'rather than cause a scene out here on the street.'

The others nodded, and they carried on. When they reached the ground floor entrance to the tenement block where they had spent the night, they slipped into the shadows, then waited. The man arrived a few minutes later. He gazed into the dark entrance hall, then walked in. Caelius crept behind him to block his escape route, while Shella and Daphne moved in front of him.

He jumped in fright.

'Hello, Thymo,' said Shella.

The younger man stared at his aunt, then he lunged at her, his fists clenched. Caelius leapt forward, and grabbed Thymo's arms, pulling them behind the Rakanese man's back.

'I wouldn't be doing that, son,' the Banner sergeant grunted, as Thymo struggled in his grasp.

Shella stepped back, her eyes wide.

'I hate you!' Thymo screamed.

'But, Thymo...' Shella said. 'I don't understand.'

'You abandoned me in Silverstream!' he cried.

'I left you with friends, and people to support you,' Shella said. 'I couldn't take you with me; we were on our way to fight the damned Emperor.'

Thymo stopped struggling, and began weeping.

'What happened to you?' said Shella.

'As if you care,' Thymo sobbed. 'My mother asked you to look after me, and then, one day, you were gone. When the war finished, I thought you would come back for me, but you didn't. I tried to look for you, but I got lost in the mountains and crossed the border into Rakana, where the militia picked me up and sent me to a home for orphans and abandoned children. That's what happened to me, Shella; that's what you did to my life. I was eighteen before I saw my mother again.'

Shella looked stunned. 'I... I... I'm sorry.'

'I hope you die alone,' Thymo said, pure hatred in his eyes; 'that's all I wanted to say to you. Alone and unloved, so that you might know how I felt for all those years.' He tried to pull Caelius's grasp from his arms, but the Banner sergeant's grip was firm. 'Let me go! I'm done. I just want to go back to my home now. I've said what I came to say.'

Caelius glanced at Shella and Daphne. Shella nodded.

'All right,' said Caelius. 'I'm going to release you now. No funny business.'

Caelius let go of Thymo's arms, and the Rakanese man turned and fled from the building.

'We should move to a different tenement,' said Daphne.

'Why?' said Shella. 'Thymo would never betray us. He hates me, but he would never do that.'

'Let's not take any chances. Are you alright?'

'No,' shouted Shella. 'How do you think I'm feeling, Daffers? You heard him; I ruined his life.'

Daphne said nothing. She tried to remember anything about Thymo that Shella might have mentioned to her over the long years of their friendship. She recalled her saying that she had briefly looked after one of her siblings' children, while Daphne had been with Killop and Karalyn in Slateford, but that was it. Could it be true? Had Shella abandoned Thymo as a boy in Silverstream?

'I'm not going to stand here and argue about it,' Daphne said in a low, calm voice. 'We should find a new tenement to hide in, and then I will call out for Karalyn. Caelius; could you please go upstairs and fetch our things, and then we'll be off.'

Caelius hurried away, then Daphne and Shella stood in silence.

'It's not what you think,' mumbled Shella, her gaze on the ground.

'I'm not thinking anything, Shella,' said Daphne. 'Let's keep our focus on getting out of here.'

Caelius returned with their luggage, then he and Daphne walked towards the doorway. Shella hesitated, then emitted a low groan and followed them. They carried on down the street, then Daphne scanned ahead. She found another empty, derelict building, and guided the others towards it. She used her vision to check they weren't being trailed by anyone, then they entered the dilapidated tenement block. The ground floor bore signs of recent flooding, so they went up the stone steps to the next level, where Caelius forced open a door.

'This will do,' said Daphne, glancing around at the bare room. 'Shella, we need to talk, but it can wait until we're safely back in Colsbury.'

Shella didn't respond. She went to the shuttered window, sat down on the floor, and lit a cigarette. Daphne glanced at Caelius, but neither spoke. Caelius dumped their luggage onto the sagging floorboards.

'Give me a moment,' Daphne said to him. 'I'll see if I can find Karalyn.'

Daphne felt for her vision, ready to send it out in the direction of Plateau City, then she gasped. Her powers weren't there. Worse, it felt as though they had never existed. She tried to draw upon a thread of battle-vision. Nothing. A rush of vulnerability and weakness surged through her, and her knees almost buckled.

Caelius raised an eyebrow. 'Ma'am? Are you alright?'

Daphne stared at him. 'My powers have gone.'

CHAPTER 17
CARRYING A SECRET

Plateau City, The Plateau – 28th Day, First Third Summer 534

Keir and Tilda smoothed down their clothes in the cramped confines of the embassy bathroom.

'We have to stop meeting like this,' Tilda whispered; 'though, at least this bathroom's cleaner than the one we were in yesterday. Next time, let me know when you're going to visit the embassy.'

'I couldn't help myself,' said Keir. 'I wanted you. I've thought about nothing else since we parted.'

She placed a hand on his chest. 'You should probably think of a better excuse to visit. Delivering the mail to the embassy is hardly the sort of thing that a high mage would do. I don't want to get caught, Keir; are you listening to me? My father would kill you if he discovered what we were up to, and doesn't your wife have the ability to stop people's hearts with a glance?'

'We won't get caught,' he said, as his fingers brushed through Tilda's hair. 'We're too smart for that.'

Worry passed over Tilda's expression. 'You do know that there's a vision mage resident in the embassy? He's not as powerful as you, but he can read minds. What if he reads mine?'

'Make sure that you're always thinking about something else when he's around.'

'That's easy for you to say. All I think about is you, Keir. Last night, for the first time, my bed seemed too big, and I wished you were with me.'

Keir frowned. 'You know I can't stay over at your apartment. I can visit, but I can't stay the whole night; people would get suspicious.'

'I know,' she said. 'Listen; I'll leave first. You'd better wait here a few minutes before coming out. Alright?'

She kissed him, then unbarred the bathroom door. She peered through the doorway, then slipped out. Keir shut the door behind her, re-locked it, then leaned against the washbasin. He closed his eyes, and pictured Tilda in his arms, then he thought about what she had said. It had probably been too impulsive of him to visit the Holdings Embassy so soon after meeting Tilda, but he had lain awake thinking about her all night, while Thorn had slept by his side. He frowned at the memory of his wife. This was her fault. If she had paid more attention to her husband, then he wouldn't have been ensnared by the first pretty young woman who had come along. With Tilda, things were more simple. He had looked into her thoughts that morning, and had sensed the raw passion that she felt towards him. It had been her desire that had made him decide to go to the embassy; her desire that had made him suggest that they walk to the bathroom. Thorn had once felt the same desire towards him, but that flame had dimmed over the years. Of course, he couldn't read Thorn's thoughts the way he had gone through Tilda's, so he never really knew how Thorn felt. Maybe that was the problem.

After he had waited long enough, Keir unlocked the bathroom door and strode out into an empty hallway. He walked down the corridor until he reached the embassy's main office. Tilda was sitting at a desk with her eyes on her work, and Keir kept his gaze away from her.

The ambassador's secretary glanced up at him. 'Ah, Lord Holdfast. I thought that you had returned to the Great Fortress.'

'I'm on my way now,' he said.

The secretary lifted a bundle of sealed papers from his desk. 'I would be much obliged if you conveyed these documents to Lord Bryce's office. It'll save me a trip later.'

'Of course,' he said. 'It's no trouble at all.'

Keir quickly entered the mind of the secretary, and was pleased to see that the man seemed to suspect nothing about his real reasons for visiting the embassy. Keir took the bundle of papers, then strode towards the main entrance. He smiled as he stepped outside into the warm sunshine. He had got away with it. His nerves were tingling with barely-suppressed excitement, and he wondered how soon he should wait before calling at Tilda's apartment. Too soon, and he might frighten her off; too long, and she might lose interest. As he began walking through the wide, neat streets of the city's New Town, he realised that he didn't particularly care if Tilda lost interest. There were always more young women; the city was full of them. There would be many, he thought, that would jump at the chance to be with the famous Keir Holdfast. He was rich, powerful and handsome – what else did women want? They were shallow creatures, easily entranced by men like him.

He walked by a side road that led to the Holdfast townhouse, and he wondered if Tabitha was there. She would be on her own, and for a moment he imagined what it would be like to sleep with her so soon after being with Tilda. He had never slept with two different women on the same day, and he felt the urge to do so grow within him. He glanced at the position of the sun. No. He needed to get back to the Great Fortress before people began to wonder what had happened to him. Besides, Tabitha was a silly bitch, who might have the gall to turn him down.

He crossed a road by the university, and turned towards the Great Fortress. He watched as a young couple pushed a pram on the opposite pavement, and, for a split second, a twinge of jealousy swept over him. His marriage to Thorn had denied him a life with children, while that evil witch Jemma kept Cole all to herself. It was unjust, but what could he do? He couldn't divorce Thorn, because he was certain that another man would come along and replace him; and that was unthinkable. He would kill any man who touched her; it was a matter of honour.

Keir crossed the bridge over the dry moat, and entered the Great Fortress. Soldiers stood to attention as he passed them, and an officer saluted, then bowed his head. Keir ignored them, and walked to the stairs, the bundle of papers under his arm.

With Bryce away, the corridors of the palace seemed quieter than normal, and Keir made for the Empress's main reception hall. Inside, beyond the line of soldiers guarding the doorways, Empress Bridget was speaking to Thorn from her raised throne. Thorn was in one of her blue dresses, and had her hands clasped behind her back, listening while the Empress spoke.

Keir approached the throne, and bowed his head.

Bridget raised an eyebrow. 'I thought you'd buggered off back to the Holdings, Keir. What took you?'

'It's a beautiful day, your Majesty,' said Keir. 'I might have dawdled on the way back from the embassy. Apologies.'

'Skive on your own time, Keir,' said the Empress. 'I pay you to be here, not to be delivering mail that could be taken by a courier. What's that under your arm?'

'The ambassador's secretary asked that I bring these documents to Lord Bryce's office, your Majesty.'

'I guess that makes you the highest-paid postman in the city, Keir. Next time, tell Mage Tabor where you're going. He's been moping around the palace looking for you. There's a great big pile of messages that need to be communicated throughout the empire.'

'I will be sure to keep him informed, your Majesty.'

'Well? Get to work, you lazy bastard.'

Keir bowed his head, then backed away. He caught Thorn's gaze, and she gave him a brief smile. She knows nothing, he thought, and smiled back.

'One moment, Keir,' said the Empress.

He turned. 'Yes, your Majesty?'

'Where's your mother? Mage Tabor says she's not in Holdings City, and she's not on the Hold Fast estate, or in Colsbury. What use is she as Herald of the Empire if I can't find her?'

'I don't know where she is, your Majesty.'

Bridget gave him a suspicious glance. 'If you find out, tell me at once.'

'I shall, your Majesty.'

He retreated from the hall, and made his way to Tabor's office, passing a classroom where Berra and Bedig were being given lessons by a Holdings tutor. Keir chuckled at the bored expressions on the teenagers' faces, then knocked on Tabor's door.

Tabor opened it, and narrowed his eyes.

'Nice of you to turn up, Keir,' he said.

'My apologies, sir,' said Keir. 'Next time, I will remember to let you know where I'm going.'

'There won't be a next time,' said Tabor. 'You shouldn't be delivering mail to a damn embassy; you have far more important things to do here.' He pointed to a heap of papers on his desk. 'I'm going for lunch – get started on those messages. I want them all sent before you finish work today.'

Keir tried to suppress the scowl that appeared on his face, as Tabor squeezed past him and left the office. Keir walked into the empty room, and closed the door. He sat down in his chair, then got up, walked behind the desk, and sat in Tabor's chair instead, then put his feet up on the table. He set down the bundle of documents that he had received from the embassy, and lifted the first message from the pile. It was addressed to a minor fort close to the border with southern Sanang, and was requesting information regarding the number of rogue bandits that had been seen over the previous few thirds. Keir sighed. Such clerical work was beneath him, but what choice did he have? If he wanted to maintain his lifestyle, he had to swallow his pride and do whatever that fool Tabor asked him to do. He opened a window, lit a cigarette, and got to work.

Keir was on his seventh message when Thorn appeared in the doorway.

He glanced up from the desk. 'What is it? I'm busy.'

Thorn's face remained expressionless. 'Oh,' she said, 'so you don't want to know that Karalyn has just arrived?'

Keir frowned. 'What does she want? I thought she was in Kellach Brigdomin.'

'Come and see. Unless you're too busy, of course.'

He got up from the desk, and stretched his arms.

'The Empress hates it when you smoke inside the palace,' said Thorn.

'I had the damn window open.'

'I can see that, but I can still smell the smoke.'

Keir shrugged. 'Tabor was being a dick.'

Thorn smiled. 'And so you thought you'd smoke in his office? Anyway, let's not argue. How was the embassy?'

'Fine, I guess,' he said, as they walked into the corridor.

'Did you meet any interesting people?'

'No.'

'I might go along, and introduce myself to the staff who work there. It's always useful to have a friend in the Holdings Embassy.'

Keir smiled, but his heart began to pound. Was Thorn playing games with him? Had she somehow discovered the truth; perhaps she was trying to trap him, or make him say something stupid that would reveal his guilt.

The sound of angry yelling reached his ears.

'That sounds like Bryce,' said Keir.

Thorn nodded. 'He's back, too, and he's not the only one.'

They passed the soldiers posted at the entrance to the reception hall, and strode inside. The Empress was sitting on her throne with her mouth open, a look of shock on her face. In front of her stood three of her children – Bryce, Brogan and Bethal, along with Karalyn, and a man Keir didn't recognise.

'I don't want him anywhere near me!' cried Bethal. 'We should have left him in Domm!'

'Be reasonable, Bethal,' said Bryce, his eyes flashing with anger. 'At least if he's here, then he can't be spreading rumours all over Kellach Brigdomin.'

Karalyn noticed Thorn and Keir's arrival, and beckoned them over.

'Now that you're here,' she said, 'I can leave.'

'You're going nowhere, Karalyn,' boomed the Empress's voice.

'But, your Majesty,' said Karalyn, 'my brother can read Brannig's thoughts. He can answer any questions about his identity.'

'Are you out of your mind?' cried Bridget. 'I don't need anyone to read Brannig's thoughts. I damn well know who he is. I need you to wipe his memories.'

The hall quietened.

'You can't be serious, mother,' said Brogan.

'Please,' said Brannig; 'I beg you – don't make me forget who I am.'

Bridget glared at him, her eyes lit with fury. 'You broke your word. You promised me that this would never happen, and I trusted you.'

A side door opened, and the Holdings tutor entered, followed by Berra and Bedig. The two children gazed at the scene before them.

'Has something happened?' said Berra.

Brannig turned to them, his eyes starting to well. 'My children,' he whispered.

'What?' said Bedig, his unruly red hair falling well past his ears. 'Mother, who is this man?'

'This treacherous bawbag is your father,' said Bridget.

'Holy shit,' Keir spluttered. 'Um, apologies, your Majesty.'

'Forget it, Keir,' said the Empress. 'That was pretty much my reaction too.'

Bedig took a step towards Brannig, then stopped, while Berra stared at her father, her eyes wide.

'It's true,' said Brogan. 'He approached us in Severton.'

'When did you all get here?' said Bedig.

'Karalyn brought us back,' said Bryce. 'Mother, should we clear the room? This fiasco should be for the family alone to witness.'

'What's the point?' said Bridget. 'Word will get out, even if we do wipe his memories – there's no stopping that now. Brannig, look at me, you useless prick; look at me and tell me why. Why have you betrayed me?'

Brannig faced the Empress, but was unable to meet her glance. 'I can't explain it, your Majesty. I didn't intend to say or do anything, but... then I saw Brogan and Bethal, and I couldn't stop myself. The urge to speak to them was irresistible. For years, I have done as you asked. I never uttered a single word to anyone about the truth; I kept it all to myself, despite the pain it caused me. I would listen to ignorant folk speculate about the children's parentage, but never once said a thing. I'm so sorry.'

Bridget continued to stare at him, her face a mask of anger. 'What do you want?'

'Nothing, your Majesty,' said Brannig. 'I only wanted to see my children.'

'Well, you've done that now. Karalyn, take him back to Domm.'

'No!' cried Berra. 'If he's our father, then I want him to stay.'

'Shut up,' said Bethal. 'You don't know what you're talking about.'

'But you've spent time with him,' said Berra. 'That's not fair. All I want is the chance to do the same thing.'

'Mother's right,' said Bryce. 'He wanted to see us, and he's seen us. We should send him away.'

'Let's not rush into anything,' said Brogan. 'Maybe we should give it a day or two, so that we can all calm down.'

'I am calm!' yelled Bethal.

'Wait,' said Berra. 'That's two votes apiece. Bedig, what do you say?'

The red-haired boy looked alarmed at the gazes directed his way. 'I don't know. Maybe... maybe he should get to stay, for a while.'

Berra beamed. 'Three votes to two. We win.'

'Hold on,' said Bridget. 'This isn't a democracy. What I say goes.'

Keir suppressed a smirk as Bridget's five children all shouted at the same time. This was far more entertaining than sending stupid messages around the empire. For the first time ever, Bridget seemed at a loss. She stared down from the throne at her squabbling children, as if she had no idea what to do. She looked ill and tired, and perhaps even a little frightened by the effects of Brannig's revelation on her offspring. Bethal had a finger pointed in Berra's face, and the identical twins seemed to be on the verge of punching each other, while Bryce was shouting at Bedig. Even the normally-sensible Brogan was raising her voice to be heard above the cacophony.

Thorn stepped forward. 'May I suggest a compromise?'

Seeing that her words had achieved nothing, Thorn glanced at Karalyn, who nodded. Karalyn raised a finger, and the hall fell utterly silent.

'Thank you, Karalyn,' said Thorn. 'I would like to make a suggestion. If Karalyn and Lord Bryce can be spared for a day or two, then perhaps Brannig could stay in the Holdfast townhouse. That way, he won't disrupt the business of the palace, and the children could visit him there. Once Karalyn and Lord Bryce return to Kellach Brigdomin to resume their search for the dream mage, then they could take Brannig back with them. Would two days seem sufficient, your Majesty?'

Bridget said nothing for a moment, then she nodded. 'Alright. Two days; if Karalyn deems her absence from Kellach Brigdomin will not cause any problems.'

'I spent an entire night hunting for Daimon, your Majesty,' said Karalyn, 'but he refused to reveal himself to me. I don't think another two days would make any difference. Also, I might need to leave for a while, to collect my mother.'

Bridget emitted a grim laugh. 'And where is my errant Herald?'

'I would rather give you that information in private, your Majesty.'

'Is she safe?'

'Aye, your Majesty. I'm waiting for her to contact me, to let me know that she's ready to leave her present location. And, if I'm here, then it will be easier for her to find me.'

Bridget scratched her cheek below where her metal eye patch sat, then exhaled.

'Listen to me,' she said. 'This is what's going to happen. Thorn, please escort Brannig to the Holdfast townhouse. Children – you are free to visit Brannig there as often as you like, or not at all, over the next two days. Brannig, I don't want you anywhere near the palace. Stay in the townhouse, and do not leave. Keir and Karalyn, come with me to my study. You are all dismissed.'

Bethal cursed under her breath and stormed from the hall, closely followed by Bryce; while Berra and Bedig approached Thorn and Brannig.

'I will summon a carriage,' said Thorn. 'Follow me, please.'

Thorn led Brannig and the two children out of the hall, then the Holdings tutor bowed and hurried away. Brogan remained where she was, a deep frown on her lips.

'Well, Brogan?' said Bridget. 'Out with it, girl.'

'There's something about Brannig, mother; something that stops me from trusting him.'

'I'm not surprised,' said Bridget. 'I trusted him, and look where that got us. He swore to me that he would never do the exact thing that he has just done. You should know, Brogan, that I have never loved your father. He appeared one day at the old palace, because he had heard that I was close to his brother. At that stage of my life, the last thing on my mind was children, but meeting him sparked something within me. I loved Bedig so much that his death nearly destroyed me, and there, unexpectedly, was his twin brother. I seduced him. I'm not proud of it, but it brought me you and Bryce, and then it brought me the triplets. Even though I slept with him several times, my heart was never his. I'm not sure if I even liked him very much; but he was Bedig's twin brother, and that was all that mattered to me. I'm sorry that you had to find out this way, Brogan.'

The Empress's daughter bowed her head. 'It's alright, mother. I think I understand. All the same, I can't help feeling that he has an ulterior motive.'

Bridget turned to Karalyn. 'Have you read his mind?'

'Aye, your Majesty. Back in Domm, I needed to check that he was telling the truth.'

'Did you see anything in there that might rouse your suspicions?'

'No, but I didn't go in very deeply.'

'I want you to raid his mind thoroughly; do you hear me, Karalyn? If Brogan is right, I want to know. Do it before you take him back to Domm.'

Karalyn frowned, but nodded.

'Right; off with you, Brogan. Plenty of your old friends missed you while you were down south; go and see them. Oh, and try to relax. Not every problem is yours to solve.'

Brogan nodded, then walked from the hall.

'You gave Brogan a nice speech, your Majesty,' said Karalyn. 'It's a pity you didn't say all that while the rest of your children were here.'

Bridget gripped the sides of the throne and struggled to her feet. 'Don't get smart with me, Karalyn. You know fine well that Brogan is the most level-headed of my bairns. She's the only one that reminds me of what I was like in my youth. Still, Bryce was born thirty minutes before her, so that's that.'

The Empress headed towards a side door, and Keir frowned. It was the first time he had seen Bridget out of a chair for many days, and she was having some difficulty walking.

'Pyre's arse,' she muttered, as she reached the door. 'My hips, my knees, my back; I can't work out which are more buggered.'

'Please, your Majesty,' said Keir; 'allow Thorn to heal you.'

Bridget glared at him. 'No chance. Don't even think about suggesting that to Thorn. I carry this pain with pride, and as a reminder of the pain each of my decisions bring to the folk of this empire. Without it, I might forget why I'm doing this job.'

'But...'

'No buts, Keir. Thorn will leave me alone; understood?'

Keir bowed her head. 'Yes, your Majesty.'

Keir and Karalyn followed the Empress into her small study, where she fell into her large armchair.

'Close the door,' she said to Keir, who did as he was told.

'Right,' said the Empress. 'Karalyn – where is Daphne?'

'She is in Rakana, your Majesty.'

Bridget's face reddened. 'What in Pyre's name is she doing there? She's supposed to be running the damn Holdings.'

'One of Shella's sisters died, and she and my mother wanted to go to the funeral.'

'So? You took them there, I assume?'

'I did.'

Bridget let out a loud groan. 'Do you realise how close we are to war with those bastards? What were you thinking? What happens if they're discovered? Shella was sentenced to death for treason by the eejits that rule Rakana, and Daphne is the fucking Herald of the Empire! If they get arrested, what are my options? Send in the troops? Do you never think things through, Karalyn?'

Keir glanced at Karalyn, but his sister seemed unruffled by the Empress's outburst.

'I did what I thought best, your Majesty,' she said.

'You're yer mother's daughter, right enough. You always jump in first, without considering the consequences, you dozy cow.' She leaned forward in the armchair. 'The moment she contacts you, get them out of there. Am I clear?'

'Aye.'

'Aye, what, Karalyn?'

'Aye, your Majesty.'

'Between Brannig's treachery, and the bloody-minded obstinacy of you Holdfasts, it's a wonder I'm still alive. My heart cannae take much more of this bullshit. The bloody Holdfasts will be the death of me. Away with the pair of ye.'

Keir and Karalyn bowed their heads, then left the room.

Keir began chuckling as they walked along the palace corridors. 'You got your arse handed to you there, Karalyn.'

His sister smiled at him. 'How's your marriage, Keir?'

Keir's laughter fell away. 'Shut up.'

'Or what?'

'You think you're so wonderful, but you're a sad, pathetic failure. Everything you touch turns to shit. At least I have a marriage, and at least my son is normal, unlike your two freaks.'

Karalyn halted. 'Say that again, Keir. Call my children freaks again, and see what happens to you. You know what I can do. I scoured your tiny mind once; I can do it again. So, come on – repeat what you just said. I dare you.'

Keir took a step back, his hands shaking. He opened his mouth, but no words came out.

Karalyn nodded, smiled, then strode away.

'Bitch,' Keir muttered, as soon as Karalyn was out of earshot. He tried to take a breath, but his nerves were raw, and he felt like screaming. He turned, and walked to the nearest stairwell, then ascended to the roof garden. He reached for his cigarettes, but his fingers fumbled the packet, and it fell to the ground. He picked it up, extracted a cigarette, and lit it, his hands still trembling.

Why was he still terrified of his sister? He had been so young when she had scoured his mind that he had no recollection of any of the events surrounding it, but the memories of his troubled childhood still shone brightly – his severe shyness, his stutter, his feelings of inferiority. He remembered his classmates laughing at his slow progress in school, and how hard he had found making friends.

It was all Karalyn's fault. Every problem of his youth could be traced back to the moment she had wiped his mind clean; and she had just threatened to do it again. She was evil, plain and simple. One day, he promised himself, one day, he would make her pay for what she had done to him.

He heard a gentle cough next to him, and saw a palace courtier standing by his side.

'What?' said Keir.

'Excuse me, Lord Holdfast,' the courtier said, 'but Mage Tabor is asking why you haven't finished sending the messages he asked you to deal with. He is demanding that you return to his office at once.'

Keir nearly exploded. He felt his fists clench and his chest tighten, and the courtier edged away, fear in his eyes. Then, from out of nowhere, he remembered Tilda, his secret proof that he could do whatever he pleased, and get away with it.

He smiled, and took a breath. 'Thank you. Tell Mage Tabor that I'll be down in a moment.'

CHAPTER 18
THE BOYS

Plateau City, The Plateau – 3rd Day, Second Third Summer 534
World's End, Domm Pass. Go.

Karalyn appeared in the street outside the old tavern. She had been expecting rain, and was surprised to see the sun shining down from a perfect blue sky. An old man was standing a few yards away, staring at her.

'I've seen you do that before, hen,' he said.

Karalyn smiled. 'Do you want to see another wee trick?'

The old man nodded. 'Aye. Go on, then.'

You cannot see me.

The old man chuckled. Karalyn turned, maintaining her illusion of invisibility, and walked towards the tavern. She wondered if Cardova would be angry. She had left him in Domm for five days while she had waited in Plateau City for her mother to contact her. She tried to place the worry she felt for her mother to one side. Holder Fast knew how to look after herself. She had been in many difficult positions over the years, and had always emerged more or less intact.

Karalyn was about to enter the *World's End* when she heard laughter and shouts from the alleyway that ran behind the tavern. She frowned, then stole down the unpaved alley. Kelpie and Kendrie were standing at the base of a ladder, their attention on the man scrambling over the roof of the tavern with a hammer and a bag of tools.

Kelpie laughed. 'He's nimble for a big lad, eh?'

Karalyn crept closer to them, and looked up. She raised an eyebrow. It was Lucius Cardova up on the roof, banging nails into new slate tiles.

'Ye missed one, pal,' shouted Kendrie.

Cardova glanced down, then looked around at the roof. 'Where?'

'On yer left, big man.'

Karalyn eased off her powers, and Kelpie and Kendrie jumped in fright.

Kelpie punched Karalyn on the arm. 'Ye'll give me a bloody heart attack doing that, hen.'

Karalyn rubbed her arm. 'Ow.'

Kelpie cackled. 'Serves ye right for sneaking up on us like that.'

'Why is Lucius Cardova on the roof?' said Karalyn.

'He's fixing a leak,' said Kendrie.

'Aye,' said Kelpie, 'and he's also repaired the back fence, unblocked a toilet that's been jammed for thirds, painted the window frames, and put up some shelves. Tell ye what, Karalyn; yer welcome to leave big Lucius here any time ye like.'

Karalyn frowned. 'You've been making him work? But I left him enough money to pay his way.'

'Aye, hen, but he's yer friend, so I wouldnae accept his money. So then he said that he would work for his board and meals. I told him no, but he's a persistent bugger; and the lad likes his food, and his ale, so fair's fair, eh?'

'Has he been getting drunk every night?'

'Well, he's not been completely sober, but he hasnae put a foot out of line. He's been very well behaved, Karalyn; a proper gent. He does ye credit.'

Cardova peered over the edge of the roof. 'I thought I heard your voice, Karalyn. Is my holiday over?'

'Are all the tiles done?' Kelpie shouted up to him.

'Yes, ma'am. One of the chimneys needs a bit of work; its bricks are loose. Do you want me to take a look at it?'

'Naw, son,' Kelpie said. 'Get yer arse down here; it's time for lunch.'

Cardova gave a thumbs up, then positioned himself next to the ladder. He grasped the sides with gloved hands, and slid down quickly in a single fluid movement, his boots landing on the ground next to Kelpie.

'I wish ye wouldnae do that, son,' said Kelpie. 'What if ye fell, eh?'

'Then I'd be in bed for a few months with a broken leg, getting served food and ale every day. Doesn't sound too bad, ma'am.' He glanced at Karalyn. 'So, now I know that when you say you'll be back soon, it might mean five days later.'

'I was delayed in Plateau City,' she said. 'Sorry.'

Cardova smiled. 'It's fine, ma'am. These past five days have been the longest I've not been on duty for years. And it rained on only two of the five days, which Kendrie tells me is something of a minor miracle. I can't remember the last time I was this relaxed.'

Kelpie shook her head. 'Ye've worked yer arse off, son.'

'Maybe that's how I relax, ma'am. Did I hear you mention lunch?'

'Aye. Come on inside. Are you hungry, Karalyn?'

'I don't want to put you out,' she said.

'Dinnae talk shite, hen. Kendrie, get lunch on for them.'

'Aye, sure,' Kendrie said.

They entered the tavern, and Cardova leaned in close to Karalyn.

'Please tell me you brought cigarettes, ma'am,' he said.

'Have you run out?'

'Almost. I've been rationing them since I found out that you can't buy them down here.'

'You're as bad as my mother,' she said. 'She starts to get nervous when she's down to her last packet.'

They entered the main room, and Kendrie strode off to the kitchens, while Kelpie went behind the bar and began to pour two pints of brown ale.

'I should have done what Kelsey and Van did, ma'am,' Cardova said, as he leaned against the bar. 'They both managed to give up smoking in the City, while I spent nights awake craving a cigarette. For over two years I had to do without, and then as soon as I got here, I'm back on them. It's a weakness, I guess.'

Karalyn brought out a packet of cigarettes. 'I'm just as bad,' she said. 'I started because my father hated it, and I wanted to annoy him. Seems ridiculous now.'

Kelpie placed the two ales onto the counter as Cardova and Karalyn each lit a cigarette.

'Thanks, ma'am,' said Cardova.

Karalyn glanced at Cardova as they made their way to a table, her eyes drawn to his bare shoulders and arms, then she looked away. Frostback had clearly made a mistake, as Cardova had never given her even the slightest indication that he was interested in her. He was friendly, but he was friendly with everyone. It was fine. She had no desire to form any kind of romantic relationship with anyone; her life was complicated enough as it was.

They sat.

'Where's Lord Bryce, ma'am?' said Cardova.

'Still in Plateau City,' said Karalyn. 'He needs time to come to terms with Brannig's arrival.'

Cardova nodded. 'How did that go?'

'There was a lot of shouting and finger pointing,' said Karalyn. 'Bridget was livid, as you'd imagine. Some of her children wanted to spend time with Brannig, and the others wanted nothing to do with him. He's living in the Holdfast townhouse. Bridget was going to send him back with me, but Berra begged her to let him stay for a few more days; so here I am.'

'Bridget is the Empress, yes?'

'Aye.'

'Then why don't you refer to her as "her Majesty", ma'am? You sound like Kelsey. She never calls Queen Emily by her proper title. What is it with you Holdfasts? Do you all dislike authority?'

Karalyn frowned.

'Brannig is the real thing, is he, ma'am?' Cardova went on. 'He's the father of the Empress's children?'

'Aye. Bridget... I mean, the Empress, she asked me to rummage through his mind, to see if he was hiding something. So I did. I searched through his memories. I could see how determined he was to keep to his vow of silence, and I don't quite understand what changed his mind. Apart from that, he seemed genuine enough. He certainly loves the children. I could feel it course through him. And, now that he's met them all, he would rather stay in Plateau City to be near them. He's not a bad guy. He feels terrible about breaking his vow, but there's no malice in him.'

'It might be good for the children to have their father around,' said Cardova.

'It places the Empress into an awkward position, constitutionally speaking. If Brannig wanted to, he could claim a measure of authority, by virtue of the fact that he fathered all five of the Empress's children. Worse, gossip has already made its way round the city. I don't know if it was a palace guard, or a courtier, or even one of the children, but word's got out that Brannig is living in the Holdfast townhouse. The street's been clogged with curious citizens wanting to catch a glimpse of him.'

'Some compromise might have to be found, ma'am. Perhaps Brannig could be persuaded to sign a statement, forswearing any intention to seek power?'

'Aye, maybe. Did Corthie and Aila get away alright?'

'Yes, ma'am. They left with little Killop at dawn the day after you were last here. They might be in Kell by now. Did you see your other brother in the city?'

Karalyn frowned. 'Aye.'

'Is there a reason for that frown, ma'am?'

'Keir is an idiot; I can't stand him. To be honest, I've been avoiding him. I even made myself invisible a few times in the palace, so that I wouldn't have to speak to him. I feel sorry for Thorn, but she seems to know what she's doing. Whenever I tried to talk to her about Keir, she kept telling me that she had it under control.'

'What did she mean by that, do you think, ma'am?'

'I don't know. I could have read it from her mind, I suppose, but I have boundaries, and I try not to read anyone's mind unless I have to.'

Cardova nodded. 'Have you read my mind?'

'No. Should I?'

'I'd rather you didn't, ma'am.'

'Why? Are you hiding something?'

He smiled. 'Everyone has something to hide.'

Karalyn took a sip of the brown ale. 'You're a Banner soldier; I would guess that you might have a lot to hide.'

'In that case, ma'am, I'll be honest with you right now. Yes, I am a Banner soldier. Yes, I took part in several operations where we were ordered to do things that most people, including myself, would categorise as atrocities. And yes, I am ashamed; deeply ashamed. In the past, I would obey every order without question; it was drummed into us from the moment we enlisted in the Banner. Obey. You must obey.'

Karalyn's heart sank. Was Cardova a killer, plain and simple?

'Now,' he went on, 'I look back on those days with something approaching incredulity. Queen Emily has never given me an order like that.' His voice dropped to a whisper. 'I have never said this to anyone else, but if she did, then I would refuse to comply. It's the same with you. I know I swore an oath to the Banner of the Lostwell Exiles, but if you ask me to kill a child, or anything of that ilk, then I will refuse. You should know that.'

'Tell me the worst thing you've ever done,' she said.

'Are you sure you want to hear it, ma'am?'

'If I didn't, I wouldn't have asked.'

Cardova nodded, his glance avoiding hers. 'I was on Dragon Eyre six years ago, ma'am, in the middle of my brief marriage. I was a second lieutenant back then, and led a half company of soldiers. We were on an island called Olkis – a nasty place, where rebels would plant explosives in our mess halls every other day, and the Banner were angry. Very angry. We'd lost eighty men in under a month, all blown to pieces as they slept. I was sent on an operation to clear out some rebels from a stretch of treacherous marshland, and we came across a dragon who had been hiding in the swamps. She had recently laid a clutch of eggs, and was guarding them. Our orders were clear – we were to eliminate any dragon that we came across. So, I gave the command to kill her. We surrounded her, and set up five ballistae in the swamps. We loosed, but despite having five damn ballista bolts stuck in her, she was still alive. Then, while she lay wounded, my men took hammers and axes to her eggs.' He paused for a moment. 'We smashed them in front of her, and then, once she had seen her young slaughtered, we killed her. I didn't loose any of the ballistae, nor did I wield a hammer or an axe, but I was responsible. I was the officer in command. When we got back to base, I was commended by the colonel in charge of the garrison. I didn't think anything of it at the time. A tiny voice was niggling away at the back of my mind, but it was drowned out by the training and discipline that had been instilled in me. I was Banner. I obey orders. It's what the Banner do. It wasn't until a couple of years later, when I was posted to Lostwell, that I properly cracked. Has Corthie told you about Yoneath?'

Karalyn shook her head.

'It was the end for me,' he said. 'I realised that I couldn't go on. Then, the most unexpected thing happened, and I found myself in the world of the City, along with three thousand other Banner soldiers, and tens of thousands of Lostwell civilians. A notorious traitor by the name of Van Logos was trying to enrol us into a new Banner, and I snatched at the opportunity to serve again. The Banner of the Lostwell Exiles saved my life. I could be a soldier, without having to worry that I would be ordered to do anything that made me feel sick. The Queen's husband, King Daniel, occasionally suggested measures that could be considered extreme, but Queen Emily would never allow them to go ahead. She made me feel that I was doing something good for a change, something honourable and just; something I could take pride in.' His eyes closed as Karalyn watched. 'I don't really expect you to understand,' he went on, 'but I don't mind. For the first time in my life, I know who I am.' He glanced up at her. 'What's the worst thing you've ever done?'

'I don't think I want to tell you that,' she said.

'Understood, ma'am. What's our next move?'

Karalyn eyed him. She had wondered if he would be angry at her refusal to share her past, but he seemed to have brushed it off. She thought back to her troubled relationship with Lennox. She had loved him, but his history in the Army of Pyre had erected a huge barrier between them. She was glad that Cardova didn't seem to be interested in her; she couldn't go through the pain of falling in love with a killer again. At the same time though, did she have any right to judge others after what she had done to the Rahain army after the siege of Colsbury?

Kendrie came over, and set down several plates from a large tray.

'Here ye go,' he said. 'This should cover fixing the roof, eh?'

'Thanks, Kendrie,' said Cardova.

'No bother, Lucius.' He winked at Karalyn. 'That's a good man ye've found there, hen.'

Karalyn said nothing, and Kendrie strode back towards the kitchens.

Cardova eyed her. 'I know you think I'm an asshole, Karalyn, but that won't stop me from doing my job. I've been ordered to protect you, and that's what I shall do.'

'I don't need you to protect me.'

'Then, ma'am, you should take me back to Kelsey.'

Karalyn sighed. 'I don't think you're an arsehole, Lucius. Finish your lunch, and we'll go to Threeways to resume the search for the dream mage.'

He nodded. 'Yes, ma'am.'

Two hours later, Karalyn and Cardova were climbing a path that ran next to a small stream, a few miles from the town of Threeways. Moss-covered boulders lay strewn to either side, and the opposite bank of the stream was lined with trees, the tips of their branches drooping close to the surface of the rushing water. Knee-high ferns brushed against their legs as they ascended the steep glen, and Karalyn could feel sweat trickling down her back from the humid warmth of the afternoon sun.

Cardova waved his hand in front of his face. 'Damn insects,' he muttered. 'I'm being eaten alive.'

'Not much further to go,' Karalyn said. 'We're nearly at the summit.'

She turned away from the stream, and they scaled a steep grassy slope, dotted with clumps of heather and gorse, their little yellow flowers swaying in the breeze. They scrambled over some loose scree, then climbed to the top of the hill, the Domm Pass below them. Karalyn sat down on a rocky lip, while Cardova gazed out at the view. The sky had remained cloudless, and the entire valley was shimmering in a heat haze of greens and browns, while the tiled roofs of the houses in Threeways were sparkling in the sunlight. On the other side of the valley, the hills stretched away into the mountainous region of the Domm highlands, where several of the high peaks were clinging onto patches of white snow.

Cardova rolled his shoulders and exhaled. 'This was worth the climb.'

Karalyn smiled. 'We didn't come here for the view.'

'I can see why Corthie would choose to live down here, ma'am.'

'That might be because we've happened upon one of the few days when the rain isn't pouring down. It's not quite as pleasant in winter.'

'If I were you, ma'am,' he said, 'I'd spend summers here, and winters in the Holdings. That way, you'd get the best of both.'

'You must have seen other places just as beautiful.'

'Dragon Eyre is beautiful,' he said, 'but you know what I think of that world. This feels different.'

'Come and sit next to me.'

Cardova smiled as if he were about to make a joke, but then he closed his mouth and nodded. He walked over and sat down on the rocky lip close to Karalyn.

'Alright,' she said. 'Here goes. I'm going to broadcast my powers far and wide. To Daimon it will be as if I've lit a bonfire in his head. If he's here, then there's no way he'll miss it. Get ready to move. If I find him, I might not have time to warn you before I transport us to his location.'

Cardova nodded again, and his hand went to the hilt of the short sword he had strapped to his waist.

Karalyn closed her eyes, and let her powers rise from her body. She reached out, sensing for other mages. She found Aila and baby Killop in seconds, almost two hundred miles away in Kell, their self-healing powers shining clearly in her mind. She then felt the presence of someone with sparking powers, and wondered if it was the same mage she had sensed before.

Come on, Daimon, she said to herself, where are you?

Why would he ask her to come to Kellach Brigdomin if he was going to remain hidden? Was Cardova's presence putting him off? The last time she had searched, Bryce had also been with them; maybe Daimon was angry that she hadn't come alone. She reached out further, combing through glens and ravines, and moved from Kell into Brig. To the north of the Brig Pass, she saw the main road that led to Threeways. While most of Brig lay empty and abandoned, the settlers who had returned were clustered around the busy thoroughfare. Farms stretched away from either side of the road, and it was dotted with taverns and hostelries that catered to the many travellers who journeyed from Domm to Kell. Her heart quickened. A thin, fragile tendril of power was snaking across the landscape, heading far off to the north-east in the direction of the Plateau. Dream powers. As soon as her senses had discovered it, the tendril began to dissolve, and she raced her vision to its source, high in the hills by the northern end of the Brig Pass. She passed through a narrow, almost inaccessible ravine, and saw an old, ruined border fortress that had once guarded the pass. In the forecourt of the castle stood a line of loaded supply wagons, and smoke was coming from a chimney. Karalyn followed the tendril of dream powers through a ruined window and into an upper storey of the old keep. A boy was sitting cross-legged on the ground, his eyes closed, while another boy was tending a fire a few feet away, where a pot of water was boiling.

Karalyn smiled as the dream powers emanating from the castle vanished.

'Too late, Daimon,' she said. 'Cardova – on your feet; and stay close to me.'

They stood.

Daimon's castle, Brig. Go.

The air shimmered, then Karalyn and Cardova appeared in a high-ceilinged chamber inside the fortress. The boy on the ground was staring up at them, his eyes wide, as Cardova drew his sword. The boy fixed his eyes on the soldier.

Go to sleep, Karalyn heard him order Cardova, but she blocked his attempt, filling the chamber with her powers to shield the Banner officer. She smiled to herself. She hadn't been sure if she would be able to prevent Daimon from penetrating Cardova's mind, but his close proximity to her was keeping him safe.

'Hello, Daimon,' she said. 'Your tricks won't work on us. You know who I am.'

The boy sprang to his feet, and backed away to the fire pit where the other boy was sitting. Both boys were dressed in expensive but ill-fitting garments, and they looked dirty and unwashed.

'I'm here to help you,' said Karalyn. 'If you want to be helped.'

Daimon raised his left hand, and Karalyn felt a surge of power come from him as he tried to breach their minds.

'I told you, Daimon; that won't work. I can shield those next to me, if I know there is a threat. Are you a threat? What do you want?'

'Don't hurt us,' said the other boy.

Karalyn sent her powers towards the other boy, but was rebuffed, as if Daimon was protecting him in the same way that she was protecting Cardova.

'Is that your twin brother, Daimon?' said Karalyn. 'I sense no powers from him. Where are your parents?'

Daimon's eyes flashed with anger. 'Why don't ye read my mind and find out?'

'You know I can't do that,' said Karalyn. 'Why are you being hostile? It was you who asked me to come to Kellach Brigdomin; well, here I am. Don't you want to talk?'

Daimon spat on the ground in front of Karalyn. 'I have nothing to say to you.'

'Have you been killing members of the Clan Council?'

Daimon's expression changed in an instant, from raw anger to guilt, and his mouth opened.

Karalyn frowned. 'You have to stop.'

Daimon shook his head. 'What about the other things that I've been doing? You have no idea, do ye?'

Cardova slid his sword back into its scabbard.

'Are ye feart, soldier?' Daimon crowed.

'You're kids,' Cardova said. 'I don't use swords on kids. I will subdue you both, though, if I have to. Karalyn, perhaps if I restrained his brother, then Daimon might tell us what he's been doing?'

'If ye touch Dillon, I'll kill you!' shouted Daimon, his hands shaking with rage.

'I could take him from you if I wished,' said Karalyn, 'but I won't. I'm not here to threaten you. Why don't you calm yourself, and then I can take us all somewhere we can sit down and talk like civilised people?'

Dillon glanced at his brother. 'Maybe we should do as she says.'

'Shut up!' cried Daimon.

'I want to help you,' said Karalyn, 'but you must promise me that you'll stop killing people. You possess great powers, Daimon.'

Daimon's wild expression softened. 'I might come, if ye tell me how ye transport yerself from place to place, and if ye show me how to make myself invisible.'

'I'd be happy to train you, but not if you're going to abuse your powers. How old are you?'

'Sixteen,' said Dillon.

Cardova raised an eyebrow.

'I saw the wagons down in the castle forecourt,' Karalyn said. 'You've been using your powers to steal from the local farms and villages, haven't you, Daimon? How long will you be able to keep it up before the local militia figure out what's been happening? Boys, you don't have to live this way. Come with me, and you can start new lives.'

'Are ye trying to buy us with cheap promises?' said Daimon. 'If ye won't teach me, then leave. I want nothing to do with ye.'

Karalyn glanced at Cardova. The tall soldier nodded, then strode towards Dillon. Daimon cried out in anger, then he lifted the pot of boiling water from the fire pit and hurled it at Karalyn. Cardova dived to meet it, putting his body between Karalyn and the scalding water, and the pot struck his chest. Daimon picked up a flaming brand from the fire, threw it at the soldier, then he dragged Dillon up, and they bolted from the chamber. Cardova groaned from the floor, his bare arms and neck scalded by the flames and the boiling water. Karalyn swore, then crouched down by him. She glanced over her shoulder, but the boys had gone.

'Little bastard,' Cardova mumbled, his eyes closed in pain.

Karalyn checked his wounds, then powered her vision to search for Daimon. It was useless. He might not be able to make himself invisible, but his powers were enough to stop her from finding him. She glanced over the ruins of the fortress, but saw no sign of the twins.

'Go after them, ma'am,' grunted Cardova. 'Don't let them get away.'

Karalyn thought about it, then shook her head.

Colsbury Castle. Go.

They appeared in the chamber that housed the Sextant, with Cardova lying on the polished floorboards, his arms and neck blistering from the boiling water. Karalyn stood, and hurried to the door. She opened it, and ran down the corridor, until she reached the large sitting room.

Agang glanced up from a comfortable armchair. 'Hello, Karalyn. I have news.'

'It can wait,' she said. 'Can you help me? Cardova's been burned.'

The old Sanang mage got to his feet, and followed Karalyn back to the Sextant chamber. He took one look at Cardova on the floor, and rushed to his side. He took Cardova's hand, and the tall soldier's eyes clenched shut, as his body began to shudder. The blisters and burns on his skin healed, and, in seconds, all traces of the injuries had vanished. Cardova opened his eyes, and gasped for air.

'Thank you,' he croaked.

'I'm glad to be of service, young man,' said Agang.

Cardova smiled, reached for his cigarettes, and lit one. 'Well, that was fun.'

'Did you find what you were looking for?' said Agang.

'Aye,' said Karalyn, 'but he got away.'

'That's a pity,' said Agang. 'There's some better news. I got a vision message from your mother yesterday morning.'

'What did she say?'

'She said that everything's fine, and that she, Shella and Caelius won't need your help returning from Rakana.'

Karalyn frowned. 'Really? They're coming back on foot?'

Agang shrugged. 'That's what she said. She told us not to worry.'

'That's odd, but I guess it's a weight off my mind. At least I'll be able to focus on the dream mage.' She glanced down at Cardova. 'You saved me back there.'

'Just doing my job, ma'am.'

She narrowed her eyes a little, wondering what kind of man threw themselves into the path of scalding water.

'All the same,' she said, 'thank you.'

'No problem, ma'am,' he said. 'I have a theory about why Daimon wanted you to go to Kellach Brigdomin, if you want to hear it.'

Karalyn nodded.

'I don't believe that he ever had any intention of speaking to you, ma'am,' said Cardova. 'That seemed clear from his reaction to us turning up like that. If I had to guess, I would say that he wanted you to leave Colsbury so that he could get at your children without you interfering. Fortunately for us, he had no idea that you'd fetch Kelsey from the City.'

'That makes sense,' said Karalyn; 'though I'm disappointed. I hoped he'd be willing to talk, at least. We need to go back down there as soon as possible, and resume the search.'

Cardova smiled. 'If we're going straight back to Domm, ma'am, will you let me enjoy this cigarette first?'

Karalyn sat on the floor next to him, and lit one for herself.

'Sure,' she said. 'Why not?'

CHAPTER 19
THE VOICE

Marchside, Kell – 7th Day, Second Third Summer 534

Corthie crouched down by the wheels of the cart, and picked up a handful of soil. It hadn't rained in a few days, and the upper layer of earth was dry, and crumbled between his fingers, while the soil beneath was still damp. It was just dirt, but it was Corthie's dirt, and, somehow, he was going to have to coax it into producing enough crops to feed him and his family.

'This field used to grow barley,' said Conal, from his seat up on the cart. 'It's too late in the year to start planting that, but. Ye might want to think about planting some vegetables for now, and maybe some turnips a bit later on.'

Corthie frowned. 'Turnips?'

'Aye; to feed the cows, eh? We're not Lach; we're not gonnae eat the damn things. The barley can wait until next spring, and then Severton will buy up whatever ye manage to harvest. Are ye thinking about buying some sheep to tide ye over till spring?'

Corthie stood. 'I don't know, Conal. This all seems like a much bigger job than I'd imagined. I need someone to come and teach me this stuff.'

'I can ask around the village,' said Conal, 'though ye'll have to remember that some of the auld farmers round here don't speak Holdings.'

'My Kellach Brigdomin's a bit rusty,' said Corthie. 'My dad taught me when I was younger, and we used to speak it in the house sometimes. It's Aila who will have to learn it from scratch.'

'Can she speak Rahain? Most of the ex-slaves remember Rahain, though there's not much call for it these days.'

'She can only speak Holdings.'

Conal nodded. 'Is she from the Holdings, then?'

Corthie smiled. 'Let's get back to the farmhouse. Aila and the others will be thinking that we're lost.'

He pulled himself up onto the cart, and Conal urged the ponies on. The cart juddered forward, its wheels following the deep ruts of the track. Empty fields lay to either side, bordered by low stone dykes and patches of trees that acted as wind-breaks. The ground sloped up to the right, and the track turned, following the line of a long drainage ditch as it ascended the low hill. The Clackenbaird farmhouse stood upon the summit – the only place on the farm from where most of the land Corthie now owned could be seen. They passed the ruins of a barn, its roof collapsed and its walls bowing inwards, and the track beneath them changed from dirt to gravel. The large farmhouse came into view, its thick stone walls having survived the long years of abandonment. Three men were up on the roof, laying down new slate tiles, while others were busy at work in the yard, sawing beams of wood to make new door frames, and shaping planks to replace the rotten floorboards. The air was full of sawdust and the scent of freshly-cut wood; while the local cats, disturbed by the noise coming from the workers, were watching from various hiding places by the edge of the yard.

Conal brought the cart to a halt, then he and Corthie jumped down. A few workers nodded to Corthie as they worked, and he wondered what they thought of him. He was paying them well, but his lack of experience was painfully obvious. They probably imagined him as a rich but clueless foreigner, who, for some unknown reason, had decided to abandon his comfortable and privileged existence for a life of toil. He had overheard a couple muttering their belief that Corthie wouldn't last one winter in Kell; that he would give up as soon as the weather turned and the evenings grew dark and cold. He remembered Karalyn and Lennox's attempt to set up home in Severton, but Lennox had been trained in all manner of practical skills by the Army of Pyre, while Corthie knew nothing about carpentry, or building; all he had been taught was how to fight.

Aila appeared at a doorway with Killop in her arms, and gestured for Corthie to approach.

'We now have two rooms that are ready to live in,' she said, as they entered the farmhouse. 'The windows, roof and floors have been finished, though there's no furniture yet.'

He glanced at her as they walked into the first room. Her baby-bump seemed to be growing bigger by the day, yet she seemed relaxed and at ease, and her skin was almost radiant with health. Her condition had provoked a few comments, with some of the older folk saying that they had never seen such a heavily-pregnant woman so fit and active.

'This will be the nursery, eventually,' said Aila, as they stood in the small room. It had one narrow window, and the new floorboards were giving off a strong smell of cut wood. 'For now, though, it might end up being where we all sleep. The kitchen is also nearing completion. We might have to live in those two rooms until the rest of the house is finished.'

Corthie nodded, the size of the task ahead threatening to over-whelm him.

'Of course,' Aila went on, 'it'll need painting first, and we still have to buy the furniture, as well as a million other things. We need to write a very long list, and hand it over to the merchants in town. Do you know when our things will arrive from the Hold Fast estate?'

'It could be thirds,' he said. 'Why? What do we need?'

'Money, Corthie,' she said.

'I thought we had tons.'

'We did, but we've already spent a small fortune on the workers and the building materials. We're going to need a lot more. The Holdfast name means that our credit is good, but we'll soon start to owe gold to just about everyone in Marchside.'

'Can we get a loan?'

'The only banks in Kellach Brigdomin are in Threeways and Severton, and they seem to be designed to assist long-haul wagon operators transporting whisky to the Plateau, not to help farmers.'

'But I don't like owing folk money.'

'What else can we do? We can't wait until our first crops are ready to sell – that'll be months away; and we need to buy seeds and equipment in order to sow the crops in the first place. The people in Marchside will be fine with waiting to be paid, as long as they know when the rest of our gold will arrive.'

Corthie felt his frustration rise. 'It would be different if I knew how to fix roofs and put down floorboards, then we could do it all ourselves, instead of paying for a dozen guys to do it for us. What can I do that will help?'

'You could look after Killop while I organise the workers putting the kitchen together.'

Corthie frowned. 'That doesn't sound very useful.'

'It would be very useful to me.'

'Fine,' he mumbled, taking the wriggling child from Aila's arms. 'I'll go for a walk with the wee guy, and get out of everyone's way.'

Aila smiled. 'I know you don't like all this, Corthie, but it's temporary. We'll be on our own up here as soon as the house is finished.'

Corthie nodded, then strode back outside into the sunlight. A few of the men glanced at the child in his arms, and Corthie could guess what they were thinking, even though none of them spoke.

'Right, wee Killop,' Corthie said, as he took the main track away from the farm buildings; 'where shall we go first?'

He walked down the hillside to the small burn that ran along the base of the slope, then set Killop down by its grassy banks, where he started to examine the smooth stones that lay by the water's edge. Corthie watched him, while his thoughts dwelt on the new life he had chosen. Maybe he had made a terrible mistake. He wondered if Karalyn had told his mother that he had decided to become a farmer. If he had gone back to the Hold Fast estate with his sister, then he and Aila could be drinking tea out on the rear porch, while servants cooked and cleaned for them.

A dark thought entered his head, that everyone was laughing at him. His family, the workers up at the farmhouse, the merchants in Marchside – they were all laughing at his stupidity behind his back. Aila was laughing, too. She knew how useless he was. In fact, she was probably having an affair with one of the men working on the house. She was a whore.

Corthie blinked. Where had those thoughts come from? He tried to clear his mind, but an image of Aila in the arms of one of the workers wouldn't leave his head. She was cheating on him, and he was blind if he couldn't see it. He should go back to the farmhouse and kill her.

Corthie's legs started to push him into a standing position, then he managed to gain control of himself, and he sat again, with an effort. He closed his eyes. What was wrong with him? He had never once entertained a violent thought about Aila, and yet he felt an almost overwhelming urge to punish her for cheating on him. The bitch deserved to die. He should smash her skull in with a brick. He gripped his legs with his arms, and sat as still as he could, and then, as quickly as they had appeared, the violent urges ceased, and he felt at peace again.

Ashamed with himself for having had such thoughts, he opened his eyes. Killop was a yard away, still playing with the smooth river stones in the bright sunshine. In a calmer state of mind, Corthie tried to think about Aila. Of course she wasn't having an affair. She was seven and a half thirds pregnant, for a start, and he had spent nearly every minute of every day with her. How could he have gone from knowing this to wanting to kill her?

'Shit,' he muttered, remembering the dream mage that Karalyn and Cardova had mentioned. Had his mind been invaded? It seemed unlikely, but how else could he explain the horrific images that had ripped through his mind? He knew that Karalyn and Sable had the power to alter someone's thoughts and perceptions, and they could convince folk that black was white, and up was down; could the new dream mage do the same thing? Worse, if it were true, then that meant that the dream mage knew who he was, and where he was. Corthie had managed to resist the voice in his head, but would he be able to keep it up forever? He leaned over and scooped up Killop. He needed to warn Aila.

He hurried back up the slope towards the busy farmhouse. One of the workers glanced over at him, a smile on his face, and Corthie nearly exploded with rage. They were all mocking him. The man with the grin had been sleeping with Aila, and everyone knew. He would rip the bastard's head off with his bare hands. The man's smile faded as Corthie strode towards him, and fear flashed across his eyes.

Corthie came to a halt a yard from the man, as a war went on in his head.

'Are ye alright, mate?' the man said, backing away.

Corthie clamped his mouth shut, lest he scream abuse and threats at the bemused worker, then Killop squealed, and Corthie realised that he had been gripping on to his son too tightly. Aila emerged from the farmhouse, took one look at Corthie, and ran over. She touched his arm.

'Get off me,' he growled. 'Don't touch me.'

Aila took a step back, then she reached out for Killop.

At that moment, Corthie wanted to hit her. The urge was so strong that his right fist clenched, and he longed for the sight of her spilt blood. He closed his eyes, and sank to his knees in the middle of the yard, a low groan coming from his lips as he fought the voice in his mind. He felt Killop be pulled from his grip, and he grasped the sides of his head with both hands.

Kill her, the voice said. *Kill them all.*

'No,' he gasped.

Someone tried to pull his hands from his head, and Corthie's right arm shot out. His fingers fastened on to the person's neck, and he squeezed.

Throttle him! Snap his neck and bathe in his blood. You are a savage; you are a warrior. You are a killer.

A plank of wood battered off the back of his head, and he collapsed to the ground; and slipped into unconsciousness.

Corthie awoke with a pounding headache, his mouth parched. He opened his eyes and the pain in his head jolted as the bright sunlight dazzled him. He glanced at his surroundings, and realised he was lying on the back of a wagon. Two men were sitting by the rear, their eyes on him.

'He's awake,' one shouted.

Corthie groaned. 'My head...'

'Ye got what was coming to you, ya mad bastard,' said one of the men. 'Ye nearly strangled the damn foreman to death.'

Corthie raised a hand to shield his eyes from the sun, as he tried to digest the words the man had spoken. His memories were foggy, though he remembered wanting to hurt Aila.

He sat up. 'Where's Aila and Killop?'

'Settle down,' said one of the men. 'A few folk want to speak to ye first.'

Corthie heard a noise to his right, and saw Conal walk out of the farmhouse, followed by Kallie and two large men. They strode up to the wagon, and Kallie narrowed her eyes.

'Well?' she said. 'Are you going to tell us what ye were thinking? Ye squeezed the foreman's neck so badly that he can barely breathe. Ye could have broken his neck, Corthie. Why?'

'Were ye drinking?' said Conal.

Corthie shook his head.

Kallie leaned her elbows on the side of the wagon. 'Speak to us, Corthie.'

'I... I can't...' Corthie stopped, the pain in the back of his head forcing out his other thoughts. 'You won't believe me if I tell you.'

'The workers are threatening to walk out,' said Kallie; 'and I'm not surprised. I didnae ken ye had a temper like that, son.'

'He was like an animal,' said one of the men sitting on the back of the wagon.

'Quiet,' said Kallie. 'Let Corthie try to explain himself.'

'I think,' Corthie began, then he quietened again. He took a breath. 'Pyre's arse, this is going to sound completely stupid, but I think there was a dream mage in my head, telling me to hurt folk. I didn't mean to strangle the foreman. I'm sorry.'

'Ye heard a voice in yer head?' said one of the men. 'Are ye daft?'

'A dream mage?' said Kallie.

'Aye,' said Corthie. 'You know, like my sister.'

'You mean, like Kalayne?'

'Aye. Did you know him?'

'A bit.'

'Karalyn told me that there's another dream mage down here. She's been looking for him. It's either that, or I'm going mad. The voice was telling me that Aila was cheating on me, and that I should kill her. I would never hurt her; you have to believe me, but the voice was telling me to, over and over. It took everything I had to resist it.'

The others glanced at each other, saying nothing.

'See?' said Corthie. 'I knew you wouldn't believe me. Maybe I have gone mad, maybe my mind is breaking down. You should lock me up, just in case.'

Kallie stared at him. 'Can ye hear the voices now?'

Corthie shook his head. 'They've gone. Are you arresting me?'

'There are no town wardens down in these parts,' said Kallie. 'As a member of the Clan Council, I have the authority to confine you to the prison in Marchside. I say prison, but it's just a wee room under the town hall, where we put folk who get too drunk and rowdy. Are ye saying that ye'd rather be in there?'

Corthie didn't answer for a long time. He thought about Aila, and how much he loved her. He wondered if he had frightened her, or made her worry that he might have hurt Killop. It was too much to take, and he hung his head, wishing that the others would stop staring at him.

'What if the voices come back?' he whispered. 'What if I'm not strong enough to stop them?'

'This is the part I don't understand,' said Kallie. 'If it really was a dream mage, then you shouldn't have been able to stop them, Corthie. Nobody could resist Kalayne's powers. If he told someone to do something, then they did it, without any hesitation. If it was a dream mage, then Aila would already be dead.'

'What should we do, boss?' said Conal.

'We cannae leave him here overnight,' said Kallie. 'It doesnae matter if his wee theory is right or not; he's admitted that he's a danger to his wife and child. I'd never forgive myself if we walked away, and something happened to Aila or wee Killop.' She sighed. 'We'll take him back to town with us, and stick him in jail for the night.'

Conal nodded. 'The whole town will know about it, boss.'

'That cannae be helped,' said Kallie. 'The workers will have already spread the story, anyway. Bind his hands.'

Corthie held his wrists out, his empty palms turned upwards, as a sense of relief filtered through him. At least if he was locked up, then he wouldn't be able to hurt anyone. One of the men leaned forward, and looped a rope round his wrists, then tied the ends in a tight knot.

'Can I see Aila and Killop before we head to town?' Corthie said.

'No,' said Kallie. 'I can arrange a visit once there's a solid door between you and them. Oh, Corthie; this breaks my heart, but I cannae see any alternative. Conal, take him into town; I'll follow a wee bit later, once I've let Aila know what's happening.'

'Aye, boss,' said Conal. 'Right, lads. I want you men up on the wagon, two on each side of Corthie, while I drive.'

The four men clambered up, and Corthie felt them squeeze in to either side of him. Conal stepped up onto the driver's bench, and the wagon set off. Corthie kept his gaze lowered, feeling shame ooze from every pore. The wagon left the yard in front of the farmhouse buildings, and descended the track to the bottom of the hill. The men surrounding Corthie said nothing, but kept their eyes on him every inch of the way.

This is a crass injustice, said a voice in his head. The men just want you away so they can take advantage of your wife while you're locked up. The whole town knows. The whole town is laughing at you. The stupid foreigner; so gullible, so trusting, so weak. Show them you aren't weak. Kill them.

Battle-vision flooded his body, and he ripped the rope from his wrists with ease. His mind clouded with violence, he moved faster than the four men could perceive. He launched his right fist at one, breaking his nose and sending him flying onto the road; then he stamped on another's leg and threw him off the wagon.

The voice crowed in his head. *Yes! Make them suffer.*

One of the final two men lashed out with a fist, but Corthie caught the blow, then snapped the man's arm over his knee. The last man tried to back away, and Corthie head-butted him in the face, spraying blood over the back of the wagon. Corthie glanced up, and saw Conal staring at him from the driver's bench. A desire to kill him drowned out every other thought, and Conal reached under the bench and pulled up a crossbow.

'I'll shoot!' cried Conal. 'Stay where you are!'

Corthie sprang at him, and Conal loosed. The bolt struck Corthie in the left shoulder, wheeling him around. He toppled to the floor of the wagon, landing on the man whose arm he had broken, as agony from the wound drove out the voice in his mind. He heard a click, and saw Conal aiming the reloaded bow at him. Conal moved forward, stepping over the driver's bench, keeping the bow trained on Corthie's head, then he turned the bow round and clubbed Corthie with the iron-reinforced butt. There was a lightning flash of pain, then oblivion.

When Corthie awoke for the second time that afternoon, a shackle was attached to his left ankle. He was lying in darkness, the only light in the cramped cell coming from a narrow, barred slit in the thick door. Pain flowed over him. His head felt the effects of being battered twice that day, while his shoulder was on fire. He raised a hand, and touched the wound. The bolt had been pulled out, and a fresh bandage had been wrapped round his shoulder and upper arm, but his left arm felt numb. He pulled himself into a sitting position, his knees drawn up to his chest, as he sat on a bed of damp straw. A heavy chain was linking the shackle to a thick iron post in the wall of the cell. Then he noticed the smell coming from the straw, and nearly gagged.

'Hey!' he shouted at the door. 'Is anyone there?'

A man's face appeared at the narrow slit in the door. He eyed Corthie, then turned and walked away. A moment later, he returned, and Corthie heard another set of footsteps follow him. He caught traces of a whispered conversation, then Aila was standing in front of the opening in the door, her eyes red.

'Corthie,' she said. 'Are you alright?'

'I've been better,' he said, trying to smile.

'I've been trying to get them to release you, but...'

'No,' he said. 'It's safer for everyone if I'm in here. Did Kallie speak to you?'

'Yes. She said that you think a dream mage has been inside your head. She doesn't believe it, though; no one does. They all think you're mad.'

Corthie nodded. 'And you? What do you think?'

'I believe you.'

'Why?'

'Because I know you, Corthie. You'd never hurt me or Killop. Not unless someone's been interfering with your mind. I remember what Karalyn did to Maddie and Blackrose, and what Sable did to many people. I get it, Corthie. Dream mages can make you do things that you don't want to do, and we know that another dream mage is out there, somewhere. He must have realised that you're Karalyn's brother.'

Corthie suppressed a sob of relief, as he realised that he had been terrified that Aila wouldn't believe his far-fetched theory.

'How did he find us?' he whispered.

'You know how,' she said. 'Me. If he can sense powers like Vana could, or like Karalyn can, then my self-healing would be easy for him to spot. I can't turn it off, but, at the same time, I can't tell the people here that. They're suspicious enough without me telling them that I'm an immortal demigod.'

'What should we do?'

'We need to get in contact with your sister, Corthie. Karalyn will be able to fix this. Listen; I can travel up to Threeways to look for her; it's four days away by wagon. I could be back in ten.'

'What if you can't find her? She might not even be there.'

'Have you got any better ideas? I can't sit in the farmhouse all alone while you're down here in a damn cell, Corthie.' She leaned in closer and lowered her voice. 'Or, I could get you out of here. I have powers, too. Remember?'

Corthie shook his head. 'I can't risk it. The voices attacked me three times. For the first two, I was barely able to keep control, but I completely lost it on the wagon. The dream mage could be watching us, and waiting to do it again.'

Aila nodded. 'Then it's Threeways, Corthie. We have no choice. The town's in an uproar, and Kallie's not going to let you out any time soon.'

'Let me see Killop.'

Aila held their son up to the slit in the door, and Corthie felt his eyes well as he looked into the boy's face.

'Did I frighten him?'

'He'll be fine, Corthie. He's two years old – he won't remember a thing. The villagers, on the other hand... well, you've put five of them in the town hospital. It's not something they'll forget for a while.' She lowered Killop. 'You had me scared. I haven't seen you like that since you were fighting beyond the walls of the City. If that man wasn't Kellach, you'd have snapped his neck like a twig.'

'I've screwed everything up, haven't I?'

'No. The fact that you were able to resist at all makes me love you more than you can imagine. I know you would never hurt us; I've known it since the first time we met. Don't give up. I'll be back as soon as I can, with Karalyn.' She smiled. 'I'll find her.'

'Good luck.'

'See you soon,' she said. 'Stay strong.'

Aila disappeared from view, and the sound of a door closing reached Corthie's ears a moment later. He leaned back against the damp walls of the cell.

'Karalyn,' he whispered, 'if you're out there, help me.'

CHAPTER 20
THE BORDER WALL

Arakhanah City, Republic of Rakana – 8th Day, Second Third Summer 534

Caelius gestured from the edge of a long row of dishevelled and grimy tents. Daphne glanced around, then she and Shella ran forward through the shadows, keeping out of the light coming from the many large fires that burned throughout the migrant camp. Daphne moved silently, but Shella was puffing and panting, exhaustion etched on to her features. They reached Caelius, and he opened the empty tent. Daphne and Shella crouched down and squeezed through the entrance, then Caelius followed.

Shella collapsed onto the filthy floor of the canvas tent, her breath ragged.

'Good work, Caelius,' Daphne said, sitting down next to Shella.

The old veteran nodded but said nothing, his eyes watching the outside through a narrow gap in the tent's entrance.

'We'll rest for an hour,' said Daphne, 'and then we'll attempt the last stage.'

'It'll never work,' gasped Shella. 'I can't run any more. I'm spent, Daffers, utterly and completely spent.'

'We only have to make it over the border wall,' said Daphne. 'As soon as we're across, the imperial soldiers will protect us.'

'I'm over sixty, Daffers; how am I expected to climb a bloody wall?'

'Dozens of Rakanese migrants make the same journey every night,' said Daphne. 'The Rakanese border guards can't keep watch over the entire length of the wall. If tired and hungry migrants can do it, so can we.'

'And what happens if we do make it?' cried Shella. 'What then? We've lost our powers, Daffers; nothing will ever be the same again. And where's your damn daughter? Why hasn't she come to help us?'

'One question at a time, Shella. Powers or no powers, I'd rather be home than here. In fact, I'd rather be anywhere but here. We can worry about what happens later, once we're safely back in the empire. As for Karalyn, I don't know what to say. The day we lost our powers, I was sure that she would come looking for us, and I don't understand why she hasn't come. Maybe she's been looking for days, but can't find us. After all, she has no powers to latch on to. Normally, she senses me by locating my vision skills. Without that, perhaps it's been too difficult.'

Shella snorted. 'You don't actually believe that, do you? Too difficult for the most powerful mage this world has ever seen?'

'What's the alternative – that something terrible has happened to her? I can't think about that. I refuse to think about it. We have to remain focussed on what we can do on our own, and not start to wallow in misery about why Karalyn hasn't turned up. Look on the bright side – we've managed to evade capture for ten days, and we've made it all the way to the border.'

'You almost make it sound romantic, Daffers,' said Shella. 'We've been raking in garbage bins for scraps, and sleeping in rat-infested housing blocks that should have been knocked down years ago. Let's face it – without powers, we are just two feeble old ladies.'

'Speak for yourself,' said Daphne. 'I feel neither feeble, nor old, thank you very much. Look at Caelius; he doesn't have any powers, and I've yet to hear him complain once about our predicament.'

'That's because the old bastard thinks we're on a jolly adventure. He's loving this; aren't you, Caelius?'

The veteran kept his eyes on the gap in the tent entrance. 'I'm merely doing my job to the best of my abilities, ma'am.'

'When we get back,' said Daphne, 'I would like you to tell me the truth about your nephew Thymo.'

Shella frowned.

'I didn't think we kept secrets from each other,' Daphne went on. 'I'm marginally offended that you decided not to reveal this little part of your past to me.'

'Well, I guess you should have read my mind when you had the chance, Daffers.'

Daphne glared at her oldest friend. 'Perhaps we should get some rest. All three of us are tired and hungry, and the last ten days haven't exactly been easy on the nerves.'

She pulled off her long cloak and folded it into a pillow. She lay down on her right side, as her left arm was sore, and closed her eyes. She shivered in the cold night air, then controlled her breathing. Just one more step to take, and they would be safe and free. Of all the powers she had lost, she missed battle-vision the most. She had lost count of the number of times over the preceding ten days that she had tried to summon it; and each time, the disappointment at finding it gone had crushed her. She and Shella had argued for days about the possible reasons why they had both been deprived of the powers that had made them high mages, but neither had thought of a convincing explanation. It couldn't be Kelsey, as Kelsey's presence didn't negate battle-vision. They both remembered when the old Emperor had caused all mage powers to cease during his experiments, but the effects of that had lasted only a few hours; whereas this had gone on for ten days, with no sign that their powers might be returning.

Daphne tried to imagine a world in which she could never access her powers again. She would be of little use to the Empress as Herald, but Bridget seemed to have made up her mind to have her replaced with Bryce, so did it matter? She would still be able to carry out her duties as First Holder, and then she could retire the following year. Would it be so bad?

Yes, she thought. Her powers were an intrinsic part of her identity; without them, she would be a different person.

'Daffers?' whispered Shella.

Daphne opened her eyes, and saw Shella lying on the floor of the tent a yard from her.

'Thymo was right,' Shella said, keeping her voice low. 'I abandoned him in Silverstream, when he was just a young boy. I took him there after Kalayne rescued me from Plateau City; it was the only place I could think of that would be safe. Then Laodoc, Bridget and Agang turned up, and persuaded me that I had to fight the mad Emperor. What could I do? Noli had asked me, begged me, to look after him. I couldn't take him to the Plateau, not when I thought that we'd probably all be killed. Silverstream was peaceful and safe, and I thought it would be better to leave him there. Then, after it was all over, and the Emperor was dead, Bridget needed me to help her regain control of the empire. Time passed, and I genuinely believed that Thymo would be better off where he was. The last thing he needed was his crazy aunt meddling in his life again. Anyway, that's what I thought. I was wrong.'

'Why have you never told me this before?'

Shella shrugged her shoulders. 'I think it was because I felt guilty about leaving him there, and I didn't want to have to deal with it. When I moved to Colsbury, I often thought about sending for him, but I backed out each time, afraid of what I might discover. And then, years later, Sable and the Army of Pyre destroyed Silverstream. After that, I assumed Thymo was dead, along with the rest of the inhabitants. I am a disaster, Daffers. I couldn't save Sami, and I couldn't save Thymo. Is it any wonder that the rest of my family hated me? I was supposed to give Thymo a new life, free from the worry of living here, in Rakana. Instead, all I achieved was to make his life even worse. A tiny part of me liked to believe that he had escaped Silverstream, and was living in peace in Amatskouri, or somewhere else on the Plateau. That little fantasy kept me going whenever the guilt threatened to swamp me. I was deluding myself; I know that now.'

Daphne knew that Shella was waiting for her to say something, but she was struggling to find a sympathetic response. The idea that Daphne would abandon even the least member of her family was utterly alien to her, and yet Shella had allowed her young nephew to slip through the cracks, spurning every opportunity to make things right.

'You hate me, don't you, Daffers?'

'No,' said Daphne. 'I'm finding it hard to understand why you acted in the way that you did, but you will always be my friend, Shella.'

'It's too late for me now. I can never repair the damage I did to him.'

'He's your nephew, Shella; it's never too late to try.'

Shella lapsed into silence, then her eyes tightened slightly. 'What about Sable?'

Daphne frowned. 'What about her?'

'She's your sister, isn't she? And yet you never express any desire to help her, or even to find out what's happened to her.'

'Don't turn this round on to me, Shella. We were talking about Thymo.'

'Yes, but I can feel your disapproval from here. You blame me for abandoning my nephew, but you haven't lifted a finger to help Sable, and she's your sister.'

'Half-sister.'

Shella snorted. 'Right.'

'Sable fought for Agatha, at least in the first stages of the war. She committed countless crimes during that conflict, and deserved to be hanged. Did I allow that to happen? No. I saved her life.'

'And sent her off to Lostwell.'

'Yes. She couldn't have stayed here. The Empress wanted her blood, and she wasn't the only one.'

'Fine. What about now, though? She could be dead on Dragon Eyre, for all you know.'

Daphne hesitated. She longed for a cigarette, but they had run out several days before.

'Do you think I have treated Sable badly, Shella?' she said.

'You tell me. You're the one who always places their family above everything else. You've got into trouble with Bridget loads of times because you put your family first. Do you think you've treated Sable badly?'

'I think I'm still angry with my father. Sable should never have been born.'

'Is that Sable's fault?'

'I can't believe you're defending her, Shella. She manipulated Army of Pyre soldiers and sent them into marketplaces in Plateau City to slaughter civilians. She forced Lennox to burn down a hospital in Rainsby. She murdered Nyane, and Ravi's sister. She abducted Thorn's mother and killed her best friend. I was disgusted when I learned that we were related.'

'You've murdered plenty of people, Daffers. Can you truly say that every one of them deserved it?'

'I'm bringing this conversation to a halt. I am not the same as Sable.'

'If you had fought on the other side, would you not have done the same things as she did?'

'No.'

'Who's deluding themselves now, Daffers?'

'Are you calling me a hypocrite?'

Caelius turned from the tent entrance. 'Sorry, ladies, but I'm going to have to request that you please keep your voices down. A squad of Rakanese militia is patrolling this area. If they hear you speaking Holdings, then the game is up.'

Daphne brought her temper under control. 'Apologies, Caelius.'

She closed her eyes, determined not to rise to Shella's bait. She was deflecting blame, because she knew how badly she had treated Thymo, and was trying to equate that with what had happened to Sable. The two matters were entirely separate. Thymo had been a young boy; while Sable was a mass-murdering traitor and war criminal. Ruthlessly efficient, she had brought terror and destruction to the empire in the service of foreign gods who had desired to rule the entire world. She and Daphne had nothing in common. Nothing at all. It was ridiculous to compare them. Utterly ridiculous.

She rolled onto her back and stared at the shadows covering the roof of the tent.

Sable was probably having fun on Dragon Eyre. After all, it was a world mired in conflict, and Sable thrived in such conditions. Unencumbered by her tortured past, she had most likely forged out a place for herself amid the chaos.

Or, she might already be dead. Daphne felt her spirits fall at the thought. Why? She loathed her depraved and twisted half-sibling. Didn't she? A pang of empathy for her lost little sister ran wild through her mind. She reined it in. There was nothing she could do to reach out to Sable. She had to focus on getting out of Rakana alive. And then? Then, maybe, she might ask Karalyn to look for her, just to check that she was all right. Maybe.

Daphne felt a hand nudge her shoulder, and her eyes opened. Caelius was crouching over her in the dim shadows of the tent. He motioned towards the entrance, indicating that it was time to go. Daphne nodded, and started to sit up, her limbs aching from the uncomfortable position in which she had been lying. Her crippled left arm was throbbing, but, without battle-vision to quell the pain, she would have to bear it. Caelius shook Shella gently, and the Rakanese woman awoke, and stretched her arms. She glanced at Daphne, then looked away, the guilt in her eyes unmistakeable. In silence, they donned their long dark cloaks, then pulled up the hoods to hide their faces.

Caelius returned to the tent's entrance and peered out. He glanced over his shoulder, nodded at Daphne and Shella, then crawled outside. Daphne gestured for Shella to go next, and the Rakanese woman scrambled through the entrance. Daphne took a breath, and followed them. Outside, the seven stars were shining down from the eastern sky, and the migrant camp was bathed in darkness and silence. A few fires were still burning here and there, and the height of the massive border wall was illuminated by the flickering flames. At the base of the wall, next to a sealed and blocked gateway, Rakanese soldiers were patrolling, watching out for any migrant who tried to scale the huge stone barrier. A pile of wrecked and broken ladders lay next to the blocked gates, and some of the militia were setting fire to them, as Daphne and her friends watched from the shadows. Caelius turned left, and they stole down between two rows of battered old tents, keeping away from the light of the fires. A few Rakanese glanced at them from the entrances of their tents, and one whispered 'good luck', as they passed. At the southern edge of the vast camp was a paved road. It led directly to the sealed gate, and a few soldiers were stationed there, keeping watch over the tented city.

Caelius crept along by the side of the road, huddling down in the drainage ditch that ran next to it, with Daphne and Shella by his side. Opposite them, two Rakanese soldiers were standing, looking bored and tired, their crossbows slung over their shoulders. Caelius glanced at them, then eyed Daphne, and she nodded. They each drew a knife, stolen from a butcher's counter at a market in Arakhanah City. Daphne signalled to Shella to remain where she was, and readied herself. With or without battle-vision, the only way across the road was through the two soldiers. She hadn't killed anyone in a long time, but she pushed her qualms to one side. What choice did they have? She gestured for Caelius to go right. He nodded, and began to crawl along the drainage ditch, a knife in his right hand. Daphne waited a moment, then crept along to the left, keeping her left arm tucked in close to her body. Caelius made a call that sounded like a bird, and the two soldiers glanced in his direction. Daphne sprang up from the ditch and bolted to the other side, where she flung herself down. She edged back towards the soldiers, until she was crouching directly behind them. She smeared mud from the ditch onto the blade of her knife, and waited. Caelius called out again, and Daphne got to her feet. She reached round with her knife, and cut the throat of the first soldier. The other started in alarm, but Caelius was on him before he could cry out. The veteran barrelled into him, knocking him off his feet, then he sank the knife into the man's heart, while clamping his mouth shut with his free hand. Caelius and Daphne glanced at each other, then they dragged the bodies off the road, and into the ditch. Daphne waved to Shella, and she scurried over the road, and jumped into the ditch, her eyes on the two dead soldiers.

Saying nothing, Daphne set off, heading away from the migrant camp and into the desolate fields that lay beyond its southern edge. She raced along, hearing the tread of the others behind her, as she put as much distance between them and the camp as possible. After twenty minutes, she veered to the right, and they turned towards the border wall. They paused in a clump of trees that was surrounded by sawn stumps, and crouched in the shadows. Caelius tapped Daphne on the shoulder.

'Ma'am,' he whispered; 'we are not alone.'

He gestured to their left, and Daphne saw a few shapes huddled in a ditch.

'They have a ladder, ma'am,' Caelius said, his low voice in her ear.

'Then we wait for them to make their move,' said Daphne.

She turned back to the wall, and watched as a Rakanese patrol marched by its base, heading north towards the camp. As soon as the soldiers had moved out of sight, the small group of five migrants hiding to Daphne's left got up, and ran towards the wall, two of them carrying a long ladder.

'Let's go,' said Daphne.

She helped Shella get to her feet, and the three of them sprinted towards the wall, jumping over the lattice-work of twisting tree roots that snaked across their path. The migrant group reached the wall first, and set the ladder in place. They jumped in fright as they saw Daphne, Shella and Caelius race towards them. Daphne placed a finger to her lips.

'We're getting out of here, too,' Shella told them in Rakanese.

'You go last,' said one of the migrants, then he signalled to the others to start scaling the ladder.

The first to climb was a young woman, and Daphne watched as she made it onto the parapet of the wall and disappeared from sight. Daphne glanced north and south, as the next migrant scaled the ladder. Her impatience started to mount, and she silently urged the migrants on. The second made it to the top of the wall, then the third and fourth. As the last commenced his climb, Caelius made a low groan. He pointed to the south. Another patrol was approaching.

The last migrant raced up the ladder, just as the soldiers were coming into view. Caelius gripped the sides of the ladder, and pulled it away from the wall, then Daphne helped him carry it as they retreated back to the clump of trees. They reached the safety of the shadows as the soldiers neared the spot where they had tried to cross the border. A few soldiers glanced down at the footprints, and the patrol stopped. They gazed around, peering into the darkness, as Daphne, Shella and Caelius hugged the ground. For what seemed an age to Daphne, the soldiers stood around, talking in low voices, and pointing at the marks on the ground left by the ladder.

The officer in charge of the patrol pulled a whistle from a pocket, and blew on it, sending a piercing blast through the night air. A few minutes later, more soldiers arrived, some with torches and lamps, and they started searching the area.

'We should have left the ladder where it was,' muttered Shella.

'Then how would we get over the wall, ma'am?' said Caelius.

'We need to pull back,' whispered Daphne. 'Come on.'

She and Caelius picked up the ladder, and they started to run to the east, away from the wall, as the torchlight got closer. Shella tripped over a trailing tree root and let out a shriek as she fell into a muddy ditch.

'Drop the ladder!' cried Daphne.

They let it fall to the ground, then Daphne reached down to pull Shella up. A torch beam flashed over them in the gloom.

'There they are!' shouted a soldier.

'Surrender or we will loose!' called out the Rakanese officer.

Caelius looked blank at the shouted words, then a crossbow bolt whistled by his face, and he dived to the ground. Another bolt flew close to Shella, and she raised her arms.

'Don't shoot!' she cried in Rakanese.

The soldiers surrounded them in moments, their bows aimed at the three fugitives.

'Well, well,' said the officer, striding into their midst. 'What do we have here? Three treacherous little runaways. You all know the penalty for trying to cross the border. We found the ladder, so there's no point in trying to protest your innocence.' He glared at them. 'Hoods off. I want to see your faces.'

Shella pulled her hood away, and the officer glanced at her without a word. His eyes widened, however, when Daphne and Caelius did the same thing.

'She's Holdings,' cried one of the soldiers, pointing at Daphne.

'I can see that, Private,' said the officer. He stared at Daphne. 'Who are you?'

Daphne said nothing, her eyes sparkling with defiance.

'If you refuse to answer,' said the officer, 'then I must assume that you are a spy.' He turned to Caelius. 'And you? Who, or what, are you?'

Caelius kept his mouth shut.

'Are you Sanang?' said the officer. 'Answer me.'

Caelius said nothing.

The officer gestured to a soldier. 'Beat him until he decides to speak.'

'Wait,' cried Shella. 'He doesn't know our language.'

'Shut up,' muttered Daphne.

'He doesn't speak Rakanese,' said the officer, 'yet he is in Rakana.' He switched to Holdings. 'Do you understand what I am saying now?'

'You'll get nothing from me,' said Caelius. 'Do your worst.'

'So, we have two spies, aided and abetted by one of our own,' said the officer. 'Sergeant, have their wrists bound, and escort them to the garrison base. I have a feeling the colonel will want to meet them.'

'Never fear, ma'am,' said Caelius; 'I will tell them nothing.'

'Shut up,' muttered Shella. 'We're sitting in a damned prison cell, Caelius, or hadn't you noticed? It doesn't matter if you speak or not – they're going to hang us all as traitors or spies.'

'But, ma'am,' Caelius went on, 'Lady Holdfast is the elected ruler of the Holdings, as well as the Empress's Herald; they cannot execute her. The empire would be forced to retaliate, and Rakana would be devastated. Their armed forces are no match for the legions under the control of the Empress; it would be walkover.'

Shella frowned. 'Damn it; you're right. Daffers, maybe it would be better if you admitted who you are to the militia. They might have to let you go.'

Daphne kept perfectly still in the corner of the cell. She hadn't told the others, but her left arm had been in agony since the moment her wrists had been bound behind her back, and she could barely speak through the pain.

'It's worth considering at least,' Shella went on. 'Daffers?'

'No,' Daphne grunted. 'I'm not leaving you behind, Shella. We got into this together, and we'll get out of it together. That goes for you, too, Caelius.'

'I cannot allow you to endanger yourself on my account, ma'am,' said the old veteran. 'If there is a chance for one of us to escape this dreadful place, then we should snatch at it.'

'I don't want to hear another word on this,' said Daphne. 'I refuse to countenance being separated from you both. If we die, we die side by side, our heads held high.'

The thick door to the cell swung open, and the occupants were blinded by the lamplight coming from the hallway outside. A high-ranking Rakanese officer walked in, flanked by crossbow-wielding soldiers, while a smattering of officers and guards stood outside.

The officer glanced down at them, his hands clasped behind his back.

'You have been tried in your absence,' he said, 'and been found guilty of murder, espionage, and attempting to cross the border illegally. Do you have anything to say?'

Daphne placed a mask of utter calm onto her features, and said nothing. Caelius did the same, while Shella kept her gaze directed downwards.

'Very well,' said the officer. He glanced at a subordinate. 'Bring him in.'

Two soldiers approached the cell, escorting another man between them. It was Thymo.

Shella gasped.

The officer smiled. 'It looks as though we might be in luck.' He turned to Thymo. 'Are you able to identify any of these prisoners, citizen?'

Thymo raised a hand and pointed at Shella. 'This is the so-called Princess of Rakana – Shellakanawara.'

A few of the soldiers started talking in excited tones, then the officer raised a hand.

'Silence,' he said. 'Citizen, are you absolutely certain that this is she?'

'Yes, sir,' Thymo said. 'She's my aunt.'

'Your aunt?' said the officer. 'Why did you not mention this before? When you said you had information concerning Shellakanawara's location, why did you neglect this detail?'

Thymo's face flushed. 'I was too ashamed. It's humiliating to have a wicked traitor in the family.'

'I see. Can you identify the others?'

'Yes, sir.' He pointed at Daphne. 'I don't know who the man is, but this is Daphne Holdfast.'

The soldiers fell into silence.

The officer's eyes widened. 'The Herald of the Empire? Can you prove it?'

'Her left arm is crippled, just as the stories say, sir. She's been a friend of my aunt's for years – this is well known.'

'Oh, Thymo,' said Shella. 'How can you do this to us?'

Thymo stared at her. 'Revenge, Shella. Did you know that there is a reward for your capture? I'm going to give it to the rest of the family; it'll be the most you've ever done for them. I hope they hang you where the people of this city can see it happen. I hope I see it.'

'That's enough,' said the officer. 'Take Thymo away, Lieutenant, and see that he receives his reward.'

'Yes, sir,' said a younger officer, who stepped forward, then escorted Thymo from the cell.

As soon as they were gone, the officer in charge glanced at a sergeant. 'Make sure Thymo does not leave this fortress alive. Distribute his reward among your men.'

The sergeant saluted, then hurried after Thymo.

'You bastard,' spat Shella.

'Silence, traitor,' said the officer. 'Were it not for the presence of the Herald of the Empire, then I would have allowed Thymo to go free. However, this has now become a matter of national security. By coming here, Holder Fast has committed an act of war against this country. I shall need to relay this information to the highest authorities in Arakhanah City. No doubt, there will be many who will wish to interrogate the prize I have scooped up this night.' He turned to the other soldiers. 'Each one of you is confined to quarters. You shall all accompany the prisoners back to the city, as soon as transport has been arranged. If any of you mention the identities of our captives to a single person, I shall have you and your families executed. This is not an idle threat – the future of Rakana is at stake, and I will do whatever it takes to secure our frontiers. Now, hood them, and place gauntlets onto the hands of Shellakanawara. Both of these women are high mages, and they will most likely try to kill us at the first opportunity. There is no need to be gentle with them.'

He turned, and smiled at Daphne. 'As I have no doubt that you sneaked into this country illegally, ma'am; let me be the first to officially welcome you to Rakana. I would wish you a pleasant stay, but we would both know that I was lying.'

He moved to the side, and soldiers flooded the cell. Daphne was shoved to the floor, then a soldier knelt on her back, and a dark hood was placed over her head.

Daphne kept calm, but the same thought kept reverberating around her head.

Where was Karalyn?

CHAPTER 21

GODFREY'S GRANDSON

P lateau City, The Plateau – 15th Day, Second Third Summer 534
Keir stirred three sugars into his coffee. 'Today is my son's ninth birthday.'

Brannig glanced at him from the other side of the townhouse balcony. 'Nine, eh? You must miss him terribly.'

'Of course,' said Keir. 'I think about him all the time, but his evil mother prevents me from playing a part in his life, and my own mother does nothing to help. Mothers think they own their children; they don't care if the fathers are discarded. Just like what happened to you, Brannig. You were used by a powerful woman, and then thrown away.'

Brannig frowned. 'My circumstances weren't like that, Keir. I willingly entered into an agreement with her Majesty. I wasn't thrown away.'

Keir smiled. 'You're still loyal to her, I see. Naïve, but loyal. I was duped by a woman when I was sixteen. She tried to trap me into marrying her. It taught me a lesson about womankind that I'll never forget. You can't trust them, Brannig. They'll lie to your face with a smile on their lips.'

Brannig glanced away, looking slightly uncomfortable. 'I'll never grow tired of this view,' he said. 'The Inner Sea looks so peaceful and tranquil.'

'You know,' said Keir, 'you don't sound much like a Kellach Brigdomin. Your Holdings is excellent.'

'Thank you. Wealth had a part to play in that. I grew up in extreme poverty, prior to the Rahain invasion, and then I spent several years as a slave. As soon as I was fortunate enough to earn a sum of money, I spent a portion of it on my own education, paying particular attention to the learning of the Holdings tongue. After all, I intended to become a merchant who dealt with the aristocrats of Plateau City, bringing them goods from my homeland.' He laughed. 'I still sound like any other Kellach Brigdomin when I converse in my own language.'

Keir frowned. Brannig was a fraud, in other words; his fancy way of speaking Holdings a mere affectation. He was a peasant who had stumbled into riches, whereas Keir was a true aristocrat.

'Your money comes from whisky, does it not?' Keir said.

'Not all. I own stakes in several enterprises in Northern Kell. Coal and iron mining, and timber, all of which is transported to Westport on the Inner Sea, and thence to here, the Imperial Capital. Some of the ships currently anchored outside the harbour probably contain goods purchased by myself.'

Keir smirked. 'It's a pity you had to ruin it all, isn't it?'

Brannig looked confused. 'I don't think I follow.'

'Well,' said Keir, 'once everyone knows that you broke the most solemn oath that you've ever made, then who's going to trust you? If you can't keep your word to the Empress, who would you keep it for?'

Brannig lapsed into silence, his gaze on the placid waters of the Inner Sea, and Keir knew he had beaten him. He sipped his coffee to hide the smug expression on his face, his eyes watching Brannig. He enjoyed teasing the older man; he seemed so gullible and trusting, and those aspects of his character reminded him of Corthie. Keir laughed to himself. Yes. Brannig was an oaf like his brother, except that he had a far posher accent than Corthie possessed.

'I must have gone over it a hundred times,' said Brannig, his face downcast, 'and yet I still struggle to explain why I broke my silence regarding the children. It was almost as though I felt compelled to approach them, as if I had no say in the matter.'

'You're not the only person lacking in self-control,' said Keir. 'However, the consequences of your indiscretion may be far-reaching. Perhaps you should cut your losses and return to Kellach Brigdomin.'

'No. Not while Berra and Bedig still desire to visit me. Bethal, I fear I have lost; but I retain hope that Bryce and Brogan may change their views.'

'You've been here, what... seventeen days? Eighteen? That's quite a long time for a man who claimed he only wanted a glimpse of his children.'

'I'm grateful that you and your kind wife have allowed me to stay in the Holdfast townhouse. If at any time, my presence becomes unwelcome, I would be happy to leave. The last thing I wish to do is inconvenience you.'

Keir frowned. He had hoped that Brannig would volunteer to leave of his own accord. If Keir insisted that he had to go, then it would mean another blazing row with Thorn, who had repeatedly assured Brannig that he could stay for as long as he liked.

'It's no inconvenience,' said Keir. 'It's been a delight having you here.' He put down his coffee cup. 'Now, if you'll excuse me, I need to get ready for work.'

Keir stood, and strode from the balcony. Would he never be rid of Brannig? And whose house was it, anyway? Thorn treated the place as if she owned it, but the name above the door read *Holdfast*, and Keir was the only proper Holdfast in Plateau City. He was being taken advantage of by everyone – his wife, Brannig, Tabor, the Empress; none of whom showed him the proper level of respect that he deserved. He came to the stairs, and saw Tabitha down in the front hall, speaking to Berra. The Empress's sixteen-year-old daughter was wearing a flowery summer dress, and was holding a wrapped gift in her hands, no doubt intended for her errant father.

Tabitha gave Keir a wary look, while Berra smiled when she saw him come down the stairs.

'Good morning, Lord Holdfast,' Berra said. 'What a beautiful day it's turning into.'

'Good morning, Lady Berra,' he said. 'Unfortunately, I don't have time to chat. I have to get to the Great Fortress.'

'I understand,' she said. 'Is my father in his rooms?'

'He's out on the balcony,' Keir said. 'I'd love to stay, but some of us have to work.'

'Of course,' she said. 'Don't let me keep you.'

Keir brushed past them and walked to the front door of the townhouse. He collected his coat, and opened the door. Outside, several nosey inhabitants of the city were loitering, hoping to catch a glimpse of the man who had fathered the children of the Empress.

'You lot still here?' said Keir, as he closed the door behind him. 'Have you nothing better to do with your time than harass that poor man?'

He walked down the wide steps and swept through the crowd, who parted for him. He climbed up into his waiting carriage, and a footman closed the door. Keir heard the driver call out to the four horses, and the carriage moved off, bumping over the cobblestones as it pulled away from the side of the road. Keir's morning newspaper had been placed on the seat next to him, and he picked it up. The main stories were all about Brannig, again. According to a supposed eye witness, the father of the Empress's children had been seen drinking in a tavern in the Kellach Quarter, and had got so drunk that he had crawled about on all fours vomiting over anyone within range. Keir laughed. It was completely untrue, but he found it funny all the same. Starved of any actual news about the man, the paper had resorted to printing any rumours reported to them, no matter how scurrilous. Keir flicked through the rest of the pages, looking for news that his mother had returned to her post in Holdings City, but there was no mention of it. She couldn't still be in Rakana, could she? Keir pushed it from his mind. It was Karalyn's job to take care of these issues, not his.

Keir managed to fit in a quick smoke after the carriage dropped him off next to the dry moat that encircled the Great Fortress. It was a hot sunny day, and he amused himself by watching the young women stroll by in their loose summer clothes. Keir loved summer in the city. The women shed their long coats, and started to reveal legs and arms, and a bit of cleavage if they were daring enough. He tossed the cigarette butt into the moat and entered the palace. He ascended to the upper levels, and announced himself to Mage Tabor, who was sitting in his cramped little office.

'Good morning, Keir,' he said, glancing up.

Keir looked down at the desk, but the usual piles of messages were absent.

'There's nothing to send at the moment,' Tabor said, noticing where Keir's glance fell.

'Why not, sir?'

Tabor shrugged. 'It sometimes happens. Go and see if Lady Thorn needs any assistance. She's working on next year's budget proposal. I'll call for you if I require your help.'

Keir raised an eyebrow, but said nothing. He was normally sent to Bryce if he was seen to be at a loose end, but he wasn't going to argue with Tabor. He nodded, then walked from the office. The hallways of the palace were almost silent as he made his way up a level to where his wife worked. Thorn's office was larger than Tabor's, and when Keir entered, his wife was talking to two young clerks, who stood taking notes.

Keir caught Thorn's attention. 'Tabor sent me. Do you need anything?'

Thorn nodded, then dismissed the two clerks.

'Close the door,' she said, once they had gone.

Keir did so, then he strode forward and took a seat. Thorn picked up a cup of tea, and sipped.

'Is something happening?' he said. 'Why is the palace so quiet?'

'There was an... incident last night,' she said.

'Is that why you stayed here?' he said. 'I notice you didn't return to the townhouse last night.'

'Yes. The Empress and her elder son had a disagreement. Both had been drinking in separate parts of the palace, and when they came together... well, it wasn't pleasant. Then Brogan got involved. She was sober, thankfully, but she was unable to calm the situation down. I've never heard the Empress so angry, Keir. The language she used towards Lord Bryce was dreadful.'

'What were they fighting about?'

'It started off with Brannig. The Empress wants to send him home, whereas Lord Bryce wants his father to live in the Great Fortress.'

Keir frowned. 'I thought that Bryce wasn't overly fond of Brannig?'

'I don't think he is, Keir; but he said that it was too late to send him back to Kellach Brigdomin. The entire city knows that Brannig is staying in the townhouse. He said that the situation was making the Empress appear weak and foolish. He thinks that if Brannig moved into the palace, then they would be better able to keep him under close supervision. Anyway, they argued about that for a long while, and then the conversation moved onto a different topic – the succession.'

'The what?'

Thorn took another drink of tea. 'Who will succeed the Empress when she either retires or dies? It was at that point I was ejected from the audience chamber, along with everyone else apart from the Empress and her children.' Her eyes stared off into nothing. 'I need to speak to your mother.'

'Good luck with that. No one seems to know where she is. She went to Rakana eighteen days ago, and hasn't been heard of since.'

'That's not entirely accurate. She's been in contact with Agang Garo in Colsbury. Didn't Mage Tabor tell you?'

Keir frowned. 'No. He did not.'

'Agang says that your mother has visoned to him, to tell him that she and Shella are fine, and that they're on their way back to the Plateau.'

'No one tells me anything in this damn place. Still, I'm relieved to hear it. I was worried she had been captured or something. Go on with what happened between the Empress and Bryce.'

Thorn shrugged. 'I heard a lot of shouting, which went on for a considerable amount of time. Eventually, I went to bed. No one told me that I was dismissed for the night, so I thought I'd better stay. I saw Lady Berra leave this morning – I think she was oblivious to what had gone on – but I've yet to see any sign of the others.' She shook her head. 'This is no way to run an empire. The Empress's drinking is getting steadily worse. She seems to be starting earlier every day, and by the evening she's incapable of standing. What if a crisis occurs while she's inebriated? What if the public learn that their sovereign ruler was knocking back a bottle of whisky every night? It can't go on. The empire deserves better than having a drunkard in charge.'

Keir chuckled. 'Treasonous talk. Are you planning a coup?'

'Don't be ridiculous, Keir. I swore an oath of loyalty to her Majesty, and, unlike dear Brannig, I keep my oaths. I'm talking about trying to persuade the Empress to cut back a little, before she kills herself with drink. Lord Bryce and Lady Brogan refuse to say anything to their mother about it, and my words lack any authority. We need your mother. Perhaps she could talk some sense into the Empress.'

'Could you not give her a subtle blast of healing powers?'

'The Empress has made it crystal clear what she thinks of that,' said Thorn. 'She told me that if I used my powers on her, I would be forced to resign my position. It sounds strange, but at times it's as though her Majesty thinks that she deserves to suffer. Maybe the weight of the deaths from the war haunt her. All those young soldiers who died defending Rainsby, and the massacres in Stretton Sands and Amatskouri. I think she blames herself. What's more, she has never quite forgiven us for forcing her to continue as Empress in Colsbury.'

'We both voted for mother; it's not our fault that the others voted for Bridget.'

'You're missing the point. Her Majesty doesn't want to be the Empress. She hates it. Perhaps we should have allowed her to abdicate with grace, rather than witness her slow decline.'

'But the empire is at peace. In fact, it's never been so prosperous and contented. Her legacy is safe.'

'For the moment. Our job is now to shield the Empress from her public. Did you read today's newspaper? Did you see the story describing Brannig's drunken antics? All false, of course, but if they start printing articles about the Empress's drinking, then her popularity will plummet. Every stereotype about the Kellach Brigdomin will be confirmed in the hearts of the citizens, and she will become a figure of ridicule. For the sake of the empire, we must not allow that to happen.'

'Why do you care? You harbour your own ambitions. If the Empress is disgraced, then does that not give you the opportunity you've been waiting for your whole life?'

Thorn put down her cup. 'I shall be Empress, one day. But what use to me is a tarnished throne? I desire a respectful and peaceful transfer of power, not the break-up of the empire. To truly succeed, I require the Empress herself to anoint me as her successor. I also need to keep my hands clean. I cannot be seen to be gloating over the Empress's misfortunes, or conspiring to have her removed from power. The same goes for you, Keir. As my husband, it would be preferable if you stayed aloof from such matters. This is why I think you should take the rest of the day off. Get out of the palace, for now.'

'What? But...'

'When the Empress and Lord Bryce finally awaken from their drunken slumbers, they will need to be handled with extreme tact and discretion. This is my area of expertise. If Mage Tabor has no work for you, then you should slip away before the arguments have a chance to restart. Mage Tabor can summon you if you are needed.'

'You don't have the authority to throw me out of the palace.'

'Don't get angry; listen to me. I'm not throwing you out – I am politely requesting that you take my advice. You have a face that cannot conceal what you are feeling, and that makes you a potential liability in circumstances such as these. Let me deal with today's events. I will tell them that you are running an errand for me, as per Mage Tabor's instructions.'

Keir simmered with rage. How dare Thorn speak to him like that, as if he were a tactless child? It was clear that she had no respect for him; that she thought he was a nothing but a fool. He stared at her, then got to his feet.

Thorn sighed. 'Don't look at me like that, Keir.'

Keir turned his back to her, and walked from the room. The two young clerks were waiting outside, and they edged away from the darkness in Keir's eyes. He glared at them, then picked up his pace, his mind whirling as he made his way down the flights of stairs to the ground floor. Several officers saluted him, but he ignored them all, his hands shaking with fury. That stupid bitch. He thought about divorcing her. See how she coped when stripped of the Holdfast name; that would teach her to respect him.

He stumbled out into the open air, and lit a cigarette. The thought occurred to him that Thorn had fabricated the whole tale, that there had been no drunken row, and that she had used it as an excuse to remove him from the palace. After all, he only had her word for it, and, like all women, she was an expert liar.

He began to walk aimlessly, heading towards the vast open-air market that sat to the north of the Emergency Wall. The crowds of people on the streets grew thicker, and Keir barged his way through, his height and bulk forcing the Holdings and Rakanese traders from his path.

He wanted to make Thorn pay, but how? His thoughts went to Tilda Holdwain. He hadn't seen her for several days, worried lest she became too attached to him. She would be working in the Holdings Embassy, but he had no reason to visit, and didn't want to arouse any suspicions. He diverted off the main road and walked down a narrow back street, which was lined with cafés. The outside tables were heaving with people who had just been to the market, and Keir carried on until he reached a deserted alleyway. He leaned against a wall, and sent his vision powers out. His sight soared up into the sky, giving him a perfect view of the New Town. He glanced around, then located the small district that contained the consulates and embassies from the various nations. The Holdings Embassy was a large detached mansion, almost palatial in size and style, and he pushed his vision in through an open window. The Holdings ambassador was entertaining a delegation of merchants from Hold Smith, while his secretary sat alongside, recording the conversation. Keir moved through the building to the first floor, where Tilda had her desk. He glanced down at her. She appeared to be hard at work, but on closer inspection, he saw that she was writing a letter to her sister back in the Holdings.

He entered her mind.

Good morning, Tilda; it's Keir. Don't react; just listen. I have the day off, and I need to see you. Make an excuse, and then go back to your apartment. I'll meet you there in twenty minutes.

He withdrew from her head without waiting for a response, then watched her, to see if she would do as he had asked. She sat still for a moment, then she folded up the half-written letter and slid it into a drawer. She glanced around, then got to her feet. Keir watched as she spoke to her supervisor, who frowned then, eventually, nodded his head.

Keir pulled his vision back to his body, and smiled.

Twenty minutes later, Keir was loitering in the shadows of a narrow lane outside the apartment block where Tilda lived. It was in a pleasant neighbourhood, with elegant three-storey houses built from yellow sandstone. Every window seemed to have its own little box hanging outside, filled with flowers in bloom, and bees were buzzing from house to house. Keir grew impatient as he waited. He was recognisable to many people in the city, as one of the only men who shared the height of the Kellach with the skin-colouring of the Holdings, and he fretted that some busybody would spot him.

Tilda appeared from round a street corner. She was hurrying along, keeping her eyes down as she strode towards her front door. Keir stepped out from the shadows, and she glanced up at him.

They said nothing as Tilda took out a key. She unlocked the door, and they entered the ground floor apartment, Keir taking a last look over his shoulder to make sure no one had seen him. Once inside, Tilda took off her coat and hung it on a peg.

'Is something wrong?' she said. 'Your message sounded urgent. Is Thorn suspicious?'

'Thorn knows nothing,' he said, taking her hand.

He began to pull her towards the bedroom.

'Hold on,' she said. 'I think we might need to talk about this.'

'Talking can wait,' he said. 'There's only one thing I need from you right now, and it doesn't involve talking.'

***

Keir opened his eyes. Had he been dozing? He glanced around Tilda's bedroom, but there was no sign of her. He listened, then made out the sounds of her shower coming from the bathroom next door. He relaxed, his mind reliving the touch of Tilda in his arms as they had lain together. He wondered what time it was. He sat up, the white cotton sheets tangling round his legs. Tilda's bedroom was sparsely furnished, with plain, undecorated walls, and just a few homely touches to show who lived there. Her clothes were scattered across the wooden floor in a trail leading from the main entrance, and he smiled at how easy it had been to get her into bed.

The noise from the shower stopped, and the bathroom door opened. Tilda emerged, one towel wrapped round her body, and another wound round her hair. Keir couldn't take his eyes off her.

'I thought you might have gone by now,' she said. 'The last time you were here, you stayed for less than twenty minutes.'

'I don't want to leave.'

'Are you not worried we'll get caught? Why aren't you at work?'

'Stop the questions,' he said. 'Part of the reason I came here was to get away from all that.'

She walked across the floor of the room towards her dresser, and Keir felt his desire for her grow.

'Come back to bed,' he said.

'No,' she said, as she opened a chest of drawers. 'I've already had one shower, and I can barely afford to pay for the hot water as it is.'

'I can give you money.'

She pulled on her underwear, the towel falling to the floor. 'You'd pay my bills?'

'Sure. Have you any idea how wealthy I am?'

'I have a fair notion.' She sat by the small dresser and gazed at her reflection, her eyes narrowing.

Keir glanced at her neck, and saw a bruise under her left ear.

'What's that on your neck?'

'You bit me, Keir. Don't you remember?'

'Uh, no. I don't.'

'I'll have to wear a scarf to hide it. A scarf, Keir; in the middle of summer. The girls in the embassy aren't stupid; they'll suss it out in two minutes.'

'Lie to them; make something up.'

'What, like I was bitten by a giant mosquito?'

Keir laughed. 'Yeah.'

She glanced at him. 'Would you really cover my bills, Keir? My father has cut off my allowance, and I'm struggling a little to survive on the wages the embassy is paying me. How would you keep it from your wife?'

He gazed at the young woman sitting in her underwear. She was so pretty that he could think of nothing but getting her back into bed.

'Thorn would never find out,' he said. 'How much do you need?'

She looked thoughtful for a moment. 'Two hundred a third? That would pay for my bills, and part of the rent for this place.' She smiled at him. 'Would that be all right?'

'Two hundred's nothing,' he said. 'And, if I'm helping to pay the rent, that means I can come round here more often. I'll be wanting a key.'

'I'd like that,' she said. She put down the brush and stood, her eyes piercing him. 'I guess that means I can have another hot shower, then.'

Keir felt as though he was about to burst as he gazed at her.

'Get over here,' he said.

She walked over to the edge of the bed. 'Do you think I'm beautiful, Keir?'

'You know I do. You're gorgeous.'

'Not as beautiful as your wife, though.'

'And how would you know what my wife looks like?'

She laughed. 'Because I've met her.'

'What?' he said, frowning. 'When?'

'The day I visited the Great Fortress,' she said. 'I was in the office with Lord Bryce, before you appeared, and Lady Thorn came in for a few minutes. Lord Bryce introduced us.'

'Thorn didn't mention that to me.'

'Why would she? She took one look at me, and said that she thought that you would like me.'

'She said what?'

'She said, "You should introduce her to my husband, Lord Bryce; I think he'll like her." And you know, she was right.'

Keir gazed at her in confusion, then Tilda leaned over and kissed him. His mind went blank, and his hands reached out for her waist. He pulled her towards him; and forgot about everything else.

CHAPTER 22
THE PIT

H old Fast, Republic of the Holdings – 16th Day, Second Third
Summer 534

The Lodge, Holdings Desert. Go.

Karalyn and Cardova appeared under the baking sun of a Holdings summer's day, each carrying a pack over their shoulder. Karalyn glanced around, desperate for a glimpse of her children. To the left of the lodge, a silver dragon was basking in the warmth of the sun.

'Good morning, Frostback,' said Cardova.

The dragon opened one eye a crack, then raised her head a foot above the hard ground.

'Good day, Lucius, and to you, Karalyn,' she said. 'I wondered when you would appear. Has your mission been successful?'

'No,' said Karalyn; 'it's been an utter failure. We've hunted Daimon all over Kellach Brigdomin, but he's been lying low, and not using his powers often enough for me to be sure of his location. This will sound odd coming from me, but I never realised how difficult it would be to find a dream mage who doesn't want to be found.'

The front door of the lodge opened, and Kelsey peered out. 'I thought I heard voices,' she said. 'I'm glad Frostback hasn't started talking to herself. Well, sis – am I done? Can I go home now?'

'It seems not,' said Frostback.

Kelsey frowned, then stepped aside, letting the twins race out into the yard. They ran over to Karalyn, who crouched down, and took them into her arms.

Karalyn beamed. 'It's so good to see you; I missed you both.' She held them in her arms for a long, blissful moment, as they burrowed their heads into her.

'Do you want a cup of tea?' said Kelsey. 'I can stick the kettle on.'

'You got any coffee?' said Cardova.

'Aye,' said Kelsey. 'Come on in, and get out of the sun before you fry.'

'See you later, Frostback,' said Cardova, as they entered the single-storey lodge. Kelsey led them to the front room, a place Karalyn remembered well. She glanced at a corner, where Laodoc had sat most evenings while Karalyn had read to him. They all took a seat, the twins on the rug close to Karalyn's legs.

'How have they been?' said Karalyn.

'Fine,' said Kelsey. 'They pined after you for a few days, but they've behaved themselves. The heat's tired them out, I think. So, tell me your woes. I assume things didn't go well. Cardova can make coffee in the meantime.'

Cardova got to his feet. 'Just point me towards the kitchen.'

Kelsey gestured towards a door. 'Down there, first on the right. Just water for me. I've had enough coffee today. Oh, and don't have a sly smoke while you're in there – that's what outside is for.'

Cardova stood to attention and saluted. 'Yes, ma'am.'

Karalyn waited until Cardova had left the room, then she told Kelsey the whole story of her unsuccessful search for Daimon and his twin brother. By the time she was finishing, Cardova was walking back into the room carrying two mugs and a glass. He set them down onto a low table, and retook his seat.

'It sounds like the whole thing was a lie,' Kelsey said. 'Daimon didn't want to see you; if he did, then he wouldn't keep hiding. What are you going to do now?'

Karalyn shrugged. 'I'm out of ideas. I've tried tempting him out into the open by displaying my powers, and I've tried sitting quietly for days on end, waiting for him to reveal himself.'

Kelsey raised an eyebrow. 'And he hasn't used his powers in all that time?'

'No, he has,' said Karalyn, 'but only in short bursts – never long enough for me to track his location. He's learned a lot since Cardova and I confronted him in the old Brig fort; and I strongly suspect that he's been continually on the move. I was sure a few days ago that he was in the Lach Pass, but the next burst I sensed seemed to be coming from the area around Threeways.'

'Has Corthie seen any sign of him?'

Karalyn shrugged. 'I haven't checked in with Corthie for a while. I didn't want to interrupt his new life as a farmer.'

Kelsey laughed. 'Corthie – a farmer. That's hilarious. Poor sap. So, this is just a visit? Damn. I'd hoped that your arrival meant that I could go back to the City.'

'Not just yet. Sorry.'

'It's not your fault, sis. Are you going to head straight back to Kellach Brigdomin?'

'No. I need a couple of days off, to clear my head. Cardova deserves a break, too.'

'I am at your service, ma'am,' the soldier said. 'Break or no break; I'm happy either way.'

Kelsey picked up her glass of water. 'You're going to take a break for a few days, sis? Interesting.'

Karalyn frowned. 'Why?'

'Well, there's something I asked you to do, but you said you were too busy. You're not too busy now, and it shouldn't take you too long.'

'Get to the point, Kelsey.'

'Fine. I want you to look for Sable.'

Karalyn groaned. 'Not this again.'

'Aye – this again. I only want to know if she's alright. Just take a look. And before you say anything, I'm perfectly aware that I'm the only member of this family who gives a shit about Sable; but you owe me, sis. You dragged me away from my home, and from Van, to look after your kids. Searching for Sable is the least you can do for me in return.'

Cardova nodded. 'She has a point, ma'am.'

'You don't even know Sable,' said Karalyn.

'I know that she's your aunt, ma'am. Your wicked aunt, if Kelsey hasn't embellished the stories she's told me about her.'

'I resent that, Lucius,' said Kelsey. 'Are you saying I exaggerate?'

Cardova smiled. 'No comment.'

Kelsey scowled at him. 'I would like to apologise, Karalyn, for inflicting Lucius Cardova upon you. He likes to imagine that he's funny.'

'I am funny,' said Cardova. 'It's not my fault if you have no sense of humour.'

For a split second, Karalyn felt envious of Kelsey's free and easy relationship with Cardova. It was clear that he was more relaxed in her sister's company than he was in Karalyn's, and it annoyed her.

'I will look for Sable,' she said, surprising herself.

Kelsey turned to her, her eyes narrowing. 'Really?'

'Aye.'

'Um, alright. Well, that was a whole lot easier than I'd imagined. Thanks, sis. You could, eh, do it now, if you've nothing else on.'

Karalyn sighed.

'You could be back here in thirty minutes,' Kelsey went on. 'Just scoot off to Colsbury, do your Sextant-thing, and then scoot back. Lucius and I can catch up while you're gone.'

'No. I'll take Cardova, just in case I need him.'

Kelsey sniggered, then raised her palms. 'Fine by me.'

Karalyn glanced down at her two children. They were occupying themselves by drawing on sheets of paper with thick crayons.

'Twins,' she said; 'mummy's going to have to leave again, but not for long.' She turned to Cardova. 'Are you ready?'

The soldier nodded.

Colsbury Castle. Go.

The air shimmered and they appeared in the Sextant room within the keep of Colsbury. As Karalyn had forgotten that they had been sitting down, both she and Cardova fell to the floor with a thump. Cardova started to laugh.

Karalyn smiled. 'That wasn't the most graceful of journeys.'

Cardova stood, and offered a hand to Karalyn. She took it, and he pulled her up. He turned to the Sextant.

'Wait,' she said. 'I want to speak to Agang first. Stay here.'

She left the room, and walked along the corridor to the main living area. Agang was sitting on what had become his chair, a book in his hand.

'Good morning, Agang,' she said from the doorway.

The Sanang man put the book down. 'Hello, Karalyn. This is a nice surprise. Are you staying?'

'No. This is another brief visit, I'm afraid. I need to talk to you about that message my mother sent you. Are you sure...'

'She has sent me another one,' said Agang.

Karalyn paused.

'Just last night,' Agang went on. 'She said that she, Shella and Caelius have crossed the border into the Plateau, and are in the process of hiring a carriage to take them to Plateau City.'

'Oh. Why has she been contacting you?'

'She told me that, as you were down in Kellach Brigdomin, she was worried that her vision powers wouldn't be able to locate you. Don't worry; I've been passing on her messages to a vision mage in the Imperial Capital, so that the Empress doesn't get too concerned.'

'Which vision mage? Keir?'

'No. A mage by the name of Tabor. He's been using his powers to contact me. The first time he did it, it was to enquire if Daphne was here, but since then, he's been checking regularly to see if I have any more messages from her. He seems like a nice chap.'

Karalyn shook her head. 'I'll be having words with my mother when she gets back. She should have told me from the start that she was going to come back on foot. I've spent days worrying about her.'

'Well, everything's fine, Karalyn. You can relax.'

'Thanks, Agang. I'll see you later.'

She slipped out of the room and returned to where the Sextant stood. Cardova was crouching by the huge device, examining it closely.

'Stand up and place your palm on to it,' she said. 'You should be able to see what I see.'

Cardova rubbed his chin. 'Sable's in Dragon Eyre, yes? I'm not sure I want to see that world again.'

'We're only going to look,' she said.

He got to his feet. 'Yes, ma'am.'

They stood next to each other, and laid their right palms flat onto its surface.

What is your desire, Karalyn?

Show me Dragon Eyre.

Mist descended over her vision, and when it cleared, she was looking down at the forested slopes of an island, set amid a sparkling sea.

Show me the temple where Sable lives.

Her sight raced across the ocean, until it reached the tip of a much bigger island, but, again, the temple complex where she had seen Sable in the past was lying deserted.

'That's the island of Haurn, ma'am,' said Cardova. 'Dear gods; I feel a bit sick.'

'What's the name of Blackrose's island?' Karalyn said.

'Ulna. That's where she was queen.'

Show me Ulna.

Her vision raced again, in the opposite direction, sweeping over the vast expanse of blue ocean, until it slowed by a large island.

Show me the palace where Blackrose lives.

Her vision moved on, crossing the rugged mountains of Ulna. She passed a volcano to her right, which was emitting a thin trail of light grey smoke, then she crossed a plain. She recognised the approaching town from her previous visits, and saw the palace built over the broad brown river. She pushed her vision down, and entered the palace. As usual, the wide hallways were almost empty. She checked the enormous reception chamber, but it was deserted. Frowning, she turned, and sped up a ramp that led to a high platform. Sitting on the platform was Blackrose. She had just landed, and Maddie was scrambling down from the harness strapped to the black dragon's back. They began walking down the ramp, as Karalyn and Cardova watched.

'I can't hear what they're saying,' said Cardova.

'Not like this, we can't.' She took a long breath. 'Cardova, will you come with me to Dragon Eyre? I know it might be difficult for you, but it's the only way we'll find out where Sable could be.'

Cardova said nothing.

'Cardova, can you hear me? Lucius?'

'Yes, ma'am; I'll come with you.'

'Thank you. We will be invisible while we're there. Blackrose and I share a past that I'd rather not revisit, and besides, we don't have time to stay for a chat.'

'You stole her Quadrant, didn't you? Kelsey told me, ma'am.'

'Aye. I did. Not my proudest moment, but I was desperate to get back to the twins. Alright. Let's go to Dragon Eyre.'

This platform, with Cardova. Go.

Karalyn and Cardova's bodies materialised on the wide platform. It was warm in the sunlight, though the heat wasn't as oppressive as it was in the Holdings desert.

You cannot see us.

'We are now invisible,' she said to Cardova, who was staring out at the view of the town.

He turned. 'I can still see you.'

'Aye. We can see each other, but no one else can see us. Have you been to Ulna before?'

'I've sailed past it, ma'am. It was thoroughly infested with green-hides back then. No dragons or humans lived here; just damn green-hides. I guess this means that Blackrose has regained her old realm.' He pointed down into the harbour. 'There are two Sea Banner vessels tied up in the docks, but both are flying the standard of a notorious pirate family that used to sail the waters of Olkis, far to the west of here. Gods, it's all coming back to me. The islands, the ocean; the sunshine. It's beautiful, but death is never far away. The memories of this place will always be with me.' He exhaled. 'Apologies, ma'am. I was getting lost in my own thoughts.'

'Let's follow Blackrose,' said Karalyn, 'and then I can enter Maddie's mind.'

He nodded, and they set off. They walked down the ramp, and were soon swallowed up within the shadows of the bridge palace. Ahead of them, Karalyn could see the black dragon making her way to the huge reception hall. Maddie was chattering by her side. They were discussing another island, called Enna, and how best to defend it from a realm called Wyst, which seemed to lie to the north. Karalyn and Cardova followed them into the hall, where they remained in the shadows.

Karalyn pushed her way into Maddie's mind and found that, although she was talking about Enna, her thoughts were focussed on a man called Oto'pazzi. Karalyn delved below the surface, searching for memories of Sable; and found them in abundance. Karalyn flinched. Each recent thought of Sable was entangled with tales of death and slaughter. Sable had not been idle on Dragon Eyre. If Maddie's memories were accurate, then Karalyn's aunt had waded in the blood of thousands; tens of thousands. Karalyn pried deeper, and saw that Sable was in the custody of the dragons of Wyst. They were punishing her for the deaths of hundreds of dragons. Karalyn started to feel queasy.

'I'm not sure I can do this,' she said.

'What's the problem, ma'am?' said Cardova.

'I think we should return to Colsbury. I know roughly where Sable is, but maybe we should leave her there.'

'Where is she?'

'In a deep dungeon on Wyst.'

'Wyst? Dear gods. Do the dragons have her?'

'It seems so.'

'Then she'll already be dead, ma'am.'

'Not according to Maddie's memories. They swore they'd keep her alive, to avoid a war with Blackrose.'

'You cannot trust any promises made by Wyst, ma'am. They hate all humans. We should find out if she lives, and if she does, we should extract her.'

'Why? Sable's murdered thousands. Why would we rescue her?'

'For Kelsey, ma'am.'

Karalyn snorted, then she realised that Blackrose was staring at their location.

'What are you looking at?' said Maddie, squinting into the shadows.

'I sense something, rider,' said the dragon. 'I have a most disagreeable notion that we are not alone.'

'I can't see anyone.'

'Which leads me to but one conclusion, my rider.' She lifted her head. 'Holdfast, if you are there, reveal yourself. If you refuse, I will flood this hall with flames. Invisible or not, you will still burn.'

Karalyn froze.

The dragon opened her jaws, and sparks sizzled and leapt from her great fangs.

Karalyn dropped her powers.

Blackrose's red eyes flashed with rage. 'You. The betrayer returns. You have one minute in which to plead your case to me; otherwise you and your friend will die this day.'

Karalyn raised her arms. 'We're not here to harm you. We're looking for Sable.'

'Karalyn?' cried Maddie, her eyes wide. 'How...? What...? Is this real?'

'You owe me one Quadrant, Holdfast,' said Blackrose.

'You got here, didn't you?' said Karalyn. 'Did Sable find a Quadrant for you?'

'She did.'

'Then your account with my family has been settled.' She entered the dragon's mind, keeping very still and quiet. 'I know Sable is being held captive on Wyst,' she said. The dragon's thoughts turned immediately to Wyst, and Karalyn gleaned the approximate location of Sable's prison from her mind. 'I can sense that you feel sympathy towards my aunt,' Karalyn went on, 'but you know that any rescue attempt will provoke a war. I can rescue her, without any dragon seeing or knowing how it was done. Do you want me to?'

'Yes!' cried Maddie. 'Would you do that? Please. Poor Sable; she won the war for us, and now she's locked up.'

'Quiet, rider,' said Blackrose. 'Karalyn Holdfast has not thought this through. If Sable returns to Ulna, then the dragons of Wyst shall blame us, even if they do not understand how the rescue was achieved.' She stared at Karalyn. 'I feel pity for Sable, but I cannot advocate a course of action that will lead to war. Therefore, with a heavy heart, I must forbid any such rescue attempt.'

Karalyn bowed. 'Then I bid you farewell.'

Where Blackrose thinks Sable is being held, Wyst. Go.

The air shimmered, then Karalyn and Cardova found themselves on a rugged mountainside, thickly forested with steep ravines and gullies.

'Where are we?' said Cardova.

'On Wyst.'

'But...'

'I don't care what Blackrose says.'

Cardova raised an eyebrow.

'I know what you're thinking,' she said, 'but it would be wrong to leave Sable here.'

'I have no problem with that, ma'am. I thought it was you who hated her.'

'No. I don't hate her. I... Alright, I do hate her. I loathe her so much it hurts. But you were right about Kelsey. How can I return home and tell her that Sable's a captive of dragons? Kelsey will be so angry with me. Kelsey and I... it's complicated. Damn it. Talk to me, Cardova. Help me reason it out. This is all too close to me, emotionally. Tell me why I should save someone who forced my husband to burn down a hospital.'

She sat on a moss-covered rock, and put her head in her hands. Cardova lit two cigarettes, passed her one, then sat next to her.

'Do you believe in redemption, ma'am?'

Karalyn said nothing.

'I know what you did to the Rahain army, ma'am,' Cardova went on. 'Kelsey has often talked about you. She told me that she used to hate you, because of something you did to Keir when he was a baby. Kelsey doesn't hate you any more; she loves you. I know this. She told me all about your reluctance to get involved in the last war, and about how much you hate killing. And yet, when it came to the final stages of that war, you were forced into destroying the entire Rahain army. A hundred thousand men and women. You ended their lives with a mere thought. You won the war, but you carry this burden around with you wherever you go.'

'I am not the same as Sable.'

'I didn't say you were, ma'am. You are a Holdfast, and so is she. You have both killed many, but there the similarities end. You feel grief and shame for what you did. Should we not at least see if Sable feels the same way? If we find her, and she is unrepentant, then leave her where she is. But, if there is the slightest hope that she feels the same way that you do about what she has done, then doesn't she deserve another chance? You were given another chance. I was given another chance, too. You, me, Sable – we are all scarred by the things we have done. The scale may differ, but the guilt we feel is the same. What is the point of life, if we don't try to do better; if we don't try to see the good in others? All humans fail. We lie, we cheat, we kill. But we also love. Be true to the goodness within you, Karalyn; and save Sable. If she stumbles again, then you will have still done the right thing.'

Karalyn started to cry.

'Forgive me, Lennox,' she whispered.

She wiped her eyes and turned to Cardova. 'I'll do as you say. If Sable is as twisted and selfish as I believe her to be, then we will leave her. If not...'

She stood, and focussed her powers. She was the most powerful mage who had ever lived, and she needed to remember that.

'Follow me,' she said, then she started to clamber down the hillside.

At the base of the hill were a few scattered wooden huts, gathered around the entrance to a cave. A group of black-clad men were sitting outside the huts next to a fire, while three enormous dragons stood at the periphery of the camp, standing guard.

You cannot see us.

Karalyn reached the bottom of the slope, and waited for Cardova to catch up. Karalyn scanned the men by the fire, and entered the mind of the closest. Sable was imprisoned within a deep pit, along with a man called Olo'osso. The pit was sealed with a double set of doors, to prevent Sable from using her powers. Food was pushed through the narrow tunnel once a day; or, it was supposed to be. In reality, the men sitting round the fire stole most of it to supplement their own rations, and the dragons turned a blind eye. The captives were being slowly starved to death inside the deep pit, and the men expected them to die soon. There was more. Inside a bag belonging to their leader, the men had placed the Quadrant that they had taken from Sable, though they had no idea how to use it.

Karalyn raised an arm.

Sleep.

By the edge of the forest, the three dragons collapsed to the ground with a crash, their bodies felling trees as their eyes closed. Around the fire, the humans toppled over. Karalyn strode forwards, stepping over the body of an unconscious man. She leaned down, opened a leather bag, and took out the Quadrant. Next to her she heard a sound. She turned in time to see Cardova kick one of the sleeping men in the face.

'That's for Van's mother, you Unk Tannic piece of shit!' he cried, his face contorted with anger.

'Stop,' said Karalyn.

'Why?' he yelled. 'These bastards deserve to die.'

'Weren't you just telling me to be better? I can feel how hurt and angry you are, Lucius, but don't kill them. Remember why we are here.'

Cardova sank to his knees as tears flooded down his cheeks. Karalyn put a hand onto his shoulder.

You are strong and brave. You are a good man. It's alright to feel pain; I feel it too.

Cardova's ragged breathed started to slow.

'I'm sorry, ma'am,' he said. 'I lost control. It all came back, like a giant wave striking me and pulling me under.'

'Let's get this over with,' she said, slipping the Quadrant into the folds of her clothes.

Cardova got back to his feet. He rubbed his eyes, his gaze cast downwards.

'I'm sorry for bringing you here,' she said. 'It was selfish of me. I wanted you close by, and didn't think how Dragon Eyre might affect you. I need you, Lucius. I need you to help me face Sable.'

Cardova nodded, but said nothing.

They walked towards the cave, and entered its gloomy interior. Piles of crates were stacked up along one wall, then the cave narrowed. It ended in a thick door, a yard high and a yard wide. It was locked from the outside, and Karalyn slid the bolt free. She yanked on the handle, then Cardova reached out to help her, and together they pulled the door open. Karalyn crouched down, and peered into a narrow tunnel. An empty basket sat there, with a chain attached to one end, and there was a further door at the end of the tunnel, with a long pole fastened to it.

'This is how they are feeding the captives,' Karalyn said. 'They must fear what Sable could do, if she got the chance to use her powers on them.'

Cardova took the pole in his hands, twisted it, and the latch on the inner door opened. Karalyn climbed into the tunnel, and crawled along to the end, her nostrils filled with the reek of rotten food from the scraps that littered the tunnel floor. She reached the second door, and pulled it open. Beyond was utter darkness, and the sound of water flowing. Karalyn crept forward, then realised that the ground dropped away after a few inches.

'I have a lamp, ma'am,' said Cardova from behind her. 'I found it in the crates.'

He passed it to her, and she shone it downwards. Below her was a cavern, where a small stream flowed. Lying next to the stream were two bodies. Cardova squeezed into the tunnel alongside her, and they clambered down into the pit. They jumped the last yard, and landed onto the ground by the stream. Cardova took the lamp, and Karalyn knelt by the first body. It was a man, his hair and beard grey and matted. He opened his eyes, then groaned and raised a hand to cover them, as if the light was painful. Karalyn moved to the other body, which was wrapped in a long cloak. She pulled the hood away, and gazed into the emaciated face of her aunt. Sable looked close to death, her skin covered in sores, and her frame skeletal. A mixture of pity and disgust surged through Karalyn.

'Sable,' she said; 'can you hear me?' She turned to Cardova. 'Shield the light.'

Cardova nodded, and closed the front guard on the lamp, leaving only a faint glow.

'Sable,' Karalyn said again. 'Open your eyes.'

Sable moved her head a fraction. 'Karalyn? Am I dreaming?'

'No, Sable. I'm here.'

Sable opened her eyes. 'You came for me?'

Karalyn entered her thoughts without replying. She needed to be quick, before her empathy for Sable's condition blinded her. She searched Sable's thoughts, and recoiled from the darkness that dwelt within her heart. It didn't take long to find regret. Guilt wracked the mind of her aunt, but not so much for what she had done on Dragon Eyre. The guilt that consumed Sable was about something else entirely. Of all the evil that she had done in her life, she regretted one episode above all the others.

Lennox.

Karalyn took Sable's hand.

Her aunt gazed into her eyes. 'I'm sorry.'

'I know, Sable. I know. I'm taking you home now.'

'Ulna?'

'No, Sable; the Empress.'

Sable nodded. 'I understand. It's time to pay for what I did; that's why you're here.'

'No one's going to hurt you, Sable. I will protect you.'

'You? You'd protect me?'

'Aye, Sable; with my life. It's time to start again.'

'I don't deserve another chance.'

Karalyn tried to smile. 'Who does?'

All four of us. The Holdfast townhouse, Plateau City. Go.

CHAPTER 23
WRITTEN BY THE VICTORS

Marchside, Kell – 16th Day, Second Third Summer 534

Corthie sat in the shadows of the dark cell, listening. Something was scurrying through the straw by the far side of the damp chamber, but apart from that, there was nothing but silence. For ten days, Corthie had done little but think about the actions that had led to his imprisonment. Round and round the thoughts went; a spiral of disbelief and despair.

The voice, if there had indeed been a voice, had vanished, but the guilt remained. He wasn't overly concerned about the five men he had attacked; they would all recover. It was the thoughts he had entertained about Aila that pained him the most. He was frightened, he realised, not that the voice would return, but that, perhaps, there had been no voice at all, and those dark thoughts had been his, and his alone.

His jailers certainly believed that his story about a voice in his head was complete nonsense. Corthie had heard them talk about him through the open slat in the cell door; gossiping about their deranged and violent prisoner. Even Kallie and Conal disbelieved his version of events, and they were among the few folk who knew that dream mages were real, both having met Kalayne many years before. Their problem, or so it seemed to Corthie, was not that dream mages were capable of twisting someone's thoughts – they accepted that this was true; but that Corthie had managed to even partly resist the urges. Such a thing was impossible, or so they had told him.

He wondered where Aila and wee Killop were. With any luck, they would be safe with Karalyn, but, if that were the case, why hadn't his sister come for him? He hadn't spent a single night apart from his family since he and Aila had arrived back from Lostwell, and he missed them more as each day dragged by. He tried to steel himself to the notion that he might be incarcerated for thirds, or maybe even years. What if he missed the birth of his second child? The thought depressed him.

The sound of boots interrupted his melancholia. A key sounded in the lock, and the cell door opened.

Corthie glanced up at four men, and said nothing.

'On yer feet, laddie,' said one. 'Hands behind yer back.'

Two of the men pointed crossbows at him as he stood.

'Turn around.'

Corthie did so, then felt hands grasp his arms. Iron shackles were placed round his wrists, with a short chain connecting them. Once the men were certain that his hands had been secured, one of them knelt down in the straw, and removed the shackle from Corthie's ankle. Corthie kept still, giving them no excuse to loose their bows.

'Face the front,' said one of the men.

Corthie turned again, and glanced at the men. He recognised two of them from the Summer's Day festival – one was a farmer, and the other a blacksmith.

'We're taking ye to see the town council,' said one. 'Make sure ye behave yerself. If ye don't, we'll smash yer kneecaps. Nod if ye understand.'

Corthie nodded.

They led him through a doorway, with the two crossbow-wielding guards behind him, and then they ascended a flight of stairs. At the top, they went through another door and entered the town hall. It was packed with people. Lines of chairs had been set up facing the rear of the hall, where a long table lay. Behind the table, a dozen men and women were seated, including Kallie, who was sitting in the middle. A scribe sat next to the table, and along from him, more armed men were waiting. Corthie was escorted through the centre of the hall, until he reached the group of armed men, who took up positions around him.

One of the members of the town council raised a hand, and the hall quietened.

'We have called this meeting,' said Kallie, 'to decide what to do with our prisoner. According to the law, he has committed the offence of assaulting five men of Marchside. For such crimes, we would usually bestow a custodial sentence of sixty to ninety days, depending upon the severity of the assaults, and the wounds inflicted, but, as the prisoner has admitted that he remains a risk, we need to decide what should be done with him.' She paused for a moment. 'Also, he claims to have an explanation for his actions. This... explanation might be difficult for folk to understand, let alone believe. But, fair's fair. We don't condemn folk here without giving them a chance to speak for themselves first.' She glanced at Corthie. 'Let's hear it. Tell us what happened.'

Corthie glanced at the crowd. Sixty to ninety days, he could cope with, but if they thought he was dangerously insane, then who knew what they would do? They might decide to keep him locked up indefinitely. At least with ninety days, he would be able to be reunited with his family in the autumn; the alternative could be far worse. He made a quick decision.

'I plead guilty to the five charges of assault,' he said. 'I lost my temper, and I'm very sorry. I will accept whatever punishment you think fits the crime. Also, if you demand that I leave Clackenbaird Farm, then I'll accept that too. For many years, I have fought in battles and wars, and I allowed my temper to get the better of me. I've let myself down; I've let my family down; and I've let the good folk of Marchside down. I apologise to the people I hurt. That's all I have to say.'

The members of the town council glanced at each other.

'I thought he had a proper explanation,' said a man with flowing red locks. 'That just sounds like he cannae control his temper.' He eyed Kallie. 'Was there any need to call a full town meeting for this, boss? Give him ninety days and then we can all go home.'

The people in the rows of seats began to chatter among themselves.

'Quiet!' yelled Conal.

'Thank you,' said Kallie. She glanced at Corthie, a frown on her lips. 'Are ye sure ye have nothing else to add?'

'Aye, ma'am. I'm sure.'

One of the members of the audience stood, a sling round his arm. Kallie nodded to him. 'Aye?'

'I was one of the men he assaulted, boss,' the man said. 'Before that happened, after he'd tried to strangle the foreman, he told us – and you were there, too, boss – that a wee voice in his head was telling him to kill folk.'

'I've heard these rumours, too,' said one of the council members. 'Well, boss – did he say that?'

'I remember saying it,' said Corthie. 'Trouble is, I had just been whacked over the head by a bloody great plank. I was babbling nonsense at the time. Sorry about the confusion.'

Kallie narrowed her eyes at him.

'Have ye been in trouble with the law before, Corthie?' said Conal.

'Not in Kell, no.'

'Anywhere else?'

'Ummm. Aye. I was arrested in a city called Kin Dai once. I got roaring drunk, fell asleep in a gutter, and then punched an officer of the watch when I came to. I might have vomited over his shiny new boots as well. He got quite upset about that.'

A few in the crowd laughed.

'Silence,' cried Conal. 'This is not a laughing matter.'

'I understand why you shot me, Conal,' Corthie said. 'I don't hold any grudge; you did the right thing. If you hand down a custodial sentence, I promise to serve my time peacefully, and then I'll go back to my farm.'

'Come on, boss,' said the red-haired council member. 'The lad likes a drink, and he likes a wee brawl. So what? This isnae the damn Holdings; it's Kell. And the lad's the son of Chief Killop; we should take that into consideration. Could we not just let the boy go, if he promises to behave himself? Slap him with a fine. A hundred gold sovereigns to each of the men he assaulted, and that'll be the matter resolved. I have fields that need tending; I cannae be sitting here wasting my time.'

'Aye,' said another of the council members. 'I would vote for that.'

Several of the others by the long table murmured their agreement.

'No,' said Kallie, her features firm. She stared at Corthie. 'Ninety days; take him away.'

The crowd muttered, as a sense of anticlimax percolated within the hall. The guards led Corthie back through the rows of seats, passing many in the audience who seemed disappointed, as if they had been led to believe that something scandalous and gossip-worthy would happen. A man and a woman stood up, looking enraged. The man was missing several teeth, and Corthie recognised him as one of those he had attacked. The woman by his side pointed a finger at Corthie.

'He's a fucking maniac!' she shouted. 'Look what he did to my man; he'll never be able to chew anything again. He'll be eating soup for the rest of his life. Where's our compensation?'

'He has a beautiful wife,' Corthie said; 'that will have to do him.'

The woman clenched her fists, and had to be held back by her neighbours.

'Let me at the wee prick!' she yelled.

Corthie was shoved out of the hall, and led back down the stairs to the basement cell. One of the guards undid his wrist shackles, and he was bundled into the cell. He slid on the wet straw, and crashed to the floor, then the door was slammed shut and locked.

Ninety days, thought Corthie, as he sat and leaned against the wall. Bollocks. Not only would he not be present for the birth of his second child, but he was going to miss the rest of the summer.

Several hours later, as Corthie was watching a rat scurry about in the straw, he heard movement outside his cell.

A woman's voice ordered the guards to leave, and then Kallie's face appeared in the barred hole in the door. She glanced at him, then Corthie heard a key enter the lock.

'Do ye swear not to run away, or to try anything stupid?' she said.

'Aye.'

She unlocked the door, and pulled it open. A chair had been positioned by the front of the cell, and Kallie sat on it.

'I'm doing this as a courtesy,' she said, 'because of who yer father was. Killop and I had our differences, and I hated him for a long time; but in the end, I realised there was little point in hating someone who didnae give a shit about me. So, I got on with my life. Did ye know that I have a husband, and four bairns of my own? They're all grown up now; four strong lads. Anyway, I'm telling ye this so ye know that I dinnae hold a grudge against ye. Now, between you and me, son – why did ye lie in the hall?'

Corthie shrugged. 'Who says I was lying?'

Kallie snorted. 'Me, ya daft eejit. Ye might have fooled the folk upstairs, but I happen to think that yer a terrible liar. What ye told me up on the farm – that was the truth. So, I'll ask ye again. Why did ye lie?'

Corthie said nothing.

'Is that how yer gonnae play it, son? Look; I want to help ye, but I cannae if ye keep lying.'

'Where's Aila?' he said.

She narrowed her eyes. 'That's funny. That's one of the questions I was gonnae ask you. No one's seen her, or yer bairn, since she visited here ten days ago. Some folk think that she was so scared of what ye might do, that she took the bairn and ran; but I'm no fool, Corthie. I know ye spoke to her before she left.'

Corthie puffed out his cheeks. He wanted to trust Kallie, but his trusting nature had got him into trouble in the past. Maybe she was trying to trick him into a confession.

'Is yer sister really a dream mage?' Kallie said.

'Aye.'

'Have ye got other brothers and sisters?'

'One of each.'

'Do they have any powers?'

He nodded. 'My other sister can block powers. And I don't just mean that she's immune to them, like I am. Kelsey's mere presence stops other mages from being able to use their powers. She creates a dead zone around her; very useful if there's a crazy god in the vicinity. My brother is a vision mage and a fire mage, all rolled into one. He's also a prick, but that's by the by.'

Kallie nodded. 'Can yer sisters resist this new dream mage?'

Corthie frowned. 'Um, well, I guess Karalyn can. I don't know about Kelsey. Maybe? Why?'

'Is it not obvious, son? If other members of yer family can resist dream powers, then, maybe, just maybe, you can too. How many times did ye hear the voice in yer head?'

Corthie decided to trust her. 'Three.'

'Describe how ye felt each time.'

He rubbed his forehead.

'I ken it's painful, son. Please try.'

'The first time, out of nowhere, I suddenly decided that Aila had been cheating on me, and that I should kill her. I actually stood up, but then, I managed to get control of myself, and sat back down. It was baffling. I mean, I completely trust Aila. I've never once suspected her of cheating on me. It was then that I remembered the dream mage, so I rushed back up the hill, so I could warn Aila. I got back to the farmhouse and some random guy smiled at me; and I was convinced that *he* had been seeing Aila behind my back. Again, I managed to suppress it, but it took a lot more effort that time, and I lashed out at that foreman guy. Then, you know, I was whacked on the head. The third time, I powered up my battle-vision without meaning to. It just happened. I was in the cart. That time, I wasn't able to resist. I acted, as if I was in a trance. Since then, though, nothing. I don't think he can sense me any more. He was locked in on Aila, and now that Aila's not here, he...' Corthie cursed to himself.

Kallie frowned. 'How would a dream mage be able to sense Aila? They sense powers, don't they? Is Aila a mage?'

'Uh...'

'There's something yer not telling me, Corthie. Something about Aila. Yer not stupid; you must know that folk have been gossiping about yer wife. She seems nice, and folk like her, but they're confused about where she comes from. She's clearly not Kellach or Holdings, and she's obviously not Rahain or Rakanese. Some folk think she must be from Sanang, but I ken what those folk look like, and Aila's not one of them. Also, there's no city called Kin Dai anywhere on the Star Continent. Most folk in Marchside are fairly ignorant about the rest of the world, but I've travelled, Corthie. What country is Kin Dai in?'

Corthie gave a half-hearted smile. 'Kinell.'

'Oh, Kinell, eh? That's lovely. Where the fuck's Kinell?'

'It doesn't exist anymore. It was on Lostwell, and that entire world was destroyed by gods.'

Kallie raised an eyebrow. 'Are you bullshitting me?'

'No. I was there, at the very end. We fought gods. We had dragons on our side. I can't explain it.'

'Is Aila from Lostwell?'

Corthie shook his head. 'No. She's from another world altogether.'

'Another world? How many worlds are out there?'

'No idea.'

'It's not natural, the way Aila acts. A woman that pregnant, and she doesnae even seem remotely affected. No sickness, no aches or pains, no nothing. One of the workers claims to have seen something, when he was up in Clackenbaird. He says that Aila was helping to carry a new doorframe, when her hand grazed off a nail that was sticking out of a wall. He saw the blood, or so he says. Anyway, a minute later, when he looked again, there was no blood, and no cut. Can ye explain that?'

'Aye.'

'Well?'

'You won't believe it.'

Kallie sighed. 'Pyre's arse, Corthie. Tell me the truth.'

'Alright. Aila's a god. My wife is immortal. When we're all dead and buried in our graves, she'll look exactly the same as she does now. She's been around for almost eight hundred years. That's why the dream mage can locate her – she burns healing powers continuously, even when she's asleep.'

Kallie kept her gaze fixed on him for a long moment, then she nodded.

'I can see why yer keeping that a secret,' she said. 'And the bairn?'

'Aye; him, too. He's a wee demigod.'

'Pyre's tits, lad. Yer fathering a line of gods? Is that wise? I mean, did yer family not help the Empress defeat a band of gods a few years back?'

'Not all gods are the same. Agatha was trying to kill the Holdfasts. My children will be Holdfasts.'

'Is that supposed to make the world feel any safer? Listen, son; I didnae meet Agatha, but I saw the old Emperor, when he transformed into a god. I was there, when Keira killed him.'

'The Empress's daughters told me that. Can I ask you something?'

'That depends. If it's about me and your father, then no.'

'It was about someone called Kylon. Conal mentioned his name, but he wouldn't say who he was.'

'Oh. Him. I suppose that it suited certain people to forget that Kylon and I were involved in what happened on the roof of the Great Fortress that night. In my case, I think yer mother was happy for my part to be forgotten. She didnae like me, for obvious reasons. That was fine by me. I didnae want any of the attention; I was glad just to walk away with my life. Kylon wasnae so lucky. Did you never wonder how yer sister Kara-lyn, a mere two year old, got onto the roof in the first place? She should never have even been in Plateau City. Kylon abducted her from yer mother and father, and dragged her onto that roof. He knew that only she had the power to stop the Emperor. So, against the wishes of everybody else, he did the unthinkable, and placed a wee bairn into extreme danger. The Emperor blew his head clean off his shoulders. But, and here's the thing – he was right. Without Karalyn, the Emperor would have killed us all. What Kylon did was essential, no matter how reprehensible. As soon as it was all over, though, no one ever spoke about him again. No one wanted to admit that Kylon had done the right thing; and so, his name was forgotten. It's a shame – he was yer father's best friend, and he loved yer Aunty Keira. Still, I can see why yer mother would rather pretend that Kylon and I didnae exist. It makes it easier for her. I'm more surprised that Bridget went along with it. She and I used to be friends.'

'I'm going to speak to my mother about this,' said Corthie. 'It's not fair that your role got ignored.'

Kallie laughed. 'Forget about it, lad. It's all in the past. Let those who want it take the credit.' Her face grew serious again. 'Back to the business at hand. Where's Aila?'

'She said she was going to travel to Threeways, to look for Karalyn.'

'And ye let her go?'

'Aye. What was the alternative? We thought you were going to lock me up indefinitely. You didn't believe the story about the voice in my head. Do you believe it now?'

Kallie frowned. 'I doubted it at first, but, as I said, yer a terrible liar, Corthie Holdfast. Yer father was just as bad. And, if it's true that other members of yer family can resist dream mages, then maybe you can, too. However, it's yer wife and bairn that I'm more worried about. If the dream mage can track Aila, then they're in danger. Has yer sister been in contact?'

Corthie shook his head.

'Shit,' said Kallie. She fell into silence, her eyes narrow. After a while, she glanced up at Corthie. 'Ye've given me no choice,' she went on. 'I cannae keep ye locked up in here while a rogue dream mage is out

CHRISTOPHER MITCHELL

there, not if he can find yer wife. If he was interfering with yer mind, then it might mean that he's trying to hurt yer family, Corthie. If you're even slightly resistant to his powers, then it gives you an advantage over the rest of us. Can ye ride a horse, son?'

'Aye.'

'Good.'

'Are you going to let me go?'

She put a finger to her lips. 'Quiet, son. I've sentenced ye to ninety days in the slammer; I cannae just "let ye go", as you put it. Yer gonnae have to escape. I notice the numpty guards forgot to put the shackles back on yer ankle. An unfortunate oversight, especially if there's folk in this town who sympathise with yer plight.' She stood. 'Stay awake this evening, lad. Someone will come. In the morning, I'll have to send out scouts to hunt for ye, so get away as quick as ye can. This might be the last time I see ye. Ye remind me of everything that was good about yer father; he was kind, strong and honest, and he always tried to do the right thing, even if it got him into trouble. I can see all that in you, Corthie. He would be very proud of you.'

She took a hold of the cell door, swung it closed, then turned the key in the lock, but didn't remove it. Corthie heard her footsteps fade away, and he leaned back against the cell wall, his thoughts focussed on Aila and Killop. Had they walked into a trap? Had the dream mage been trying to separate them? But why? Corthie had done nothing to antagonise the new dream mage; he had just been trying to get on with his life, far away from the politics and troubles of the world. Then it occurred to him that perhaps he and his family weren't the real targets. What if the dream mage was trying to hurt Karalyn, and was using Corthie to get to her? Kell was supposed to be his own little safe haven, but maybe there was no escape from being a Holdfast. For the first time, the walls of the small cell felt oppressive, and he knew he had to get out.

Corthie stared at the cell door for hours, hearing nothing. A distant bell sounded out its regular midnight chime, and he began to wonder if Kallie had changed her mind. The door was thick and strong, and had been reinforced with a lattice of iron strips. Maybe, if he powered his battle-vision to its maximum extent, he might be able to rip it off its hinges, but he hesitated from pursuing such a course, in case it alerted the dream mage to what he was doing. If at all possible, he needed to slip away without using his powers; and to do that, he required assistance.

The key turned in the lock, and the cell door swung open. Corthie blinked. He hadn't heard anyone approach. He got to his feet, and saw a hooded figure standing in the dimly-lit hall outside the cell.

'Who are you?' Corthie whispered.

'It's best if ye don't know,' said a man's voice. 'Scram, boy. Go. Up the stairs and out through the rear door of the town hall. A horse is tied up there, waiting for ye. I'll lock this door after ye've gone, and the guards won't know a thing about it till the morning.'

'Thank you.'

'Don't thank me, son. Thank the chief. I'm just doing what she asked. Go on; beat it.'

Corthie turned, and ran up the stairs. He entered the large hall, which was still and empty, and hurried between the rows of chairs to the back of the building. He found a door, and eased it open. Outside, the seven stars were shining down from the eastern sky, and the town was bathed in thick shadows. Lights were coming from behind the shutters of a few houses, but the rest of the settlement was dark, and the streets deserted.

Corthie stepped outside, and saw a grey gelding standing a few yards away, its reins tied to a thick post. Corthie approached the horse, and ran a gentle hand down its flank, while he whispered a few words of encouragement. He lifted his left foot into a stirrup, then brought his right leg up and over the saddle. He loosened the reins from the post, gripped them in his hands, and dug his heels into the gelding's flanks, coaxing it into a slow walk. The clip of the gelding's hooves on the cobbled streets sounded like thunder in his ears, but he kept going, slowly and carefully. The moment the cobbles disappeared, replaced by soft earth, he kicked his heels again, and the gelding started to trot. They reached the edge of the town, and Corthie took one last look over his shoulder at Marchside, then he urged the gelding on, and it raced off, speeding along the road that led north to the Brig Pass, and Threeways.

CHAPTER 24
THE HEAD OF THE SNAKE

A rakhanah City, Republic of Rakana – 16th Day, Second Third Summer 534

Daphne shuffled along the cold floor, her head wreathed within a thick hood, and her arms shackled behind her back. Hands gripped her arms, guiding her bare feet somewhere. She was hungry and thirsty, and her left arm was more painful than it had been for many years. For eight days, she had been transported from one place to another, never seeing a glimpse of Shella or Caelius in that time. She had been on several wagons, and on a canal barge, but, throughout it all, no one had uttered a word to her.

They were softening her up; trying to weaken her resolve. If they hoped she would crack under the pressure, she told herself, then they clearly had no idea who they were dealing with.

The hands gripping her brought her to a halt, then she heard a door open, and they pushed her onwards again.

'Bring the prisoner forward,' a voice said in Rakanese.

Daphne was jostled along, then she halted again. Something jabbed into her back – a crossbow, she imagined.

'Should we remove her hood, sir?' said another voice. 'I want to see for myself if this is really the Herald of the Empire standing in front of us.'

'I think that would be unwise,' said the first voice. 'Her vision powers are well known. Give her the slightest chance, and she will try to escape.'

'Very well, sir. Shall I commence the interrogation?'

'Yes. Proceed.'

'Prisoner?' said the second voice. 'Can you hear me?'

'I can,' said Daphne.

'I would like you to confirm your name for us.'

'Who is "us"? To whom am I speaking?'

'You are standing before a special tribunal, brought together to decide your case. Some extremely serious charges have been laid against you, and we are here to deliver a verdict. We are acting with the full authority of the rulers of the Republic of Rakana.'

'Is this an official tribunal?'

'Semi-official. It is being conducted behind closed doors, to protect the security of the Republic. I'm sure you understand. Now, your name, if you would?'

'You know who I am.'

'I want to hear you say it. If you refuse, it will be counted against you.'

'Have I been assigned a lawyer?'

'No. This is not the Holdings; you have no such rights here.'

'I see. You are conducting a farce. I presume you have already settled upon a verdict? How nice for you. I expect my throat will be slit two minutes after you pronounce me guilty, and then my body will be dropped into a canal. Remember to weight it – you wouldn't want me bobbing back up again.'

'If you believe that to be the case, then there is no harm in providing us with a record of your name.'

'You're taking records of this? How brave. I wouldn't have thought that you'd want to leave any evidence behind. Perhaps you're too stupid to realise that.'

There was silence for a moment, then Daphne felt a fist strike her stomach. She gasped, and doubled over for a moment, gritting her teeth.

'Your name, prisoner,' barked the first voice.

Daphne straightened herself with an effort. 'No,' she said. 'I don't think so. You're going to have to do better than that.'

She braced herself for another blow, but none came.

'I think we can dispense with the need for her to provide her name,' said a third voice. 'We know who she is.'

Daphne smiled behind the hood. It wasn't much of a victory, but she would take what she could.

'Daphne Holdfast,' the third voice went on; 'First Holder of the Holdings Republic, and Herald of the Empire, you have been charged with espionage. It is alleged that you illegally entered the Republic of Rakana with the express intention of spying on this nation, and were caught trying to return to the Plateau. How do you plead?'

'I want to see my lawyer. He happens to be in Holdings City; he's very good. He's Rakanese, actually; one of your fellow countrymen who has had the excellent fortune of being able to escape this wretched land. Why is it that so many Rakanese want to leave?'

'The man who was captured with you,' the second voice said, 'one Caelius Logos, has already admitted the charge of espionage. He testified that you were in charge of the operation, and that Shellakanawara was assisting you. What do have to say to that?'

'Not much,' she said. 'It's clearly fabricated nonsense. Why should I dignify it with a response?'

'Tell us; what was the purpose of your visit to Rakana?'

'To visit a grave. Shella's sister had died, and we wanted to pay our respects. Is that too much for your tiny brains to understand?'

'Lies,' said the first voice; 'all lies. The Herald of the Empire would not risk breaking a dozen laws for such a ridiculous reason.'

'It's only ridiculous because your laws are ridiculous. Does your paranoia know no bounds? If you opened your borders, then people could come and go as they please. What are you frightened of?'

'This Republic has good cause to be suspicious of its neighbours, as you well know. For years, the Empire has attempted to undermine us. The Holdings manipulated the Migration, allowing the Rahain to slaughter three hundred thousand of our citizens. Then, the old Emperor invaded, and thousands more lost their lives. It cannot be paranoia if the threats are real.'

'These events occurred almost thirty years ago,' said Daphne. 'Maybe you should move on.'

'I want to know the names of every person with whom you had contact while you were here,' said the second voice.

'Alright. There was one man we spoke to. His name was Thymo. Where is he?'

The voices lowered as the people in the room consulted one another. Through the hood, Daphne couldn't make out what they were saying, but she didn't care. She had but one thought in mind – utter defiance.

'Who is your contact in Rakana?' said the third voice. 'Who did you speak to for information?'

'Your voice sounds familiar. Yes, it was you. You were my contact. You are in charge of a massive, underground espionage organisation, trying to bring down the Rakanese government.'

She heard a long sigh.

'This is getting us nowhere,' said the second voice. 'Perhaps we should reconvene in ten minutes, so that Holder Fast has an opportunity to... reflect upon her attitude.'

'Agreed,' said the first voice.

Daphne heard the sound of seats moving, their legs scraping off the smooth, cold floor.

'Don't break any bones,' said the third voice.

A door opened, and then closed again. A fist collided with the side of Daphne's head, then someone kicked the back of her knee, and she fell to the floor. Boots swung in, but with her wrists shackled behind her back, she couldn't protect her face, and she felt her nose crack as a kick made contact. She retreated into herself, the pain reverberating throughout her body as the guards beat her. A boot stamped down on the fingers of her right hand, and Daphne clamped her mouth shut, as blood and tears mingled on her face. She tried to think of happy memories, but the thought occurred to her that she was unlikely to live long enough to create any new ones. What she wanted more than anything, she realised, was to see all of her children and grandchildren in the same place at the same time. With Kelsey back, such a thing was once again possible, at last, and she felt a violent loathing toward anyone trying to prevent her from fulfilling her dream.

She realised that the beating had stopped. She could hear the guards chatting together in low voices, their job done. A door opened, and the chatting ceased. Chair legs squeaked.

'Lift her up,' said the first voice. 'I'd rather not have to speak to the Herald of the Empire while she is lying on the floor.'

Hands gripped Daphne's shoulders, and she was hauled to her feet.

'Let us hope that the prisoner shall be a little more receptive to our questions,' said the second voice. 'Daphne Holdfast, how do you plead to the charge of espionage that has been laid against you, and corroborated by the evidence of Caelius Logos?'

'I refuse to recognise the authority of this tribunal,' she said, her voice slurring from her broken nose.

'Who is your contact within the city?' growled the first voice.

'I've already answered that question.'

'Do you wish us to torture this information out of you?'

'If you let me go now, then I'll consider not coming back and killing you all.'

'You are known to be a killer,' said the third voice, 'but your threats mean nothing to us. With your experience, I am sure you can grasp the difference between a quick, merciful death, and a long drawn out death by torture. Consider that. If you change your tone, and decide to assist this tribunal, then there will no need for any more pain. You were caught in the midst of carrying out an illegal act; we have all the evidence we need not only to secure your conviction, but to ensure that you receive a sentence of death.'

'It does not have to be this way,' said the second voice. 'Holder Fast, don't you want to see your home and family again? Give us what we need, and there remains a possibility that you may be released.'

'There remains a possibility that the sky will turn green,' said Daphne. 'I think that and my release are about equally likely.'

'Send her for special treatment,' said the first voice. 'I tire of her games.'

'One moment, sir,' said the second voice. 'Daphne Holdfast, I do not wish to see you taken away for special treatment. I have seen what happens to people subjected to such an ordeal; they emerge broken, as shadows of their former selves. We will get the information we require out of you one way or another, so why not spare yourself the agony of torture? We know that you were here to spy on us. We also know that there exists a small number of subversives – traitors living within Arakhanah City who wish to betray their country. Tell us who you spoke to; give us the names of your contacts, so that we may uncover this plot.'

'The only plot that exists is inside your own heads,' said Daphne. 'We were here to visit a grave. If I had wanted to bring down your government, do you think I would have come in person? I take that as a grievous insult to my intelligence. And why would I bring Shella if my purpose was to spy on you? Believe me, there are plenty of anonymous Rakanese living in the Plateau who would have been only too happy to volunteer for such a task. Now, I have a question for you – tell me; what do you imagine will happen when the Empress discovers what you have done to me? Take your time in answering; think it through.'

'The Empress will never know,' said the third voice. 'You will, presumably, be reported as missing, but the government of the Republic of Rakana will deny all knowledge of having ever seen you. If the Empress pushes the matter, then she will have to admit that she knew you were here to spy. She would never do such a thing. She may feel a small pang of guilt at having abandoned you, but, ultimately, you are expendable. She will not go to war over hearsay and rumour. As for your guilt, it is painfully obvious, despite your crude attempts at pretending you were only here to visit a grave. Really, one would have thought that you would have come up with a more imaginative story.'

'This is your last chance, Daphne Holdfast,' said the second voice. 'Furnish us with the names of the traitors in Rakana that you have met, and you will be spared special treatment.'

'I can confidently predict the same outcome, whether you torture me or not, as pain will not induce me to furnish you with something that I do not know. I have been tortured before. I did not crack then, and I certainly will not crack now. How could I crack, if I have nothing to tell?'

The first voice laughed. 'Oh, we have a very long list of questions to present to your torturers. As Herald, you know the defensive plans of the Empire, their communications network, and the identities and locations of countless imperial agents. You have plenty of information locked up inside your head that the Republic would like to know. And, within a few hours, you will have told us everything. Take her away.'

'This is not over, you cowards,' said Daphne, as hands steered her away from the voices.

She was shoved through a doorway, and down a corridor. They stopped, then turned right, and entered another room, where the floor was even colder than before.

'Ah,' said a new voice; 'our famous prisoner. I had hoped she would come my way.'

'The prisoner's hood is to remain on at all times, sir,' said one of the guards.

'That won't be a problem,' said the new voice. 'Tie her to the table.'

Daphne was shoved along the cold floor, then her legs were gripped along with her arms, and she was hoisted into the air. The guards set her down onto a flat surface, and her shackles were attached to another chain. Her ankles were then also fastened to something. Daphne stilled herself. No matter what happened, she would say nothing. It wasn't just her own dignity at stake; there was also the matter of preserving the respect due to a Herald of the Empire. More than that, though, she was a Holdfast, and she would never have anyone say that a Holdfast was broken by mere pain.

'Here are the questions, sir,' said a guard.

'Thank you. You may leave us.'

Daphne heard the door close.

'Well, well,' said the new voice. 'Daphne Holdfast. Might I say that I consider it an honour to be the one who will extract the answers to these questions from you?'

'You can say whatever you please,' said Daphne. 'But let me tell you – this shall be the only time that you will hear me utter a word. I shall not scream, nor beg, nor complain. I do not fear you, because I know that you cannot truly hurt me. I am beyond your reach. You may begin.'

She heard a soft laugh, then she focussed on the faces of her children, and prepared herself for more pain.

Daphne regained consciousness as she was being dragged along a hallway. Despite the agony wracking her body, she knew that she had won, and that was all that mattered. Her last memory was of her torturer losing his temper with her adamant refusal to say a word. He had raged and ranted at her, and she wished he could have seen her smile beneath the blood-soaked hood. They would kill her soon, but she had no regrets.

A door opened, and she was thrown inside. She landed awkwardly onto a stone floor, her left arm screaming in agony. She tried to lie still then, as the door slammed shut, she felt a hand touch her shoulder. She gasped, and struggled beneath the touch.

'It's me, ma'am; it's Caelius. Dear gods, what have they done to you?'

Daphne rolled onto her side, then felt fingers unbuckle the straps that were keeping her hood on. The hood was lifted clear of her head, and she blinked in the dim light of another prison cell. Caelius's bruised and bloody face was gazing down at her, and his eyes were recoiling from horror and anger.

'Do I look that bad?' she gasped.

Caelius gathered her up in his arms, and sobbed as he embraced her. The contact with him was painful, but welcome at the same time, and she felt her breathing slow as she pressed her face against his chest.

'They told me that you'd confessed,' he said, pulling away to look at her, 'but I knew they were lying. I told them nothing, ma'am; nothing. I imagined them as Unk Tannic, and my contempt for them bore me through the pain.'

She nodded, though she wasn't entirely sure what he was talking about.

Caelius laid her head back down, using her folded-up hood as a thin pillow, then he checked her injuries.

'Did you get special treatment, too?' she said.

He shook his head. 'They were more crude with me. I was beaten with rods, but they didn't break any bones. I've suffered worse.' He glanced down at her feet, and his face paled.

'How many?' she said.

'Ma'am?'

'How many toes are missing?'

'Two, ma'am,' he said, his voice barely a whisper, 'and three of the others have had their nails pulled out. What did you tell them?'

'Nothing.'

Tears came to his eyes. 'You should have made something up, ma'am. You should have said something, to make them stop.'

'I couldn't. I refused to give them the satisfaction.'

'I will kill every last one of the bastards for this.'

Daphne tried to smile. 'You'll have to get to them before I do. Why did they put me in here with you? They must have known that you'd take my hood off. Do they know that I've lost my powers?'

'I don't know,' he said. 'I can't think straight. I can deal with pain, but it makes it hard for me to take in everything that's going on. How long have we been prisoners?'

'This is our eighth day, Caelius.'

'Is that all?' He leaned back against a wall. 'If they don't care about us conferring any longer, that can only mean one thing.'

'Yes.'

'I'm not afraid to die, but the thought of them executing you, ma'am, makes me angrier than I thought possible.'

'Hold my hand,' she said.

He reached out, and took her right hand.

'Don't be angry,' she said. 'If these are our last moments, don't waste them on anger.'

Caelius closed his eyes, his hand gripping Daphne's.

'Have you seen Shella?' she said.

'No, ma'am. Not since the day we were captured.'

'I wonder if they'll make her arrest public,' she said. 'I can understand why they're keeping me hidden, but I'd have thought that they'd want to make a show of hanging Shella.'

'They might desire that, ma'am, but the Empress would learn of it, and know that you had also been captured. It will be more convenient for us to simply disappear.'

'I'm sorry about getting you into this mess, Caelius.'

'Don't apologise, ma'am; I knew what I was doing when I decided to come along with you; I knew there would be risks. The decision was mine.'

Daphne nodded. She tried to rearrange her limbs on the cold stone floor, but every part of her seemed to be aching, and the pain coming from her feet was making it hard to think. She leaned on to her right side to relieve the pressure on her left arm, and the shackles dug into her wrists. Caelius moved his hand, and rested it on the side of Daphne's face, his thumb gently brushing the hair from her eyes. They remained silent for a long while, each bearing the weight of their pain with as much dignity as they could muster.

Daphne's thoughts went back to Karalyn. Surely her daughter must know that they were missing? It was incomprehensible that she would fail to search Rakana for them. There still hope, she thought. Perhaps Karalyn was searching for her at that moment.

A laugh echoed through her mind.

Karalyn will not be coming.

Daphne blinked.

That's right, Holder Fast, said the voice in her mind; *yer oldest child knows nothing of yer situation. Do ye want to know why?*

Daimon?

I said – do ye want to know why?

I'm sure you'll tell me, Daimon. You sound like you want to tell me.

Karalyn won't be coming, crowed the voice, *because I told Agang Garo that ye were safe. I tricked him into thinking that the messages I've been sending him were from you. And then Agang Garo told Karalyn and the Empress not to worry about ye – that ye were on a carriage, bound for Plateau City. Is that not funny?*

Why?

Why what?

Why would you do that? I have never done anything to hurt you.

The voice paused. When it returned, it was a low whisper.

Where are the twins?

You are in my head, Daimon. If I knew that, then you would see it.

How is Karalyn hiding them from me? Oh. I can see that. Kelsey. Kelsey Holdfast has them.

Why do you want to hurt the twins?

Hurt them? The voice said. *I don't want to hurt them; I want to save them from the Holdfasts. I've looked into yer minds, and I've seen the terrible things that yer family have done over the years. Massacres, betrayals, death. The twins are like me, and you'll pollute them with yer blood-soaked hands. I want to save them from that; I would never hurt them.*

You're wrong. Karalyn has a good heart...

Karalyn slaughtered a hundred thousand Rahain as they lay sleeping in their tents! Daimon cried. *She's as bad as the rest of ye; maybe worse. She tried to snatch me, did ye know that? She came to my hiding place, with a soldier, and tried to harm me and my brother. We were lucky to escape. You'll not be so lucky, Daphne Holdfast. You're the head of the Holdfast snake, and yer death will make the world a better place. Did ye like what I did with that eejit Thymo? I made him betray ye! He didn't want to, but I knew it was for the best.*

They killed him, Daimon.

The voice went quiet.

Did you hear me? Daphne went on. *The Rakanese killed Thymo, right after he had identified us. What did Thymo ever do to you? Does his death mean nothing to you? Don't lecture me on morality, not when your hands are just as bloody.*

They... they killed him? But there was a reward; I read it from the mind of a soldier. Thymo was gonnae be rewarded.

He knew too much. He knew that I was also in Rakana. You didn't think of that, did you? You didn't think it through, and now he is dead.

Daimon said nothing, and for a few moments, Daphne thought he had left her mind.

Are you there? she said.

Aye.

Did you take my powers, Daimon?

Aye.

That means you can restore them, too.

Aye.

Then it's not too late, Daimon. Give me back my powers, and I'll be able to locate Karalyn.

No.

Do you want more blood on your hands?

I want justice; and that means you have to die, Daphne Holdfast. Yer crimes demand it. Without you, the other Holdfasts will despair, and yer family's power will crumble.

You underestimate my children.

No. You overestimate them. Kelsey doesn't want to be here. Keir is too selfish to care about anyone else, and Corthie is nothing but a savage murderer. And Karalyn? She won't lift a finger to help this world; all she cares about is hiding away, and pretending that her conscience is clean. Yer family have been granted great power, and ye've wasted it. When they lead ye to the executioner, Daphne Holdfast, I want ye to remember that I'll care for Kara-

lyn's twins, once I've killed their mother. I will mould Kyra and Cael into my own image, and save them from the Holdfasts. Let the end of yer family be yer last thought, Daphne, before the axe swings.

The voice vanished from her mind.

She glanced at Caelius, who was still leaning back against the cell wall, his eyes closed.

'Caelius,' she said.

'Ma'am?'

'Karalyn won't be coming.'

CHAPTER 25
DIVORCE

Plateau City, The Plateau – 16th Day, Second Third Summer 534
Keir lit a cigarette. He knew he wasn't supposed to smoke inside the Holdfast townhouse, but Brannig was out on the balcony, and Keir couldn't be bothered having to speak to him. Besides, it was Keir's damn house, and he could smoke if he wanted to. He heard laughter filter through from the balcony. Tabitha was out there with Brannig, and the two of them were getting on well together. The Brig man was always polite to the servant, but Keir knew he was a fraud. He probably just wanted to sleep with Tabitha, and, as far as Keir was concerned, he was welcome to her.

He stood, and paced the floor of the sitting room. It had once been the master bedroom, but Thorn had had it converted to allow others access to the townhouse's only balcony. It was ridiculous that he was cooped up within the townhouse. He was a high mage, and yet the Empress seemed to have no need for him. He had only been in the Great Fortress for fifteen minutes that morning, before Tabor had informed him that there was nothing for him to do. His first thought had been to contact Tilda, but she had insisted that she was too busy to take another day off, and so he had gone home, to pace the floors while Brannig ate their food and drank their wine.

Another peal of laughter reached his ears from the balcony, and Keir's fury grew. It was time for Brannig to leave. He had been scrounging off the generosity of the Holdfasts for too long, and Keir was sick of Bridget's children turning up at any hour they chose to visit him. He had to go. Keir would break the news to him, and then suffer the anger of his wife later. Thorn would no doubt shout at him, but he didn't care. He was so tired of her. She treated him as if he were a lodger in his own home, when Brannig was the interloper. He needed to put his foot down. If she didn't like it, then she could cease being a Holdfast. Keir strode to the balcony doors. Tabitha was clearing away plates and glasses from the table, while Brannig was making her laugh. Keir scowled at the scene. He would wait until Tabitha had left the balcony, then he would tell Brannig to pack his things.

He smiled as he imagined the look on the oaf's face.

There was a loud crash behind him, and Keir jumped in fright. He turned, and saw four people in the sitting room. He recognised his sister immediately, but the other three seemed unfamiliar. Two of them were lying on the floorboards, as if injured, while the other was tall, and dressed as a soldier. Karalyn was crouching by one of the prone bodies, and was acting as if Keir wasn't there.

Keir coughed.

Karalyn turned to him. 'Where's Thorn?'

'What?'

'You heard me, Keir – where is Thorn? I need her.'

'Is that it?' said Keir. 'You appear here without any warning, and you want to know where my wife is?'

Keir felt a dull sensation behind his temples, then Karalyn turned to the soldier.

'Thorn is in the Great Fortress, Lucius,' she said. 'Stay here while I fetch her.'

The soldier nodded, and Karalyn vanished.

Tabitha and Brannig appeared by the balcony door.

'What's happening?' said the servant.

The soldier bowed his head slightly. 'Good morning, ma'am,' he said. 'Karalyn and I have returned from an operation. Could you perhaps get some water and food for the two prisoners that we rescued?'

Tabitha stood frozen for a moment, then she ran off.

Keir strode forwards to take a closer look at the two bodies on the ground. The man seemed to be at death's door, his cheeks sunken. His body was shivering as if from cold. The woman was in a worse state. She looked almost skeletal. Keir frowned as he peered down at her. There was something about her face that seemed familiar. He tried to enter her head, but was rebuffed; and he gasped.

'Is that Sable?' he said, staggering back a pace.

'Yes, sir,' said the tall soldier. He seemed Kellach Brigdomin, but his accent belied that.

'She can't be here!' cried Keir. 'Get her out of this house at once!'

'Perhaps we should wait for Karalyn to return, sir,' said the soldier, his eyes narrowing as they followed Keir.

'Did you not hear what I said, soldier?' Keir shouted. 'Sable is a traitor. Karalyn must have lost her mind. If you don't remove Sable from this house, then I will.'

The soldier straightened, and positioned himself between Sable and Keir.

'I advise you not to touch her, sir,' he said.

'How dare you?' Keir cried. 'Do you know who I am?'

'Oh, Keir,' Sable gasped from the floor. 'I see that you're still a nasty little shit.'

Keir's face twisted with fury. 'Shut up!'

Keir felt a sudden calm settle upon his mind, and he backed away. There was no reason to argue with Sable or the big soldier, he thought; everything was fine. He walked over to a chair, and sat.

'Does your wife know what you're up to?' gasped Sable.

Keir said nothing, his mouth refusing to open.

'What happened to them?' said Brannig.

'They've been starved, sir,' said the soldier.

The Brig man walked forward. 'And who is this Sable?'

'I'll let Karalyn answer these questions, sir. You're Lord Brannig, aren't you? I remember you from the *World's End*.'

'Aye,' said Brannig; 'although, forgive me, I do not recall your face. I was rather occupied with greeting my children at the time.'

'It's quite all right, sir. My name is Lucius Cardova, and I've been assigned to guard Karalyn Holdfast.'

The air shimmered in the corner of the room, and Karalyn appeared with Thorn next to her. Thorn's eyes passed over Keir, then Karalyn urged her towards the two bodies.

'Oh my,' said Thorn. 'Sable? What...?'

'Questions later,' said Karalyn. 'Can you heal her?'

Thorn frowned, her eyes narrowing as they stared at Sable.

'Please,' said Karalyn. 'She's dying.'

'I'll need to touch her,' said Thorn.

'I won't bite,' Sable croaked.

Karalyn glanced at Keir while Thorn knelt by Sable. Keir wanted to say something, to shout at the fools invading his house, but he couldn't open his mouth.

Karalyn smiled. 'I see your powers are still working, Sable.'

Her aunt looked up. 'He was getting on my nerves.'

Thorn shook her head. 'Sable is too weak. She's not ill; she's starving to death. She has no spare energy to allow me to heal her.'

'Take some of mine,' said Cardova.

Thorn glanced at the tall soldier. 'I don't think you understand what you're saying.'

'I understand, ma'am,' said Cardova. 'Take some of my life force, and give it to Sable. She needs it more than I do.'

'I don't like this idea,' said Karalyn.

'We didn't go all the way to Dragon Eyre just to let her die on your sitting room floor, ma'am,' said Cardova. He walked over to Thorn, crouched down, and extended an arm. 'I'm ready.'

'What about the man?' said Thorn. 'Who is he?'

'His name is Olo'osso,' said Karalyn. 'He was imprisoned with Sable; I couldn't just leave him there on his own to die.'

345

'He is in a similar condition,' Thorn said.

'One thing at a time,' said Karalyn.

Thorn nodded. She took Cardova's hand in hers, and placed her other hand onto Sable's forehead. Cardova closed his eyes and shuddered, the skin on his face paling. On the floor, Sable started to convulse. At that moment, Tabitha reappeared, carrying a tray loaded with dishes and mugs.

'Set it down on the table,' said Karalyn, 'and fetch some more. There will be a few hungry mouths in a moment or two.'

Sable groaned, then opened her eyes. Her face seemed healthy again, and the sores had disappeared. She sat up, and glanced around, is if realising where she was for the first time.

'Thorn,' she said; 'that's twice you've saved my life.'

'And I'm already starting to regret it,' said Thorn. She released her grip on Cardova's arm, and the soldier grunted.

'And you,' Sable said to him, 'whoever you are – thank you. Are we in the Holdfast townhouse in Plateau City?'

'How do you know that?' said Karalyn.

Sable pointed at the view through the balcony door. 'I can see the Inner Sea. Where's the Empress?'

'She's sent Bryce to arrest you,' said Karalyn. 'She seemed a little put out when I arrived to fetch Thorn. I may have overestimated the Empress's capacity for forgiveness.'

Sable nodded. 'Then, you won't mind if I get out of here as quickly as possible? I want to talk to you, Karalyn, but not if it means I've exchanged a dungeon on Dragon Eyre for one under the Great Fortress.'

'Eat first,' said Karalyn. 'You, too, Lucius. Eat.'

The soldier opened his eyes. He looked sick, but obeyed Karalyn. He sat by the low table and began to eat, pushing the food into his mouth. Sable joined him. She glanced at his face, then also started to eat.

'That was very brave,' said Brannig. 'Might I volunteer to assist the other victim? I am strong, and have a healthy constitution. I can take it.'

'It's your decision,' said Thorn.

Brannig walked over, and Thorn repeated the same process as before. The frame of Olo'osso shook violently, then he lapsed into a deep sleep, his features drawn but at peace. Brannig joined the others by the table, and Thorn got back to her feet.

'Why, Karalyn?' she said. 'Why Sable? You know what she did to my family. When you took her to Lostwell, I thought I'd never see her again. Even looking at her now brings back bad memories.'

'I pitied her,' said Karalyn.

'Does she deserve pity?' said Thorn. 'She showed Bracken none.'

Sable stopped eating. She looked up at Thorn, then stood.

'Thorn,' she said. 'I'm sorry for what I did to your friend. It was cruel.'

'Are you expecting me to forgive you?'

'No. I just want you to know that I understand why you hate me. I have done... many bad things. I'm not sorry for all of them, but I'm sorry about your family, and I'm sorry about Bracken.'

Thorn glanced at Keir. 'And what about my husband? I presume his sitting there like a statue is your doing?'

'Keir wanted to throw Sable out of the house, ma'am,' said Cardova.

'I see,' said Thorn. 'Sable; release him.'

Keir felt a weight lift from his mind, and he sagged, then gasped for air.

'That damn witch!' he cried, jumping off the chair. 'The Empress is going to hang you, Sable, and I'm going to watch as you swing from the noose.'

Sable put a hand on her hip and smiled.

Keir felt his rage explode. Was he the only sane person in the entire house? His sister had just rescued a mass-murdering maniac, and then his own wife had healed her. He clenched his fists.

'Be careful, Keir,' said Sable. 'I've been in your head; remember? If you attempt to strike me, not only will I kick your sorry arse and throw you off the balcony, I might also be tempted to share a few thoughts I found floating around in that skull of yours.'

'That's enough,' said Thorn. 'Keir – behave yourself. Sable, I think you should wait until Lord Bryce gets here. If you run, it will only confirm in the Empress's mind that you cannot be trusted.'

Sable laughed. 'Who says I can be trusted? I want to go back to Dragon Eyre; I have unfinished business. The Unk Tannic stole my Quadrant, and I need it back.'

Karalyn tapped her side. 'I have it,' she said, 'but I can't allow you to return to Dragon Eyre. Blackrose told me that your presence would start a new war.'

Sable shrugged. 'She's exaggerating. I ended the last war.'

'I know what you did, Sable,' said Karalyn. 'The trail of carnage and destruction you left behind is... unparalleled, even for Dragon Eyre.'

'What did she do, ma'am?' said Cardova.

Sable frowned down at him. 'Your accent... Are you Banner?'

'Yes, ma'am.'

Sable's eyes flashed. 'Would someone explain to me what a damned Banner soldier is doing in Plateau City? Has this world been invaded?'

'I brought him from the world of the City,' said Karalyn.

'The what? Oh, the salve world? They have Banner there?'

'I'll explain it all later,' said Karalyn. 'Right now, we need to discuss how to handle Lord Bryce. He'll be here any moment.'

'Lord Bryce?' said Sable. 'The Empress's son? What's to discuss? I'll be arrested, and then the Empress will resurrect her old sentence of death against me, and that will be that. No. I don't think so.'

'What did you do on Dragon Eyre?' said Cardova.

'Do you really want to know, Banner soldier? I destroyed the occupying forces, from Alef to Throscala. Port Edmond is gone; Ectus is in smouldering ruins, and the slaves of Gyle are free. That's what I did. And if I happened to kill tens of thousands of Banner soldiers like you along the way, then that's no great loss.'

Cardova got to his feet, his eyes dark.

Sable laughed. 'Hit a nerve, did I? The gods have abandoned Dragon Eyre. You're looking at an Ascendant-killer, soldier.'

Cardova snorted. 'Impossible.'

'Karalyn, tell your boyfriend the truth.'

Karalyn nodded. 'She's right, Lucius. She killed an Ascendant called Kolai on Dragon Eyre.'

'I could have killed Bastion, too,' Sable said, edging closer to Cardova. 'Instead, I filled him full of abject terror and sent him back to crawl at the feet of his master.' She glanced at Karalyn. 'That reminds me – Edmond is marrying Belinda. I thought you should know.'

Karalyn's mouth fell open. The front doorbell rang, and everyone froze; everyone except Sable. She threw herself across the room, colliding with Karalyn and knocking her to the floor. Sable plucked the Quadrant from Karalyn's clothes, and, in an instant, she was gone.

'See?' cried Keir. 'You stupid cow, Karalyn; now she's on the loose.'

Cardova extended a hand, and pulled Karalyn back to her feet.

'Shit, Lucius,' she whispered; 'what have I done?'

'You did the right thing, ma'am,' he said. 'You gave her another chance. It's not your fault if she spurns it.'

'Of course it's her fault,' said Keir. 'This is a disaster.'

Tabitha opened the door of the sitting room, and Bryce strode in, accompanied by a dozen burly Kellach soldiers.

Bryce's eyes scanned the room. 'Where is she?'

'Karalyn let her escape,' Keir cried. 'Sable took a Quadrant and vanished.'

'Is that true, Karalyn?'

'Why did you bring all these soldiers, Bryce?' said Karalyn. 'It's no wonder she fled. I didn't rescue her so that you could hang her.'

'She is a wanted criminal,' said Bryce. 'The law applies to everyone, even members of your family.' He glanced down at the sleeping body of the older man on the floor. 'Who is this?'

'His name is Olo'osso,' said Karalyn. 'He has nothing to do with Sable; he just happened to be locked up in the same place as she was. He killed a dragon.'

'He hasn't broken any of our laws,' said Karalyn. 'He can stay here until he has fully recovered.'

'Out of the question,' said Keir. 'This house is busy enough as it is.'

Karalyn ignored her brother. 'Tabitha, please make up one of the guest rooms for Olo'osso, and treat him with all kindness.'

Tabitha bowed. 'Yes, ma'am.'

'Never mind about that old fool,' said Keir. 'Sable bloody Holdfast is on the loose! She could be anywhere; we are all in danger, thanks to my idiot sister.'

'Losing your temper isn't going to help matters,' said Bryce.

'Indeed,' said Thorn. 'We should go to the Great Fortress, and inform the Empress of everything that has occurred here this day.'

Bryce smiled. 'Thank you, Thorn; I think that is an excellent idea.' He glanced at the soldiers. 'Return to the palace; we shall be following shortly.'

The soldiers saluted and left the sitting room.

Bryce eyed his father. 'You are to come to the palace, also,' he said. 'My mother has decided that it would be better if you no longer resided with the Holdfast family. Come; there are carriages outside waiting for us.'

'Thank you, my son,' said Brannig, standing.

Bryce frowned. 'Are you alright? You look... ill.'

'I shall be fine in time,' his father said.

'He sacrificed some of his health to aid Olo'osso,' said Cardova.

'And from the look of you, Lucius, you did the same for Sable?'

Cardova nodded. 'A few meals and plenty of rest, and we'll both be fine.'

Bryce nodded, then he turned to Karalyn. 'I trust that you will not disappear without warning? The Empress will need to speak to you. You can imagine what mood she will be in when she hears that Sable has slipped out of our grasp.'

'She was never in your grasp, Bryce,' said Karalyn.

'Let's not argue over words. You shall accompany me in my carriage, along with Brannig and Lucius. Thorn, you can take the other carriage with Keir.'

They walked from the room. Keir trailed along at the rear, watching as Karalyn whispered something to Lucius Cardova. He wondered if there was something going on between them.

'Well, you got your wish,' said Thorn, as she walked by his side down the stairs.

'What?' said Keir.

'Brannig is leaving the townhouse.'

'Yes, to be replaced by another old guy I've never met before. My home is turning into a refuge for waifs and strays, it seems.'

Thorn nodded. 'I was surprised to see you in the townhouse when Karalyn brought me here.'

'Why? I live here.'

'I thought you would be out.'

Thorn turned away before he could reply, and he waited for her as she spoke to Tabitha. The servant accompanied them to the front door, then closed it once everyone had left. Two carriages emblazoned with the imperial insignia were sitting on the cobbles by the side of the road. Bryce, Brannig, Karalyn and Cardova boarded one, and Keir and Thorn walked to the other. They climbed up onto the comfortable benches, and the carriages moved off.

'It's time for a little chat,' said Thorn.

'Yeah?' said Keir. 'I doubt you have anything to say that will interest me.'

'Let's see. I'll keep it brief. I am aware that you are conducting an affair with Tilda Holdwain. If you attempt to divorce me, I will inform your mother of your indiscretions. Once your mother knows, she will adopt me as a full Holdfast, and disinherit you. Am I clear?'

Keir said nothing, his eyes wide and staring.

'I said, am I clear, husband?'

'But... I'm not having an affair with Tilda.'

Thorn laughed. 'Come now; it was I who engineered your meeting. I knew you wouldn't be able to resist your baser temptations, and I had an inkling that Tilda would reciprocate. She's a little immature, don't you think? Pretty, but not very wise.'

'I won't see her again; I swear it.'

Thorn shrugged. 'See her if you want; it makes no difference to me. In fact, I think I would prefer it if you maintained your relationship with young Tilda – it'll keep you out of my way. You haven't pestered me since you met her, and I've enjoyed the peace and quiet. Only, keep it discreet. The Holdwains are a powerful family; not one I would like to gratuitously upset.'

Keir felt his self-esteem shrivel. 'I don't understand.'

'I don't care if you understand or not, dear husband. As long as you desist from any foolish notions about seeking a divorce, then I shall be satisfied.'

'You don't love me any more.'

'I haven't loved you for quite a while now, Keir. I was dazzled by you when we were young and foolish, but now I think I can see the type of man that you are. I don't regret our marriage, as it has eased me into the higher echelons of power, but I no longer respect you. When we get to the Great Fortress, you will act as if this conversation has not taken place. Oh, and I need to work tonight, so I want you out of my hair. Go and visit your little Tilda; but, Keir, be nice to her. If you act in your normal manner, you will drive her away, and then I will have to find you another diversion.'

She turned away to look out of the carriage window, and Keir stared at her, as unable to speak as when Sable had subdued his mind in the townhouse. How had she known about Tilda? Had she truly planned it all? He felt stupid, and small. He started to cry, and Thorn passed him a handkerchief without a word.

He barely noticed the carriage come to a halt. Thorn raised an eyebrow, then glanced at the side door of the carriage. Keir wiped his eyes with the handkerchief, and opened the door for her. An imperial soldier was standing outside, and he assisted Thorn to descend to the ground, her long, sapphire dress gathering around her ankles. Keir stepped down from the carriage, and glanced up at the towering bulk of the Great Fortress. He wanted to run, anywhere, rather than follow Thorn into the building, but he had no choice. She had him by the throat. His mother would probably do worse than merely disinherit him if she discovered his infidelities. Daphne Holdfast had a trenchant loathing for people who betrayed their spouses, ever since she had been told that her own father, Godfrey, had been sleeping with Queen Miranda of the Holdings. Keir would be lucky to depart from any confrontation with his life.

Keir and Thorn followed Bryce and the others into the fortress, and they ascended the many stairs to reach the palace levels. Bryce led them past guards and courtiers, and they entered the Empress's informal meeting chamber, where Bridget was sitting at the head of a table, a large glass of whisky in her left hand. She stared at Karalyn as soon as they entered.

'Don't speak,' Bridget said, in a voice that was controlled but edged with fury. 'The soldiers have already informed me that you allowed Sable to escape. Bringing her back was one thing, but then letting her go? It's beyond belief, Karalyn. The Holdfasts have finally gone too far. Sable could do anything right now; go anywhere. A deranged killer with a grudge and a Quadrant. You, Karalyn, have placed the entire empire in peril.'

Karalyn said nothing.

'I have two tasks for you,' the Empress went on. 'If you fulfil them both, then the path to rehabilitating your family's name may reopen. First, I want you to accompany my son Bryce back to Kellach Brigdomin. There, you will help him promulgate an amnesty that I have written.'

'What amnesty?'

Bridget stared at her, her fist gripping the whisky glass as if she were about to break it.

Karalyn sighed. 'What amnesty, your Majesty?'

Bridget took a drink, then nodded towards Bryce. He took a folded document from a pocket and passed it to Karalyn. She opened it, her eyes scanning the page.

'Is this a joke, your Majesty?' she said. 'You're offering Daimon a full pardon and a job in the palace?'

Bridget nodded. 'That's right. I need a reliable, loyal dream mage to serve me. You had your chance, Karalyn, and you have repeatedly defied me. When you were the only dream mage, I had no choice but to pander to every one of your naïve notions and foolish ideas. If Daimon kneels before me, and swears allegiance, then I will wipe his record clean.'

'But he's killed several members of the Clan Council.'

'The Holdfasts have done much worse over the years. If Daimon is remorseful, then I will forgive him. You will leave with Bryce this day, and not return until you have received a reply from Daimon. I want this amnesty posted all over Kellach Brigdomin, so that even the crazy old hermits dwelling in the caves of the Domm Highlands will have heard of it.'

Karalyn passed the document back to Bryce. 'I'll do it. What's the second task?'

Bridget smiled. 'I would have thought that was obvious. Catch that bitch Sable, and bring her to me. She has a meeting scheduled with a noose that I don't want her to miss.'

Thorn stepped forward, 'Your Majesty, if I may, I would...'

'Shut up, Thorn,' said Bridget. 'You and Keir are both fired. Get your things and fuck off.'

Thorn blinked. 'But...'

'You heard me, Holdfast. You love that name so much, let's see how you enjoy being tarred with the same brush as the rest of the family. Until Karalyn completes both of her tasks, the Holdfasts are no longer welcome in this palace.'

Thorn bowed her head, her composure intact. 'As you wish, your Majesty.'

Bridget chuckled. 'Well, Karalyn? The hopes of the Holdfasts now rest upon your shoulders. The moment you return from Kellach Brigdomin, you will set off on the second task. Do not fail me again.'

Karalyn glanced at Cardova, who nodded, then she turned to Bryce. 'Are you ready?'

'I still have luggage in the *World's End*,' said Bryce. 'Shall we go there first?'

Karalyn gave a brief nod, then, without another word, she, Cardova and Bryce vanished.

Bridget glanced at Brannig. 'On to you. I have decided that you will remain here in the palace, but that does not mean I have forgiven you. It's more that I don't think that you should be associated with the Holdfasts any longer. Their power and fame is on the decline, at long last. Servants will show you to your new quarters. Do not leave them unless I call for you. Dismissed.'

Brannig bowed low, then walked from the room, leaving only Keir and Thorn remaining. Bridget turned from them, and lifted her glass to her lips.

Keir and Thorn bowed in the direction of Bridget's back, then retreated out of the meeting room.

'Holy shit,' muttered Keir, as they began to make their way down to the lower levels of the Great Fortress. 'Karalyn has screwed everything up this time. It's not fair. We didn't bring Sable back. This is unjust.'

'Oh, shut up, Keir,' said Thorn. 'This was always expected; it's just come a little earlier than your mother and I had planned.'

'What?'

'You're so naïve at times; maybe that's why you and Tilda get along so well. The schism between the Holdfasts and the imperial crown has begun.'

Keir stared at her.

She smiled. 'It's finally time to see who really rules this world.'

CHAPTER 26
THE GUILTY ONES

Threeways, Domm Pass – 20th Day, Second Third Summer 534
Karalyn sat on the roof of the tall, stone-built hostelry, her eyes scanning the town as it stretched out in every direction. To the east were the huge wagon marshalling yards, where cargo destined for the markets of the Plateau was being loaded, and goods that had arrived were being stockpiled, ready to be sold in Kellach Brigdomin. The rest of the sprawling town looked like a shabbier version of Severton; the streets were muddier, the tenement blocks less elegant, and the town stank of leather, ale and cow manure.

For four days, she, Bryce and Cardova had waited for Daimon to respond to the Empress's amnesty, but there had been no sign of the dream mage. The waiting had been good for Cardova, and he had recovered from his role in Sable's healing; but Karalyn felt nothing but frustration. She longed to be back with her children, and was dreading telling Bridget that she would refuse to carry out the second task that had been allotted to her. She had promised Sable that she would protect her from the Empress, and she would keep her word. However, it wasn't Sable that was occupying her thoughts as she smoked a cigarette on the roof – it was Belinda. Sable's almost absent-minded comment had changed everything. If Belinda was alive, then Karalyn knew what she had to do, but the scale of the task seemed insurmountable. She would have to go to Implacatus and rescue her, if, that is, she wanted to be rescued. Corthie and Aila had told her about Edmond, and his position as ruler of Implacatus and the gods. Was Belinda marrying him willingly? If she was, then it could only mean that she had decided to rejoin the gods who had once been her friends. Karalyn realised that she wouldn't be able to rest until she knew for sure, but how could she face leaving her children behind to find out? It would help if she could see Implacatus through the Sextant, but when she had asked, several thirds before, it had declined to answer. Perhaps, now that it had a Quadrant inserted into its flank, it would be more cooperative.

'I thought I'd find you up here, ma'am.'

Karalyn glanced up, a hand raised to shield her eyes from the sun. 'It's the only place we're allowed to smoke.'

Cardova sat down next to her and lit a cigarette for himself. 'Are you thinking about the Third Ascendant again?'

'Aye.'

'I remember seeing her in Yoneath, ma'am. She was with Arete and Leksandr, but not *with* them, if you know what I mean. She seemed detached. The reason I remember is that it seemed unusual to see an Ascendant who looked so unsure of themselves.'

'I regret the way we parted. I was brusque and ruthless with her, and I hurt her. I was angry, but it's no excuse.'

'Does the rest of your family feel the same way about her?'

'No. She's a bit like Sable in that respect, which is a little unfair on Belinda. Sable was a traitor throughout the war, whereas Belinda was loyal, right up until the final stages of the siege of Colsbury, when she panicked and opened the gates to Agatha. That was enough to turn the Empress against her. It was no coincidence that I took both Sable and Belinda to Lostwell – I was saving them from Bridget's wrath. But, just as Sable has Kelsey; Belinda has Corthie.'

'Corthie, ma'am?'

'Aye. Belinda and Corthie became good friends. He was devastated when he returned from Lostwell without her. Belinda loved him like a brother. When he finds out that she might still be alive, then I imagine he'll forget all about wanting to become a farmer.'

Cardova looked at Karalyn, his eyes troubled. 'Ma'am, please don't tell me that you're actually thinking about intervening in the affairs of the Ascendants on Implacatus?'

'I might be. Kelsey was there; that's where she met Van's father.'

'Yes, ma'am, and according to them, the gods were aware that a Holdfast was in Serene. Lord Bastion was practically knocking at Caelius's front door when they managed to escape. Going to Implacatus would be suicide, plain and simple.'

Karalyn smiled. 'Not if you came with us. You must know every street in Serene.'

'Maybe I do,' he said, 'but the Third Ascendant won't be in Serene, ma'am. She'll be in Cumulus, along with the rest of the Ancients and Ascendants. Only the most favoured mortals are ever allowed to enter Cumulus; and, believe it or not – I wasn't particularly favoured.'

She frowned. 'Let's return to this conversation another time. We have enough to do without burdening ourselves with thoughts of Implacatus.'

'I heartily agree, ma'am. By the way, Lord Bryce has left the hostelry. He's gone to speak to the Clan Council again, to lobby them to increase their publicity regarding the Empress's amnesty.'

'I'm not sure what the point of that is. Daimon will know about it by now, and where is he? Bridget doesn't seem to understand that I can't find him if he doesn't want to be found. He could be fifty yards away, but unless he broadcasts his powers, he's as good as invisible. And then, once this is over, I'm going to have to tell Bridget that I will not be hunting Sable down.'

'Do you know where she is, ma'am?'

'I haven't looked, to be honest. It hardly matters; she won't be in Kellach Brigdomin, and my range doesn't reach the Holdings from here. That's where she probably is, although she might be hiding in one of her old haunts in Rahain. You know, when she disappeared like that, at first I was angry and disappointed, but not any more; not after seeing Bridget's reaction. If I was Sable, I would have fled, too.'

'She doesn't seem to like Banner soldiers very much.'

Karalyn glanced at him. 'Try a little experiment. Imagine that you were from Dragon Eyre. Would you like Banner soldiers?'

Cardova lowered his gaze. 'Not if you put it like that.'

'They occupied that world for... how long was it?'

'Nearly thirty years, ma'am.'

'If you were a native of Dragon Eyre, you would probably be fighting the occupation.'

'But the Banner soldiers are only doing what they're told, ma'am.'

'Aye, but didn't you tell me that they had ordered you to carry out atrocities? At some point, soldiers have to take some responsibility for their actions – they cannot always blame it on following orders.'

'I know that, ma'am. All the same, many of those Sable killed will have been decent people, who thought they were doing the right thing. What will happen to the survivors? If it's true that the gods have abandoned Dragon Eyre, then the remaining Banner soldiers will be stranded, and probably desperate. Serene will be in mourning when they discover what's happened. Thousands of families will be heartbroken, not knowing if their loved ones are alive or dead.'

'Do you hate Sable?'

'No, ma'am. She was fighting for her cause, and, if I'm being honest with myself, her cause was righteous. We had no business being on Dragon Eyre. We should have left it well alone.'

'Why did Implacatus invade?'

'I have absolutely no idea, ma'am. The Banner stay out of politics; we don't weigh up the rights and wrongs of any individual campaign. We sign up, and then we do as we're told.' He stretched his arms. 'If you don't need me right now, I might nap for a couple of hours. I still feel a bit off after the healing.'

'Brannig was right,' she said. 'It was brave of you.'

He shrugged. 'Someone had to do it.'

'What do you think of Thorn?'

'In what respect, ma'am?'

'Just your general impression.'

He looked thoughtful for a moment. 'Well, I think that your brother is a lucky man.'

'Why, because Thorn is so beautiful?'

'I wasn't thinking of that, but I guess you're right. I was more thinking that she seems too smart and self-assured to be with Keir.' He laughed. 'Apologies, ma'am. That sounded as though I think your brother is an idiot.'

'My brother is an idiot.'

'Thorn seems like a natural leader; she wants to lead, I could feel it. I could be wrong, though, ma'am; that was just the impression I got. Bryce seems more suited to her.'

'Why?'

'They seem similar. Everything I said about Thorn also applies to Bryce. Whereas, your brother...'

'Go on.'

He shook his head. 'No. I don't want to start dissecting Keir's personality. You know him far better than I do, ma'am.' He stood. 'I'm going for that nap, before I say something stupid about your family. Wake me if you need anything.'

Karalyn watched as Cardova walked across the flat roof and entered the stairwell. She was glad he was there, as relations with Bryce had been tense since leaving Plateau City, and Cardova's easy-going manner had helped dispel any arguments. The Empress had been clear – she wanted Daimon to replace Karalyn as her dream mage, and Bryce was determined to follow his mother's course. On one level, Karalyn hoped the Empress's plan succeeded. If she was no longer needed to assist the Empress, then it would free her to spend more time with her children, but could Daimon be trusted? So far, the sixteen-year-old had given little indication that he could be brought into the fold, and Karalyn had no idea what Daimon's aims were. If she could discover why he had killed five members of the Clan Council, that would be a start. She crossed the roof, and descended the four flights of stairs to ground level.

If Bryce was out, and Cardova was sleeping, then she had an opportunity to strike out on her own, without having to worry about protecting her two companions.

You cannot see me.

She stepped out on to the busy street, dodging pedestrians and ox-drawn wagons. It hadn't rained in a few days, and the unpaved road was rutted but not muddy, and the wagon wheels were sending fine particles of dust into the air. Karalyn started to walk toward the town centre, her senses soaking in the sights, sounds and smells of the bustling streets. While Severton was clean and well ordered, Threeways had a shambolic and chaotic air about it, but there was no denying the boisterous sense of life emanating from the town. She saw a few Holdings merchants drinking outside a huge tavern, their voices raised to compete with the cacophony of noise. One side of the tavern bordered a large square, where posters proclaiming the amnesty for Daimon had been nailed up next to signs looking for recruits to join wagon teams. Beyond the square lay the administrative district of the town, and Karalyn noticed a large militia presence patrolling the streets.

Karalyn crossed the square, and entered the mind of a militiaman wearing officer insignia. The militia were hunting for someone, and at first, Karalyn assumed it might be Daimon, but then she realised her mistake. A member of the Clan Council was missing, seemingly abducted from his own bed the previous night. From the soldier's mind, she gleaned that the Clan Council was in a state of near panic. Despite the varied circumstances surrounding the deaths of the five council members that had already occurred, many were refusing to see the deaths as a coincidence. They were right, Karalyn thought to herself. Daimon had killed them and, presumably, he was now responsible for the missing council member. Did that mean Daimon was in Threeways? Not necessarily. He could have told the council member to leave his own house from a safe distance, and then persuaded him to throw himself into one of the rivers that wound through the Domm Pass. His body would most likely be found in a day or two, she thought. But why him; and why the other five?

A flash of powers caught her attention, and she withdrew from the officer's mind. She turned, and focussed. Aila. Karalyn blinked. What was Aila doing in Threeways? She pinpointed the location of the demigod's self-healing powers. She was in one of the town's many hostelries, a solid, stone-built tenement block that rented rooms to travellers. She sent her vision to the room, and saw Aila sitting with little Killop on her knee. Aila seemed healthy enough, but she looked as though she could give birth at any moment. Why was she alone? Karalyn hurried along the street. If she could sense Aila, then Daimon would be able to do the same. She ghosted through the town centre, and arrived at the stone block. The main entrance was unlocked, and she entered, then climbed the steps to the third floor. She dropped her powers and knocked on the door.

A bolt slid free, and the door opened.

Aila peered out. 'Karalyn? What are you doing here?'

'Working,' she said.

'You'd better come in,' said Aila.

The demigod led Karalyn into a small room. Its walls were damp, and there was a nasty odour left behind by the previous occupants. Aila sat down, a hand on her swollen abdomen.

'Corthie's been arrested,' she said.

'What? When?'

'Thirteen days ago. He went wild in Kell, and attacked five men.'

Karalyn paused, her eyes narrowing. Something about Aila seemed odd, as if she was hiding something, or as if she had forgotten something important.

'If Corthie is locked up in Kell, then why are you in Threeways?' said Karalyn.

Aila blinked. 'I... I don't know. But, I have to stay here. I'm not to leave this room.'

'Who told you that?'

Aila looked confused. 'I don't know. Corthie's dangerous. He might hurt the children.'

'Corthie would never hurt a child.'

'You didn't see him, Karalyn; he was like a wild beast. It's not safe to give birth anywhere near him. I'm going to have my baby here, where we'll be safe. Yes, that's it. I want to be safe.'

'Have you seen Daimon?'

Aila said nothing.

Karalyn stared at her, then entered the demigod's mind. Within seconds, it was clear that something was wrong. Aila's memories had been chopped up, and re-arranged into a bewildering mess that made no sense. She saw a memory of Corthie strangling a man by a farmhouse, but it lacked any context, and seemed isolated from her other memories. Karalyn went deeper, and saw more interference in Aila's mind. She had been compelled to remain in the hostelry; if she tried to leave, then excruciating pain would be her punishment. Karalyn started to unpick the layers of compulsion and manipulation that had reduced the demigod to blind subservience, but Aila gripped the sides of her head and groaned in agony. Karalyn pulled back, her anger growing. Aila started to pant, her breath ragged and heavy.

'Please, don't hurt me,' said the demigod.

'Daimon is manipulating you,' said Karalyn. 'He is holding you here like a prisoner.'

'No,' said Aila. 'I'm safe here. Please leave. I don't want you to hurt me again.'

Karalyn hesitated. She knew that she could probably sweep away what Daimon had done to the demigod's mind with a strong burst of her own powers, but what would remain? Aila would be left with nothing but pain and a large hole in her memories. To repair the damage properly, Karalyn would need time and patience, and it would be too dangerous to attempt such a plan within the dank room where they were sitting. Daimon knew where Aila was, but he might assume that she was safely confined; if Karalyn moved her, then he would be able to track her self-healing powers. She could temporarily turn off the demigod's self-healing, but with her due to give birth, that would be more dangerous than doing nothing.

Aila stood, and pointed at the door. 'Leave.'

At that moment, the door swung open, and Dillon walked into the room, a box of groceries clutched in his right hand. His eyes widened as he saw Karalyn standing in front of Aila, and he froze.

'Where is your brother?' said Karalyn.

Dillon dropped the box and fled. Karalyn raced after him into the stairwell, and Dillon disappeared through a door into another rented room.

'She's found us!' he cried.

Karalyn ran into the room. The shutters were closed, and in the dim light she saw a man tied to a chair, his face bruised and beaten. He gazed at Karalyn with terror in his eyes, as Dillon raced past him. Karalyn looked for Daimon, then turned in time to see a stout club swinging towards her head. She dived backwards, and the club clipped the side of her jaw. She fell to the floor, and Daimon lashed out with the club again, striking the back of her head. Still conscious, she pulled her hands up to protect her head, as the pain drove out her other thoughts.

'Have ye killed her?' said Dillon.

'I don't think so,' said Daimon. 'Should I?'

'No! She's not on the list we made, brother. She had nothing to do with our mother's death.'

'I know that, but she's a threat. She keeps coming to Kellach Brigdomin to hunt us.'

'But you asked her to come here.'

'Aye, so I could contact her children without her interfering. If I don't kill her, then she'll keep coming.'

'What about the amnesty? Daimon, please. The Empress says that she'll forgive us if we hand ourselves in.'

'They're lying to us, brother,' said Daimon. 'They're just trying to force us out into the open. And besides, I've gone too far. It's not just those bastards in the Clan Council who have died; not any more.'

There was silence for a moment, and Karalyn lay still, her eyes closed as her head drummed with pain.

'Who else?' said Dillon.

'Some poor bastard in Rakana,' said Daimon. 'I didn't mean it.'

'Rakana?' said Dillon. 'What were ye doing there?'

'Setting a trap for Daphne Holdfast. She's just as evil as those councillors, brother. She's a cold-blooded murderer. Maybe we'll have to kill all of the Holdfasts.'

'Ye cannae mean that,' Dillon cried. 'I thought we were doing this for justice; justice for our mother.'

'It's gone beyond that,' said Daimon, as he strode across the floor.

Karalyn opened her eyes, and saw Daimon standing over her, the club lifted above his head.

'The amnesty is genuine, Daimon,' she gasped. 'But if you kill me, or hurt Aila and the children, the Empress will never forgive you.'

'Why would I hurt Aila, or her bairn?' said Daimon. 'I rescued them from yer brother. I looked into Corthie's heart. He's a beast. It was only a matter of time before he hurt them.'

'You made him attack those men in Kell?'

'Aye, I did. But, he would have done it anyway, on his own. I was just speeding things up. I wanted to show the world what kind of man he really is.'

'Is my mother still in Rakana?'

'Aye. She's been sentenced to death. They think she was spying on them. It's not true, but Daphne deserves to die for the crimes she's committed. You Holdfasts thought ye could get away with yer crimes forever. I never intended to hurt yer family, but ye've left me no choice. I'll try to make it quick.'

'Don't do it, brother!' cried Dillon. 'If we kill Karalyn Holdfast, we'll be hunted until we die.'

'I have to,' said Daimon.

'No. She could be a hostage. We could use her to negotiate with the Empress.'

'I'm sorry, brother. I have no choice.'

'Wait! What would mother think? We're doing this for her, or I thought we were. Ye told me this was about justice; about punishing the men and women responsible for mother's death. Karalyn had nothing to do with any of that. If ye kill her, then I'm walking away.'

Karalyn saw the conflict in Daimon's eyes as he held the club, then he lowered his arms.

'Help me tie her to a chair,' he said.

Dillon ran over.

Daimon pointed the club in Karalyn's face. 'If ye struggle, yer brains will end up on the wall; understand?'

Dillon lifted Karalyn by the shoulders, and dragged her to a chair, which stood a few feet away from the beaten body of the member of the Clan Council. She tried to send out her vision, to warn Cardova, but Daimon's powers were flooding the room, and in her weakened state, she was unable to force her way through them. Dillon pulled her arms behind the chair, and bound her wrists, then Daimon pulled a knife from his belt.

'What are ye gonnae do with that?' said Dillon.

'We can't allow her to use her powers to alert the militia,' said Daimon. 'If she's suffering, then she'll be too distracted to send a message.'

He drove the knife into Karalyn's right thigh, then twisted the blade. Karalyn opened her mouth to scream, and Daimon held his hand against her face, muffling her cries. He pulled the knife from her thigh, and blood flowed from the wound, running down her leg and dripping onto the bare floorboards.

'Check on Aila,' said Daimon. 'I'll scout the area, to make sure no one followed Karalyn here.'

Both boys left the room, and Karalyn clenched her teeth. Just as Daimon had predicted, the pain from her head and thigh were drowning out everything else. After all that she had faced, had she been defeated by a sixteen-year-old with a club? It didn't seem possible.

'Karalyn Holdfast?' gasped the man tied to the other chair. 'Can ye hear me?'

Karalyn nodded, her eyes closed.

'Save us,' the man whispered, his voice filled with pain.

'Why you?' she gasped. 'Why do they want you dead?'

'Revenge for their mother,' the man said. 'Every councillor who has died recently; they were the ones who voted to send soldiers into the Domm Highlands, to clear out the bandits. Some... tragic mistakes were made. Civilians died in the raids. Daimon and Dillon's mother was one of those killed by our soldiers. They razed the village to the ground. I told them I was sorry, but they don't care. They're going to kill me. You have powers; I was listening to what they said. Use them. Save me, if ye can.'

Daimon and Dillon walked back into the room, closing the door behind them. They approached the two chairs. Karalyn looked into their eyes. Dillon looked almost ill with nerves, while his brother was radiating a restless anxiety.

'You should do it,' said Daimon, holding out the knife.

'What?' said Dillon. 'No. I can't kill him. You do it. You killed the others.'

Daimon slapped Dillon across the face. 'How many times do I have to tell ye? I didn't kill the other councillors; I just filled their minds with guilt, for what they did to our mother. They killed themselves.'

'Is that true?' said Karalyn.

'Aye, it is,' said Daimon. 'I'm not a murderer, no matter what ye think. Those councillors – each one of them knew what they had done. All I did was make them focus on the guilt that they already felt, until they couldn't bear it any longer.' He gestured to the man tied to the chair. 'Except for this one; he feels no guilt or shame about what he did. He still thinks it was right to send thousands of soldiers into the glens of the Domm Highlands, to slaughter and burn. Isn't that right, Councillor?'

'The Domm bandits were attacking peaceful farmers and traders,' the man gasped. 'They had to be dealt with. I'm sorry about your mother, and...'

Daimon punched the man in the face. 'Liar! You're not sorry. Dillon and I watched what happened to our mother. The soldiers beat her, then locked the doors of our house and set fire to it, while she was still inside.'

'It got out of hand,' said the man, as blood streamed from his nose.

'I read the minds of some of the soldiers,' Daimon went on, his face red. 'Their orders were clear – show no mercy. Clear the glens. Destroy the villages that support the bandits. Was my mother a bandit? She never hurt a single person in her entire life. She hated the bandits; we all did. They stole from us, too.'

'If you let me go,' the man said, 'then I will set up an inquiry; I swear it. Anyone who broke the law will be punished.'

Daimon leaned forward, until his face was inches away from the man. 'Too late.'

He moved the knife closer to the man's neck, as Dillon shrank away, his eyes wide with terror. As Daimon stared at the blade, Karalyn felt his powers recede a little, as he struggled with the enormity of what he was about to do. She pushed past her agony, and sent a tendril of power flashing out of the tenement. It sped through the streets, and into the hostelry where she, Cardova and Bryce had their rooms. She found Cardova, asleep in bed, and rammed her location into his dreaming mind.

She felt a slap across her cheek.

'Stop that!' cried Daimon.

'You don't have to do this,' gasped Karalyn. 'Let us go, and speak to Lord Bryce. The Empress's son has been empowered to grant you both an amnesty. Explain to him what happened with the councillors, and allow me to save my mother from Rakana.'

Daimon's hands shook as he gripped the knife, and his eyes were wild with mixed emotions.

'I can't,' he said. 'I can't stop now.'

A loud cry came from the room next door, and Daimon blinked.

'See if Aila is alright,' he said, and Dillon ran off.

'Let her go,' said Karalyn. 'Aila is no threat to you, and Corthie would never hurt her.'

'Yer wrong,' said Daimon. 'Corthie is a beast. Why don't ye realise that? Have you never looked into his heart?'

'Corthie has his struggles, and I have seen the darkness that lies within him; but he's trying, Daimon; he's trying to live a peaceful life. The Holdfasts are not your enemies.'

'No? Tell me, Karalyn; how many people have ye killed? And Corthie – how many have lost their lives at his hands? Keir, too; and let's not forget yer mother. I watched her kill a guard in Rakana. It was easy for her. She didn't hesitate, and she has no regrets. In fact, she forgot about it almost right away. That guard had done nothing to hurt her. Yer mother is a monster, and her children are no better.'

'If you kill the man sitting next to me,' said Karalyn, 'then you will also be a murderer. You will have become what you say you hate. Is that what you want?'

Daimon hesitated. He glanced at the knife, then at the terrified councillor.

Dillon burst into the room. 'I need help!'

'Why?' said Daimon. 'What's happening?'

'Aila's gone into labour,' cried Dillon. 'Her baby – it's coming!'

CHAPTER 27
THE BEAST

Threeways, Domm Pass – 20th Day, Second Third Summer 534

Corthie's grey gelding staggered into Threeways. He had pushed the horse to the limits of its endurance, and it would need to rest for days, but Corthie didn't care. Up on the saddle, he felt almost as tired as the gelding. He hadn't used an ounce of battle-vision during the four-day journey from Kell, and he was nauseous with hunger. Racing away from Marchside at midnight had seemed like a good idea, but he had left without bringing any food, blankets, clothes or money, and he probably looked fearsome and wild in his bedraggled state.

He dismounted when the road surface changed from hard-packed earth to cobblestones, and tied the reins of the gelding to a fence. Someone would probably steal it, he thought, as he patted the gelding's flank. At some point, he would have to repay Kallie for the horse. More than that, he knew that he should return to Marchside to serve the rest of his sentence. If he didn't, then he would never be able to go back to Kell, and the thought made him uncomfortable. Several of the locals had predicted that he wouldn't last a winter in Clackenbaird; if he didn't return, then he wouldn't have even made it through his first summer.

He glanced up at the four-storey buildings of Threeways, wondering where to start. Aila could be anywhere. If she had booked into a hostelry, there were over two dozen to choose from within the bounds of the town. He set off down the main street leading from Brig, and passed through thick crowds. No one glanced in his direction – to them, he was just another Kellach Brigdomin. He saw a large six-storey hostelry on the left-hand side of the road, and ducked through its wide entrance. A reception counter was on the left of the hallway, and Corthie approached it.

'Excuse me,' he said. 'I'm looking for my wife; is she staying here?'

The old man behind the counter glanced up at him. 'What's her name?'

'Aila.'

The man frowned. 'I'm sorry, sir, but it's our policy not to reveal the identities of our guests.'

'Then why did you ask for her name?'

'So that, if she's here, we can pass on a message to her once you've gone. You wouldn't be the first man to be looking for a woman who doesn't wish to be found, sir.'

Corthie swore under his breath.

'Do you have a message, sir?'

'Does that mean she is here?'

'I haven't checked the book, sir. And I won't; not until you've left the building.'

'Tell her that her husband is looking for her. I'll... um, I'll be staying in the *Merchant's Rest*. She can leave a message for me at the desk there.'

'Very good, sir.'

Corthie turned, and eyed the staircase. With a burst of speed, he could be up the first flight before the old man would be able to emerge from behind the desk, but what then? He couldn't knock on every door. He strode from the building, and walked back out on to the street. When he had been in Threeways before, while he had been travelling with Brogan and Bethal, they had stayed in the *Merchant's Rest*. They had also visited the Clan Council buildings. Maybe someone there would remember him. He was tempted to pull on his battle-vision, but it was just as likely to attract Daimon as Karalyn. He walked towards the town centre, along busy streets and past wagons groaning under the weight of their cargo, until he saw the high roof of the main Clan Council building. Dozens of militia were patrolling the nearby streets, and Corthie walked up to one.

'Hey,' he said. 'What's going on?'

'The council buildings are closed to the public,' the militiaman said. 'All appointments have been cancelled. Try again tomorrow.'

'Why?'

'Do I look like a fucking news-teller? Beat it, son.'

Corthie stepped back, and eyed the guarded entrance to the council building. A small crowd had gathered, and some were arguing with the militiamen and women posted outside the front doors. Corthie frowned. One of the men trying to gain access to the building was Lucius Cardova.

'Lucius!' he called out, waving his hand in the air.

Cardova turned, then spotted Corthie. He retreated from the doors, and hurried across to where Corthie stood.

'What are you doing here?' said Corthie.

'I'm trying to get inside to speak to Lord Bryce; but no one's getting in or out.' The tall soldier glanced around. 'Are you here on your own?'

'I'm looking for Aila,' he said. 'I've just ridden four days from Kell.'

Cardova nodded. 'Will you help me?'

'Sure. To do what?'

'I received a garbled message from your sister while I was sleeping. An address, that's it; just an address. I was trying to see if Lord Bryce would authorise some militia to come with me, in case there's trouble, but I'll settle for you, Corthie. You're worth at least ten militia.'

'Why would Karalyn place an address into your head?'

'I'm not sure, but we should go and find out. I was having a nap, and her message woke me. She wasn't in her room, so I'm guessing that she wants me to go to the address. Will you come?'

'Of course.'

Cardova smiled. 'Thanks, Corthie.' He pulled a pencil and a scrap of paper from a pocket, then crouched down by the side of the road and jotted out a brief note. He folded the piece of paper, then glanced at Corthie. 'Wait here.'

Corthie watched as Cardova ran back towards the front entrance of the Clan Council building. He barged his way through the crowds, leaned in close to a militiaman, and passed him the slip of paper. The guard seemed reluctant, but he eventually nodded, and shoved the message into his coat. Cardova worked his way back through the crowd to Corthie.

'I'm not sure if Lord Bryce will get that message,' he said, 'but I don't want to waste any more time. Let's go.'

They set off, with Cardova leading the way.

'Are you still searching for the dream mage?' Corthie said, as they hastened down the busy streets.

'Yes. The Empress wants to offer him an amnesty, and...'

Corthie's anger tipped over, and he clenched his fists. 'An amnesty – for that little prick? If I find him, I'm going to rip his head off.'

Cardova raised an eyebrow. 'Why?'

'He's been in my head, Lucius, telling me to do terrible things. He tried to make me attack Aila, and... I nearly did. He won't be getting any amnesty from me.'

'If,' said Cardova, 'and I'll admit it's a big "if", but if he's hurt Karalyn, then I'm tempted to agree with you. If we do it, though, if we smash the little bastard to a pulp, there will be consequences.'

'I don't give a shit,' said Corthie.

Cardova nodded, his eyes grim. 'You know, Corthie, I'm not sure I do, either.'

Corthie frowned, as they turned left at a junction. 'Thanks for looking out for my sister, but are you not taking this a bit personally? I mean, I'm happy to kill the little runt, but Aila's my wife. Are you and Karalyn, eh, together?'

'No.'

'Then..?'

'If I tell you something, Corthie, will you promise not to tell Karalyn?'

'I hope I don't end up regretting this, but alright.'

'I think I might be falling for your sister.'

'Is that a bad thing?'

'Your mother made me swear that I wouldn't do anything about it. Karalyn doesn't know. I'm meant to be protecting her, and I have to act like a damn professional. It's been driving me crazy.'

'I hate to be critical, but if you're supposed to be protecting her, then how did you manage to lose her? Napping all afternoon doesn't strike me as particularly professional.'

'I was exhausted from helping to heal Sable. I gave her some of my life force.'

Corthie's mouth fell open, and his feet stopped moving. 'What?'

'Karalyn and I rescued her from Dragon Eyre.'

'Sable?'

'Yes, Corthie; Sable bloody Holdfast, as Keir called her. She's back. Empress Bridget was not very pleased.'

'That sounds like an understatement.'

'It was. Come on; we can't stand here in the middle of the street looking like numpties.'

'Interesting choice of words.'

'I picked it up from Kelsey; let's go.'

Corthie's mind turned cartwheels as they hurried along the road. Sable? He smiled to himself. Aside from Kelsey, he seemed to be the only member of the Holdfast family who didn't think Sable was the incarnation of pure evil, but then he hadn't been around when she had committed her worst crimes. The only time they had ever met was in Old Alea, on Lostwell's final day, and they had got along well enough, as they had stood shoulder-to-shoulder with Belinda against Edmond and his forces.

'Did you see Maddie and Blackrose?'

'Yes,' said Cardova.

'And?'

'The dragon forbade us from rescuing Sable, but you know what Karalyn's like.'

'I'm a bit surprised that Blackrose didn't eat her.'

'She'll probably wish she had, once she finds out that we rescued Sable anyway.'

They went down another street, then Cardova slowed and came to a halt. He slipped into the shadows of an alleyway, and Corthie joined him.

Cardova pointed at a stone tenement on the other side of the road. 'That's the building.'

'Do we know the room?'

Cardova shook his head.

'You're the officer,' said Corthie. 'What do you suggest?'

Cardova gazed at the building for a few moments. 'We can't go in screaming, shouting and kicking down doors,' he said. 'If they're on an upper floor, all that will do is announce our arrival. Remember, Corthie, we don't know if Karalyn or the dream mage are in there. We'll have to be stealthy. Floor by floor, listening at each doorway. One of us should stay by the stairs, so that we don't get out-flanked, while the other one checks the doors. And, you'll have to keep your battle-vision under wraps until the last moment.'

Corthie nodded. 'What if they're not here?'

'Then we go back to the hostelry where we're staying, and I'll buy you a beer.'

'Alright. Do you have any weapons?'

Cardova pulled back the side of his long coat, revealing the hilt of a short sword. 'You?'

Corthie shook his head.

Cardova unbuckled his sword belt and passed it to Corthie.

'Are you sure?' said Corthie.

'Damn right. I'm pretty handy in a fight, but I'm certainly not the greatest mortal warrior of all time.'

Corthie fastened the belt round his waist, and pulled his cloak over to conceal it.

'Let's double back a bit,' said Cardova, 'in case anyone is watching from the windows.'

They retraced their steps, then crossed the road when they were out of sight of the tenement. They stayed close to the line of buildings, and reached the main entrance to the stone block. Cardova tried the door, and it opened. There was no reception desk in the hallway, and they climbed the stairs to the first level, where four apartment doors sat against the wall facing away from the stairwell.

Cardova signalled for Corthie to remain by the stairs, then he crept forwards, and crouched by each door in turn, listening. Cardova shook his head, and they ascended to the second level, where they repeated the process. Corthie suppressed his frustration as he waited by the stairs. He tried to remember that Karalyn's message might have been benign, garbled or mistaken, but his hand lingered by the hilt of the short sword, ready. Cardova shook his head again, and they began to steal up the next flight of stairs, keeping as silent as they were able. Halfway up the stairs, a low cry echoed from the floor above – a child's cry. Corthie and Cardova glanced at each other, and raced up the rest of the stairs. Cardova listened at the doors, then pointed at one. Corthie approached, and placed his ear against the door. He heard a child cry out again, then Aila's voice responded, clear and unmistakable, followed by a man's voice.

Cardova eased Corthie to the side, then made a few hand gestures that Corthie didn't understand.

'I'll kick the door down,' Cardova whispered, seeing Corthie's blank look; 'then you go in.'

Corthie nodded, and stepped back. Cardova took a short run-up, then battered the door open with a powerful kick. Corthie surged his battle-vision and charged into the cramped apartment. Aila was lying on the floor of the small room, blood pooling by her legs, while little Killop was crouching by her, holding her hand. Standing a few yards away was a young man, holding a newborn baby in a blanket. The young man stared at Corthie, his eyes widening in shock.

'Don't touch me!' he cried.

'That's one of them!' shouted Cardova. 'That's Daimon's brother.'

Corthie battle-vision-powered rage took over; the sight of his wife lying bloody on the floor enough to bring his fury to boiling point. Some small part of his unconscious mind knew that the sword would be too much, and he clenched his right fist. He sprang at the young man, his movements a blur. He plucked the child from the man's grasp, then buried his fist into his face. There was a nasty sound of bones cracking, and the young man flew backward, clattering off the wall, and falling to the bare floorboards, where he lay motionless. Corthie turned from him, his left arm cradling the newborn.

'Aila,' he said, 'are you alright?'

Aila was staring up at him, terror emblazoned across her features. She clutched onto Killop, and tried to crawl away from Corthie.

'Aila,' he said, 'everything's going to be fine. I'm here.'

'Get away from me!' she cried. 'You beast!'

Corthie gazed at her in confusion as his rage subsided. The baby in his arms began to cry, and Aila's face twisted with torment. Corthie passed the baby to her, and she gathered it up in her arms, then backed away until she was against the far wall.

'Don't touch us,' she said. 'Leave us alone, you monster.'

'I don't understand,' he said. 'We're here to rescue you.'

'Um, Corthie,' said Cardova.

Corthie glanced up. Cardova was crouching by the body of the young man Corthie had punched, a hand placed gently against the man's neck.

'There's no pulse,' he said. 'He's dead.'

Aila screamed.

'But,' said Corthie, 'I only hit him once.'

'It was enough,' said Cardova. 'We need to get out of here.'

Corthie turned back to Aila. The demigod was weeping, her eyes filled with abject terror as she stared at Corthie. His heart broke at the sight. Aila had never been frightened of him before. When others had called him a thug, or a ruthless killing machine, she had always shrugged off such comments, believing that she knew him better than anyone else; and yet, from the look on her face, she now seemed to think that he was nothing more than a mindless monster; a danger to her and her children.

Children, he thought. Aila had given birth to their second child, and he didn't even know if it was a boy or a girl. His shoulders sagged, as the last echoes of anger dissipated away, leaving an ashen emptiness.

'Corthie,' said Cardova, 'we can't linger here. Daimon might be in the building; he will have sensed your battle-vision.'

'What does it matter?' Corthie said. 'Aila hates me.'

'She's in shock,' said Cardova. 'We need to move her to a safer place.'

A guttural cry came from the doorway. Corthie and Cardova turned. A young man, similar in age to the man Corthie had killed, was standing by the entrance of the apartment, his eyes lit with rage.

'What have ye done to my brother?' he said.

Aila pointed at Corthie. 'That beast murdered him, Daimon. Dillon was helping me, and that monster took his life.'

Daimon clenched his fists and let out a howl of grief and anger, his face contorting with pain.

'Where is Karalyn?' said Cardova.

Daimon pointed a finger at the tall soldier. Cardova's eyes rolled up into his head, and he toppled over, crashing onto the floorboards by Dillon's body.

'You will pay, Corthie!' screamed Daimon. 'Ye'll pay for what you did. I'm gonnae flay ye alive; make ye suffer. You will beg for death.'

'Kill him!' cried Aila.

Daimon raised his hand, and Corthie felt the worst pain imaginable rip through his mind. He clutched the sides of his head and fell to his knees, blinded. He tried to scream, but no sound would leave his lips.

'Do ye like that, beast?' said Daimon, walking forwards. 'Do ye feel the knives inside yer mind, cutting and tearing through yer thoughts and memories?'

Corthie closed his eyes, but it was too late; Daimon was in his head, burning his way through his mind like a spark devouring a dry forest.

'Beg for yer life,' said Daimon.

Despite the agony, Daimon's words struck home. Corthie felt an urge to whimper and plead with the dream mage, but something stopped him, and he resisted.

'Yer strong,' Daimon said, 'but I already knew that. I'll enjoy breaking ye, but nothing will make up for what ye did to my brother.'

Daimon snapped his fingers. The pain soared in Corthie's mind, and he fell to the floor, unconscious.

Corthie opened his eyes. He was standing up, but couldn't move, his limbs frozen. He tried to turn his head, but it, too, was fixed in position. In front of him, three chairs sat in a line. Cardova was bound and gagged in the seat closest to Corthie, then, in the next seat along, Karalyn was tied up. She was gazing at Corthie, but she looked weak and in pain, then Corthie noticed the wound on her leg. Blood had soaked through her clothes, and had formed a pool by the base of the chair. On the third seat was a man Corthie didn't recognise, his face beaten and bruised.

'Corthie,' Karalyn gasped. 'Be strong.'

'Shut up,' said Daimon, though Corthie couldn't see where the dream mage was located. 'He killed my brother,' Daimon went on, his voice breaking.

'I saw what happened,' said Karalyn. 'It was an accident.'

'No,' said Daimon. 'Corthie was following his true nature. Did I not tell ye about him? Ye didn't listen, Karalyn, but I was right. Yer brother is a savage beast. How many widows and orphans live in grief because of him? There's no pity in his heart; no goodness – only darkness. Tell her, Aila.'

'Yes,' said Aila's voice, from out of sight. 'Corthie is a monster. The children aren't safe with him. Kill him, Daimon; he scares me.'

'Oh, he will die, Aila,' said Daimon. 'There's nothing more certain than that.'

'Good,' said Aila. 'The sooner he's dead, the better.'

A solitary tear rolled down Corthie's face. He tried to move again, but felt as though his body had been fixed in a vice.

'Don't listen to them, Corthie,' said Karalyn. 'Daimon has twisted Aila's thoughts – she doesn't know what she's saying.'

'Do ye also wish to die, Karalyn?' spat Daimon.

'I know you're hurting,' said Karalyn. 'Corthie didn't mean to kill your brother. This is a mess; a terrible mess, but please don't make it any worse.'

'Yes,' cried the man in the chair along from Karalyn. 'Please let us go!'

Daimon strode forward, entering Corthie's line of sight. The dream mage struck the bound man across the face.

'Silence, Councillor,' he said.

'If you kill me,' sobbed the man, 'then you will also be a murderer.'

'No; I'll be a bringer of justice. It can't be wrong to kill someone who massacres civilians. With your death, Councillor, my campaign for revenge will be over, and my mother will sleep more easily in her grave.' He turned to Corthie. 'As for you, beast, I'm gonnae take my time with you.' He walked towards Corthie. 'I will tear ye to pieces for what ye did. Then, when I spit on yer corpse, maybe everyone ye've wronged will feel some comfort.'

Daimon clenched his fist, and struck Corthie in the face. Unable to move, Corthie absorbed the blow, his eyes watering as his nose streamed blood down his chin. Daimon struck him again, and again, his face twisted with grief as he punched Corthie.

'Stop,' cried Karalyn. 'Daimon, please stop.'

Daimon took a breath, his chest heaving. 'I can't stop. I've never wanted to kill someone as much as I want to end the life of the bastard who took Dillon from me.'

'Do it,' cried Aila. 'Kill him, Daimon.'

Daimon walked out of sight, then returned with the short sword. He held it up, its point pushing against Corthie's neck.

'Yes,' said Aila. 'Cut his throat.'

Corthie gazed down at the tip of the sword. Maybe they were right.

Maybe he was a lost cause; a savage killer whose attempts at trying to live a normal life had failed, because of his inner nature. Hadn't he revelled in battle? Hadn't he enjoyed killing greenhides and soldiers? Didn't he thirst for combat; and long for the feeling of dealing death to those weaker than himself? He had punched Dillon without a thought for the consequences, his temper driving him to violence. It was who he was, and there was no escape.

Daimon's hand began to tremble. 'Why can't I do it? Oh, Dillon; I'm too weak to avenge ye.'

'It's not too late,' said Karalyn. 'Put down the sword, Daimon. Let the law deal with this.'

'The law?' said Daimon. 'The same law that sent soldiers into the Domm Highlands, to burn down villages? That law? No. I've got a better idea. Corthie will do it. I'll keep my hands clean.' He stared into Corthie's eyes. 'Beast, strangle the three people in the chairs, and then I'll give ye the sword to end yer own life.'

Corthie took a step towards Cardova, then halted, his mind attempting to resist the command of the dream mage. Sweat and blood streaked down his face, as Daimon urged him onwards.

Corthie grunted. 'No...' he gasped.

'What's that?' said Daimon. 'Do ye believe ye can resist me, beast? Yer Holdfast blood has made ye strong, but I'm stronger. Kill them!'

Corthie raised his hands, and took another step towards Cardova, who was watching him from behind the gag with wide eyes.

'Break his neck,' cried Daimon, 'then do the same to yer sister. This shall be a terrible day for the Holdfasts. Corthie kills his sister, and then himself. Yer family will wail and mourn this awful tragedy. And then, the bairns will be mine. Two wee dream mages and two wee demigods, under my control. Ye cannot resist, Corthie; do it!'

Corthie's feet took another stride, leaving Cardova's neck just inches from his outstretched fingers. He felt another presence in his mind, as his weakened sister attempted to battle Daimon for possession of his thoughts. Every time Karalyn seemed to be in the ascendancy, Corthie's hands halted, or drew back from Cardova, then Daimon's powers would surge again, and his hands would creep closer to the soldier's throat.

The battle in his mind ceased, and Corthie froze again.

'This is getting tiresome,' said Daimon. He walked up to Karalyn, the sword still in his hand. 'I'll need to weaken ye a wee bit more.'

'Your powers are almost spent,' gasped Karalyn. 'You have tried to do too much, and have spread yourself too thinly. But, there is still good in you, Daimon. Drop your powers, before you exhaust yourself.'

'Ye'd like that, eh?' sneered Daimon. 'The moment I lower my guard, ye'll vanish, saving yerself. No. Ye'll not trick me again.'

He pushed the sword forward, slowly but firmly, and the blade cut into Karalyn's waist. She cried out in pain, her eyes closing.

'That's better,' said Daimon. He turned, and placed the hilt of the sword into Corthie's right hand. 'Forget the soldier,' he said. 'Kill yer sister, while she's weak.'

Corthie felt the surge of power through his mind, and he shook, his resistance faltering without Karalyn's support.

'That's it,' said Daimon. 'Ye can't defy me. Yer sister must die.'

Blistering pain ripped through Corthie's mind, and he slumped to his knees.

'There's only one way to stop the agony, Corthie,' said Daimon. 'Kill yer sister; or the pain will never end.'

The last vestiges of resistance faded from Corthie's mind. He forgot who he was, or where he was. All he knew was that he had a sword in his hand, and that the woman tied to the chair in front of him had to die. Nothing else mattered. He got to his feet.

'Corthie, no,' gasped the woman, but Corthie had forgotten who she was.

'Her death will free ye,' said Daimon. 'Kill her.'

Corthie nodded, and raised the sword.

CHAPTER 28
EXECUTION

Arakhanah City, Republic of Rakana – 20th Day, Second Third Summer 534

'The commanding officer had no idea what to do,' Caelius said. 'We had four dragons attacking our positions from the north, and a horde of armed Dragon Eyre natives assaulting our lines to the south. With a few others, I managed to drag our last working ballista through a hundred yards of thick mud, while flames roared all around us. We pushed it up onto the brow of a low hill, and were preparing to loose, when a dragon swooped down, his claws out. In mere seconds, our ballista had been reduced to a heap of tangled metal and broken wood, and every man who had been operating it, apart from myself, was dead.'

Daphne glanced at him from the darkness of the cell. 'How did you survive?'

'A god appeared,' he said. 'I can't remember her name, but the air crackled, and there she was, standing in the midst of our battered and ragged regiment. She raised her hands, and two dragons screamed, then plummeted to the ground. The natives lost heart, and fled in a panic, dropping their weapons in their haste to flee from the god. The regiment lost over three hundred men that day, but Implacatus trumpeted it as a great victory. That was the last time I was ever on Haurn. I heard that the gods released greenhides on to the island, to extinguish the last flames of resistance.' He snorted. 'Damn greenhides. How I loathe them. The gods view them as just another weapon in their arsenal, but greenhides don't stop until every living thing within their reach is dead – men, women, children, animals. That's not war; it's an abomination.'

They fell into silence. Daphne shifted position on the damp straw, trying to alleviate the pain coming from her feet. Some of her wounds had got infected, and she couldn't bear to look too closely at what remained of her toes. Perhaps the Rakanese were going to leave them to die in the cell; at the rate she and Caelius were weakening, it wouldn't take too much longer. Racked with hunger, thirst and pain, and with their wounds untended, their bodies were beginning to fail.

'Do you have any regrets, Caelius?' she said.

'A few.'

'Tell me.'

'One of my biggest regrets was the way I had parted from Van. That ate into me for years. At least, if I die now, I'll know that he doesn't hate me any more. That's a source of relief, though, not regret. I regret not standing up to the stupid orders handed down by gods and officers, but there's nothing I can do about any of that. My old Banner life is over. If I have any regrets that affect me now, then it's that I won't be able to spend more time with you, ma'am.'

'We've spent five days together in this cell.'

'Yes, but I can see the pain you are in, and it breaks my heart that I can do nothing to help you. You are a fine woman, Daphne Holdfast; a jewel amid the ash. I also regret not telling you how I feel about you.'

'Are you sure that isn't the pain talking?'

'I'm sure, ma'am. I had long resigned myself to being alone. I spent so many years in Serene, after my wife died, and while Van was away, with no one close to me. I grew isolated, and bitter; a friendless, contrary old man, with nothing to offer. There is something about you, Daphne, something that grips my soul. I would say that you are a kindred spirit, but that sounds too bold an assumption. You have captured my heart.'

'I wish things had turned out differently, Caelius. I wish we had gone to Holdings City, instead of Rakana. I wanted to show you round; take you up to the Old City, so you could see the old palace, where Queen Miranda ruled. We could have strolled the streets each evening by the university; it's so beautiful there. It sounds foolish, I know.'

'No, ma'am; it doesn't. It sounds like a dream.'

'Caelius, if we're going to die, then I want to ask if you would do something for me.'

'Anything, ma'am.'

'Kiss me.'

Caelius leaned forward in the gloom, and his lips touched hers.

'Now hold me,' she said.

He gathered her up in his strong arms, and held her close. She shut her eyes as he gently rocked her, and, for a brief moment, she forgot the pain wracking her body.

Boots thumped in the passageway outside, and the door screeched open. A figure was bundled into the cell, then the door was pushed shut. The figure groaned, then looked up.

'Shella?' said Daphne.

'Hi, Daffers,' the Rakanese mage said. 'Fancy meeting you here.'

Shella pushed herself up, and sat back against the door, her hands enclosed in thick metal gauntlets.

'Did they torture you, too?' said Daphne.

'No. Why? I can't see anything in this murk. Are you hurt?'

'Holder Fast received "special treatment" from her interrogators,' said Caelius. 'I was beaten, but her injuries are far more severe. She needs a physician.'

Shella's eyes widened. 'Oh shit; they tortured you, Daffers?'

'They wanted me to answer a long list of questions about the empire,' Daphne said. 'I think they took my refusal personally.'

'You told them nothing, didn't you?' said Shella. 'You stubborn bitch. I might have known. They didn't ask me anything; I've been in solitary confinement for days. The first contact I've had with anyone was ten minutes ago, when they dragged me out of my cell.'

'They're going to execute us, aren't they, ma'am?' said Caelius.

'Yeah. Soon. That's why they moved me. We're going to get our heads chopped off, and then our bodies will be burned; and the ashes strewn into the nearest canal. They seemed a little disappointed. I think they would have liked to have paraded me through the streets, but they're too scared that Bridget will retaliate if she finds out what's been going on. So, they're going to hush our deaths up, and deny everything. Still, I'm hopeful that Karalyn will turn up to save us.'

'Karalyn isn't coming,' said Daphne, 'because Karalyn doesn't think we're in Rakana.'

Shella's demeanour changed, and she gasped. 'What? But...'

'Daimon has been sending messages, purporting to be from me, telling all and sundry that we are making our way to Plateau City. No one is coming, because no one has the faintest idea of our predicament.'

'Daimon, the dream mage? Why would he do that?'

'The boy is clearly deranged,' said Daphne. 'Perhaps the power has gone to his head. Does it matter?'

'The thought that someone was coming was the only thing keeping me going,' said Shella. 'I can't believe that this is the end, and what a bloody miserable way to go. Damn it, there was still so much I wanted to do with my life.'

'Such as?' said Daphne.

'Oh, I don't know. Sit about Colsbury getting drunk, I guess.'

The cell door opened again, and guards piled in. Two reached for Daphne, and Caelius swung his fist, knocking one off his feet.

'Restrain him,' shouted an officer.

Four guards jumped onto Caelius, and pushed him to the floor of the cell. Two more dragged Daphne out into a dim corridor, while others did the same with Shella, who didn't resist. Daphne was pulled to her feet, but she couldn't put any weight onto them, and she fell back to the ground. In the chaos, Caelius was hauled out by his legs, still struggling despite the beating he was receiving.

'Get them to the execution chamber,' yelled the officer. 'Quickly.'

The three prisoners were dragged and shoved down the corridor. They were bundled into another room, and pushed against a wall. In the centre of the floor was a large block of wood, and a man stood next to it, carrying a long axe.

'Let's get this done as quickly as possible,' said the officer. 'The man first, then the Herald, and finally, the former princess.'

Four men dragged Caelius forwards, holding his arms as he writhed and struggled.

'Curse you!' Caelius cried. 'Curse you all! Cowards! You will pay for this!'

The guards tried to push Caelius down to the block, but his rage had given him strength, and another two guards rushed over to assist their comrades. Caelius was forced down, his head shoved flat against the block of wood.

The officer nodded to the axe man. 'Do it.'

Daphne stared in horror, as the man lifted his axe.

The air shimmered, and a woman appeared in the room, armed with a sword. She plunged the blade deep into the throat of the axe man, then ran her thumb over the small copper-coloured device in her left hand. The air shimmered again, and Daphne found herself on roof of the Great Fortress in Plateau City. Shella stood wide-eyed to her left, while Caelius was still kneeling, his eyes clenched shut as he awaited the blow that would end his life.

Daphne sobbed from shock, then stared at the woman who had saved them.

'Sable?'

Sable smiled at her. 'Sister.'

The air crackled, and Sable vanished. Daphne fell to her knees, weeping on the grass of the rooftop garden.

'What... what happened?' said Caelius, his eyes opening.

Shella began to laugh hysterically.

'Where are we?' said Caelius.

He got to his feet when neither of the women responded. He glanced around, as if in a daze.

'Good old Sable,' cackled Shella, tears spilling from her eyes as she laughed. 'Oh, Daffers; you never told me she was back.'

'I didn't know,' said Daphne. 'She saved us. Sable saved us. I... I'm speechless.'

Shella went to slap her on the back, then remembered that she was wearing thick metal gauntlets.

'I'd better not do that,' she said. 'Dear gods, I could do with a smoke. What a beautiful day.'

'What is this place?' said Caelius.

'It's Plateau City,' said Shella, 'and we're on the roof of the imperial palace. Daphne and I have been here before, but that's another story. Wait here, and I'll find some help.'

Shella hurried off to one of the corner stair turrets, then Caelius walked over to Daphne, and helped her sit on the grass. Daphne was too overcome to speak, and felt as though she were dreaming.

Sable. Her demented little sister had saved her life. It seemed too much to take in, and yet it was true.

'I remember you talking about Sable in Rakana,' said Caelius, sitting down next to her on the grass. 'I thought she was on Dragon Eyre, ma'am.'

'So did I, Caelius.'

He looked into her eyes. 'I need you to know, ma'am, that I meant what I said in that cell. It wasn't the fear of death that made me say those things; it was a fear that I was about to lose you forever.'

Daphne nodded, though the pain from her injuries was making it hard to think. A group of soldiers and courtiers burst out of the stair turret. They ran over to Daphne and Caelius, and set down two stretchers next to them.

'Thank you,' said Caelius, 'but I can walk. Give all your attention to Holder Fast.'

Daphne was lifted by four men onto a stretcher, then they carried her towards the stairs. With great care, they lowered her down through the stairwell, then brought her into a small chamber, where the Empress was sitting.

'Your Majesty,' Daphne gasped. 'Hello.'

'Pyre's arse, Daphne,' the Empress said. 'Look at the state of you. Is it true what Shella said; did those Rakanese bastards torture you?'

'I might be missing a toe or two.'

'I've summoned Thorn to the palace, and Keir, too. They'll be here soon.' She glanced at the courtiers. 'Set the Herald of the Empire down next to me.'

Daphne was carried across the room, and her stretcher laid down between two chairs. Bridget frowned at her, and shook her head.

'That's it,' she said. 'I'm going to smash those Rakanese pricks for this. Who do they think they are?'

Shella walked into the room, rubbing her bruised wrists and hands.

'That feels good,' she said. 'I've spent fifteen days unable to scratch my nose.'

'Take a seat,' said the Empress. 'You, too,' she said to Caelius. 'Who is this, Shella?'

'His name is Caelius Logos,' Shella said. 'Karalyn brought him back from Kelsey's world.'

Caelius bowed low before the Empress. 'Your Imperial Majesty, my greetings.'

Bridget chuckled. 'I see that one of you remembers my correct title. Thank you, Caelius.' She sighed. 'Alright; let's hear it. Start at the beginning, and leave nothing out.'

Daphne glanced at Shella, who nodded. The Rakanese woman began telling the Empress about everything that had happened to them. Caelius joined in now and again, while Daphne drifted off on the stretcher, the pain dulling her thoughts. Bridget said nothing throughout the entire tale.

'Well,' said the Empress, when Shella had finished; 'that's quite the story. I'm taking away three things from it. First, you two have lost your powers; second, the Rakanese deserve an arse-kicking; and third, Sable knew where you were.'

'Did you know she was back?' said Shella.

'Aye. Karalyn decided to fetch her from Dragon Eyre, though Sable escaped the moment she arrived. How did she know where to find you?'

Shella shrugged. 'She's a vision mage, isn't she?'

'Aye, but so's Keir, and he didn't find you. How did Sable manage it?'

'I haven't the slightest clue, your Majesty,' said Shella. 'I barely know Sable; I have no idea what her motivations are.'

A courtier opened the door. 'Your Majesty,' she said, bowing; 'Lord Keir and Lady Thorn Holdfast are here.'

'Send them in,' said Bridget.

Daphne opened her eyes a crack, and saw her elder son and his wife walk into the room.

'Before you say anything,' Bridget said, 'I'm well aware that it was only a few days ago that I barred you both from entering the palace. However, I am not a brute. Daphne's health outweighs my feelings about the Holdfasts in general. Do what you can, Thorn.'

Thorn bowed low. 'Thank you, your Majesty.'

She walked up to the stretcher, Keir a pace behind.

'What happened, mother?' said Keir, his eyes wide as he gazed down at the stretcher.

'Give her a moment,' said Thorn. 'Holder Fast is in considerable pain.'

Daphne felt Thorn's hand on her brow, and her pain lessened, then ceased altogether. Daphne gasped in relief.

'I've stabilised her pain, your Majesty,' Thorn said. 'It appears that Holder Fast has been tortured. It might not be possible to heal her completely.'

'I know,' said Bridget. 'That's why I said "do what you can". I'm not expecting miracles.'

Thorn nodded, then Daphne felt a tremendous burst of healing powers ripple through her body. She convulsed on the stretcher, as a dozen different wounds closed up. She felt her broken nose heal, and her fractured ribs. The surge subsided, and Daphne took a long breath.

'Well?' said the Empress.

'I have done what I can,' said Thorn. 'Holder Fast is healed, apart from the two missing toes. I cannot re-grow them, your Majesty.'

Bridget snapped her fingers. 'Get Daphne a glass of wine and a cigarette. I guess today's the day for breaking rules.' She leaned over, took Daphne's hand, and smiled down at her. 'How are you feeling?'

'Like it was all a dream, your Majesty,' she said. 'A particularly bad dream.'

'Did you really tell the interrogators nothing? Don't reply. I know you well enough to guess the answer to that question. The Empire owes you a debt of gratitude for your silence, but you shouldn't have gone to Rakana in the first place.'

Daphne sat up. 'We had to, your Majesty. Cael had a vision of the future.'

Bridget frowned. 'Karalyn didn't mention that.' She glanced at Thorn. 'Could you also heal their friend? Caelius, his name is.'

'Certainly, your Majesty,' said Thorn. She raised a finger in Caelius's direction, and the man's bruises and cuts healed in an instant.

Caelius bowed. 'You have my gratitude, ma'am; although it was Holder Fast that concerned me. My injuries were slight compared to hers. It pleases me immensely to see her well again.'

'You're very welcome,' said Thorn. 'What about Shella? Does she require healing?'

'Nah,' said Shella. 'I'm fine. They didn't touch me.'

A courtier entered with a tray, and Daphne, Caelius and Shella each took a glass of red wine. The courtier then deposited a packet of cigarettes and a box of matches onto a low table.

'Can you walk, Daphne?' said Bridget.

Daphne took a sip of wine, then placed the glass onto the table. 'Let's see.'

She gripped the sides of the stretcher, then swung her legs over and set them onto the floor. She reached down, and removed the filthy, blood-soaked rags that had bound her feet. The swelling and infection had gone. On her left foot, the lower toe was missing, while the middle toe was absent from her right foot.

'There are a few toenails missing,' said Thorn. 'They will grow back in time.'

'Who did this to you, mother?' said Keir.

Daphne ignored her son's question for the moment, and got to her feet. She swayed, as if her balance had been affected, then took a single step forward.

'It's going to take a little practice, I think,' she said.

'That settles it,' said the Empress. 'You will all stay here tonight, so that Daphne can rest.' She pointed at a doorway. 'There's a small apartment through there; make yourselves at home. I have an announcement to make. It was going to wait until Bryce got back, but it will be good if you're all here to hear it. It'll be at sunset, so don't go anywhere.'

The Empress got to her feet. She reached for a walking stick, then used it to support her weight.

'I'll leave you in peace before you start smoking,' she said. 'Ring the bell for food, or anything else you need.' She glanced at the courtiers. 'Everyone out. Leave the Holdfasts and their friends in peace.'

'Your Majesty,' said Daphne, as she sat. 'Thank you.'

Bridget smiled. 'You and I go back a long way, Daphne. We may have had our disagreements, but you will always be my friend.'

The Empress walked from the room, her steps slow, as if each one gave her pain. Once she had left, a courtier closed the door behind her.

Daphne lit a cigarette, then Keir and Shella did the same.

'Right,' said Daphne; 'now that I can think clearly again, I have a few questions. Thorn, Keir - why did the Empress bar you from entering the palace?'

Thorn sat. 'It was because of Sable, ma'am. The Empress was angry that Karalyn brought her back without permission, and even angrier that Sable then made her escape. The Empress has assigned two jobs for Karalyn to complete that would allow us to return to the palace – find Daimon, and find Sable.'

Daphne nodded. 'Why did Karalyn bring Sable back?'

'Because she's a damn idiot,' said Keir.

Daphne gave her son a glance. 'I don't think comments like that add much to the conversation, dear. Karalyn must have had a reason. Let's move on. Is Karalyn currently in Kellach Brigdomin?'

'Yes, ma'am,' said Thorn. 'With Lord Bryce and Lucius Cardova. The Empress stated that she wants Daimon to become her court dream mage. She is considering an amnesty for him.'

'An amnesty?' said Daphne. 'Interesting. Is the Empress aware that young Daimon was responsible for our capture in Rakana?'

'What?' said Shella. 'I didn't know that.'

'He manipulated Thymo,' said Daphne. 'Your nephew was innocent of our betrayal at the border.'

Shella slumped in her seat, her eyes welling. She put a hand to her face.

'The Empress is unaware of that,' said Thorn. 'Might I ask how you managed to escape?'

'It was Sable,' said Daphne. 'My sister rescued us.'

Thorn laughed.

'It's hardly funny,' said Keir.

'I happen to disagree, husband; it's very funny. This confirms what I suspected – Karalyn brought Sable back because she believes that she has changed. Ma'am, can I ask – did Sable gloat over the rescue?'

Daphne shook her head. 'No. Not in the slightest. She had the perfect opportunity to lord it over me, but, instead, she was frightfully efficient and business-like. Maybe I have misjudged her.'

'You can't be serious, mother,' said Keir. 'Sable's a twisted maniac. Have you forgotten about Thorn's mother, or Bracken and Nyane? And what about Lennox?'

'No one felt the pain of what Sable did to Lennox more than Karalyn,' said Daphne, 'and yet she was the one who brought her back from Dragon Eyre.'

'She was in a terrible state, ma'am,' said Thorn. 'She had almost starved to death. She had been imprisoned by dragons, or so Karalyn said.'

'So, Karalyn saved her, and then she saved me, Caelius and Shella?' said Daphne. 'What will be her next move, I wonder?'

'The Empress wants Karalyn to hunt her down,' said Keir.

Daphne frowned. 'I don't think I will allow that to happen.'

'If you don't,' said Keir, 'then the Empress will never let us near the palace again. She's already removed me and Thorn from our positions; and she's on the verge of replacing you as Herald with Bryce. You might be her "friend", as she put it, but she doesn't want the Holdfasts to hold influence any longer; not unless Karalyn obeys her commands.'

'My husband is correct,' said Thorn. 'The schism we discussed has begun.'

'Then we should return to Colsbury as soon as possible,' said Daphne. 'All of us – the Holdfasts, and our allies. If Karalyn returns in the next day or so, then she can take us. If not, we shall travel by carriage.'

Daphne noticed Caelius sitting quietly to one side. His expression was neutral, but his eyes were betraying pain that he had been so quickly pushed to the side while the Holdfasts debated events. She remembered their intimacy in the cell just a few hours before; they had kissed, and he had opened his heart to her.

'You should all know,' she said, 'that Caelius Logos behaved with outstanding bravery before and during our capture. Without him, I'm not sure I would have survived the ordeal. When the time comes for Kelsey to return to her world, I would very much like Caelius to stay here. It's his choice, of course, but that is what I desire.'

Caelius smiled. 'I would be honoured to stay with you, ma'am.'

Daphne smiled back at him.

Shella shook her head. 'Do you all see what I had to endure in Rakana? Those two, gazing into each other's eyes. I was almost relieved when we were captured.'

Keir glanced at Caelius with wary suspicion.

'I'm delighted to make your acquaintance, Caelius,' said Thorn, her smile radiating kindness. 'Thank you for looking after Holder Fast. We owe you our gratitude.'

'You're most welcome, ma'am,' said Caelius, his cheeks reddening a little.

'I have one final question,' said Daphne. 'About this announcement at sunset – do you know what it entails?'

'I have my suspicions, ma'am,' said Thorn.

Daphne nodded. 'Let's hear them.'

'I might be wrong,' Thorn said, 'but I suspect it will touch upon the issue of the imperial succession.'

Daphne suppressed the anger that flared within her heart.

'I see,' she said. 'If that turns out to be the case, then you were right, Thorn. The schism is underway.'

CHAPTER 29
NEXT IN LINE

Plateau City, The Plateau – 20th Day, Second Third Summer 534

'What a day,' said Thorn.

Keir nodded, but said nothing. He lit another cigarette, staring down at the view from a bench in the roof garden. Ahead of them, the sun was lowering in the western sky, and the roofs and towers of Plateau City were bathed in warm red tones.

'The Empress might decide to reprieve Sable,' Thorn went on. 'Her Majesty can't ignore the fact that she saved the life of the Herald of the Empire.'

'I don't think the Empress cares,' muttered Keir. 'Sable was merely paying back the favour. Karalyn rescued her, so Sable probably thought that she had to do the same. It doesn't magically turn Sable into a good person.'

Thorn frowned. 'I know.'

Keir shook his head. 'I still can't believe that you healed that evil witch. Sable abducted your mother and handed her over to the Rahain; and she killed your best friend. Have you forgiven her?'

'No. However, as much as it pains me to say this, Sable is a Holdfast, and right now, the Holdfasts need all the help they can get. Imagine if

Sable decided to join with the rest of the family. Such a reconciliation would alter the balance of power.'

'That's another reason for the Empress to execute her. Bridget can't allow that to happen. Right now, she has us exactly where she wants us. You and I have lost our jobs; Corthie's decided to become a peasant; Kelsey wants nothing more than to bugger off back to her adopted world; and Karalyn keeps disobeying orders. And, to top it all, dear old mama has lost her powers. She's just another useless old woman.'

Thorn glared at him. 'Do you say these things in an attempt to provoke me, husband? Or, are you actually that stupid?'

'Piss off,' he mumbled.

'No, I don't think I will, Keir. I'm going nowhere. Your mother needs our unqualified loyalty and support, and I intend to give her that. Do you?'

He shrugged.

'Let me ask you again – are you loyal to the Holdfasts?'

Keir's temper surged. 'I'm the only bloody Holdfast sitting here right now! You're nothing – just a wife. You're not a damn Holdfast – you're an opportunist from the remote reaches of Sanang who got lucky.'

Thorn smiled. 'You are amusing when you're angry, dear husband. Remember, one word from me to your mother regarding a certain Miss Holdwain, and we'll see who the real Holdfast is. Do you want me to tell her what you've been up to?'

Keir felt his spirits deflate.

'Well, husband?'

'No,' he muttered.

'Good. I will keep silent about your sordid little activities, and you will remain loyal. It's quite simple. One day, Keir, you will be consort to the Empress, and then I will allow you to have as many discreet affairs as you like. Once I hold supreme power, you can screw all the servants you desire.'

'What about you? Will you have affairs?'

'I very much doubt it, Keir. I'll be too busy ruling the world.'

'Tilda means nothing to me.'

'I know. If I thought you were falling in love with her, then I might be concerned. I'm more worried that the silly girl will fall in love with you. The Holdwains could make things difficult for us in the Holdings, especially with the election for First Holder due next year. If they were angry with us, then they could use their influence to try to block the Holdfasts' candidate.'

Keir frowned. 'But mother has to step down. What Holdfast candidate?'

'You really are a simpleton at times, Keir. Holder Fast has nominated Weir of the River Holdings to replace her in office. A more doughty, loyal servant of the Holdfasts would be difficult to find. With Weir as First Holder, our control over the Holdings would be assured.'

Keir shook his head. 'You really are a conniving witch.'

'If that is true, then so is your mother. Do you think I have planned this in isolation? Holder Fast has been grooming me for power for many years. That is why I am more valuable to her than you, dearest husband. The only thing you bring to the table is your marriage to me. Does that make you the lucky opportunist?'

'If I am a fool, then it's because I was stupid enough to believe that you loved me.'

'I did love you, once.'

He glanced at her. 'When did you stop?'

'Let me see,' she said, narrowing her eyes. 'Yes, I think it was around the time when I had to care for Karalyn's two children, and you refused to help. For four long years, the twins were in and out of my head, manipulating my emotions. What they felt, I felt. It was hard, I won't lie to you; very hard. I almost gave up, more than once. I loved the twins, loved them deeply, and I still do; but they drove me to despair. I have never felt such highs and lows. When they called me "mother", my heart would break with joy, and then, if I was firm with them, they would make me feel like ending it. I wept most nights, but you didn't seem to notice or care. You didn't lift a finger to help me, even when I was desperate. I think it was around then, Keir.'

'But,' he said, 'I was trying to get involved with Cole back then. I was trying to be a part of his life.'

Thorn laughed. 'Tell yourself that if it makes you feel better. I needed you, and you weren't there.'

'If Jemma had been less of a bitch, then it might have worked out.'

'Don't blame Jemma for this. I have more respect for her than I do for you, despite our many differences. Jemma wants the best for her son, and I can understand that. What I will never understand is the ease with which you shrugged off your responsibilities for Karalyn's children. Why was I left alone to deal with it all? Not once did you get up in the middle of the night when they were crying; not once did you feed them, or change their nappies, or bathe them, or soothe them to sleep.' Thorn paused, and took a breath. 'I shouldn't let myself get angry. I did what I did because it was the right thing to do. You did what you did because... well, only you can answer that. I should have married Corthie; now, there's a real man. I look at the way he treats Aila, and the way he dotes on little Killop, and I feel envious. And then I look at you...'

Keir sat in silence, dumbfounded by his wife's outburst. He longed to escape into the arms of Tilda, someone who didn't judge him; someone who didn't loathe him.

'It's almost sunset,' said Thorn, as if nothing had happened. 'We should go downstairs.'

She stood, and smoothed down her azure dress. Keir got up from the bench, and they walked to the nearest stair turret, then descended the steps into the upper floors of the palace. They went into the apartment that Bridget had set aside for them, and Daphne glanced up from where she was sitting with Shella and Caelius.

'Is it time?' said Daphne.

'The sun will be setting in a few minutes, ma'am,' said Thorn.

Daphne nodded, then reached over for a set of crutches.

'Do you require assistance, ma'am?' said Thorn.

'I've already tried to persuade her to accept my help,' said Caelius, 'but Holder Fast is a stubborn woman. She insists that she can manage on her own.'

'I am not an invalid,' said Daphne, using the crutches to get to her feet. She slipped them under her shoulders. 'I mean to enter the grand reception hall without being carried.' She glanced at the others in the room. 'Remember, if this announcement is what we think it is, then I want no reaction from any of you. Remain calm and dignified. Our response will need to be measured and proportionate. Once the announcement is over, we shall make arrangements for the withdrawal of the Holdfasts to Colsbury. Understood?'

'Yes, ma'am,' said Thorn.

Keir frowned. He didn't want to admit it in front of his wife and mother, but he had no idea what they were talking about. He remembered Thorn saying that she suspected the announcement had something to do with the succession to the throne, but what did that have to do with the Holdfasts? Thorn's ambitions were barely credible; she was deluding herself to think that she would ever become Empress – was he the only one who realised that?

'I shall go first,' said Daphne. 'Caelius, I would be honoured if you were to walk by my side. Then Shella, and then Keir and Thorn.'

Shella chuckled. 'Is this necessary? Who cares what order we walk in?'

'I do, Shella,' said Daphne. 'When we enter the hall, every eye will be upon us. Plateau City is full of supporters of the Empress, and many of them have a low opinion of my family. It's vital that we present a united front.'

Caelius stood, and opened the door, then they filed out into the corridor. Daphne swung her crutches as though she had been using them all her life, and they made their way to the palace's largest reception hall. The sound of a crowd chattering reached their ears before they saw it, then courtiers opened the high, double doors for the Holdfasts, and they entered. The hall was packed with people, with several hundred sitting on rows of chairs, while others stood at the back. At the other end of the hall, upon a raised platform, sat an empty throne. Four of the Empress's children were standing there, with Brogan and Bethal on the throne's left, and Berra and Bedig on the throne's right. The crowd murmured as they watched Daphne approach the front row of seats, where places had been reserved for her and her family and friends. Daphne nodded to the crowd, then sat. Caelius took his place to her left, then Shella, while Keir and Thorn sat by Daphne's right.

A courtier stood before the crowd. 'Please be upstanding for her Imperial Majesty, Empress Bridget ae Brenna, Holder of the World.'

The crowd stood. A side door opened, and Bridget strode through, using her stick to help her along. The crowd broke into spontaneous applause, and Bridget smiled as she made her way to the platform. Brogan stepped forward, and took her mother's hand, helping her sit upon the throne.

'Sit, sit,' said Bridget, waving her hand at the crowd.

The hundreds gathered in the hall retook their seats, and the place fell into silence.

'We have asked you to come here this day,' Bridget went on, 'so that you can learn about a few decisions that have been taken to secure the future of the empire. We were originally going to convene this gathering once Lord Bryce had returned, but as we are currently honoured by a rare appearance of the Herald of the Empire, we decided not to wait.'

Keir saw Daphne and Thorn exchange the briefest of glances.

'First,' said Bridget, 'as I am sure you all know, the father of my children has recently come forward, after spending many years in blissful anonymity. Brannig, please stand.'

The crowd hushed as Brannig got to his feet. He had also been assigned a chair in the front row, a few yards to Daphne's right.

'We have decided,' said the Empress, 'to welcome you into the imperial household. From this moment, you, Brannig of Brig, are a full member of my family.'

The crowd broke out into applause again, and a few cheered.

'However,' said Bridget, 'let me make one thing clear. Brannig will possess no authority over the empire. His position will remain as imperial father, but I shall not devolve any sovereign power into his hands. He shall live in this palace, so that he can become a part of the family, able to guide and support his children to the best of his abilities. What say you to this, Brannig?'

Brannig bowed his head, as tears fell down his cheeks. 'Thank you, your Majesty. You have granted more than I ever dreamed.'

Bridget smiled. 'Come up here and stand by your children.'

Brannig strode forward, to tumultuous applause from the crowd. He ascended the platform, where Brogan, Berra and Bedig embraced him in turn. Only Bethal seemed a little distant, though she shook her father's hand.

'With that out of the way,' the Empress said, 'I want to move on to a matter of vital importance for the empire. For twenty-seven years, I have sat upon this throne, and, while I hope to be sitting here for a few years yet, I have decided that the empire would benefit from some clarity about what comes next. Prior to my reign, Emperor Guilliam ruled these lands. He died without heirs.' The hall fell back into complete silence. 'I have heirs,' Bridget said. 'In Lord Bryce, my eldest child, I also have an intelligent, brave, honourable young man. I am fortunate, and the empire, too, is fortunate.' She gazed out at the crowd. 'Therefore, I hereby proclaim that Lord Bryce is my appointed successor to the imperial throne. When it is time for me to depart this world, Lord Bryce shall be Emperor!'

The crowd erupted in a roar as hundreds leapt to their feet. Bridget smiled and sat back, allowing their jubilant emotions free rein. In the front row, Daphne sat expressionless, and Thorn mirrored her features. Caelius glanced around, as if unsure how to react, then took his cue from Daphne. Shella applauded politely, then sat on her hands. Bridget gazed down at Daphne, and their glances met.

Bridget broke off the glance, then raised a hand in the air. The crowd settled down, listening intently.

'Once Lord Bryce has returned from Kellach Brigdomin,' she said, 'there shall be an official ceremony, formally appointing him as successor. Until then, feel free to spread the good news.' She nodded. 'Dismissed.'

Courtiers opened the doors at the rear of the hall, and the crowd began to stream out, many with broad smiles on their faces. Daphne remained motionless. Keir started to get to his feet, but Thorn gave a subtle shake of her head, and he retook his seat. Within a few moments, the hall had emptied, except for Bridget and her family upon the platform, and Daphne, Thorn, Shella, Caelius and Keir in the front row of seats.

Bridget laughed. 'Something tells me that the Herald of the Empire does not approve of my decision.'

'That's something of an understatement, your Majesty,' said Daphne. 'It's not every day that one hears the Empress betray the entire foundation of her rule.'

'Is that so, Daphne?'

'Yes, Bridget, it is so.'

'Scurry back to your apartment, Holdfasts,' the Empress said, 'before I have the guards eject you from this hall.'

Daphne gripped her crutches, and pulled herself to her feet. 'This is the most grievous mistake you have ever made, Bridget.'

Bridget laughed, but it sounded forced. 'Really? Is your opinion of Bryce so low?'

'Not at all. I happen to regard Lord Bryce as a young man with exceptional promise. Tell me, though, what will happen to the Empire if his offspring turns out to be cruel and devious, or corrupt and self-serving? By that point, it will be too late; the hereditary principle you espoused today will be set in stone. Have you forgotten how you became Empress, Bridget? This Empire chooses its sovereign; it does not have one imposed upon it.'

'And who would you choose, Daphne? Thorn?'

'That is irrelevant. The next Emperor or Empress must be selected in the same manner as you were, with a conference of the world's high mages, and a transparent vote. If Lord Bryce were nominated and his candidature successful, then I would be the first to pledge allegiance to him as Emperor. What I will not stand for, however, is having your son thrust upon us.'

Bridget sighed, and leaned forward on her throne. 'Tell me, Daphne; what are you going to do about it?'

'You shall see. I hereby resign as your Herald, effective immediately. I shall not serve a ruler who flouts the most basic law of the Empire. The succession is not yours to choose, Bridget; this day, you have usurped power from the people you purport to rule. What you have done is a crime against the Empire. It will not stand, and, deep down, you know this.'

'You're living in a dream world, Daphne,' said Bridget. 'Power is power. I thought you would understand that.'

Daphne smiled. 'I understand that you have given way to your basest instincts. You are a traitor to the Empire, and I shall resist you with all the strength I can muster.'

'Oh, fuck off, Daphne. Get out, and take your little minions with you. I want you all gone from the palace by dawn tomorrow. If you repeat to others what you have said to me, I shall have the entire Holdfast clan arrested and charged with treason. You have been nothing but a pain in the arse for many years; that ends today.'

Daphne glanced at Thorn, and they made their way from the hall. Caelius leapt up to follow them, then Shella shrugged at Bridget, muttered something under her breath, and went after Daphne. Keir lingered, uncertain about what to do. He glanced at Daphne, then at Bridget, torn.

'Got something to say, Keir?' said the Empress. 'Pick your side, boy.'

Keir looked at the faces of Bridget's children. Bethal looked a little smug, while Brogan wouldn't meet his glance.

'Well?' said Bridget. 'Are you a Holdfast, or are you not?'

'I didn't want this,' Keir said, his voice a whisper. 'This is not right.'

'Tell that to your fucking mother. Now, piss off.'

Keir trudged from the hall, despair clinging to him like a bad odour. He made his way to the small apartment, and entered. Daphne, Shella and Thorn were huddled together, speaking in low tones, and none of them registered his arrival. Caelius glanced at him, and walked over.

'I'm not going to pretend that I understood all of that,' the old soldier said. 'Perhaps, if you have time, Lord Keir, you might explain to me the complexities of the imperial constitution.'

'Read a damn book,' Keir muttered.

He walked to a cabinet, took out a bottle of brandy, and poured himself a large measure. He glanced at the scheming women whispering together. His mother, his mother's best friend, and his wife, all plotting and conspiring, as if the Empire were theirs to play with. His temper exploded, and he hurled the full glass against a wall, shattering it and streaking brandy across the floor.

The women turned to him, and Daphne raised an eyebrow.

'What have you done?' he shouted, his rage boiling over. 'Are you insane? Bridget will hang us all for this treachery!'

Daphne kept her face calm. 'One must do the right thing, son, even if it leads to unpalatable consequences.'

'The right thing?' Keir screamed. 'Are you utterly deluded? Bridget is the Empress; whatever she says is the law, whether you like it or not!'

Daphne glanced at Thorn. 'My apologies. It seems that you accurately predicted my son's reaction; whereas I held out hope that he would take it in his stride. I was wrong.'

'Perhaps I should walk him to the roof, ma'am?' said Thorn. 'He needs a moment to calm down.'

'You deranged little witches,' Keir yelled. 'If the Empire collapses or descends into war, it will be your fault! Yours!'

Keir ran for the door, went through, and slammed it behind him. He had to go back to the Empress, to tell her that he wanted no part in his mother's rebellion. He was a vision mage, and a fire mage; maybe she would forgive him. He could be useful to her. Damn his stupid wife, and his delusional mother; damn them both. Keir picked up his pace, and raced back to the grand hall. He barged through the doors, then swore. It was empty. A large Kellach guard was stationed by a side door, and he hurried over.

'Is the Empress in her quarters?' he asked the soldier.

'She is, my lord.'

'Then, let me past. I need to speak to her.'

'I'm afraid not, my lord. The Empress has forbidden any Holdfast to enter her private rooms.'

'But I'm on her side! I don't agree with anything my mother said in here; not one damn word.'

'Orders are orders, sir.'

'You don't understand; it's vital that I speak to her.'

The soldier ignored him.

'Damn you!' Keir cried. He turned away, then a desperate notion entered his mind. He turned back to the soldier.

Sleep.

The armoured soldier's eyes closed, and he toppled to the ground with a crash. Keir glanced around, but there was no one else in sight. He dragged the soldier out of the way, then eased the door open. Beyond, the floors were carpeted, and he could hear Brogan's voice coming from another room. Keir stole into the Empress's quarters, then listened to Brogan by a side door. She was voicing her misgivings to her siblings about what had happened, urging them that a compromise with the Holdfasts could be found. Bethal answered in angry tones. In her view, the Holdfasts had condemned themselves as traitors, and she wanted them all to be arrested before they could leave the palace. Keir shook his head in despair as he listened, then he crept onwards, heading for the Empress's private study.

The door to the study was open a few inches, and Keir peered through the gap, trying to prepare himself for what he was going to say. He would plead with the Empress to allow him to stay; he would swear renewed allegiance to her, and denounce his own mother before her. He swallowed. Could he do it? His mother would never forgive him. He would be cast out from the family; but so what? None of the other Holdfasts liked him, not even Kelsey, who had once been his closest friend. Even his wife loathed him; she had made that plain on the roof.

He steeled himself, and gazed through the gap in the door. Bridget was sitting in her favourite armchair, a glass of whisky in her right hand. She looked sombre, as if she had relished nothing of what had taken place in the hall. She had probably expected Daphne to behave in the way she had, but it was clear that the confrontation had wounded her deeply. Keir took a breath, then he noticed that Brannig was also in the room. He was lingering behind where the Empress sat, and he was holding something in his hand.

'Get a drink and sit yourself down, Brannig,' the Empress said. 'We need to talk.'

'In a moment, your Majesty,' Brannig said.

Keir frowned. What was the man doing? Brannig crept up to the rear of the armchair, and lifted his right hand. Keir gasped. Brannig was wielding a long knife, and was raising it, ready to plunge the blade down into Bridget. Keir glanced at Brannig's eyes. They seemed clouded over, as if he were in a trance.

Keir burst into the room, his one thought to save the Empress. He charged into Brannig, knocking him over, and they fell to the floor of the study. Brannig lashed out, and struck Keir's chin with his left fist. Keir recoiled from the blow, then gripped Brannig's right hand. The knife twisted, then Brannig rolled over, and Keir pushed up with all his strength. The blade rammed into Brannig's chest, up to the hilt. Brannig howled in agony, then he went limp, falling on top of Keir.

Bridget screamed, and, within seconds, soldiers were piling into the room. Two of them hauled Brannig from Keir, then Bridget stared at the knife in Keir's hands.

'You Holdfast bastard!' the Empress cried.

'No,' gasped Keir. 'He was trying to kill you.'

'You fucking liar!' Bridget screamed. 'Arrest him! Arrest them all!'

Bridget's four children ran into the room. Berra screamed at the sight of her dead father, lying bloody on the floor, then she ran to him, crouching and weeping over his body. Two soldiers dragged Keir away, pulling his hands behind his back, as Bridget joined Berra on the floor by Brannig's corpse.

'Did you hear me?' Bridget cried to the soldiers. 'I want every Hold-fast, and their friends, in chains. Get this bastard out of my sight!'

Keir stared, as the four children embraced their grieving mother over the body of Brannig. Amid tears and howls of grief, soldiers bundled Keir out of the room.

'You treacherous little shit,' one of the soldiers shouted in Keir's face. 'You'll swing for this; you and your traitor family.'

'This is a mistake!' Keir cried. 'Brannig was trying to kill the Empress.'

'Gag him,' said an officer, 'and throw him in the cells. Then gather the squads. We're going to raid the Holdfast apartment. If they resist, you have my permission to beat the living crap out of them. Go.'

A thick strip of cloth was pulled over Keir's mouth, then a soldier punched him in the face. Keir's head jerked back, he saw stars, then he slipped into oblivion.

CHAPTER 30
DISSOLUTION

Threeways, Domm Pass – 20th Day, Second Third Summer 534

Corthie raised the sword above her.

No, brother. This is not you; you are a good man. Fight this.

Corthie's eyes looked down at Karalyn, but they were blank. Weakened by the wounds in her thigh and waist, Karalyn directed all of her remaining powers at her brother.

Drop the sword.

Her brother's hand began to shake. Daimon's powers surrounded him like a dense fog, but even so, some small part of Corthie's mind was still resisting. He was stronger than Karalyn had guessed; stronger than anyone had guessed.

Daimon is wrong about you. You have darkness within you, but there is also light, and love. You love Aila, and your family... and you love Belinda, too. Belinda is alive, brother; Sable told me. Do you remember the Holdfast townhouse, when we cared for her? You told her stories, and you got her those cats that I didn't like. Belinda loved them; she loved you, too, like a brother. Remember who you were before Gadena took you. Remember the little boy who always smiled, who was always kind. That little boy was you, Corthie.

'You are mine to command,' yelled Daimon. 'Yer nothing but a savage beast.'

Corthie's face twisted in anguish. He cried out in pain and torment, and the fingers of his right hand began to loosen their grip on the hilt of the sword. He dropped the weapon, then clutched the sides of his head, his hands over his eyes, as blood trickled from his nose. He made a choking, gargling sound, then crashed to the floor of the shabby room and lay still.

Daimon stared down at him, his eyes wide.

'Stop,' Karalyn said to him. 'Stop, before it's too late. I am not your enemy.'

Daimon began to weep. 'He killed my brother.'

'I know, Daimon, but he didn't mean it. What happened to your mother was wrong, but this won't bring her back.'

'I want justice!' he cried.

'This is not justice, Daimon; this is revenge. What would your mother want? What would Dillon want? We are dream mages, you and I; let me help you.'

'We are not the same,' Daimon said. 'Ye don't know how I suffered as a child with this... this curse. These powers are nothing but a curse; I hate them!'

'I suffered, too, Daimon. I almost killed my other brother when he was a baby. My parents sent me to live in the desert so I couldn't hurt anyone. I was alone; so alone. I know how it feels to be feared and mistrusted. I understand you, Daimon; I might be the only person in the world who knows how you are feeling. Let me help.'

Daimon slumped to the floor, sobbing. 'Dillon, I'm sorry. I can't do it without you.'

Next to Karalyn, Cardova moved his arms. The tall soldier had managed to untie the cords that had bound his wrists, and he pulled them free of the chair. He glanced at Karalyn, then slowly got to his feet, as Daimon wept on the floor.

'Daimon!' cried Aila. 'The soldier is standing up!'

Cardova raised his hands in the air. 'I'm not going to hurt anyone. I'm just going to help Karalyn; she's losing blood. She'll die if she doesn't get help.'

Daimon glanced up, his eyes red with tears.

Cardova stepped behind the chair where Karalyn was bound, and reached down. His fingers loosened the knots of the cords, and Karalyn's hands slipped free.

Aila backed away, clutching her two children to her chest. 'Stop them, Daimon!'

'No,' he said. 'It's over.'

Daimon raised a hand, and Aila convulsed, her eyes closing. She fell back onto the floorboards, then her eyes opened again, and she looked around, as if in a daze. Her glance fell on Corthie, and her face paled. With her newborn pressed against her, she crawled over the floorboards to where Corthie was lying, and took his hand.

'What happened?' she said. 'Corthie, can you hear me?'

Cardova eased Karalyn from the chair, and set her down on the floor. His hands went to the wound on her thigh. He pressed down on it, then he took the cords that had bound her wrists, and tied them round her leg, staunching the bloodflow.

Someone knocked on the door of the small apartment.

'Lucius? Are you in there?'

Anger returned to Daimon's face.

'Who's that?' he cried. 'Have ye betrayed me?'

'It's Bryce,' Karalyn gasped. 'The Empress's son.'

The door opened. Karalyn expected a dozen soldiers to charge in, but Bryce was alone and unarmed. He walked into the room, his eyes taking in the scene.

'Is everyone alive?' he said.

'No!' Daimon cried. 'Corthie killed my brother.'

Bryce nodded, his palms open. 'Let's all remain calm. My name is Bryce. My mother, the Empress of the world, sent me here, not to arrest you, Daimon, but to help you. Read my mind; you will see the truth of what I say.'

Karalyn drew on her weakened powers, ready to defend Bryce from attack, but Daimon did nothing more than scan the mind of the Empress's eldest child.

'I don't understand,' said Daimon. 'I've done bad things; I don't deserve an amnesty.'

'Have you killed anyone?' said Bryce.

'He murdered five councillors!' cried the man tied to the third chair.

'Is that true?' said Bryce.

'Aye,' said Daimon.

'No,' said Karalyn. 'They killed themselves, through the guilt at what they had done.'

'Why are ye defending me?' said Daimon.

'Because you are lost, like I once was,' said Karalyn. 'Bryce, Corthie did kill Dillon, but it was an accident.'

Bryce's eyes narrowed. 'Who wounded you?'

'I did,' said Daimon, weeping. 'I wanted to kill them all. I was so angry when Dillon died. What will I do without him? He was the only one who loved me.'

Bryce crouched by Aila. 'Are you alright? When did you give birth?'

'I don't remember,' Aila sobbed. 'I can't remember anything.'

'And Corthie?'

'He's unconscious,' said Aila. 'I don't know what happened to him.'

Bryce nodded, then he glanced at Karalyn. 'This is too much for me to decide on my own. Karalyn, is there still time to save Daimon? Help me decide what to do.'

Karalyn turned her eyes to the weeping dream mage. He looked like a little boy, his earlier rage gone. Despite all that he had done, she felt pity stir her. He was only sixteen. At that age, she had been out of control, a danger to everyone she came across. If her mother and brother had been killed while she had been that age, would she have acted in the same way?

She glanced at Bryce. 'He deserves a second chance. He was blinded by grief.'

Bryce said nothing for a while, then he nodded.

'Release the councillor, Lucius. There is no need for any more suffering this day. Karalyn, can you take us to Plateau City?'

'Aye,' she gasped. 'As long as Daimon doesn't try to block me.'

Bryce stepped forward, and helped Cardova free the councillor from the chair.

'This is an outrage,' the councillor spat. 'This boy is nothing but a murderous menace. He needs to answer for what he has done.'

Daimon lowered his head in shame.

'I'm taking him to the Empress,' Bryce said. 'She will be the judge of what happens next.'

The councillor's face rippled with anger. 'But...'

'I know why Daimon chose you,' said Bryce. 'I know about the villages that were destroyed in the Domm Highlands, and your part in that. Be grateful that I am allowing you to walk out of here with your life, honoured Councillor.' He nodded to Karalyn. 'Now, please. The Great Fortress.'

Karalyn closed her eyes, and focussed her dwindling powers.

The Great Fortress, Plateau City. Go.

The air shimmered, then everyone who had been in the room, with the exception of the councillor, appeared in an empty chamber of the palace in Plateau City. The first thing Karalyn noticed, as she lay bleeding on the carpeted floor, were roars of anger and the thump of soldiers' boots.

Bryce frowned. 'Something's happening. Daimon, come with me. Everyone else, stay here. I will fetch assistance.'

Daimon stared into space. Bryce strode over, and extended a hand towards him. Daimon seemed bewildered, then he took Bryce's hand and got to his feet. He glanced down at Karalyn, then followed Bryce from the chamber.

'Hold on, Karalyn,' said Cardova; 'you're going to be alright.'

'What's wrong with Corthie?' sobbed Aila, as her children cried. 'Why won't he wake up?'

The door of the chamber opened, and Brogan ran in. She stared down at the bodies of Karalyn and Corthie, and then at Aila and the children.

'Karalyn and Corthie need help,' said Cardova. 'Is Thorn here?'

'Thorn's under arrest,' said Brogan, 'along with the rest of the Holdfasts. Get out of here, Karalyn; quickly. Keir murdered Brannig, and I've never seen my mother so angry; I don't know what she'll do. Go, and take Corthie with you!'

'I need to find my mother,' gasped Karalyn.

'Daphne is in the cell next to Thorn's; and Shella is in the next one along. Only Caelius is still on the loose in the palace. If mother finds you here...'

Karalyn's resolve snapped.

Colsbury Castle. Go.

The air crackled again, and they appeared in the Sextant chamber inside the Great Keep of Colsbury.

'Get Agang,' Karalyn gasped, her powers falling away.

Cardova bolted from the room, and Karalyn closed her eyes. She had lost too much blood, and could feel her life drain away. Had it all been for nothing? Had she endured so much, only to return to find her family had been imprisoned? Maybe it was time to give up. For too long, she had felt the weight of the world on her shoulders. If she gave up, she could drift away like a leaf on the autumn breeze, and her pain would be over.

An image of Kyra and Cael playing on the same rug where she lay entered her mind. She couldn't give up. Her children needed her. She tried to resist, but the pain was too much.

A hand touched her forehead, and she screamed as a massive jolt of healing powers entered her body. She rolled onto her knees, and vomited blood onto the rug, splashing the side of the Sextant. She panted, her pain gone.

She looked up, and saw Agang's kindly features gazing at her.

'Thank the gods,' muttered Cardova. 'I owe you a drink, Agang.'

Agang smiled. 'I'd better heal Corthie before I drink anything.'

'You can't help Corthie,' said Karalyn, wiping the blood from her chin. 'Only I can do that.'

She turned, and stared down at the body of her unconscious brother.

'What's wrong with him?' said Aila. 'Why will no one tell me what's happening?'

'You were under Daimon's control,' said Karalyn. 'He didn't hurt you, or the children, but he was manipulating your mind.'

'I can't even remember giving birth,' Aila sobbed.

Karalyn closed her eyes, and sent her powers into Corthie's battered mind.

Be at peace, brother. You are safe; Aila and the children are safe.

She repaired the damage caused by the trauma of resisting Daimon. Unlike Aila, Corthie would remember everything when he awoke, and she soothed his bruised consciousness.

Come back to us, my beloved brother.

Corthie opened his eyes. He gazed at Karalyn, then saw Aila, little Killop, and the newborn baby in her arms. He burst into tears, and embraced his wife.

'I'm so sorry,' he sobbed, as Aila gripped onto him, her head buried in his chest.

'Don't be sorry,' said Karalyn. 'Your strength saved us all.'

'I almost killed you,' he wept.

'I know, but you didn't. You resisted, right to the end. You proved Daimon wrong, Corthie; you are not a monster.'

Corthie shook his head. 'I am.'

'No,' said Aila; 'don't say that.'

'Let me see our new child,' he said.

Aila held out the bundle of blankets that wrapped the baby.

'I don't even know if it's a boy or a girl,' he said, taking the baby in his arms.

'It's a girl, Corthie,' said Aila. 'We have a daughter.'

Corthie held the child close, and dissolved into tears.

'Let's give them some peace,' said Karalyn, glancing at Agang and Cardova.

'I'll prepare a bath for Aila and the baby, and some food and drink for you all,' said Agang. 'There are spare baby clothes somewhere; I'll dig them out.'

'Thank you, Agang,' said Karalyn.

Karalyn, Cardova and Agang left the room, and the Sanang man hurried off.

'How are you feeling, ma'am?' said Cardova.

'Physically, or mentally?' said Karalyn.

'Both.'

'Did you hear what Brogan said?'

'I did.'

'Then you know what I have to do now.'

'I do.'

'Are you not going to try to stop me?'

'Tell me what it means, ma'am. Why would Keir kill Brannig?'

'I don't know, Lucius, but they're my family. My mother always spoke of a day when the Empress and the Holdfasts would become divided. I think that day is today. If I rescue them, then the Holdfasts will be in open rebellion against the Empire. I can't ask you to come with me. This is not your fight.'

'Bollocks to that, Karalyn. You're taking me with you, and that's that. You're powerful, but Daimon proved that you're not invincible. All it would take is one crossbow bolt in the back of your skull and it's over. I'll watch your back. Let me do my job, ma'am.'

They locked glances for a moment, then Karalyn looked away, unable to bear the intensity with which Cardova was gazing at her.

'Don't die for me, Lucius.'

'I'm a soldier, ma'am. I'd be pretty useless if I shirked my duty when things got rough.'

'You don't owe me any duty.'

He smiled. 'Allow me to disagree. Let's go, before the Empress decides she's in the mood for some executions.'

'We'll talk to her first, and try to reason things out.'

Cardova nodded.

She looked back into his eyes. 'You're a good man, Lucius.'

'I think my ex-wife would have something to say about that, ma'am.'

Karalyn exhaled.

The Great Fortress, Plateau City. Go.

Their surroundings shimmered, and they appeared in the same chamber within the Great Fortress that they had left from. Cardova raised a hand, then strode to the door and peered out.

'It's quietened down, ma'am,' he said. 'Maybe old Caelius has finally been run to ground.'

Karalyn joined him by the doorway, and they walked out into a wide hallway. Two soldiers standing outside a set of doors spotted them.

'Halt!' one cried.

Karalyn raised her arms. 'We're here to speak to the Empress. I've done what she asked. I brought Lord Bryce and Daimon here. Please tell her I need to talk to her.'

The two soldiers trained their crossbows on them, then one banged on the door behind him.

'Karalyn Holdfast is here!' he yelled.

More soldiers emerged from the entrance, along with Bryce.

'Don't shoot,' Bryce said. 'My mother wants to speak to Karalyn. Let her through.'

Cardova and Karalyn kept their arms aloft as they were escorted through the double doors and into a meeting chamber. Bridget was sitting at the end of a table, her head in her hands as she wept. Sitting next to her were her other children. Berra and Bedig were also crying, while Bethal looked in shock. Brogan stood, her eyes narrowing, as Bryce led Karalyn and Cardova forwards.

'Mother,' said Bryce. 'Karalyn is here.'

Bridget raised her head. 'Another damn Holdfast? That's all I need.'

'Karalyn had nothing to do with what happened here, mother,' said Bryce. 'She acted with honour and compassion in Kellach Brigdomin. Without her, Daimon would never have willingly handed himself into our custody.'

'Don't defend her, son,' said Bridget. 'The Holdfasts murdered Brannig, and she is one of them.'

'Why would Keir do that?' said Karalyn.

'You tell me,' snapped Bridget. 'It was surely no coincidence that your mother openly rebelled against my rule not ten minutes before Keir plunged a knife into Brannig's heart.'

Karalyn frowned. 'My mother did what?'

'You heard me. She called me a traitor to the Empire, to my face. Keir was probably trying to impress her. I think maybe that I was the target, and that Brannig got in the way.'

'I thought my mother was in Rakana. Why did she call you a traitor?'

Bridget wiped the tears from her cheek. 'Because I announced that Bryce would be my successor.'

'Oh.'

'Is that all you have to say, Karalyn?'

'My mother has... strong feelings about the imperial succession.'

Bridget snorted. 'So it seems. Do you share those feelings?'

'Is it true that you have jailed my mother? Keir, I can understand, but Shella? And Thorn?'

'And Caelius, too,' said Bridget. 'They were all conspiring against me. Answer my question, Karalyn – do you think I am a traitor?'

'No, your Majesty.'

'Then, you agree that I am perfectly within my rights to appoint my own successor to the throne?'

'No, your Majesty. I think Bryce would make a good Emperor, but I also believe that the decision does not belong to you. The next Emperor or Empress should be chosen in the same way that you were chosen. Did we not agree this in Colsbury, seven and a half years ago? When you abdicated, we voted you back into power.'

Bridget laughed, but it was a bitter sound. 'In other words, you think that the Holdfasts should decide.'

'Not necessarily, your Majesty. The high mages of this world should decide.'

'Aye, and how many of them are Holdfasts, or friends of the Holdfasts? You're just as bad as your mother.'

'Will you please release her from prison? And Shella, Thorn, and Caelius. They have broken no laws, as far as I can see.'

Anger rippled across the Empress's features.

'Do you want the Empire to fracture?' said Karalyn. 'Let me take them back to Colsbury. If you keep them here, locked up for something Keir did, then the Holdings and Sanang will feel betrayed. If they leave the Empire, what will remain?'

'I will not be blackmailed, Karalyn.'

'Listen to her, mother,' said Brogan. 'Daphne is adored throughout the Holdings, and Thorn is the pride of Sanang. Should they be held accountable for Keir's actions?'

'Shut up,' said Bethal. 'We can't trust any of the Holdfasts.'

Bridget glanced at her eldest child. 'Bryce?'

The young man bowed his head. 'Forgive me, mother, but I cannot abide the thought that my appointment as successor to the throne will cause the Empire to split. Show clemency. Release them all, and let them go home. Ban them from the Plateau, by all means, and strip them of all imperial titles, but do not execute them; I beg you.'

Bridget said nothing for a long while, then she emitted a deep sigh. 'Very well, I shall bow to the judgement of my successor. Karalyn, you may take your mother, Thorn, Caelius and Shella home with you. Keir will be placed on trial for the murder of Brannig. However, you must treat this as the last chance the Holdfasts have to stay out of imperial affairs. If I discover that Daphne is fomenting revolution, then I will grind your family into dust. This world has one ruler, and it is I, not Daphne Holdfast.'

Karalyn bowed her head. 'Thank you, your Majesty. Might I ask about Daimon?'

'The young dream mage is sleeping in his new quarters,' said Bryce. 'I think the ordeal in Threeways exhausted him. Once he has had time to settle in, I shall present him to the Empress.'

'Be careful,' said Karalyn. 'That boy has a lot of anger in his heart, and his powers are formidable.'

'Don't lecture me about dream mages, Karalyn,' said the Empress. 'I've had to deal with you for years, remember? Go. Take your family, and do not return.'

'It pains me to part in this manner, your Majesty.'

'Really? Tell me honestly, Karalyn; would you have obeyed my second command – to catch Sable and bring her before me?'

Karalyn smiled. 'No, your Majesty; I would not.'

'Then we have nothing more to say. Bryce, accompany Karalyn and her soldier friend to the dungeons.'

Bryce gave his mother a brief nod, then escorted Karalyn and Cardova from the chamber.

Cardova puffed out his cheeks. 'Thank you for what you said in there, sir.'

'I didn't do it for the Holdfasts,' said Bryce.

They descended several flights of stairs, leaving the palace behind, and entering the fortress levels of the building. They passed soldiers and courtiers, each bowing before the Emperor-elect, and entered the dungeons in the cavernous basement of the Great Fortress. They came to a row of prison cells, lit by oil lamps. Bryce directed soldiers to the first four cells, and commanded that they be opened. Karalyn and Cardova stood back as Daphne emerged from a cell, limping, but with her head held high. She saw Karalyn, and gasped in relief. Thorn, Shella and Caelius joined them in the dark hallway, as soldiers kept their weapons ready.

'Her Majesty has decided that you are to be freed,' said Bryce; 'but there are conditions. You must not set foot in the Plateau again, and you must desist from any treasonous activities.'

'We can go back to Colsbury?' said Shella, looking tired and dishevelled.

'Yes,' said Bryce, 'and I strongly advise you to stay there. The Hold-fasts have served the Empire well, but that time is at an end.'

'What about Keir?' said Daphne. 'I refuse to believe that my son deliberately murdered Brannig. Such a thing defies logic.'

'Why didn't you read his mind to find out, mother?' said Karalyn.

'Because Daimon stripped all powers from Shella and myself, dear daughter. How else would the Rakanese have captured us?'

Karalyn frowned. She darted into her mother's head, and immediately sensed what Daimon had done to her mind. She removed the blocks with ease.

'Try it now, mother,' she said.

Daphne narrowed her eyes, then smiled. 'Thank you, Kara-bear.' She limped over to the cell where Keir was confined. 'Son? Open your eyes.'

Karalyn and the others joined Daphne by the cell entrance. Karalyn peered through the bars, and saw Keir lying on the cold, damp ground, his face beaten and bloody.

'I'm sorry about the beating,' said Bryce. 'The emotions of the palace guards were running high.'

Daphne said nothing, and her eyes glazed over for a moment.

'My son is innocent,' she said.

Thorn pushed her way forward to look at her husband. 'Keir said that he was trying to protect the Empress. Is it true?'

'Yes,' said Daphne. She turned to Bryce. 'Release him, or put me back into my prison cell. I will not be leaving without my son.'

Bryce frowned, then glanced at Karalyn.

Karalyn hesitated for a moment. She loathed her elder brother, but if her mother was speaking the truth, then not even Keir deserved to die for something he hadn't done.

She entered Bryce's mind.

Bryce, she said, *I am going to take you into Keir's mind, and then we shall both see the truth for ourselves.*

She gathered Bryce's consciousness, and took it with her as she sent her powers into the cell. They entered Keir's head through his open eyes.

Keir; show us what happened.

The images swirled, and Karalyn felt the anger and torn emotions of the moments before Brannig's death. Keir had been on the verge of betraying the Holdfasts, and proclaiming his loyalty to the Empress. Bryce and Karalyn watched as Keir peered through the doorway into Bridget's private study, then they saw Brannig raise the knife.

Enough, said Bryce. *I've seen enough.*

Karalyn withdrew from their minds, and Bryce took a breath.

'I don't understand,' he said. 'Why would Brannig, my father, want to kill my mother?'

'I don't know,' said Karalyn. 'You saw the same as me. It doesn't make any sense. I read Brannig's mind after I brought him here, and I saw no malice or evil there.'

Bryce raised a hand to his face, and shielded his eyes from the others. Karalyn put a hand on his shoulder, feeling nothing but pity for Bridget's eldest child.

Bryce wiped his face, then turned to the soldiers. 'Open the cell. Karalyn, take Keir with you. I will explain what happened to my mother.'

'She might not understand.'

'You're right; she won't, but it's my decision, and I shall accept the consequences. Go, before I change my mind.'

Two soldiers opened the cell door, and Daphne limped in. She crouched down by her son's body, and embraced him.

'Go!' said Bryce.

Colsbury Castle. Go.

The air crackled, and they appeared in the Sextant chamber in Colsbury. Thorn sighed in relief.

Karalyn took a step back, as Daphne, Caelius and Thorn gathered round Keir.

'Holy shit,' said Shella, 'am I glad to be back here. Agang had better not have drunk all the damned whisky.'

———

Three hours later, Karalyn and Cardova were on the roof of the Great Keep of Colsbury Castle, as the seven stars shone down from the night sky. Cardova lit two cigarettes, and passed one to Karalyn.

'Thanks,' she said, taking it.

'What now?' he said.

'I don't know, Lucius. If you're looking for grand plans and schemes, you should ask my mother.'

'Will you be fetching Kelsey soon?'

'I guess so. Are you looking forward to going home?'

Cardova shrugged. 'Caelius is staying.'

'I know. He and my mother seem to have hit it off. Will Van be upset?'

'Probably not. I mean, you can travel back and forward to the City whenever you like. Maybe the Holdfasts should relocate to Tara.'

Karalyn smiled. 'That's not a terrible idea, though I imagine that my mother might object. Thank you for all your help; I don't think I could have got through it all without you.'

'Just doing my job, ma'am.'

'Is that all it was, a job?'

Cardova glanced away, his eyes masking his feelings, and Karalyn was tempted to peer into his mind to see what he was thinking.

'I'm a professional soldier,' he said.

She nodded. Why did she feel disappointed?

'Don't laugh at me,' she said, 'but I'm going to miss you, Lucius.'

He gazed at her, his eyes widening a little, then Daphne appeared by the stairs.

'What are you two doing up here all alone?' she said.

'Nothing, ma'am,' said Cardova, his features closing.

'Come downstairs,' Daphne said. 'We need to talk; we have much to do; much to prepare. Karalyn, I want you to bring Kelsey, her dragon and the twins here first thing in the morning. I'm not going to miss this opportunity to have all of my children in the same place at the same time. Once she is here, then together, as a family, we will decide our next moves.'

'What moves, mother? You know, I think Bryce would make a fine Emperor.'

Daphne smiled. 'The succession to the imperial throne is not for you to decide, dear; it is for all of us to decide – and that is what we shall do.'

'All of us? What about Sable?'

'Yes, her too; if you can find her.'

'Do you really intend to do this, mother?' said Karalyn. 'You know what it will mean.'

Daphne limped forward, and leaned on the parapet between Cardova and her daughter.

'I am well aware of what it means,' she said. 'Tell me – what is the alternative; that we acquiesce in the dissolution of the Empire? If Bridget hopes that the Holdfasts will sit here quietly while she gifts power to her son, then she is much mistaken. The time has come to take a stand.'

'Hasn't this world suffered enough?'

'Fighting tyranny requires sacrifice, daughter; for make no mistake, that is what we are facing.' Daphne gazed out into the dark sky. 'Whatever the cost, Bridget and her new dream mage must be stopped.'

AUTHOR'S NOTES
AUGUST 2022

Thanks for reading Dreams of Kell – I hope you enjoyed it.

If you have made it this far in the series, then you will probably know that you have just finished the first book of the last part of the Magelands arc – only three more to go! Dreams of Kell was a difficult book to write, and not only because of the persistent troubles I had with fitting all of the plot points together; it was also because I knew I was embarking on the beginning of the end. For seven years, this story has dominated my thoughts, along with the characters, and the places they visit. I am looking forward to finishing it, but, in other ways, I don't want it to end.

RECEIVE A FREE MAGELANDS ETERNAL SIEGE BOOK

Building a relationship with my readers is very important to me.

Join my newsletter for information on new books and deals and you will also receive a Magelands Eternal Siege prequel novella that is currently EXCLUSIVE to my Reader's Group for FREE.

www.ChristopherMitchellBooks.com/join

ABOUT THE AUTHOR

Christopher Mitchell is the author of the Magelands epic fantasy series.

For more information:
www.christophermitchellbooks.com
info@christophermitchellbooks.com

Printed in Great Britain
by Amazon